BOUND BY EDEN

BOUND
BY EDEN

Eden series

TOLBA: BOOK 2

LEXI POST

BOUND BY EDEN
EDEN SERIES
TOLBA: BOOK 2

By Lexi Post

One night with two alien strangers changed everything.

Risk manager, Rowena Lewis, threw caution to the wind when she drowned her sorrows in a bottle of tequila and two hot Edenists. These seemingly perfect men aren't making it easy for her to return to her planet and the career she loves. But what if she's already bonded with them? For life?

Takoda's heart will always belong to another, so he is anxious to prove that he and Awan have not bonded with Ro. But as he learns more about her, he discovers a danger that is far too close, and it's impossible to ignore.

Awan's unshakeable belief that everything happens for a reason has him excited about what their future will hold with Rowena in their life. Finally, they will be happy. But when she rocks his faith, he realizes he must take action…that is, if he's not too late.

Acknowledgments

For Bob Fabich, who has bound me to him with his love for over twenty-five years. I am so incredibly lucky to have you.

Thank you to my sister Paige Wood, who always provides great insights that make my stories better.

Thank you to my Legends for some awesome names when I got stuck - Bonnie Davis for Salpinos, Rochelle Ireland for Moorg, Penny Brosze for Vorian and Pamela Reveal for Condor. Also, I want to thank my reader Anne for creating shevi, a new alien breakfast pastry that sounds yummy.

As usual, I need to thank Marie Patrick, my critique partner, not only for her readiness to give feedback on my work, but for allowing me the pleasure of reading her work in progress as well.

I had some great final readers before this went to print, so I need to thank Denise Hendrickson, Michele Hedgcock, and KC for their sharp observations. I couldn't do this without you all.

Author's Note

Bound by Eden was inspired by Emily Dickinson's poem, "He touched me, so I live to know," which was first published in 1891.

This poem is clearly one of Dickinson's more sensual poems. The narrator has finally touched the one she loves physically, and she is overwhelmed by her feelings, losing her self-identity. By the second stanza she is a changed person because of her connection and now she feels she's found her home. By the final stanza, she is anxious to solidify the relationship which will bring her such joy it borders on heavenly.

But what if the woman is fiercely independent when she discovers not one but two men who can sweep her away? Will she be able to give up a career she enjoys for the men she loves? And what of the men? Are they ready to make equal sacrifices so they can all be together, or will their past make the ultimate joy impossible?

XVIII.

He touched me, so I live to know
That such a day, permitted so,

I groped upon his breast.
It was a boundless place to me,
And silenced, as the awful sea

    Puts minor streams to rest.
And now, I'm different from before,
As if I breathed superior air,

    Or brushed a royal gown;
My feet, too, that had wandered so,
My gypsy face transfigured now

    To tenderer renown.
Into this Port, if I might come,
Rebecca, to Jerusalem,

    Would not so ravished turn—
Nor Persian, baffled at her shrine
Lift such a Crucifixial sign

    To her imperial Sun.

A short dictionary of Eden words is available at the end but is not needed to understand the story.

For free books, updates, sneak peeks, and special prizes, it's easy to sign up to receive the latest news from Lexi at http://bit.ly/LexiUpdate

The bond of Eden is unbreakable. It should be entered into with much forethought and consideration. There is no worst fate than to choose unwisely. But oh, for he who chooses well, an eternal joy to rival the celestial spirit awaits you. E.D.

– from the Preface to Dickinson Law

CHAPTER ONE

By the Crius, what had *they done?*

Takoda rubbed the sleep from his eyes with his free hand, the other pinned beneath the woman sleeping next to him. He stared at her. She was not his chosen one, not the woman he thought he would spend the rest of his life with. His chest tightened.

No, instead he'd visited a Pleasure Dome to bury his sorrow in the willing body of a meekwee. Looking over her, he found Awan, his arm and one leg thrown over her.

He tried to remember last night, but his brain was cloudy from the Tolban ale and whatever the woman had given them. Some drink from Earth that he blamed for the pain in his head.

"Awan." He kept his voice to a whisper, not wanting to wake the woman up. That he couldn't remember her name proved how much her drink had affected him. He *always* remembered a woman's name.

1

Awan didn't respond, his breathing continued in that blissful state of sleep.

An uneasy feeling about their night to escape their heartbreak caused Takoda's gut to tense. Everyone knew it was poor judgement for two men to enjoy one woman in the Pleasure Domes. It could be done, but only if the men were well in control to avoid bonding. Unfortunately, he had grave concerns about his control throughout the night. He *had* to know what Awan remembered.

Slowly, he pulled his arm out and slid from the bed. He only hoped she slept as soundly as Awan. He leaned over the bed, but quickly stood straight again, his head feeling as if a feroon sat upon it. He whispered again. "Awan. Awan, wake."

The brother of his heart didn't move. As much as Takoda wanted to slip out and pretend he hadn't been there, it wouldn't avoid the ramifications of what they might have done. He had to know.

Did they bond with a woman they'd just met?

Walking around to the other side of the bed, he could see why they'd both been happy to spend the night with the red-haired beauty. Her body was full and curvy and her legs long. A woman a man could embrace without fear of hurting her. Her face, even in sleep, was exquisite with high cheekbones, a slender nose, and full lips that even now stirred his desire. But she wasn't Xavia - the woman they were *supposed* to have bonded with.

His stomach rolled, the not-knowing making him sick. It was either that or the Earth drink she called teekeela. Carefully, he lifted Awan's arm off their bedmate and tugged. His blonde-haired friend rolled his head toward him and his eyes opened slightly. "What?"

Takoda crouched down, careful to keep his head perpendicular to the floor. "Shh, we need to leave. Now." He gestured toward their companion. "While she sleeps."

Awan frowned and jerked his hand away to rub his temple. Lifting his leg from the woman, he sat up on the edge of the bed, holding his hand over his eyes, despite the muted light coming in from the high windows of the domed sleeping room. "I need a healer."

"So do I. Come." He locked onto Awan's arm and pulled him to a standing position.

Awan tilted.

Tugging his friend toward him, Takoda almost lost his own balance and let go, the pain in his head intensifying. By the Crius, what had been in that bottle? He glanced back toward the bed, concerned that she might be in pain as well. Should they bring a healer back or were Earth women immune to teekeela?

The sound of Awan bumping into the archway that connected the sleeping room to the meekwee's living quarters had him quickly moving out of the room. She must have been familiar with the properties of the drink. They could come back later and see how she fared…once he knew what happened last night.

It took all his concentration between the pounding in his head and an unusual lack of balance to maneuver them both out of the Pleasure Dome and onto the packed dirt of the thoroughfare still empty in the predawn hour. He was thankful both for the quiet and the gray start to the day that portended rain. Thankful too that there were no cold drops hitting his still warm bare body. He focused on simply putting one foot in front of the other in a semi straight line.

"Which way?" Awan's voice seemed as loud as the screech of a gokokhoko flying down for the kill. From the way Awan grabbed his head, he thought so too.

Takoda kept his voice to a whisper. "East." He pointed toward the lightening sky. They had wandered out of their hatchoc last night, their pain over losing both their beloved and the brother of their heart too much to bear. They'd walked and talked until one of the new patrols had spotted them in the pink light of the Bendis moon.

Once the patrol determined neither of them were Kindred of Eden, Awan had pulled him into the Pleasure Dome, presumably because he'd threatened to levitate the patrol higher than the top of the dome and drop them to the ground. He remembered that much.

"She felt so good." Awan's whispered words held a sense of awe.

"Do you remember what happened?"

Awan's grin turned to a cringe when he started to nod. "I remember how good it was to be inside her. And she smelled of sweet fruit. So beautiful."

At the mention of the sweet fruit scent, the vision of the meekwee in the throes of her ecstasy flashed through his mind, spiking the pain in his head while at the same time causing his cock to react.

Awan must have noticed. "I see you remember, too."

He sighed. "Just a little. What I can't remember is if we bonded with her."

"Bonded?" Awan halted. "Why would we bond with her? We just met her."

Since it had taken him a moment to react to Awan's sudden stop, he turned back to face him. "I know that, but I don't remember if we were careful last night. You remember being inside her. I can't remember if I was, too."

If they had both reached fulfillment with her one right after the other, they could be bonded. While it chilled him to think that had occurred, his body continued to react to the idea in a positive way. Walking the pathways with an erection was not considered normal for adult Edenists.

If he could just remember! But the harder he tried, the more pain filled his head.

"What if we did? It just means we no longer need to look for a beloved." Awan smiled crookedly, the teekeela obviously still coursing through his body. "We must have liked her enough to enjoy her, so why not bond with her?" He lifted both hands, palms up. "I would not mind returning to her dome and continuing our evening." He turned around, lost his balance, and abruptly sat on the packed dirt of the pathway.

Takoda's head started to pound like a rockslide but he couldn't calm himself. "Why?" He stepped in front of Awan. "Why? I'll tell you why. Because we love Xavia!" His voice rose of its own accord and he grabbed at his head.

Awan's face paled before he leaned over and vomited.

At the sight, Takoda closed his eyes trying to calm his own stomach. *Don't think about Awan being sick. Think of something pleasant. Something calming.* His brain filled with the vision of a woman's neck and his nostrils filled with the scent of sweet fruit. The pounding in his head eased and his stomach began to settle.

"Help me up."

At the sound of Awan's defeated voice, Takoda opened his eyes. The brother of his heart sat with shoulders slumped looking up at him, all the heartache they had tried to drown out in the past night stark upon his face.

"Here." He held his hand out.

Awan grasped his forearm and pulled himself up, but he continued to hold on until his equilibrium returned. His amber eyes appeared unusually bright in the muted light. "Thank you."

Takoda didn't dare nod. Instead, he let go and ignored the obvious pain in his friend's gaze. "Let's go home." He began to walk again, slowly.

Awan fell into step beside him but didn't say a word.

They continued in silence as they made their way east toward their lonely home. What had been a warm and inviting place with the four of them now held no appeal. Their filoz was broken and their beloved bonded to another. *Xavia.*

They finally came to their hatchoc and took the path to the left. As they made the turn, Awan halted again.

Takoda stopped to look at him. "What is it?"

Awan pointed ahead. "Bendis." The word came out on an awed breath.

He moved his gaze from Awan to find the giant pink moon slowly sinking below the horizon, its proximity making it appear as big as Eden itself. He was rarely awake so early and never in a position to see such an awe-inspiring sight.

"It's a sign." Awan's voice remained reverent.

A sign? "What kind of sign?"

Awan kept his gaze on the quickly sinking orb. "It's meant to be."

Takoda ground his teeth in exasperation. Clearly, Awan had not yet emptied enough of the contents of his stomach. "Everything is meant to be. Bendis does not make it so."

"No." Awan finally looked at him. "But it's a sign that what occurred in the dark of night beneath its light was meant to be. We must wait and see."

Now his gut was back to feeling as if it were burning from the inside out. "What do you see?" He fisted his hands as Awan closed his eyes for a moment then opened them.

"I see four scenarios where we bonded, seven in which we didn't with two in which we each had a different woman."

No sooner were the words spoken than images of all eleven possibilities filled his head as Awan sent them to him. Another woman? He found the odd images in his mind and frowned. He'd forgotten her. Then again, he'd forgotten most of last night. Still, the odds were in their favor that they hadn't bonded. Awan would know which was correct. He always knew when he was involved. Takoda opened his mouth to voice his thought, but found Awan watching Bendis.

Takoda moved his gaze to catch the final sliver of the moon dipping below the horizon. A bright purple flash almost blinded him before the moon was no more. Something about that odd light had him fisting his hands again. If the odds were in their favor that they didn't bond, then why did he feel like his life was about to change…drastically?

Rowena Lewis stretched, her whole body feeling satisfied and happy. As she opened her eyes to the light of day, pain shot through her head and she moaned. "Crap."

She just needed to stay still and go back to sleep. She was physically tired enough, but the second she remembered why, her brain jumped into warp speed. "Son of a bitch."

Without opening her eyes, she sat up and crossed her legs. The pain in her head took all her concentration. She needed to breathe. Slowly, she did so, counting to ten as she inhaled before letting the breath release to the same count. Her muscles were more than ready to relax, but it took another ten minutes of deep breathing for the pounding in her head to ease to more manageable rumbles of pain.

Carefully, she opened her eyes again. Immediately, the pain increased. Forcing herself to rise, she donned an old extra-large men's collared shirt, pulled her hair into a ponytail, and meandered toward what she called a kitchenette in the large dome of her home to pour a glass of water. Drinking a few sips to test her stomach, she was relieved to find it didn't object.

Without hesitating, she pulled her purse from the cupboard and found her precious bottle of ibuprofen, thankful she'd restocked when visiting Earth last month. Regular visits to Earth had been one of her requirements for staying on Eden. As wonderful as it was, there were a couple necessities missing. Luckily, visiting Earth only took a couple Edenists pressing the Crius chip beneath their arm and she simply walked through the portal to home.

She swallowed a couple of tablets and carefully sat on her very comfortable couch, or what Edenists called a longseat. She focused on breathing and sipping the water. Her gaze fell upon the empty bottle of tequila and she groaned. Memories of the night tried to flood her brain, but she forced them away. Unfortunately, she had no such control over her emotions and defeat had her shoulders rolling inward.

She'd saved that high-end bottle of tequila for a particular special occasion. She'd given herself six months on Eden to find her own filoz, two to five men who would call her their beloved and enable her to have what no woman in her family had achieved – a happily ever after. At the age of thirty-two, it was time in her estimation.

Why hadn't Sist and Micco asked to bond with her? It wasn't as if there were a lot of women to choose from since none were born on Eden. The women that Edenists could bond with were those from Earth. That's why women had to accept at least two men. Her favorites were Sist and Micco. They'd known of her deadline, and she was sure they felt strongly about her.

Obviously, not strong enough.

Finishing her glass of water, she contemplated getting up for another, but she was too depressed to move. It was a good thing she'd kept her brownstone in Boston. At least she'd have somewhere to—

The bells at the entrance to her dome clanged and she covered her ears. She hadn't been this hungover since she turned twenty-one. She knew better. "Enter at your own risk."

When no one came in, she gritted her teeth in anticipation of another head-pounding clang, but it didn't come.

Instead, Calliope Bowers peaked around the corner of the door. "Ro, are you alone?"

She started to nod, then thought better of it. "Yes."

"Oh, good." Cali strode in, a happy spring in her step, something Ro was usually pleased to see, but at the moment, it was irritating as hell.

Her friend of only a month, and the only other woman there

who had come to the Pleasure Dome compound under unusual circumstances, fell back on the longseat directly across from her and crossed her bare feet on the wide stump that served as a coffee table. She grasped the tie of her pale pink terry cloth bathrobe and grinned. "So how was it? Everything you expected? Everything they said it is? You have to tell me every detail." She shook her finger with a mock frown. "I'm no wuss. I want to know it all."

Ro stared at Cali as if her head had just spun around like a possessed woman in a scary movie. Her friend's short brown hair didn't actually float on air, but it did sway as she leaned forward, her brown eyes filled with curiosity. How could such a petite bundle of energy be so clueless about the day? She'd told Cali last night was her deadline. "What are you talking about? They didn't show."

Her friend's brow furrowed. "What do you mean? I talked to them. You all left the Pleasure Dome and came here." She let go of the bathrobe tie and swept the room with her hand then stopped and stared at the empty tequila bottle. "Don't tell me you don't remember?"

She began to shake her head, but the pain intensified and she stopped. "I remember enough."

At her friend's quizzical look, it was obvious she was missing something. "Ro, you said you planned to open that bottle to celebrate your bonding. You were with two men last night, which I know you would never consent to unless it was the filoz you've told me about."

She groaned and closed her eyes.

Immediately, she heard Cali move. "Are you okay? Oh, I bet you need water. Let me get you some. The Jerk always needed water after getting drunk. He wasn't…

As Cali continued a steady stream of the usual chatter about her ex, Ro allowed herself to think about last night. The first thought had her whole body flushing. She forced her mind to focus on the actual men she'd been with. It wasn't Micco and Sist, of that she was sure.

Last night, the two men were in the same sour mood as she. They didn't sport the usual smiles most Edenists wore to a Pleasure Dome. That's why rather than drink her sorrows away by herself, she'd invited them to join her. In fact, she remembered thinking that it was the perfect scenario for a night of drinking. Drowning her sorrows and all that.

She rarely went to the Pleasure Dome to meet Edenists to bring back to her place. Though it was the purpose of the Pleasure Domes in each hatchoc, no woman who lived on the compound was required to interact with any Edenist. It was simply where they had the single women live whose filoz didn't work out.

Her filoz may have worked, but then she didn't know what a filoz was. On Eden, at least two and up to five men who were very close friends could form a filoz. Then they would choose a woman on Earth, their "chosen one" and watch her through their portal. When they thought the time was right, they would bring her to Eden and ask her to be their "beloved" or "agapayto" which meant wife. Though the rate of success was high, things didn't always work out, hence the Pleasure Dome compound.

The Pleasure Dome itself served as a place for the single women to meet men and sleep with one if they so choose. Some women even opted for teaching men how to ensure a woman enjoyed their lovemaking. Not her thing, but there were plenty of women who enjoyed the hunky naked men of the planet, so they visited the Pleasure Dome to find prospects, but only *one* at a time to avoid bonding.

"Here you go."

A glass of water appeared in front of her. She looked up at Cali which was rare since the woman was so short. "Thank you." Taking a good swallow, she let out a breath in relief that her stomach continued to cooperate. So far so good.

"So, start at the beginning." Cali resumed her seat and returned her feet to the coffee table. "Last night you brought two men back here. One was blonde, super tall, with bulging muscles and had the Kindred of Mind birthmark on his arm. If he was from Earth, I'd say he was Eastern European maybe."

Cali was clearly warming to her story. "The other was a little shorter and way too cute in a guy-next-door kind of way. He had some dots on his back. If I remember from our orientation," she said the word with air quotes, "his birthmark was Kindred of Air. He definitely had a lot a woman would be interested in, if you know what I mean." Cali wiggled her brows to make it clear she was remarking on the Edenist's cock.

At the mention of his anatomy, Ro flushed and hid it by taking another good gulp of water.

"You told me the only two men you'd ever bring back to your place together were Micco and Sist. You also said you were saving that bottle for when they asked you to be their beloved." Cali pointed at the empty tequila bottle. "So did you bond or are you taking it slow?"

Instead of answering, Ro glared at the culprit of her woes. She knew better than to throw caution to the wind. As a risk manager, it was her specialty to calculate risks and minimize them. But every once in a long while, she rebelled. One of those times was when she first agreed to come to Eden. It appeared last night was another time. "No, I didn't bond with Micco and Sist. Those two men were not them."

Cali's eyes rounded in surprise, the woman's face one of complete shock. "Wait? What?"

Ro focused on the half empty water glass in both her hands. After taking Cali under her wing, how could she admit she'd been completely irresponsible? "I wasn't drinking the tequila in celebration. I started drinking it in consolation. I told Micco and Sist that I had six months to find men who wanted a beloved. They each knew my timetable. But last night they didn't come, so I started to drink."

"I can't believe it." Cali shook her head. "You told me you lose all control with tequila and that's why you were saving it to have with your fiancées."

She turned the glass of water around in her hands as if she could find the answers in it that would make sense, but her weakness didn't make sense. She was always in control, except on those rare times when she wasn't, and then she ignored logic. Is that what happened last night? "I know. But what I didn't tell you was that whether I find men to have a future with or not, I'm going back to Earth."

"You can't!" Cali pulled her feet off the coffee table and leaned forward. "Ro tell me you're not leaving. Please."

At the fear in her friend's eyes, she paused. It had never occurred to her that Cali depended on her. Crap. The woman had seemed to regain her confidence in herself so quickly. Stalling for time, Ro finished off the water, pleased that at least the pounding in her head had settled down.

Cali reached across the table and grasped her wrist. "You can't go. What's six months have to do with it? What if two days from now, Micco and Sist come to ask you and you're gone? Would you really risk that? Why only six months?"

It was a legitimate question. She'd spent years on Earth trying to find a meaningful relationship. Yet, she'd given Eden only six months, but it was all she could afford. She'd taken a six-month sabbatical from her job, from her amazing career. She had to go back or lose all she'd worked for. If she lost her position, she'd have to start over. "I have to get back to my job. Besides, I'm getting too old to start a married life."

Light laughter filled the room. "No, really. Why six months?"

She just stared at her twenty-four-year-old friend. This was no laughing matter. She'd known many women in their late thirties, two in her own family, who had tried marriage, but it just didn't work for them. They were too used to their independence, to only having to worry about themselves. She didn't want to be like that, but that's what would happen if she waited any longer. She knew it in her gut.

She had a successful career, and she was financially independent, but on a scale of one to ten, she could only say her life was at a nine. Something was missing. She wanted a companion, not just a best friend. The night she'd been swept away to Eden with the two men who couldn't get enough of her, she thought she finally had a chance.

"You're serious." Cali shook her head. "You're not old. It's just a job. You wouldn't seriously put your job over your happiness."

She sighed. "My job is my happy place. I had just hoped to share the other parts of my life with someone."

Cali's gaze flitted away. Ro could almost see her mind working, looking for new arguments. Then her face brightened. "It isn't six months on Earth yet. You have…about three weeks yet."

She stilled. Cali was right. Eden days were only twenty-two hours long and the calendar was different based on two moons, but her burgeoning hope quickly dissipated. "True, but why should a few weeks make a difference? It's obvious that none of the Edenists I've met have been interested enough to ask me."

"You don't know that." Cali sat back and propped her feet up on the table again. "Maybe Micco and Sist are preparing their dome right now to invite you to move in? Maybe those two Edenists last night are sitting at the breakfast table talking about taking you to the arboretum thingy they have in the next hatchoc."

If the two men who were with her last night had drank as much as she had, she'd be surprised if they could even function. Earth alcohol affected Edenists much faster and harder than Eden alcohol and vice versa.

"So, what were their names?"

Cali's question caught her off guard. "Who?"

"The men you brought here last night. Really, Ro, you must be seriously hungover."

She was that. "Their names were…" She knew this. It was right there on the edge of her brain. Hah. "Dakota and…" and what? Irwin? No, too Earth like. Ono? No, to Asian sounding.

"And? Don't tell me you spent all night with them and can't remember."

"I remember. It was Dakota and Ion."

Cali cocked her head. "I don't think so. Those sound too Earth-like."

Well, hell, she was right. "Well, we did finish off that big bottle of tequila, so my brain is still a bit fuzzy."

"Is that all you did is drink?" Cali's feet came down again. "Or did you do it with both of them? Safely, of course. I know there's ways, even if I've never had more than one man." She snorted. "Unfortunately."

For a moment, Cali's statement took her mind off her own life and reminded her of the limited experience of her friend. Cali had only had one man in her bed, and he'd totally screwed her over figuratively and literally.

"Tell me, did you have sex with both of them?" Cali's eyes glittered with excitement.

Had she? She remembered drinking. All three of them bemoaning their fate. They had lost a beloved to someone else and one of their filoz to exile. She hadn't asked if he was a lawbreaker. All lawbreakers were exiled to live or die in the jungle as fate determined, but she also knew of two who had been exiled and weren't lawbreakers. It made it a bit confusing.

Was talking all they did last night? Suddenly, heat filled her body as a memory surfaced of lying on her back with a man inside her, thrusting deeply and bringing her to her climax more than once.

"Oh my gosh, you did!"

Cali's excited exclamation had her frantically searching her memory. The feeling of four hands on her body, pleasuring her in all the right places had her sheath tightening even as she sat there. She couldn't have. She wouldn't. Just because she remembered them pleasuring her, didn't mean they both had orgasmed inside her one after the other. That would cause the bonding. They wouldn't have bonded.

She rose and walked to her kitchenette to pour herself more water, cold water. A vision took shape in her mind of herself standing, held against one man while another pumped into her, bringing her to climax. Her breathing faltered as water spilled over the top of the glass and into the sink. She stopped the flow and concentrated. Her body heated at the feelings of remembered ecstasy. She had to concentrate. Was it the same man?

"Now, you're stalling." Cali's voice interrupted her focus.

She turned, grasping the glass like a life buoy, leaning her butt against the wooden counter for support. "I'm not stalling. I'm trying to remember everything."

Cali crossed her legs under her and clasped her hands. "Yes. I want to know it all. Did you have them both at once or one at a time? I've always been curious how that works."

"Both were involved but I only had one." At least she hoped that was the case.

"Oh." Cali sighed. "And I bet they made sure you were satisfied first. These Edenists are so different from Earth men."

She frowned at that. "That's not a fair conclusion. You haven't exactly experienced Earth *men*. But you're right. They were all about me." At least she hoped so. None of them were in the mood when they first started drinking, and she'd made it clear she wasn't interested. They'd respected that. So how did she end up having sex with them?

"Start from the beginning. When you left the Pleasure Dome, they walked on each side of you. To be honest, you looked tiny next to them."

Cali's words brought another wave of pleasure coursing through her body. She *had* felt small, not a normal occurrence for her with Earth men. At five-foot eleven-inches tall, she often felt rather large. She wasn't petite like Cali either. As her mom would say, she was "big-boned." But last night she'd felt feminine, dainty, and incredibly sexy.

"What happened when you arrived here?"

She blinked. "We opened that bottle." She pointed to it, scowling as if it was the cause of all her troubles. "They were as deflated and depressed as I was."

"They did seem quite serious, but I didn't realize they were sad. I'm not sure I've seen a sad Edenist yet. But it makes sense that not everything on this amazing planet would go their way. What were they—"

The clanging of the bells at her door sent a sudden surge of excitement and trepidation through her. Were they back?

Cali's eyes rounded. She pointed to the door and mouthed the words, *is it them?*

Ro tried to remember if they had made any plans, but that tidbit of information was beyond her foggy mind's reach. She shrugged.

Frustrated, but not deterred, Cali rose and went to the door. She winked at her then opened it wide and stared. "Oh, hello."

Ro wasn't surprised by Cali's breathless greeting. Directly in front of her were Micco and Sist, twin towers of naked handsomeness, smiles on their faces, and from the look and smell of it, bearing breakfast.

Chapter Two

Awan stepped outside his working dome in the Discoverist Complex to take a seat in the shaded courtyard that held all the Resource Edenists. No one else was there and for the moment he was pleased to have the solitude. Leaning back, he stared up at the branches of the yahaw trees, watching the green-feathered lintue birds as they flitted about the branches, their bird song light and happy.

He was not happy, but nor was he unhappy. In essence, he felt unbalanced. A rare state for him. Takoda was always up and down, not him.

Part of it was most likely his lack of memory about last night. No matter how many times he reviewed the eleven scenarios in his mind regarding what had occurred, none of them spoke to him. That in itself was odd because whenever he used his Kindred of Mind ability to generate situations that involved himself, he *always* knew the right one. He wasn't used to experiencing the not-knowing feeling that others had once hearing or seeing his possibilities.

Perhaps that was what had thrown him off this morning. He sat forward and looked back through the open archway of his working dome to the door on the other side as if he could put to rest the odd feeling he'd received from Salpinos.

Salpinos was relatively new and worked in the Social Discoverist circle. Awan had helped him once before when he'd requested scenarios on what the Tolbans' reaction to the HPs, or Hatchoc Patrols would be. That those very patrols had been put into place hadn't been a surprise. Of his eleven outcomes, only two had had any negative repercussions.

Then why had he been reluctant to share the eleven scenarios today regarding doubling those patrols? It made no sense. They were in place to keep all Tolbans safe in case a Kindred of Eden lost control. It might be his own sorrow over losing a brother of his heart to exile because he was Kindred of Eden.

What bothered him was Lyka had never lost control. In fact, he wouldn't hurt an amobe. The possibility of more HPs was most likely because the cheetans had heard the rumors that the dirgon returned every Bendis moon.

Turning back to the serene courtyard, he shook his head. If he were a dirgon, he'd return under the cover of no moon to avoid detection. Rumors were rumors. He'd run the scenarios and not a single one confirmed that was the case…until last night when the dirgon came home.

The loss of both Xavia and Lyka squeezed his heart all over again, despite his best efforts to make peace with what was done and unable to be undone. His beloved and brother of his heart had bonded with Davos, the dirgon, while outside the city walls and had come back to tell him and Takoda last night—the night of the Bendis moon.

Unfortunately, that event last night was as clear as the sky over the city in his mind. Later, walking the dirt thoroughfares of Tolba and entering the Pleasure Dome to meet the beautiful red-haired woman was also very clear. There had been a sense of defeat about her, which he couldn't understand. Even he and Takoda did not feel defeated —set back, maybe, but there were many women on Earth that they could court. Yet even at the thought, he didn't feel the usual excitement at something new. His heart was still with Xavia.

Was that why their bedmate of last night seemed to have given up hope? Though she never said it directly, he had the distinct impression that she'd lost her own love and faith in Eden, maybe even in happiness. That had tugged at his heart, despite its wounded state. All this he could remember, but their time in her sleeping dome was nothing but disconnected images and physical—

The bells outside his resource room rang, pulling him from his musings. He rose. It was just as well. What he was meant to remember would come to him. Striding to the arched door, it opened before he reached it.

"Awan? Do you have time for an old friend?"

He smiled widely at Kenjada, his neighbor from childhood. "Always. Come, sit, tell me how you are and the rest of your filoz." They often met for meals or to attend events.

The man was his equal in height though dark-haired with a smaller nose and eyes the color of the flash he'd witnessed last night. Now why did he think of that? That Kenjada never sought him out while he was at the Discoverist Complex told him this was an important visit.

Kenjada scanned the office as if to be sure no one else

occupied it. "You have space all to yourself. I imagine many of the discoverists prefer to keep their ideas private until they can prove their success."

He motioned his friend toward the sitting area and gestured to a chair as he maneuvered around a short, small table that sported a pitcher of ambrosia. "Would you like some?" He pointed to the pitcher he kept for anyone who needed his services.

"No. I just finished my morning meal." Kenjada crossed his arms, looking as if he didn't know where to start.

Too intrigued by the odd behavior, Awan gave his friend another warm smile. "Tell me what has you seeking me out. Is it to share exciting news or do you need to know something?" That Kenjada and his large filoz had been courting an Earth woman was well known. Could it be no more than that they had asked her to be their agapayto, their bonded wife?

His friend dropped his arms. "I want to know something."

"Please, tell me what you wish to know."

Kenjada took a deep breath then another. Whatever it was had to be of grave import.

Sensing the man needed reassurance, Awan leaned forward in his chair. "I promise your request will not be made known to anyone unless you request I reveal it."

"You know me well." Kenjada smirked. "It would be a wasted effort to have come all the way here to not ask."

Still, no question came, but the frown on Kenjada's forehead proved the weightiness of his concern.

As much as Awan wished to alleviate his friend's worry, there was no guarantee he could do so, so he remained silent, leaning back in his chair. He'd found those who wished information that was personal were often slow to reveal their request, but he could be very patient. With the discoverists in the complex, the questions came quickly as if they had just had the idea and needed to find out what the possibilities could be.

"There is tension among my filoz members."

At Kenjada's quiet voice, Awan fixed his thoughts on his friend. "What kind of tension?" He purposefully kept his voice to as little inflection as possible, not wanting to show any judgment.

"It is a woman…or rather women."

Now he understood. Kenjada was one of five men in his filoz. If there was a disagreement about who they should court then issues could arise, including a split. Though rare, it did happen. "Tell me about these women, so I may better help you."

"There is our chosen one." At his own words, Kenjada's tension seemed to disappear. "She is everything we wanted, adventurous, loving, kind, and full of life." His tone grew in volume to match the widening smile on his face. "You should see her. She would change her world if she could."

"And she wishes to come to Eden?" It was rare that a chosen one so attached to Earth would agree to leave it.

Kenjada nodded. "Yes. She has dreamed about life on other planets where the troubles that plague Earth do not exist. More importantly, she loves us all and has the stamina to enjoy us all."

She sounded almost too good to be true. Filoz of five were not as common because with that many males and only one female, it did narrow down choices significantly. Awan was pleased that his friend had found the right person for his filoz. "I am happy for you. If she is right for you all, then who is this other woman?"

"Caliope." Kenjada's face softened like it did when he spoke of his mother. "She is the woman we saved on Earth six Bendis moons ago."

"I had forgotten. You settled her into a Pleasure Dome, correct?"

"We did. She is doing very well and is happy there, but has not even begun to look for a filoz." Kenjada's brow furrowed. "That is the problem. Some of the brothers of my heart believe we should not bond with our chosen one until we know Caliope is bonded with a filoz."

"Why?" He always asked clarifying questions, but this one had him truly mystified.

Kenjada rose and walked around his chair, facing away from him. Finally turning, he bent forward and placed his hands on the back of his chair. "The best explanation I can give is that we think of her as a sister and feel that we should ensure she is happy before we allow ourselves to be happy. But others, like myself, feel we need to be sure that our chosen one is happy as well."

Now he understood. As boys, they were taught from the time they could walk and talk to revere women. It was a simple lesson since they were born into families of all men with their mother the only woman. She, of course, found happiness with their fathers long before they were born, so when it was time to find a chosen one from Earth, there was no conflict since they had no sister.

But a sister changed everything, even if she wasn't blood-related. "I understand now. What is it you wish to know?"

Kenjada let go of the chair and stood straight. "I wish to know what we should do. What are the possible outcomes of bonding with our beloved now and what are they if we wait possibly a year or even two?"

They were good questions. He quickly tapped into his Kindred of Mind ability and found eleven scenarios for each. He grinned, pleased at what he discovered.

"Why are you smiling? Is it good? In what way?"

The anxiousness in Kenjada's voice immediately made Awan want to reassure him. "May I send these to your mind?"

At Kenjada's nod, he walked to his friend and laid his hand on the man's shoulder. Instantly, all twenty-two possible outcomes filled Kenjada's mind.

Awan removed his hand at the same time Kenjada's lips broke into a wide smile.

"Thank you!" His friend embraced him, slapping him on the back before stepping away. "I must go. I need to tell my filoz there is only one clear direction. Thank you."

Awan smiled as his happy friend strode toward the door. "I hope I am one of the first to hear of your chosen one becoming your beloved."

Kenjada looked at him over his shoulder as he stepped through the doorway on his way out. "The very first. I promise."

As the door closed, Awan stared at it, the happiness at Kenjada's excitement dissipating as his own bonding troubles resurfaced. Had he and Takoda bonded with the beautiful, intelligent, but defeated woman of last night, or must they look for a new beloved?

And if they had bonded, would they come to feel love for each other? Slowly, he resumed his seat. There was only one way to find out. He had to convince Takoda to return to the Pleasure Dome and ask her.

Now, if he could just remember her name.

Rowena's stomach filled with the usual butterflies at the sight of the two men standing in her archway. At least she hoped it was butterflies and not her stomach reacting to the thought of breakfast. Not after all they'd done to bring her favorite kafez and shevi.

She set down her glass and walked toward them. "How thoughtful. Here let me take this."

Micco shook his head, his light brown wavy hair remained perfect despite his movement. "No. We are here to serve you." At the look in his dark eyes, it appeared he planned to do so in a very intimate way.

The excitement that usually followed such a statement from the six-foot-four athletically built man did not occur, and she hid her disappointment by turning back toward her couch.

"Ahem."

At the sound of Cali's voice, Ro quickly turned back. "I apologize. Micco, Sist, this is Cali, my friend I told you about."

Both men were kind in their greetings, asking after Cali's transition to living on Eden and giving Ro a chance to gather herself. Though the men had made it clear they were interested in her, they were aware that while she lived on the compound of the Pleasure Dome, she could see, and possibly even have sex, with other Edenists.

But since meeting Micco and Sist she's only been with either of them…until last night. Now, she felt awkward, like she had betrayed them somehow, but they'd never committed to her. Their feelings for her could be all in her own head. They weren't even aware that she hoped they would ask her to be their beloved.

Turning back toward the couch, she caught sight of the damned tequila bottle and quickly snatched it up and set it in the trash.

"I'll leave you all alone. Ro, I'll be back later to get the full scoop."

She looked up in time to see Cali's wave before she closed the door behind her.

Sist moved forward, his arm outstretched toward the couch. "Come, sit. We wanted to surprise you."

Her heart jumped, but from excitement or nervousness, she wasn't sure. "Surprise me?" She sat as requested. "If breakfast served is my surprise, I have to say I like surprises."

Micco chuckled, the sound so pleasant it usually made her toes curl, but she was too distracted to notice. "This is good to know." He glanced at the brother of his heart and a secret communication floated between them.

It wasn't the first time she'd seen such an exchange, and to be honest, she envied that. To be so close to someone that with a simple look, a thought was understood. It was that closeness that she'd sought when she came to Eden over two Earth months ago.

With the very men she'd hoped would choose her in front of her, she tried to push her deadline out of her mind.

Sist spread a small cloth over her lap and then knelt, whipping another cloth off the dish in his hand and allowing the lemony aroma of the shevi to waft up to her nose, before setting the plate on her lap. "You said these were your favorite, correct?"

She gazed into his violet eyes and almost sighed. To have a Kindred of Heart kneeling at her feet and presenting her with warm shevi should make her giddy. So why did she feel nervous. "Yes, they are. Can I share them with you?"

Sist shook his head, his bronze hair catching the light coming in through the upper windows. "No. These are all for you."

Before she could insist that he have some because five shevi would certainly add another inch to her hips, Micco knelt on the other side of her.

"And I believe the pecone Kafez is your favorite morning beverage. Am I right?" He held out a cup and poured the steaming, nutty coffee into it from a large carafe.

Luckily, her stomach didn't protest, and she closed her eyes in pure bliss at the scent. Opening her eyes again, she looked at each of them in turn. If they were men on Earth, she would guess they had done something she wouldn't like and were paving the way for an apology or they wanted something. But Edenists, at least the ones in Tolba, didn't have hidden agendas. "Thank you. This is very much appreciated though equally unexpected. Are we celebrating something?"

She held her breath as another look passed between the two men. Was this it? Were they going to ask her? What she'd been waiting for the last four months? She should be excited, her stomach in knots, but that wasn't the case.

Instead, panic rose. She wasn't in love with them. The realization hit hard and fast. She just liked them a lot and thought there was potential. What did she really know of them? Her mouth went dry. Maybe she could simply move in for a while and see if they were all really compatible. After all, they hadn't even spent twenty-two hours in a row together.

Completely ill at ease now, she hid her feelings by taking a sip of the kafez, what tasted most like coffee on Eden, as she waited for one of them to speak.

Micco stood only to sit next to her, but Sist remained on bended knee and set his hand over his heart. "We merely wanted to mark the occasion of your residence here in Tolba. You did say that as of yesterday, you would be here six months and that was significant, correct?"

Her heart lurched. Had they simply waited until after her six-month deadline to be sure she was willing to stay? Had she drunk herself into oblivion for no reason?

Micco took the plate from her hand, drawing her attention. Picking up a shevi, he held it to her mouth. "We understand that it has not yet been a full six months on Earth, but we wanted to celebrate your time on Eden in some small way."

Obediently, she took a bite of her favorite pastry. What should have been heaven, basically a puff pastry filled with a lemony filling and tiny chunks of avocado, tasted like straw, her stomach tightening as her mind raced. Were they simply waiting for her six Earth months to be almost over? Had she given up too soon? Had she damaged her chances with them after last night? Even as her anxiety escalated, she couldn't remember exactly what had happened in her bedroom. Surely, the Edenists she'd been with last night wouldn't let any bonding occur. After all, they grew up in this culture, and bonding was a biological connection…for life.

Micco's brows lowered over his dark eyes. "Is it not to your liking?"

She gave him a weak smile. "I'm sorry, it's very good. I was just thinking about my time here." More specifically, last night.

He smiled. "Yes, you have acclimated to Tolba well. We," he nodded to indicate Sist, "are particularly pleased you have stayed."

Was this it? Would they ask today? Now? The panic swept

over her like a northeastern snowstorm, and she abruptly stood. "Where are my manners? You must let me offer you ambrosia, water, something."

Sist rose, his hard body no more than two feet from her own. He cocked his head. "Something is wrong."

Crap, she should have known a Kindred of Heart would sense her unease. Sist had the ability to make people feel any emotion he wanted, but it would leave soon after he did. That didn't mean he could tell what she was feeling. It could simply be her awkwardness that clued him in. She lifted her hand to her head. "I have a headache, head pains. I'm sure they'll go away soon. I'm probably just dehydrated." She lifted the mug of kafez to her lips and took another sip.

"Then you should rest."

At Micco's words, she looked down at him. "You're probably right." She gave him an honest smile. "But not before I finish that shevi." She forced herself to sit back down. She was making a mountain out of a mole hill as her grandmother was fond of saying.

Micco lifted it to her lips once again and she took another small bite, chewed, and swallowed. "These are so delicious. Just one of the many things I love about Eden."

Sist sat on her other side. "What else do you love about our planet?"

Now this was a safe subject. "I love that there is such respect for women, of course. By I also love how everyone works together for the betterment of the community. I know you've said that Tolba is divided into eleven hatchocs to make that easier, but I've found the way people look out for each other is particularly admirable."

Micco touched her hand to gain her attention. "I believe it

is like this in other cities as well. Have you ever wished you could visit those, or are you content here?"

Now that was an odd question, but she gave it serious thought. "I don't know much about the other cities. If they are like Tolba, I imagine they would be interesting to experience, but that is not why I'm here. There are other cities on Earth as well that I could have visited, but the human thought process would be the same. Edenists have a refreshing way of looking at life. That is why I decided to stay here for so long."

Micco nodded as if he were happy with her answer.

Did he plan to travel and request she accompany him?

"And would you consider living here longer than your proposed time?" His question surprised her.

She swallowed hard, unwilling to commit to anything at the moment. What had changed? Last night she was drinking away her sorrows over these two *not* asking her to be their beloved and now she was hoping to avoid the question all together? She was never one to avoid an issue, and she wouldn't start now. "If I found the right filoz, I would live both here and on Earth with my beloved." She didn't smile to be sure they understood how serious she was. She wanted to know where they stood before she made a commitment. She also needed to find out what happened last night.

Micco nodded sagely. "We appreciate your honesty. It is one of elevendy things we enjoy about you."

She warmed at his comment and eyed Sist to find him smiling in agreement. She returned his smile. "It is what I like about you, too."

At her words, Sist seem to freeze, and she switched her gaze back to Micco to find him holding the shevi out for her to take a bite. Was he avoiding her comment or just taking it in stride? If she didn't know any better, she'd say they were hiding something, but she'd never known them to hold back. Maybe they were planning another surprise for her?

She pulled the rest of the shevi from his fingers and chewed before switching to a safe topic that Micco would probably enjoy discussing. "How are your experiments going?" After the Kindred of Eden men who had brought her to Tolba had been hauled away, she hadn't planned to have anything to do with that Kindred, but she considered Micco safe.

He didn't meet her eyes as he placed the plate on the coffee table. "They go well. Soon we will have results that will change how Tolbans see their city." As if he'd said too much, he rose. "We should leave and let you rest. Would you like me to send for a healer?"

Surprised by the abrupt end to their conversation, she stared at him uncomprehending for a moment. No proposal? Had she read them wrong? She slowly shook her head.

Sist also rose. "I do not like that you are in pain." He kissed her on her forehead. "If you do not feel better by midday, send for us."

She started to say she'd be fine but swallowed her words. "I promise."

"Good." Sist followed Micco to the door. When he reached it, they both turned to look at her. "Be well."

She gave them a weak smile for their concern and then they were gone. She stared at the closed door. What the hell just happened? Did she single-handedly avoid a proposal she'd been hoping for for months, or was there something those two weren't telling her?

Chapter Three

Takoda lowered the cyndistone slab into place. It would serve as the foundation for another residence in this expanded section of Tolba. Next the toleric blocks would be shaped to form a two-level dome.

He found it ironic that despite the number of lawbreakers and Kindred of Eden who had been exiled, the Tolbans still needed more space. These additional hatchocs, to him, were merely postponing the inevitable. They were outgrowing their city, but it wasn't his concern. He left that to the cheetans.

The planner signaled to him that the slab was well situated, so he floated downward to the disturbed gravel of the site. When the same man pointed to someone behind him, he turned. "Awan." The brother of his heart stood well back from the building area.

Takoda glanced at the sky. Helios was still far from setting, though no longer at its zenith. Why was Awan here? It was a rare occasion that Awan left his position and visited him during the day. The last time was when Xavia had gone missing. He hoped this was not equally disturbing.

He strode toward the brother of his heart, the only one he had left. Despite Awan's outward calmness, Takoda had long known the tell-tale signs that his friend was feeling "unbalanced," as he phrased it. A tightness in his jaw and a stiffness in how he held his head, gave him away.

"What is it?" He stopped in front of Awan. "Something troubles you."

"Yes, and it is something we must face." Awan scanned the area before putting an arm around his shoulders and walking them toward the exit of the new hatchoc.

He wanted to stop him and demand an answer, but Awan could be as immovable as a male feroon protecting his female. Finally, they were close enough to the exit for Awan, and he released him.

His impatience growing equal to his concern, he couldn't keep it from his voice. "What must we face now?"

Awan's amber gaze remained serious. "We must face the possibility that we bonded with our bedmate last night."

He stepped back as if hit by a block of toleric. It was what he feared and at Awan's determined look, his heart refused to listen. "Did you remember something?"

"No more than I did at the dawn of the day, but we must confirm that we did or we didn't."

Again, Takoda's heart balked. He loved Xavia. His brain understood that she would never be his, and that he was supposed to find a new chosen one, but he loved *her* and he couldn't change that. "Why? I'm sure if we bonded, we will know soon enough."

"Soon?" Awan's brows rose. "That could be days from now. Does that mean you do not mind if another makes love to our beloved?"

Fury flashed through him so quickly it made his muscles jerk. Shocked by the immediate emotion, he scowled. "No."

"Then we need to know now. We cannot wait."

While Awan's logic made sense, he was still reluctant.

"You hesitate." Awan placed a hand on his shoulder. "Tell me. Why? Do you not want to know?"

No, he didn't want to know. He wanted to stay ignorant and hope that all was as it had been before last night. But nothing would be the same since discovering the woman he loved, and the brother of his heart, had bonded with another. "I am at a loss as to what I want. I only know what I do not want."

Awan nodded. "I understand. I feel as you do, but this unknowing is worse."

"But you said there were only four scenarios in which we bonded. Can you not see which scenario of the eleven occurred?"

"No. I cannot. That is what concerns me."

A chill seemed to grow around his heart at Awan's words. Awan always sensed which path to follow when those opportunities involved him. That he couldn't, didn't bode well. "What do you suggest?"

"We must go back to the Pleasure Dome and ask our meekwee."

Even as his mind agreed with Awan, his heart searched for excuses, but nothing would come to him. "Very well." Turning, he walked to the planner and let him know that he would be leaving, secretly hoping the planner wouldn't want him to go so he'd have an excuse to delay the inevitable. But the man was far too accommodating.

Finally, he made himself return to Awan. At least the hatchoc of the meekwee was far from where he labored for Tolba. It could take them until the setting of Helios just to arrive. Maybe by then he would remember something.

Awan gave him a half-hearted smile. "It is not as if we are being exiled. Come, let us discover the truth and move forward with life."

It was a characteristic of Awan that he both liked and disliked at the same time. Awan had an abundance of faith in what was meant to be and a strong belief that what was meant to be was always for the best. Sometimes he wished for such faith.

"Come, Takoda. We may discover that we still have years to find our beloved. Why not know that now?"

He had a point. "You are right, as usual. Let us go." He nodded toward the exit of the new hatchoc.

Awan shook his head. "No. We should levitate there. It will take far too long to walk."

He stifled a groan, not wanting Awan to know how much he wanted to stay in ignorance. Walking would take longer because the city thoroughfares were packed with Tolbans going about their labors ever since the cheetans banned the use of the Crius chips for anything but visiting Earth or other cities. He was one of the very few Kindred of Air in Tolba who could levitate and he regularly used his ability to move about the city. In fact, he preferred it to walking…usually.

At Awan's questioning gaze, he let out a breath in defeat. The feeling reminded him of their bedmate last night. What did she think of this? Did she expect them to have stayed? For the first time, her feelings loomed before him, and guilt for being so selfish surfaced to spur him on. "Yes, let us discover the truth."

Flipping his hand over so his palm faced the sky, he lifted them above the new opening of what had been the wall that protected Tolba from the jungle beyond and floated them over three hatchocs before slowly lowering them to the pathway at the front of the Pleasure Dome.

Awan led the way inside, striding confidently to the Lead Protector, who sat high on a dais for a full view of the Pleasure Dome. The women of the Pleasure Domes were held in high esteem. They were waited upon and protected by those trained for such service. Every young Edenist wished to become a Meekwee protector at some point in his life. It was not only an honorable position, but the only one where the males were not the majority.

Noticing Awan slowing, he caught up to him. The large, main chamber where men interested in a night of pleasure waited in the hopes a meekwee would invite them to their personal dome was empty now and their footsteps echoed off the curved walls. Last night, the longseats and tables with chairs were filled, the sounds of music and conversation filling the room, but not now. He kept his voice low. "What is it?"

A flush stained Awan's cheeks. "I do not remember her name."

He understood his friend's embarrassment. They were taught their entire lives to think of women before themselves. Had they at least given her pleasure first? He rebelled at the thought that they could have been so selfish not to have done that. "We will describe her and accept our shame."

Awan's eyes widened. "You do not remember either." Though said as a statement, Awan's voice held shock. They always supported each other. Always. To discover that they had been so self-absorbed as to have failed to do that as well was beyond—

"Well, look who's back." The female voice came from the opposite end of the dome.

Takoda spun, but it was not the woman they'd come to see.

This woman was short and tiny of frame, especially compared to the protector next to her. A vague memory of seeing her in this room made him wonder what state he truly was in the night before.

Awan recovered before he did. "Yes, we have returned."

She strode directly across the room toward them, her protector keeping his distance but watching nevertheless. She must be going into the city.

Her gaze roamed over them appreciatively as she approached. "Ro is certainly getting a lot of company today, and it's not even nighttime." She laughed softly before coming to a stop before them. "If I were you, I'd get over there pretty quick. You're not the first filoz to visit her today, you know."

The rush of anger that swept through him caught him off guard. He forced himself to stand perfectly still despite his body's need to race from the dome and find whom he sought.

The diminutive woman put out both her hands as she spoke to Awan. "Whoa, I'm just the messenger."

Takoda studied his friend. What he saw on Awan's face reflected his own sudden response. Forcing himself to relax his facial muscles, he addressed her. "I apologize, but I do not remember your name." He sensed more than witnessed the protector stiffen.

She waved him off. "Oh, we never exchanged names. You were far too into Ro to notice anyone else. My name is Cali. And you are?"

Before he could answer, Awan did. "This is Takoda and I am Awan."

At Awan's pronouncement, she giggled. "It's very nice to meet you. I'm on my way out, but if you head through that archway," she pointed behind her to the middle of three openings, "and take the second path on the left, you'll find Ro." A sparkle came into the woman's brown eyes. "I'm sure she'll be surprised to see you." Something in her knowing glance had him wondering if she knew more than they did?

He bowed his head but watched her carefully. "Thank you."

She gave them a wide knowing smile. "Happy to help. Rowena Lewis is one lucky lady." She nodded. "Yup, very lucky indeed." With that pronouncement, she stepped around them and headed for the front archway that led to the public path.

The protector quickly caught up to her and opened the door to let her out. As soon as the door closed, he nodded toward it. "This Cali knows something we do not."

Awan scowled. "Yes. She knows that another filoz visited today."

He was about to remark on Awan's clenched hands but stopped as he forced his own to release. He lowered his voice. "At least we know that Rowena is the one we seek."

"Rowena. Yes. She said her friends call her Ro." Awan's face softened. "I called her Rowena last night."

That Awan's memory returned was important, but Takoda didn't want to discuss it in the Pleasure Dome. "I think we need to see Ro now." Without waiting, he strode for the archway Cali had indicated. Had she given them directions because she didn't think they remembered which way to go? How would she know they had very few memories of the night before?

Once outside in the courtyard, he halted.

"What is it?"

He looked Awan in the eye. "You remembered something. Tell me."

"I only remembered her name when it was mentioned."

"Nothing else?" He searched his own memory as well, not able to bring up any image beyond the woman in the throes of her delight. At least they'd brought her that somehow. Beyond the image was only the soft scent of sweet fruit.

"I remember much about her. How smooth her skin felt, how strong her body was, and how she grasped me as I pumped inside her." Awan's face took on the look of a man lost in his own pleasure.

Suddenly, Awan's face as he experienced his own ecstasy flashed through Takoda's mind. He had been looking at the brother of his heart and holding Ro against him as she faced Awan. If that was the only time one of them released inside her, they were safe. Relief flooded him. "Then I suggest we find her and ask her what happened last night, so we can go back to grieving the loss of our beloved."

Awan's eyes widened in surprise. "Now you are anxious to discover the truth? Why?"

He shrugged his shoulders, unwilling to share his confidence that no bonding occurred. "As you said, it is better to know now."

Awan lifted his brows, a clear sign he didn't completely believe him, but he nodded. "Yes. Let us go."

He didn't wait a moment longer. Striding down the second path on the left, he tried to remember walking it the night before, but he couldn't. At the end of the path, he halted. Before him were three private domes. Which was Rowena's?

"Why do you stop?" Awan looked quizzically at him.

"Do you know which residence is hers?"

Awan studied the three structures and pointed at the one directly in front of them. "Yes. It is this one."

"You are sure?"

Awan nodded, confident.

Jealous that his friend seemed to have more memory of their night with Ro, Takoda reached for the bells that would announce their presence then froze.

The bells. A shiver raced up his spine and a chill filled him.

"What is it?"

Awan's voice had him dropping his hand, but he didn't stop staring. "Look. These are not Tolban bells." Only complexes had bells. All private residences had crystals. He was not an expert on crystals, bells, artwork, or any of the finer things in life, but even he recognized these were from Earth.

"You are correct." Awan examined the similar trapezoid-shaped objects. "They look like Tolban bells, but they are made of another material and the painted designs are different yet similar. We must ask about them."

The bells made Takoda uncomfortable, but he didn't know why. "I think we have more important matters to discuss." And once it was clear they were not bonded, the bells would no longer be of concern.

"You are correct." Then without further thought, Awan rattled the chord attached to the bells and a strange sound vibrated through them.

Takoda felt the sound in his bones, but before he could contemplate the deep-rooted feeling, the door swung open.

"Well, that was shortest shopping trip—oh."

As his breath left him, he stared into wide eyes so green as to rival the yahaw tree leaves in full canopy. Flashes of images crowded his mind with expressions he remembered —sorrow, anger, hopelessness, wit, curiosity, ecstasy—ecstasy. His body heated even as a cold chill shook him. Rattled, he spoke, trying to ignore the tightness in his gut. "I am Takoda and this is Awan."

ROWENA SWALLOWED HARD, HER THROAT suddenly dry as sensual excitement swept through her at the sight of her lovers from last night. Her body obviously remembered more than her mind.

She couldn't say she was surprised. How could she have thought she could drink herself into oblivion with two such gorgeous, muscular hunks and not have sex? Had she really been that far gone?

The one called, Awan, chuckled and she moved her gaze from the dark-haired Edenist with the deep blue eyes to the tall blond one, whose amber eyes smiled with amusement as he spoke to his friend.

"Takoda, I think she already knows that." Those warm eyes moved to focus on her. "Please excuse him, we did not get much sleep last night."

A wave of heat rushed through her body and her cheeks warmed. At her reaction, he too appeared to flush. Now this was uncomfortable. Quickly, she stepped back holding the door open wider. "Please, come in."

As the two men walked by her, the scents of citrus and ginger filled her nostrils, and she closed her eyes in pleasure. Her aromatic memory kicked in to provide her with the image of being sandwiched between the two of them, one holding her as the other slid inside.

She pulled in air and snapped her eyes open before shutting the door to hide her body's reaction though it probably didn't help since Edenists could cue into pheromones. Why had they come? Had they bonded and come to claim her? A spike of fear sliced through her even as her body reacted well to the idea. They could just be here to see how she felt after their night together. That would be in keeping with an Edenist thought process.

Might as well brazen it out.

Turning back to face the room, she found both of them looking at her as if reacquainting themselves with who she was. She wanted to do the same, but while she was dressed in a pair of workout leggings and oversized button-down shirt, they were nude, and to study them would make an awkward situation worse.

"Please, sit." While standing, they seemed to crowd the room. "Can I offer you water, ambrosia, kafez?" At the word kafez, guilt crept up her spine. Micco and Sist were the ones who had brought her the kafez.

"No, please. We'd like to talk to you." Awan reached his hand out to indicate the couch across from them.

Right. Talk. "Of course." She moved to the other couch and sat crossed legged on it. "We are very good at talking." She gave them a tentative smile. She hadn't remembered their names until Takoda had blurted them out, but she had remembered they talked. She increased her smile, more grateful to the dark-haired man for being embarrassed by his supposed faux pas so that she appeared to know their names.

Awan's smile widened. "Yes, we are." He gave Takoda a triumphant look that she didn't understand.

Takoda didn't catch it, his gaze focused on her like a man who couldn't believe he was meeting someone he'd always hoped to meet. That made no sense since they were all together just last night.

When neither spoke, she cocked her head to the left. "What would you like to talk about?"

Immediately, Takoda looked away. Was that embarrassment or shame?

"We would like to discuss last evening." Awan had lost his smile and didn't quite meet her eyes.

She disliked it when people "beat around the bush" as her mother used to say. Her family always addressed issues head on. It was more expeditious and often avoided bigger problems down the road. Suddenly, her stomach tightened. Or were they hesitant because they bonded last night after all and didn't know how to tell her?

Despite her intentions of getting to the point, she grasped at anything besides that. "I have to apologize for dumping my problems on you last night."

As if relieved at her choice of subject, Takoda's gaze came back to her. "But we did the same to you." His knit brow made it clear he was honestly confused by her apology since they'd all shared their woes.

She really did like the way Edenists thought. "True, but the tequila I added to the conversation probably brought us all down even more. It's known on Earth that alcohol is a depressant and it was the last thing we all needed."

Awan raised his palm to his head. "My head pains are almost gone. Is that teekeela also known for leaving behind such pain?"

She grimaced. "It all depends on the person, but that is a common side effect."

"Does it also take away memories?"

At Takoda's question, she nodded. "I'm afraid that is another common side effect."

At the relief that crossed his face, she moved her attention to Awan, who also appeared pleased with her answer. Wait. Did that mean they didn't remember last night either? That could be both good and bad.

Before her brain could go into risk-management mode, Awan spoke. "We appreciate knowing this. We seem to have lost our memory about last night."

"Not all of it though." Takoda's kind smile, probably meant to reassure her, did anything but.

She widened her eyes. "Are you saying you don't remember much of our conversation?" *Please let that be it.*

The two men looked at each other before Awan took a deep breath. "No, what we are saying is we do not remember if we bonded with you last night."

And there it was - the elephant in the room - the one piece of information they *had* to have but didn't. Her mouth went dry.

Takoda reached his arm across the table and put his hand on her knee. The almost electric shock that action caused had her flinching unintentionally. His blue eyes darkened in response. "We do not mean that we don't remember *anything.*" He glanced at Awan before returning his gaze back to her. "We value you and the pleasure we all shared. "His gaze searched hers as if needing reassurance.

She nodded, not sure why he would need that, but her body was too wound up by his touch to get her vocal cords working. Moving out from beneath his hand, she rose and walked to her kitchenette for her cold morning kafez.

Awan's voice followed her. "We came here to discover if you are our agapayto."

In other words, their beloved, their bonded one, their wife!

She took a sip of the cold caffeine, forcing herself to swallow. They didn't remember. She didn't remember. She could lie and say they didn't bond and hope for the best, but that wasn't her style.

Finally, she turned, the half-finished kafez still in her hands. She would tell them the truth and see where it led. She had no choice. Bonding was a biological connection that could not be broken. All she could do is hope it hadn't happened. "I do not know. The tequila had the same effect on me as you."

Takoda scowled. "But surely you are used to this type of drink, otherwise, why would you drink it?"

It wasn't difficult to see he was angry, but his question was more than fair. "That's the problem, I don't normally drink it. I was saving it to..." she paused, not sure how much she'd already told them, "...for a special occasion, but when that didn't happen, I used it to drown my sorrows."

At the confused look on their faces, she explained further. "On Earth, it's common to drown one's sorrows by seeking an outside distraction. Some use alcohol like I did last night. Others might turn to drugs, another human, or simply to sleep. Some bury themselves in work to keep their mind off their troubles, unless of course, work is the trouble." She barely held back a snort at how well that didn't work. At least, not for her.

Once she'd been made director of risk management for her German-owned pharmaceutical company with offices in Boston, she'd started looking for someone to share her life with. She'd been completely focused on her career goal for years, but once achieved, she'd easily put the same dedication into meeting Mr. Right.

Only Mr. Right always turned out to be Mr. Wrong. Every time that happened, and there were dozens of times, she'd thrown herself into her work. But it never took her mind off her failed search for a life partner.

"This we didn't know."

At Awan's statement, she moved her focus to him and found him deep in thought. His face in that moment brought another image to her mind from last night. He'd been listening to her whine about the state of her life back home with that same focused look, then had met her gaze with such empathy that her heart had responded. She quickly lifted the cup to her mouth and finished off what was left of her morning kafez.

Having no other reason to stay in her kitchenette, she forced herself back to the sitting area and sat.

They both stared at her, Takoda still frowning a bit and Awan contemplative.

She didn't know much about them. After last night, all she knew was that they lived in a different hatchoc, they were heartbroken, and they were good in bed. No, make that amazing in bed. She flushed as her body tingled with remembered feelings.

But they were also good listeners, and she was pretty sure that they had all talked well into the night before they found themselves in each other's arms. An idea formed. "Maybe between the three of us, we can remember enough to figure out what happened."

Both men seemed to relax a little. How odd that she could tell. With Takoda, it was in his shoulders, but with Awan it was more in how he held his head.

Awan nodded. "This is a good plan. Takoda and I have discussed this. I remember reaching my release inside you. Takoda remembers seeing you reach yours."

Her cheeks heated. To talk about sex with two men who were in all actuality strangers was both embarrassing and arousing. But there was no help for it. Not exactly one of her most comfortable moments on Eden.

She closed her eyes, trying to remember. She saw Awan on top of her, his gaze intent on her and the excitement coursing through her. She opened her eyes and took a calming breath. "Yes, I remember you."

Awan's smile was pure male satisfaction on any planet. "Good."

"What about me?"

Takoda's gaze was intense. She wasn't sure if that was because his ego needed reassurance or that he wanted to know whether they had bonded. She closed her eyes again and tried to recapture the image of being sandwiched between them. Her sheath tightened as the image came to life.

She'd been on the bed with both men, facing Takoda, of that she was sure. She remembered burying her nose in the soft, dark hair on his neck. Awan was behind her, his hand everywhere. Hell. It felt amazing.

"Rowena?" Takoda's softened voice sent a shiver of need through her even as she opened her eyes.

"Yes."

His lids had lowered slightly and his nostrils flared. "Your memories of our pleasure are shared."

What? She lowered her gaze to find his body had reacted.

Crap, she forgot about the pheromones. With a quick surreptitious glance toward Awan, she confirmed her simple memory had aroused them.

"I apologize. I was just remembering the three of us, all…" She swallowed. "Together."

Takoda shook his head. "Do not apologize. It is what we need to know."

"And we enjoy your pleasure." Awan grinned, obviously pleased they could make her feel so good.

They definitely had. Way too good. Was it simply because she had both of them making love to her as opposed to one at a time like she'd had with Micco and Sist? Just the thought of the two men she'd hoped to find love with had her ardor cooling.

Takoda threw Awan a scowl before turning back to her. "Do you remember which of us was inside you when we were all conjoined?"

Nothing like being blunt. Her stomach sank as she nodded. "I do. It was you."

At her statement, his eyes widened in surprise.

"You don't remember?" Now she knew how it felt for a man if a woman wasn't pleased with his performance in bed. Takoda's reaction made her feel lacking in some way though that made no sense. The tequila had taken his memory.

"I do not, and for that I am disappointed." His shoulders fell as if he had failed in some way.

She couldn't let him feel bad. "It's the tequila. It's what it does if you have too much. That was a very big bottle. I'm actually lucky you shared it with me. If had drunk the entire thing by myself…" She shivered, as that had been her intention. "I would have needed more than a healer." She gave him a tenuous smile, even though he didn't look at her.

Awan placed his hand on Takoda's shoulder. "This is not you. It was the alcohol we drank. It is not your fault you cannot remember. We must look at what we *do* know."

Takoda finally lifted his gaze to her. "From what you say, we both enjoyed your satisfaction. Do you know if we found our release inside you one after the other?"

Her whole body flushed at his direct speech. She was probably red from her feet to her forehead, but she wasn't about to look at her bare arms to confirm that. Instead, she shook her head.

Takoda shot up and walked behind the longseat, his strides angry or maybe frustrated. She couldn't be sure. She didn't blame him.

"Wouldn't you two be in the habit of being careful? Do you really think the tequila could have made you lose all your innate inhibitions as to bond with me, a stranger for all intents and purposes?" If there was one thing she knew, it was that practice and habit saved many a mishap.

Takoda stopped pacing. "She's right. We have always been careful until Xavia."

Xavia? She searched her mind for who that was. Nothing came, but it must be their beloved who left with the brother of their heart and bonded outside the walls of Tolba.

Awan turned his head to look at Takoda, giving her an unimpeded view of his large neck muscles, not to mention the arm that she was sure could crush a boulder if he so chose. Again, heat filled her body. She really needed to keep focused on their problem.

Awan answered his friend. "That may be true, but remember, I see four scenarios which say we bonded."

At that pronouncement, her body cooled. "Scenarios? What scenarios?"

Awan faced her again. "It is my Kindred of Mind ability. When given a problem or issue, I can see eleven possible scenarios."

What she wouldn't have done to have someone like him working in her office. "Why eleven?" That odd number was always cropping up in Tolba. She found it weird.

Awan shrugged his shoulders. "It is not for me to question. It simply is."

She wasn't sure how she felt about his acceptance, but even with four out of eleven, the odds were that they hadn't bonded. "That's still under forty percent chance, or actually closer to only a thirty-percent chance we bonded."

Then again, he didn't have all the information when he last ran those scenarios. More information always gave a clearer picture of the possibilities. "What if you include what I just told you and run your scenarios again?"

Awan shook his head. "That is not how it works. When I request possible outcomes, nothing I know has to do with it. My knowing more won't change them."

That was confusing. "I thought this was your special ability, to gather the information and predict possible results, like a super math whiz."

"I do not know what is a 'math whiz.' For me, it is not a conscious synthesizing of information to run the scenarios. It is a gift from Eden. Knowing more won't change them. My mind simply fills with eleven visions of what could be."

The whole situation was getting more frustrating by the minute. Eden abilities were far beyond her realm of experience. And they were getting them nowhere.

Awan sighed. "Since we cannot be certain, I propose that you come live with us until we can confirm the existence of a bond or lack of one."

"No."

"No."

She whipped her gaze to Takoda, who had answered in unison with her. A rush of hurt hit her square in the chest even as his eyes widened. What the hell was wrong with her?

She rose, needing to do something, anything. She strode to the archway of her bedroom and stared at the still unmade bed, willing her brain to remember. Wouldn't she know if she'd bonded? How could she not? This was crazy!

Large hands covered her shoulders, and she had the weirdest impulse to turn around and accept the offer of comfort they communicated, but that wasn't her. So as not to offend, she simply turned around, figuring Awan would step back, but he didn't. Instead, he simply laid his hands back on her shoulders as his warm gaze met her own. "Do not panic. We need not make any decisions right now. All will become clear within the next few days."

Of course. If they had bonded, they each would feel some kind of connection within the week, or so she'd been told. She nodded. "Yes. Then we will know either way."

Awan leaned forward and kissed her on the forehead. "Do not worry. What was meant to be will be."

It was a common Tolban sentiment and usually she didn't pay it much attention, but right now, it did give a little comfort…a little.

The fact was, there was nothing they could do but wait. Patience was not her best quality, but there was no other choice.

Awan gave her a reassuring smile before lifting his hands from her shoulders and turning to Takoda, who still stood behind her longseat, only now he was back to scowling.

She completely agreed with his sentiment, but it transformed him from the good-looking guy next door to someone who was about to pound his fist through a wall.

He turned that look on her. "You cannot have anyone here until we know."

"Excuse me?" Heat spread from her chest upward as anger took hold. "This is my home and I'll have whomever I—"

Once again Awan's hand rested on her shoulder though he spoke to Takoda. "We cannot demand anything, but perhaps Rowena will see the wisdom of not having other Edenists to her bed before we have confirmed her availability." He turned his head and simply looked at her.

How could the man be so calm in the face of their situation? She wanted to yell at someone, but the only person she could blame for this whole fiasco was herself.

At that realization, guilt crept in for dragging these two, obviously good Edenists, into her mess. The least she could do is agree to what was a reasonable request and hardly a problem for her anyway. She nodded.

Awan let out a silent breath, revealing how important her decision was to him.

Takoda's shoulders relaxed and his scowl disappeared.

That just made her guilt double. And what would she say to Micco and Sist next time they came to see her? Maybe she'd get lucky and they'd be too busy this week. Yeah, and the temperature on Eden might dip into the fifties. She'd really made a mess.

Awan moved past her toward the door, but Takoda walked around the longseat and came to stand before her, his dark blue gaze intense but not threatening. "Your eyes."

At first, she thought he wasn't going to continue, he paused for so long, but then he did.

"They touch one's soul."

Her heart seemed to stop for a moment at his words, his own eyes mesmerizing in their own right.

Then, as if he shouldn't be looking at her at all, he spun away and followed Awan to the door. Within seconds the door closed, her last sight of them, their naked broad backs and muscular butts.

She blinked, to get her mind to function again and when it did, she laid her hand on her face and spoke to the oppressively silent room. "Now how the hell am I supposed to know if there's a bond?"

Chapter Four

Awan strode through the courtyard, his frustration impossible to hide any longer. His excitement of what could be possible with Rowena was thwarted by not knowing what had happened. His hands curled into fists of their own accord and he had the rare inclination to pummel something, anything.

"Awan."

He entered the Pleasure Dome and skirted the furniture, barely keeping himself from picking it up and throwing it across the room.

"Awan!" Takoda grabbed his arm.

Without thinking, he wrested his arm away and swung.

Luckily, the brother of his heart knew him that well and ducked. Instead of getting angry, Takoda chuckled. "I was wondering how long you could hold back your anger."

He took deep breaths, fisting and unfisting his hands, attempting to find the control he'd lost. And failing.

Takoda nodded to his right at the Lead Protector who watched with obvious concern. "Maybe we should exit before discussing this further."

He scowled. "That is what I was doing." Ignoring the smile

that played about Takoda's mouth, Awan continued toward the large archway with double doors and threw them open, only to halt as a man with two trays of baka buns walked by him, oblivious to how close he'd come to having his wares knocked to the ground.

"Breathe."

Takoda's word had him turning. "I know that. Believe me I'm trying."

"Why is it so bad this time? The only other time I saw you lose control so much was when Xavia disappeared."

At that observation, his breathing slowed. He could always count on Takoda to bring him back into balance. "You're right. It is odd that my psyche is so disturbed by this turn of events." It made him want to ponder the issue more. "This will be resolved in a matter of days, yet I am uneasy."

"If you could be like me and allow the anger to surface as it occurs then you would not have this issue."

He wasn't sure that was true. His responses were instinctual or possibly conditioned. He'd never once seen his fathers even scowl at his mother, never mind speak their mind in Takoda's tone of voice. One of his fathers took him aside after his first "episode" and said it happened to him as well, which meant there was no changing it.

But as his father said, it was simply meant to be that way for them. "I think it best if I go home. I will let the Discoverist Resource director know that I will be taking a few days to re-balance."

Takoda frowned. "It is that bad?"

He nodded, not willing to voice how unsettled he felt. It was as if his body and brain weren't functioning correctly and every move, every thought itched like the rash from a naswa plant. Trying to describe it to Takoda would be a hopeless endeavor.

After another moment of introspection, Takoda held out his arm in invitation toward the thoroughfare which bustled with men going about their daily lives. "Then let us walk. It will be good for you to do something physical."

"You're coming with me?"

"Yes. The planner will not need me again today. I will check tomorrow and see if he can spare me a few days." Takoda glanced behind him at the closed doors of the Pleasure Dome before turning his back. "I am angry, frustrated, and worried and no fit company for anyone anyway."

"Then let us be unfit company away from all others." Awan moved into the stream of men striding purposefully toward or from their activities, some carrying various goods while others moved freely. He wondered, not for the first time, how many of them had lost a brother of their heart to exile and had to find a new way forward.

The ache in his heart was far harsher than he would admit to Takoda. Though they shared all, he didn't want to burden him with his own pain when Takoda, very obviously, was so unsettled himself.

Awan stepped to the side as two men maneuvered a cart of longseats out of a rut in the pathway. Xavia had said that Tolba reminded her of old western towns near where she'd lived, but much busier.

"We can't finish the additional hatchocs soon enough." Takoda's irritation at the crowded thoroughfare mirrored his own.

"Perhaps walking is not as conducive to our moods as we thought."

Immediately, Awan found himself rising above the throng

and floating toward home. There were definitely advantages to having a member of his filoz whose ability was to levitate.

From this vantage point, Tolba spread out before him in all its organized domed beauty. All homes, establishments, and public gathering buildings were constructed of toleric block and formed into a dome. The thoroughfare and pathways between buildings were packed dirt, but the courtyards of all building were filled with lush green vegetation.

The city was modeled after a tolba shell, each hatchoc a scute as delineated by wide walls of stone no taller than two men on top of each other. These had large wide arches to allow easy egress from one hatchoc to another.

Within each hatchoc, individual residences or places of industry were set apart by narrow short walls no higher than a man's shoulders. All were welcomed everywhere. It was the Tolban way. So why were Kindred of Eden being exiled? The recurring thought since Lyka's exile, further unbalanced him, and he pushed it away. All was as it was meant to be.

Takoda pointed beyond their home to the high walls at the edge of the city that protected them from the lawbreakers that were exiled to the jungle. "There is where our next extension will begin." On top of the thick walls could be seen painted stripes where the next break in the outer wall would occur.

"That does not look as large as where you work now."

Takoda began lowering them to the ground. "It is not. Where we work now will be a much larger hatchoc because it is to appear as the head of the turtle."

As his feet touched the dirt in their rear courtyard, Awan felt another surge of irritation. "And who is to populate that?"

"That is not decided yet." Takoda strode across the courtyard, past the round sunken hot pool and beneath the covered patrio before stopping at the rear door. He shook his head. "There is talk of moving the cheetans to new quarters there, of making it only for those who are well-established, or providing for new yeneas. From all I've heard, there is only one qualification they have agreed upon."

Awan didn't ask the obvious. The brother of his heart knew what he wanted to know.

Takoda opened the door and stopped, his eyes narrowed. "No Kindred of Eden will be allowed."

The surge of anger that hit him was so unexpected that he stepped back. Heat surging through him.

"Awan?"

He spun, his eye catching the outdoor eating area. Four wooden chairs surrounded the carved stone table. Striding to it, he grabbed a chair and smashed it on the table. Splintering wood flew across the courtyard. The sound and sight of the destruction eased the anger inside him.

He remained still, his breathing hard. What good was four chairs when they were no longer a filoz of three in search of a beloved anyway?

Steps behind him had him turning.

"Feel better?"

He nodded. "I do. But this is not me."

"No, it isn't. You need to find your balance again." Takoda's concern showed in his blue gaze. "How can I help?"

He pulled out one of the remaining chairs and sat. "I don't know. I don't think anything can be done until we know if we are bonded or not."

"What about one of your fathers. He might have practical advice."

Yes, this was true. "That is an excellent idea. I will visit them this evening."

Takoda shook his head. "No. I will bring them here. I have never seen you this out of control."

Though he grasped the chair arms tightly, he managed to nod. His mind acknowledged the wisdom of Takoda's words, but his emotions were winding up at the smallest resistance. What *was* wrong with him?

"I will leave you to your thoughts. Make them good ones." With that, Takoda walked into their home, leaving him alone.

Make them good ones. It was good advice if he could get his mind to cooperate, but Takoda was correct. This was not like him. Even when Lyka had been exiled and Xavia vanished, though he'd lost control then it was nothing like this.

A flash of memory had his whole body tensing again. During his transition, this had happened once before, before Takoda or Lyka had become his friends, before he'd learned his mind was stronger than his emotions. The transition, when his Kindred of Mind ability started to manifest, had caused a severe imbalance for him. It also signaled something important.

Life change.

Immediately, he rose and walked to the hot pool. Kicking off his clear footwear, he stepped down into the warm water to his waist. Then he'd known his life would change, but now?

He moved beneath the fountain and let the warm water wash over him, trying to find solace in his faith that whatever the outcome, it was meant to be. But even as he tried to focus on the concept, his mind wandered to Lyka, Xavia…and most of all, Rowena.

Takoda floated closer to the Pleasure Dome and scanned the residential domes emanating out from it. After three days, Awan was no better. In fact, despite his fathers' visit, he seemed to have grown worse.

He'd never seen the brother of his heart so out of control. Awan was always the calm one.

It had forced him into the role of being the calm one and it didn't sit well with him. He'd gravitated toward Awan when they were younger because of his ability to take everything in stride, while he'd always felt as if he were at odds with the world, like a changeling left in the stead of a true Edenist. Awan had made him feel as if he belonged and Lyka had fit in perfectly to their filoz.

He fisted his hands as he hovered over Rowena's home, not really sure why he was there except he needed to do something.

Was she there? Had she sensed anything yet? Neither he nor Awan had noticed anything different except for Awan's volatility. Could that be the bond? He couldn't imagine that was it. Each bonding was unique to the Earth woman and Edenists involved, but it never made an Edenist worse. In fact, it usually filled a need of some kind.

He had no needs, except for wanting back Xavia, his chosen one, and Lyka, the brother of his heart, but nothing could accomplish that. They had bonded with Davos, the dirgon shifter, the first Kindred of Eden to be exiled for simply being Kindred of Eden. The fact that Davos could change into what was thought to be a long extinct dirgon had instilled a fear in all Tolbans that had only grown with the passing years. Now all Kindred of Eden were looked upon with trepidation.

He didn't understand that. A shifting Edenist in itself was a bit concerning, yes. And he certainly comprehended the possible danger of a prehistoric animal wreaking havoc and destruction among the citizens of Tolba, but that was radically different from Lyka, the brother of his heart, who could simply blend in with the scenery. How could that be dangerous?

Takoda shook his head to disrupt the now familiar spiral his thoughts were heading down. First, he had to make sure they had not bonded with Ro. Then he could go about the task of living while trying to let his feelings for Xavia go. He hadn't told Awan yet, but he wasn't sure he would ever be ready to seek a new beloved.

Activity below caught his attention. A man was exiting Ro's residence! She'd promised!

Instinct had him rushing down to tackle the man, his rage uncontrolled.

"Hello? Anyone here?"

At the sound of Ro's voice, he halted not far from the ground. Giving the back of the man a final glare, he turned to see her walking around to the rear of her dome. He levitated higher to better view her progress. She stood in her small courtyard, hands on her hips, scanning the area as if an Edenist could be hiding behind the salis bushes.

She shook her head. "You're totally losing it, Ro." Dropping her hands, she started around the other side of her dome, still looking about as if she were in search of someone.

When she reached her door, she hesitated, once more scanning the immediate area before stepping inside and disappearing from view.

Not sure what that odd behavior meant, he rose higher to see if the man that had been in her residence had exited the Pleasure Dome, but there was no sign of him.

Tamping down his anger, he lowered himself to the ground and strode to Ro's door, determined to find out why she'd broken her word to them. His stomach churned so much, he felt like he would be sick.

Reaching up to ring the bell, he snatched his hand back. He didn't like those bells. They weren't Tolban but tried to be.

Before he could decide how to let her know he was there, the door swung open.

"Takoda. I knew it!"

Taken aback, he stared into her triumphant green gaze.

"Come in." She swept her arm to the side in invitation. Her wide sleeved clothing at odds with her tight leg wrappings.

He strode in, quickly scanning the living area before turning to face her. "You promised." His words came out in a growl, but he didn't care. Hurt and rage fought for control.

Her brow lowered in confusion. "I don't know what you mean. The only thing I promised you and Awan was that I wouldn't take another man to my bed."

Her eyes widened and she threw her hands up. "Oh, for criminy sake, it's only been three days. What do you think I am, a nympho? I'll have you know that at least half the women who live here don't do so because they want to have sex with every hot Edenist who walks through the door. We live here because it's the only place you have in this city for single women."

Her raised voice had him folding his arms, his fingers biting into his biceps as he struggled for control. He wanted to yell right back, but his upbringing prevented him. "I saw him."

"You saw…oh, you mean Kuruk. He's Cali's protector. We're planning a little surprise for her birthday. You thought I'd slept with him?" Again, her voice rose to a higher pitch.

But as her words settled in his brain, his rage dissipated as quickly as it had come. He opened his mouth to apologize when her eyebrows lowered and the gaze he found so fascinating narrowed.

"You were spying on me. How dare you?" She pointed her finger at him, her cheeks flushing.

By the Crius, he'd upset her. Why couldn't he do anything right with this woman? Uncrossing his arms, he held them out to the side. "I wasn't spying on you. I came to talk to you."

This time she crossed *her* arms which were covered in a maroon swirl patterned material. "How did you get here? I just walked all around my dome and there was no one anywhere nearby. Then you suddenly appear."

"I levitated."

"You what?"

He held out his hand and lifted it parallel to the floor to approximate his ability. "I levitated."

"Like a magician?" Her brow furrowed again.

He searched his brain for any knowledge he may have learned in school about something called a magician but couldn't find anything. "It's my Kindred of Air ability."

She raised a brow in clear doubt. "I haven't heard of an Edenist being able to do that."

She could accept that Awan could see eleven scenarios, but

not that he could levitate? Unhappy about that for no apparent reason, he lifted his hand higher and raised her two steps off the floor.

"What? You didn't say anything about levitating other people." She looked frantically about as if afraid she'd fall. He'd never let anyone fall.

He brought her toward him until she was within arms-reach then carefully placed her back on the floor. He took a step closer. "I can levitate whatever I wish." He'd meant the words to come out like his father when he would scold, but they lost their power with her proximity.

She stared at him in surprise before she appeared to swallow hard. "I didn't know that was a thing."

With sheer willpower, he resisted the urge to wrap her in his arms and kiss her slightly opened mouth. "It is."

They stood nose to nose, barely apart, breathing each other's air. She broke the stand-off first, stepping back. "Well, no wonder I felt like someone was watching me. Where were you?"

He pointed to the ceiling above them. "There."

She looked up, her slender neck enticing him.

He took a step back, widening the space between them. "I travel across the city above the domes. It's much faster that way."

She brought her gaze back to meet his. "That makes sense. If I could levitate, I'd use it as a means of travel as well. Tolba, during the day, is busier than Faneuil Hall at lunch time. At least I know why I felt as if you were nearby. You were."

Takoda's breath stuck in his chest. It couldn't be. He forced his lungs to function. "Me? I thought you said you sensed someone nearby."

She shrugged. "Yes, but you were the first person to come to mind." Turning away, she walked to her meal area and picked up a glass. "I was just about to pour myself some byunca juice. Would you like some?"

"No. I am fine. I do not care for it. Too tart."

She waved away his objection. "Oh, I agree, which is why I load it up with sugar from Earth." She held her finger over her lips. "Don't tell though. I know the cheetans frown on taking anything from Earth…besides women." She smiled before turning back toward her counter.

That was true. The cheetans were strict about that. Sugar was only produced by the City of Kif and it was very rare. There wasn't an Edenist he knew who would pass up something with sugar in it, including him. "Then I would enjoy a small amount."

He walked to the little area that provided what she needed to heat up meals and keep food cold, but it was not a full meal room. It had never occurred to him how meekwee lived. His experience with the women who were willing to have intercourse with men outside a filoz was always focused on their sleeping rooms. Suddenly, how she lived mattered. "How do you make your meals?"

She handed him a small glass. "I don't, though I suppose I could with the inducer. I get my meals from my favorite restaurants, I mean meal domes. Then if I have leftovers, I use the inducer to heat them up." She moved to her longseat and pulled one leg up on it, wrapping her arm around her bent knee. "If I'm feeling lazy, I ask my protector to go out for my food."

He followed her to her living area but didn't sit. He needed to get back to Awan soon. Leaving him alone for any length of time in his condition wouldn't be wise.

"So why did you come to see me." She gave him a half-hearted smile. "Where is Awan?"

He took a sip of the sweetened juice to think of his answer, but as the sweet yet tart flavor washed over his tongue, he closed his eyes. It was remarkable! If it always tasted like this, he'd have it every morning, but it didn't. She was right, it was so much better with sugar. Opening his eyes, he found her brows raised in question.

"You like it then?"

He smiled like he had when his mother caught him eating his fifth baka bun before the evening meal. "It is very good this way."

"I know. It takes a lot of sugar, so I don't drink byunca juice that often, but this afternoon, I just had a craving for it." She shrugged. "One thing I like about Eden, is that it's so easy to satisfy a craving here. My responsibilities are few and my time is my own." She sighed as if it would soon disappear.

He took another sip, savoring the flavor while he scanned the room. It was much like other meekwees' except that there was a lack of personalization in it. Either she preferred a sparse appearance or she hadn't been on Eden long. There were no decorations of any kind on the counter or walls. No fresh flowers graced the tables or what his mother called knick-knacks on shelves.

"You didn't answer my question. Where is Awan? Is he at the Discoverist complex?"

Her voice brought his gaze back to hers. If he avoided her direct gaze, he did better concentrating. "No, he is at our residence today." Awan preferred that no one know he sometimes had difficulty balancing, so Takoda didn't elaborate.

She studied him then put down her cup. "Takoda, why did you really come here?"

He crossed his right arm over his chest and held his left shoulder. "I came to discover if you felt anything. It's only been three days, but a majority of bonds happen in that time." He wouldn't tell her that he feared for Awan's sanity.

"Have you?"

Her question caught him off guard. "No. I haven't."

"And Awan? Has he sensed anything?" She picked up her cup again, but there was a slight tremble in her hold before she grasped it with both hands.

Was she afraid? Nervous? Did she hide something? If she did, she had to know it would reveal itself. The bonding was unbreakable. "No, Awan has not."

She gave him a relieved smile. "Then I guess there was no bond."

The flush of irritation caught him unawares. Why would he dislike her feeling relieved when it was exactly what he hoped as well? He wanted to erase that relief from her face. "As I said it *usually* only takes three days. Many times, it takes five and sometimes seven."

She cocked her head. "I thought you didn't want there to be a bond."

At her accusation, he winced. Bonding was sacred, no matter how it occurred. That she recognized his hesitation over it proved how poorly he'd spoken to her. "You misunderstood. Bonding is a gift to be treasured."

She dropped her leg over the side of the couch and set the cup on the table, not looking at him. "Just not with me."

The words, said so softly, cut him like a knife to the chest. He inhaled harshly at the feeling. "No, it is not about you."

She looked at him, defeat in her eyes. "I know. It's not me it's you. Don't worry about it. If we aren't bonded, I'll be fine."

Rising, she straightened her shoulders then walked to the door. "I'm thinking maybe we should wait another four days to be sure. If you'd like to check in with me then, I'd be fine with that."

Her message was clear. She wanted no more visits until then. His chest constricted with the knowledge he'd hurt her. He wanted to say something that would make her feel better. Awan was good at that, but right now even he wasn't himself. Maybe that was it. Like Awan, he wasn't "balanced" either. "As you wish."

He strode to the door she now held open but couldn't help stopping in front of her.

She raised her gaze to meet his.

"I'm sorry if I saddened you." He set his palm to the side of her cheek as he gazed into her eyes, willing her to accept his apology as sincere.

"No harm done."

But there was. He could see it. The deep sadness that had he and Awan seeking her out in the Pleasure Dome that night was still present. Instead of removing his hand, he wanted to lower his head and kiss her.

Before he could act on the unbidden inclination, she stepped back. "Have a good day."

He returned her nod and walked out. As the door closed, his gut constricted. A yearning to go back in had him turning around, but what could he do? What could he say? She wasn't interested in speaking with him right now. Defeated and oddly disappointed, he walked out from beneath the covered patrio and stood in the sun.

Accepting the fact that he must wait four more days before

returning, he levitated himself high above the Pleasure Dome compound and floated back to his hatchoc. It was for the best. He'd already left Awan alone for too long. He was bound to be unhappy.

As their home came into sight, he stared at the disturbance in the rear courtyard. What had happened?

Speeding up his flight, he recognized the area for what it was…a hole. It covered half the yard and almost abutted the hot pool. As he descended, it was clear the hole was growing larger and the reason for that moved with speed at one end. "Awan!"

Awan's frantic efforts ceased as he looked up, scowling and breathing heavy. "Where have you been? It has been a day since you left."

It had been no more than three hours, but from the damage to the courtyard, it appeared as if he'd been away three days. "I went to see Ro."

"Rowena?" At the mention of her name, Awan's breathing seemed to slow.

"Yes, Rowena. What are you doing?"

Awan observed the area around him as if coming out of daze. "Digging?"

He swallowed a chuckle. "Obviously, but why?"

The brother of his heart shrugged. "I needed to."

"Are you ready to come out of there and hear about my visit?"

Awan nodded, so Takoda levitated him out of the pit, not sure how he'd expected to get out on his own since it was deeper than he was tall. Before his feet hit the ground next to the outdoor table, Awan was already speaking.

"How is she? Has she felt anything?"

He leaned his ass against the back of a chair as he faced Awan.

"No. Though she did have a 'feeling' that I was nearby, but I'm not sure that means anything. It doesn't appear that she has many visitors and guessing that someone is in the vicinity may or may not be a bond."

"True. Did you feel anything while with her?"

He shook his head. "No, and I think I hurt her."

Awan pulled out a chair and sat, his calmness a stark contrast to the man he was just minutes before. He hadn't been this relaxed since before they'd left Ro's dome three days ago.

Whatever the reason, Takoda was glad for it. He needed the brother of his heart he could talk to. "I may have intimated that if she was not our beloved, I would still be content."

Instead of the anger Awan would have displayed at that news just this morning, his gaze filled with understanding. "I see. And she thinks it is because of who she is. She probably does not remember that just four days ago, we were in love with our former chosen one."

"*I am* in love. You may be able to accept it is meant to be, but I cannot. I cannot stop my feelings of love for Xavia." Takoda took two steps away, his anger and hurt too fresh to stay still while discussing it.

"I hurt too."

At Awan's quiet admission, Takoda calmed. They had both been hurt. He needed to remember that. Turning, he found Awan drinking from a cup, the liquid inside clearly a deeper pink than the Bendis moon.

Byunca juice.

He pointed at Awan's cup. "Where did you get that? We haven't had any in the dome for days."

"This?" Awan raised the cup. "I went to Nadee's meal room while you were gone. I had a craving for it and couldn't wait. You know I enjoy it. Why are you staring at me like that?"

Every fiber in his body suddenly came alive with joy and anger. It was as if he would shatter into elevendy pieces.

"Takoda? What is it?"

It couldn't be coincidence. Ro sensed his presence *and* she craved byunca juice.

Awan rose and walked to him, laying a hand on his shoulder, his concern clear. "Takoda?"

He stared into the tawny gaze of the man he cared about, depended on, and loved as part of his family and forced the words from his throat. "We have bonded."

CHAPTER FIVE

ROWENA LEANED HER BACK AGAINST the door, fisting her hands. Rejection hurt, no matter what words were used. She understood Takoda had just lost the woman he loved to another. It wasn't his fault. But what luck? Why did she even try?

Pushing away from the door, she strode toward her bedroom. Maybe she should just call it quits. Eden had been a nice place for a six-month sabbatical. A nice vacation, but obviously, she couldn't even find that illusive thing called love on a planet of naked men who practically worshipped women. If she couldn't find it here, she wasn't going to find it anywhere. She must be meant to live her life alone. For all she knew it was genetic.

Stopping in front of her bed, she fought the urge to lay down and cry. It wasn't the worst thing in the world, or rather universe. She had a great career, a comfortable bank account, and could do whatever she pleased without having to compromise with someone...or even two someones.

Then why did she feel such utter devastation? She'd been through this before with men she'd truly thought she loved. She barely knew Takoda, so why did it hurt so much. Her brain understood that he'd just lost the love of his life, so why did she feel that about him?

Get your shit together, Ro. You forgot his name for criminy sake! What about Micco and Sist?

That was a good question. She walked to the side of her bed and sat. She really liked those two men. Not only were they kind, thoughtful, and seriously attractive, but each was an excellent lover. More importantly, she had a feeling they'd be willing to spend time on Earth with her, one of her many requirements for bonding.

With Takoda and Awan, she had no idea what they thought about that. Hell, she didn't know anything about them except their kindred abilities, place in Tolban society, and snippets of their lovemaking. Even as she thought of it, another image flashed through her mind. She was on her hands and knees and Awan held her hips from behind while Takoda beneath her chest was— "No. I'm not thinking about that anymore. Way too distracting."

She rose, not sure what to do, but she needed to do something. Striding to the rounded chest on the back wall of her room, she opened it and took out a suitcase. If Micco and Sist didn't ask her to be their beloved in the next fourteen days, she'd go back to Earth. It was that simple, no matter how she felt about it. At least there she had a career and a couple of friends.

Throwing the suitcase on her bed, she opened it. She caught her breath at the framed photo she'd left inside. It was of her mom at her last promotion. Ro's eyes started to water and she pressed them closed.

She practiced her deep breathing. Why was she so emotional? This wasn't like her at all. Opening her eyes again, she lovingly laid the picture back down on the bottom. Moving to the table that served as a place to keep her clothes, she lifted a pile and set it in the suitcase over the photo to protect it. Tolbans didn't have dressers or closets because they didn't wear clothes. From what she understood, no one on Eden did.

She paused as she picked up the second pile, this one mostly tunics and leggings. Did the women who settled here really go nude? She walked to her suitcase. In the shops, such as they were, she'd seen other women, and they all wore clothes or wraps. Did they take them off when they returned home?

She'd never actually thought about it since her intent was to bring her Edenists home with her. Settling the pile of clothing in her suitcase, she lifted the case off the bed and placed it on her almost empty table. The only other items on it were her brush, her hair ties and clips, and her Chamomile perfume. She loved the way they made it in Tolba.

What else could she pack now? Scanning the room, she noticed a book she'd borrowed from the Knowledge Dome. Micco and Sist had brought her there, introducing her to what she considered a library. She'd been more interested in their company than the books but had gone back numerous times since.

As if the thought of Micco and Sist had brought them back, she snapped her head up, sure that she'd see Takoda scowling at her through her window. She walked to it and scanned the backyard. No one was there. Was he hovering over her dome? If he was, he had four more days to wait.

Refusing to think about him, she picked up the book that had obviously been hand-bound and opened it. *The Animal Life of Eden.* She'd only made it halfway through. It started with prehistoric life and slowly, with emphasis on "slow," moved forward. She'd made it to the beginning of the last century in Eden time and hadn't picked it up again.

She frowned at her impetus for borrowing it. There had been a bit of drama in the Pleasure Dome one night when a patrol had come in to take away a man who was Kindred of Eden. It had brought back memories of her first morning on the planet. So the day after the incident, she went to the Knowledge Dome to see if she could find information on that specific kindred, but there was nothing. She found information on Kindred of Mind, Heart, Water, Light, and Air, but nothing on Eden. She'd assumed it was lent out, so she'd settled for the history of animal life, since Kindred of Eden had abilities that came from the planet itself, both plants and animals.

It had given her more understanding of Micco who told her he had abilities from the prehistoric bird called a zander, which was unusual. She assumed that was why he was a discoverist. She would have never become involved with Kindred of Eden, but discoverists were held in high esteem, just below cheetans, so she was sure he was safe from exile.

With no interest in finishing the book, she brought it into her living room and laid it on the coffee table. She should let Takoda read it. It was amazing how some species mated for life. She smirked as she stared at her curved ceiling. "I'm not going out there just to see if you're here. Go away."

Looking around to see what else she could pack, she walked to her kitchenette. She had a few items she'd take with her, but she'd need them over the next few weeks.

Turning back toward her bedroom, she was surprised by the sound of her bells. It couldn't be Cali because she was supposed to be getting a massage. It better not be Takoda expecting her to see him.

Curious, she moved toward the door. She'd want to take her bells with her, but they were obviously still needed. She'd make a list so she didn't forget anything. Once she left the planet, that would be it. She wouldn't even remember Eden existed. It was part of Crius Law.

Opening the door, she froze. "Awan?" Confused, she tried to look over his shoulder. She was positive it would be Takoda.

Awan smiled. "And Takoda." He moved aside to reveal the man she'd just told not more than an hour ago that she didn't want to see him for another four days.

"Why are you here? Did you remember something?" She was both excited and nervous.

Awan smiled apologetically. "I know you weren't expecting us, but we need to talk with you."

There was something about his warm gaze that made her feel as if everything was going to be fine. Her grandmother had had that knack, and she was always right.

She gave a brief nod and backed up to allow them in. The scent of citrus and ginger wafted by. She couldn't help taking a deep breath. They *did* smell good.

Closing the door, she expected to see them moving to her couch, but they remained standing just inside. "If you want to know if I've remembered anything else from that night, the answer is no. At least nothing significant."

Awan shook his head as he took her hand. "Rowena, we believe that we are bonded."

An unexpected thrill shot through her before her brain rebelled. Snatching her hand away, she stepped back. "Why?" She couldn't have bonded with strangers. Panic closed her throat and she shook her head, unable to say anything else.

Awan motioned to her sitting area, but her body wouldn't move. She'd come to this planet to find love, not a biologically forced marriage. This wasn't supposed to happen. *Except you let it happen.* Her conscience snapped her paralysis. She did. This was all her fault.

She glanced at Awan, whose sympathetic gaze made her want to cry, so she looked at Takoda. His eyes were dark and turbulent. He understood what a mess they'd made and didn't like it any more than she did. But they actually didn't make the mess, *she* did. She'd known the risks when she'd invited them both to her dome that night. She hadn't even had a drink yet before she'd walked in the Pleasure Dome.

"Rowena, would you like to sit?"

At Awan's question, she nodded, thankful for the excuse to turn her back on them both and gather her thoughts. First, she needed to assess the situation. How did they know? If true, what were the logical steps? What were her options? She glanced at her bedroom doorway, her suitcase out of sight, before settling onto the couch and crossing her legs beneath her.

Awan sat across from her once again, but Takoda remained standing behind him.

She had to admit, not only was Awan attractive, but he had some significant musculature going on.

Awan gave her a warm smile. "I know this is a surprise to you, but we all knew it might happen."

"True, but I'm confused on why you think we're bonded. I have had no indication that we are connected." She needed to analyze every piece of evidence or interpretation and look for flaws.

He continued. "You told Takoda that you felt him nearby before he arrived."

She waved her hand. "That's just women's intuition. That happens on occasion on Earth too."

Takoda frowned. "Does this intuition cause you to walk around your residence looking for the person you sense is nearby?"

She swallowed, desperately trying to remember if she ever had done something like that.

"And do you sense that person even though you have no idea they could be floating above you because they can levitate?"

She stared at Takoda in surprise. From the sound of his voice, he was insulted that she dismissed a supposed connection between them. Did he or did he not want this bond? Confused, she crinkled her brow and shook her head. "That could just be this planet somehow enhancing my instincts."

She returned her gaze to Awan. "The bond would be with both of you. I have not felt any connection to you at all."

He glanced at Takoda before facing her again. "Did you have a craving for byunca juice early this afternoon?"

"Byunca juice? Yes, but what does that have to do with the bond. Is craving byunca juice a sign of it?" From what she knew, there were no specific signs because it was supposed to be unique to each of the parties involved.

He gave her a soft smile. "No, not usually. But I craved byunca juice early this afternoon. It was such a strong craving that I left my home to obtain some."

Part of her brain started a happy dance and she squelched it. What the hell? "That could simply be coincidence?"

Awan shook his head. "It is not. It is the bond. I do not know if it is just the juice or what I want to drink, or if it is any craving I have or any craving you have, but whichever it is, we share it."

"That can be a bond?" She was obviously not well educated about this process.

Takoda answered. "Yes. And that you sense when I am nearby, that would also be a bond. Many times, it manifests as a protective or calming asset."

It was obvious he was quite proud of his supposed bond with her. What happened to him not wanting her? She could feel the panic creeping up her back again. It was as if she were trapped, which if the bond was real would be the case. "But the bond is supposed to go two ways, right? It's not just about me connecting to you, you would have a connection with me, right? Have you felt anything unusual?"

Awan's smile was wider now. "I have."

She blinked. She hadn't expected that. "What?"

"You balance me."

"Balance? Do you usually have difficulty walking?" She didn't remember him falling down the night she'd met him or even the next day when he came to visit.

He chuckled. "No, not physically balance. You mentally balance me. I…"

As he trailed off, his gaze moved away from hers.

Finally, he continued. "I have not been…well since I last saw you. My mental balance has been severely compromised. So much so that I had to remain at home. It has not happened often, but this time was the worst."

He paused again as if searching for the right words. She understood mental balance. Her sister had often struggled with mental health issues.

"It is as much physical as mental." Takoda stepped around the couch to stand next to Awan. "Awan is always in balance. It is what makes it possible for him to accept the scenarios that come with his Kindred of Mind ability. As soon as I returned from visiting you today and told him where I was, his balance stabilized."

She was getting the feeling that there was more to this "balance" thing than she understood. She looked at Awan. "Your balance returned just like that when Takoda told you where he was?" She snapped her fingers to emphasize her point.

He finally faced her. "Yes."

Her doubt must have shown on her face because he explained further. "When Takoda arrived home, I was digging a hole in our courtyard."

"A hole? For what? To plant a tree?"

Awan cringed, but a wry smile lifted the corner of Takoda's mouth. "We could plant an entire forest in this particular hole."

Awan shook his head but didn't explain.

Takoda lost his grin. "He was using his extra energy to cope with his imbalance."

"Extra energy?" She imagined Awan in a big hole shoveling mounds of dirt. "Oh, you mean he was letting off steam."

"Yes. I was letting off steam. As soon as Takoda mentioned he'd been with you, I calmed because the bond had revealed itself to Takoda. I didn't even know that yet, but the steam disappeared. Everything is now right. I need the bond to be."

It was a bit hard to believe, especially because she'd *never* had that effect on people. At work, when they saw her coming, they either groaned or tensed, knowing she would point out a risk, safety precaution or communicate a new procedure.

Even Cali wasn't calmed by her, but then again, her friend was a bit like a pinball and "balance" was not a word that would ever describe her.

Ro didn't know all the ins and outs of Eden bonding, but this one seemed to be a reach. "Couldn't it simply be that you were distracted by something else, say, the topic of me maybe?"

Awan shook his head, a confident smile lifting his lips.

He seemed so confident. She wished she could be as well. "But you aren't having any effect on me right now, and what about Takoda?" She moved her gaze from Awan's smile to Takoda's frown.

"I do not know. I have not felt anything."

"Yet." Awan looked at Takoda. "You haven't felt anything *yet*. The bonding is neither instant nor uniform. It could be a few more days before you understand your connection to Rowena."

She grasped onto that point. "Then we should probably wait and be sure. All you have told me could be coincidence. We need to be sure before we make any life changing decisions. That would be the proper way to approach this."

That sounded rather reasonable, not at all like her nerve-endings were firing off in different directions. It was as if her fight or flight instincts were kicking in at the same time, which was impossible. She wanted the bond to be real as much as she didn't.

"You resist what is meant to be." Awan's statement sent a cold chill through her while at the same time her heart filled with excitement. What the hell?

She returned her attention to him to find his eyes lightening from a tawny brown to a pale yellow. For the first time on Eden, she truly recognized that the Edenists were aliens. She sucked in her breath.

As his eyes returned to their normal color, his brows lowered. "There are others in your life."

She let out her breath. Of course! Micco and Sist. What if they had feelings for her? What if they still planned to propose?

Awan leaned forward, his elbows on his knees. "You do not want to be bonded with us." His confusion was clear.

How could she explain her reluctance when part of her was excited by the idea? This duality of feeling made it hard to figure out the safest course of action. "It's not that I don't want to be bonded with—"

"Of eleven scenarios, five show you have feelings for another filoz." He clasped his hands together tightly. She could see white under his skin because he was cutting off the blood supply.

How could he care that much when he didn't even know her? "Actually, I think if we got to know each other, I would very much like to be bonded with you. But you are correct, I have been interested in another filoz, but they have not asked me to bond."

His hands loosened. "I am sorry that hurts you, but I'm pleased that you have not committed to others."

At that statement, she snapped her gaze back to his. His caring look made her feel like she'd really messed all their lives up. "You said you saw eleven scenarios. What were the other six?"

He grinned. "Three are that you are excited to be our beloved."

Takoda moved away at that pronouncement, turning his back on them, reminding her that he'd rejected her. Only three out of eleven. He definitely had that right. Something inside her pushed her toward them. Luckily, she had willpower.

Unless it was the bond. Her mouth dried up instantly. There was no way to escape a biological connection. She had learned that her very first week on Eden. It was why two men never visited a meekwee together unless they were interested in a long-term relationship, as in forever.

Even as the thought filled her head, her body filled with fear. The bond when wanted was bliss, but if not, it was a life sentence.

"The other five are that you are afraid." Awan's words though barely above a whisper, startled her, hanging in the air almost echoing around them. It was as if he'd read her mind.

She pulled one leg up and wrapped her arms around her knee. "Why would you say that?" Her voice came out higher than she would have preferred, but at least it didn't shake.

"Yes, why is she afraid?" Takoda had turned around and studied her, his stance revealing that he was affronted for some reason. Really?

Awan sat back against the couch. "Rowena is afraid of the bond and what it means, but there is more, right?"

She couldn't sit still another moment. She rose and walked around to the back of the couch as if having it between them would protect her from the inevitable. "Of course there is more. I'm not afraid of bonding. It's why I've stayed on Eden so long. I'd hoped to bond."

She didn't need to explain she'd given up on Earth men. "But I wanted to bond with a filoz of my choosing, who cared for me as much as I cared for them." She speared Takoda with her gaze, refusing to back down as he stared right back.

She gripped the back of the couch, frustration rifling through her. It was far too complicated to explain even to Cali, never mind to two aliens, one who obviously thought it was wonderful and the other who disliked the idea as much as she did. *But you like the idea.* No, she liked the idea in general. *No, you are excited by them.*

Ignoring her conscience, she pointed to Takoda. "Ask him if he wants this. Ask if he fears being bonded."

Takoda's eyes widened. "It is not about what I want. If we are bonded, then it is so."

She grasped onto that tiny little word—*if*. "Ah, you are not convinced that we are bonded either."

He glanced at Awan then back at her. "If Awan agrees we are bonded then I trust it is true."

She threw her hands up, unable to keep her frustration to herself. What the hell? If they truly were bonded, they might as well know the real Rowena Lewis, not just the polite one. "It's meant to be. I trust Awan knows." She repeated their words. "This faith is admirable, but I can't change my life on faith. I need facts. Irrefutable facts." She slapped the back of her right hand into the palm of her left hand. "If you can prove to me that we have a bond then I'll accept it." At the thought that they could prove it, an odd peace settled in her chest.

She strode back to the front of the couch, part of her hopeful. "Can you do that?" She looked each in the eye. Unfortunately, in Takoda's gaze was resignation and in Awan's was pure confidence.

Awan stood, smiling. "We can." He scanned her living space. "Is there anything here you would like to bring with you?"

"Bring with me?" What did that have to do with proving they were bonded?

"Yes. You will need to come live with us."

Her heart started to race. She understood that if she were bonded with them, they would live together, but she hadn't lived with anyone since she was in grammar school. She'd lived with her aunt after her mom died, but she'd basically had the house to herself, since her aunt was a successful businesswoman and was gone before she woke up and home late at night. With her older sister in the treatment center, it had been just her.

She cocked her head. "What does proving we are bonded have to do with me moving in?"

Awan pushed the coffee table to the side with his leg and took her hands. "Do not be afraid. You must come and be our beloved in order to see and feel the proof of the bond."

She leaned to the right to see what Takoda thought of that.

He nodded. "This is true."

This couldn't be happening. *But it's what you wanted. It's why you stayed so long.* But she'd expected to choose her men, not have them chosen for her. *This is what mom wanted. What she missed.* At the memory of her mother's dying words, her panic lessened.

Her mother had been the youngest vice president of the financial firm and had been poised to move up when the CEO retired. Then she'd been diagnosed with stage four metastatic breast cancer. Her mom's only regret was she'd never had a true partner, a man who loved her as much as she loved him. Her mother made her promise not to follow in her footsteps.

That's why after achieving her career goals, she'd set out to achieve her personal goals with the same drive and dedication. So where was that dedication now?

She pulled her hands from Awan. "Very well. You have almost three weeks. At that time, I must return to Earth to keep my position at my company."

Awan's brow furrowed. "But you are bonded to us. You must stay here on Eden."

She shook her head. "That's not true. If we are bonded and if I am happy being with you then we can figure it all out. If I'm not happy and not bonded, I'll return to my old life." She'd been alone before. She could do it again.

Takoda stepped forward to stand shoulder to shoulder with Awan. "You'd break a bond?"

His shock was real. Despite the fact he didn't want this anymore than she did, he expected to simply live with it. "Yes. I'd rather return to lead a single life until I die than be in a relationship that makes me miserable. If I remember correctly, you said something similar the night we met."

Awan's eyes widened and he turned to Takoda. "You said that?"

"Probably. I do not remember."

She remembered that part clearly. "Yes, he did. He was bemoaning your beloved when he said it."

"Do not take our questions as doubt. We do not doubt you." Awan opened his arms, palms upward. "We simply do not remember, but we believe you."

She hadn't expected them to back down so quickly. "Then you accept my terms?"

Takoda looked to Awan, clearly having never encountered someone like her.

She swallowed a sigh. Maybe an Edenist had been the wrong route to take, but she was here now and possibly bonded. As long as she could leave if and when she wanted to, she should try it. On one hand, she refused to end up like Cali had on Earth. On the other hand, she did need the practice of living with other people. *And most importantly, you could fall in love.*

"I believe I understand now. You are not sure that you could come to care for us and we you."

Relieved that Awan understood at least, she gave him a half smile. "Yes."

"I believe that you will be surprised. Eden's plan for all of us is always for the best."

She stared into tawny eyes that glistened with excitement and she wished she could believe him, but in the back of her mind was the memory of Wym and Condor who had been pulled from their home at the break of day and exiled to the jungle full of criminals. That didn't seem to be what was best.

Chapter Six

Now that he knew there was a bond, Awan couldn't wait to learn all there was about Rowena and have her learn about them. She must have been the reason he and Takoda had lost Lyka and Xavia. They were obviously happy bonded to Davos. That had to mean that he and Takoda would be happy with Rowena. "We don't have to take everything with us now. Just what you prefer to have with you to make you feel comfortable."

He scanned the room, finally taking his attention from their new beloved. He received no feelings about who she was from the décor. It was as if she'd moved into the dome the day before. Nothing personal was readily seen. Perhaps in her sleeping chamber.

She pointed to the meal area. "I do have some baka buns in the cold box and other food items."

Takoda moved forward. "I can gather those."

Awan strode to the doorway of her sleeping area. "I'm sure you have items in here you would like to bring with you."

She hurried ahead of him as if she didn't want him to see inside. "I do. Give me a few minutes. I have a suitcase. I'll just throw some clothes in there."

He frowned. That Earth women preferred to cover their

bodies was well known and grudgingly accepted, though for an Edenist, it was the rudest insult. Still, he'd always dreamed that *his* beloved would be willing to forgo hiding her body to better fit into Eden society.

He moved away from the archway, shaking his head. He needed to give her time. This was new for all of them.

While Takoda filled a sack with her food, Awan meandered around the room. It concerned him that there were no clues as to what she liked or valued. He wanted to know everything about her. His memories of the night they spent together remained limited. She'd seemed to have given up. She'd felt like a failure for some reason, but he couldn't remember if she told them why.

That she was intelligent had been clear. Even today he'd seen it and only when he pulled the scenarios had he finally understood her reluctance. Anyone with such a logical mind would not have argued so long if not motivated by fear. He should have recognized it sooner.

He stared out the window, the dome next door blocking the view. What would she think about their residence? They could make changes for her to make her more comfortable. He grimaced. The courtyard appeared as if a pack of direlots had clawed it up and left it. Maybe he could—

"What do we tell our parents?" Takoda's whispered words jerked him from his thoughts.

It was a good question. "I think we should wait until we know each other better."

"In three weeks?" At the irritation in Takoda's voice, Awan snapped his head to look at him.

"What do you mean by that?" He kept his voice low as well.

"I mean that they never met Xavia. I don't want them to meet Ro either if we are left with a broken bond."

Awan's gut tightened at Takoda's words. "There will be no broken bond. She is ours."

"Maybe."

He waited for Takoda to continue, but instead Takoda turned away and set the sack he carried on the table between the two longseats.

It appeared he was the only one who understood this relationship was meant to be, but it wasn't the first time he'd had to convince others of the beauty of life's happenings. This time though, he held three hearts in his hands, or rather he would once they learned more about each other. This type of work was better suited to a Kindred of Heart than Mind, but he was determined to succeed for all their sakes.

"Okay, I'm ready." Rowena stood in the archway of her sleeping chamber, a big box with a handle in one hand and a book in the other. "I was going to return this to the Knowledge Dome tomorrow." She held the book aloft as if it was of the utmost importance.

Takoda moved forward and took it from her. "I can do that for you."

Her empty hand found her hip. "But what if I want to borrow another?"

"Then I can take you with me."

Awan watched the awkward exchange, his task already at hand. He strode toward them and faced Rowena. "He is considering your safety. Once you leave the Pleasure Dome, you will no longer have a protector. That will be our responsibility."

She dropped her hand. "Right. I forgot about that." Though she professed to understand the bond, even want it, she had no experience with it. He and Takoda had witnessed their parents' bonds and they both knew what it was to have a beloved. "I'm sure it will take us some time to adjust to our new living situation."

He took the box from her, surprised by how light it was. "But first, will you need to return here at a later time to gather more belongings?"

She swallowed. "Yes, I just packed what I want with me right now."

His instinct was to have her gather everything, but he tamped it down. No doubt it was the bond reacting to the idea that she might consider leaving them. This was an unusual and awkward situation. He'd only heard of such an event happening once before in his parents' generation. It had not ended well, according to the stories.

But this was unique, and they'd make it a different story. They already had by allowing her to come to terms with the idea in some way. In addition, she did appear to know quite a bit about Eden and its ways.

Takoda moved toward the door. "Then we can depart."

Still, she hesitated, looking around the room. "I feel like I'm forgetting something. It wasn't as if I had a long time to prepare for this move." She gave Takoda an accusatory look as if he were responsible.

The fact was they were all, in part, responsible and that is why he was so sure they were meant to be together. They were comfortable enough that night to share their grief, pain, disappointment and take comfort in each other. If they could share that, they could definitely become a true yenea.

The bells outside her door rang.

He understood the sudden scowl on Takoda's face. He too had the urge to keep whoever it was away from Rowena. It was a good omen.

Rowena moved forward, but Takoda pulled the door open, garnering him another scowl before she relaxed and smiled.

The small woman, Cali, stepped inside, her eyes moving from Takoda to himself. As her gaze fell to his hand and the item therein, a look of fear crossed her face with such intensity that his gut tightened in response.

She turned to Rowena and threw herself at her. "You can't leave me. Ro, don't go back yet. Please."

Rowena's eyes widened in surprise before she wrapped her arms around her friend. "I'm not going to Earth."

Cali pulled her head from Rowena's shoulder and peeked up at her. "You're not? Then where are you going because you are definitely leaving?"

"Yes, I am. I'm going with Takoda and Awan to their house."

Cali's fear and distrust immediately vanished, and happiness infused her face. "Oh, Ro. This is excellent! It's what you wanted and just in time." She winked. "Is it all you dreamed it would be?"

Rowena swallowed, obviously not sure what to say.

Cali stepped away from her. "What was I thinking? Of course you don't know yet. It's brand new." Just as quickly, Cali's expression changed again, this time to sadness, her brow crinkling in despair. "But how can I talk to you? It's not like they have phones here." Irritation flashed across the woman's face. "You'd think a society that could transport through space could have some mode of communicating."

Takoda's mouth opened, probably to explain, but Cali didn't stop talking as she suddenly smiled. "Then again who needs communication devices when you can just portal over to see someone." The frown returned. "But I can't portal."

He was beginning to feel lightheaded watching the woman's changing emotions and started forward.

"Oh, but maybe I can get Kuruk to walk me over to visit." Her frown returned. "Your poor protector. I wonder if he'll have to find another job now."

Just as he reached the two women, Rowena broke in. "Cali, I'm sure you can visit me whenever you like. I'd welcome your company, even on a daily basis."

Awan smiled kindly at Cali. "Yes, you are always welcome. I can explain to your protector where we live and you can visit. What makes Rowena happy makes us happy."

Cali shook her finger at him. "I knew I liked you. The minute I saw you two come into the Pleasure Dome last week, I knew you were good folk." She looked over her shoulder at Takoda who dropped his scowl just in time. "She's waited a long time for this, so you better not let her down."

From Takoda's lifted eyebrows, Awan imagined Cali gave Takoda a stern look. She obviously cared about her friend very much. "No need to worry. We plan on making Rowena very happy."

Cali turned back to him, a sly expression on her face. "Oh, I'm sure you do."

Rowena linked her arm in her friend's and walked her toward the door. "I'm counting on you to give me daily reports."

"My reports? Oh, yes. I promise."

"Daily?" Takoda's displeasure was clear in his lowered voice.

Quickly, Awan moved to stand next to the brother of his heart. "What he means is that perhaps a day in between would be more agreeable to all." He smiled, willing the young woman to understand that they needed time alone together.

Her eyes widened then she gave him another wink. "Of course. They don't take long, so I can just stay longer every other day."

Her meaning was clear. She wasn't leaving Rowena to them until she was sure her friend was happy. He appreciated that yet resented it as well, but he wouldn't reveal his feelings. "That would be welcomed."

Cali turned back to Rowena. "Are you sure about this?"

Rowena studied first him and then Takoda before returning her gaze to her friend. "No, but I'm doing it anyway."

Cali nodded as if she understood then suddenly threw herself at Rowena once again. "Good luck. I'm going to miss you."

Confused, he stared at the odd woman. Had they not just established that she would be visiting every other day? Personally, he hoped she visited while he was at the Discoverist Complex because he'd never been around someone whose balance was so off that it threatened that of others. Why would she miss Rowena when she'd see her soon?

"It's okay Cali. This will be good for you." Rowena's whispered words concerned him. Did Rowena doubt she'd be able to stay friends with Cali?

"I know." Cali sniffed as if holding back tears before she stepped back. "I'll see you the day after tomorrow."

"Yes, you will." Rowena smiled kindly.

His chest warmed. Though Rowena was unsure about them

and they knew little of each other, her small reiteration of Cali's visit schedule confirmed his trust in the bond.

Cali opened the door and stepped through, but before she closed it, she popped her head back in. "Day after tomorrow."

Rowena nodded and the door closed.

He breathed a silent sigh. He sincerely hoped there was a filoz in Tolba for Cali, though he couldn't think of a single one who could handle her quick changes of emotion. Definitely no Kindred of Mind or Heart.

"She's not always like that. It's only when she feels very strongly." For the first time, that he remembered, Rowena seemed vulnerable. She truly cared about Cali.

Takoda must have noticed as he gave her a crooked grin. "Then I'd say she feels very strongly about you."

Rowena blushed. "Yes, well, I helped her adjust once she arrived here. She looks at me like a big sister, and no, I don't mean in size." She gave him a stern look before breaking into a smile. "I should have said older sister."

Awan grinned as Takoda realized Rowena was teasing. He straightened as if he'd been granted the greatest honor. For someone who protested this bond, Takoda certainly wasn't fighting it.

Swallowing a chuckle, Awan opened his arm to the closed door. "If you're ready, we can leave now."

Her smile disappeared and she scanned the room again. Then turning back to face the door, she lifted her head and gave a single nod. "Let's do this."

Takoda opened the door and they stepped out into the shade of her front patrio. The sun shone brightly in the courtyard between the resident domes and the Pleasure Dome, but it was a pleasant temperature without cloth coverings. For the hundredth time, he questioned women's need to cover their bodies.

"I'll let the Lead Protector know you are leaving with us." As Takoda strode away, Rowena's gaze followed him.

Another sign she was meant for them. That she appreciated them was a good start. Above where she stood were the bells that Takoda didn't like. He moved closer to examine them more carefully. They were like Tolban bells, yet not.

"I bought those up north, on Earth, in New England. They are an Abenaki tribe design."

He immediately brought his attention back to her. "They are from a city like ours?"

She scrunched up her nose. "Not exactly. There are not many Abenaki people left, but some keep the traditions alive. I didn't know much about them until I took a vacation in Maine, a place like a city."

All the signs were revealing themselves. "You obtained these before you knew of Eden, correct?"

She smiled. "Long before I knew of your planet. That was back when I still took vacations regularly. You don't get ahead if you take all that time off."

"Off. You mean not labor?" Why would she think laboring all the time was good?

"Yes. I used to travel quite a bit with friends." She pointed to the bells. "I was in a museum on Native American peoples and I saw this design on a pouch. I liked it so much that when we got to the gift shop and I saw it on these bells, I had to buy them."

Ah, she had been drawn to something their very ancestors had created on Earth. It no longer surprised him that she was on Eden and in Tolba specifically. "Did you bring them with you when you first visited?"

She looked away, toward where Takoda had disappeared beneath the arch of the Pleasure Dome. "No, I brought them back from Earth when I decided to live here."

From her reaction, he had to assume her first filoz did not capture her heart and she had chosen to live at the Pleasure Dome rather than return to Earth. Again, another sign that she was meant to be theirs. "They fit in well here. Do you know what the design means?"

Still not looking at him, she shook her head. "I just wanted them because the design was pretty. I've thought about seeing if it meant anything, but never got around to it."

As Takoda emerged through the archway, she returned her attention to him. "Why do you ask about the bells?"

He motioned toward Takoda with his head. "Because he reacted strangely to them."

"To bells?" She returned her attention to Takoda as he halted before them.

"We may leave now. The Lead Protector will communicate with your protector and keep your residence for you until such a time that you tell him to release it."

There was a barely perceptible change in Rowena's stance that if he hadn't been studying her, he would have missed it. But he did notice and the fact that she could return to her residence had relieved her. That he did not like.

Takoda picked up the book and the sack then stood next to the box of Rowena's belongings. "I believe walking would be inadvisable at this time of day."

He nodded his agreement. Until the new hatchocs were complete, the city at midday was crowded and it would take them too long. He was anxious to see what Rowena thought of their home and everything in it.

In the next moment, Takoda levitated the box and all three of them.

"Oh." Rowena grabbed Awan's arm with both hands.

He laid his hand over hers. "Don't worry, we would never let you fall." She stared wide-eyed at the ground as she grasped onto him, trusting him to keep her safe. Bringing her home even without the bond complete was the right course of action. This was a very good idea.

THIS WAS A BAD IDEA. Rowena stared at the ground, her stomach in her throat. She'd never considered herself afraid of heights, but to be lifted into the air with nothing holding her up was another experience altogether. Not just above the ground, but above the Pleasure Dome!

"Don't look down. Look at the beauty of Tolba."

At Awan's words, she snapped her head up, anything to get rid of the sick feeling in her stomach. With no railing or even floor beneath her, it took her a few moments to focus. On the risk scale, this was off the charts!

Keeping her tight hold on Awan's substantial arm, she finally managed to bring her attention to the view. She'd never seen the city from this angle. She'd portaled into a home her first night here and had only been in the streets of her hatchoc. The streets were packed dirt that matched everything else with no greenery of any kind.

Now as she took it all in, she understood the significance of the layout. It *was* similar to a turtle shell. It also looked like a conglomeration of turtles. Every building had an adobe domed shape. They just varied in size though not in color. The sandy stone, so much like her brownstone in Boston, continued throughout the entire city, but accents varied, and dividing walls appeared to be painted among what she assumed were the residences. There was plenty greenery in yards and common spaces, but the streets, from this height, appeared just a conglomeration of people.

There were no murals surrounding the Pleasure Dome. Was that because it was considered a multi-residential property?

"That is where I am currently helping to expand the city." Takoda pointed to the far east area where construction was taking place. "I levitate the pieces that four men cannot lift or reach."

The pride in his voice was unmistakable, but before she could comment, Awan pointed to an area directly in front of them near what appeared to be the center of the city. "That is the Discoverist Complex where I labor to help Tolba move forward."

It was a large complex with many domes of all different sizes and designs. It was also where Micco worked. At the reminder that she'd hoped to bond with him and Sist and was now on her way to do a trial living arrangement with two men she barely knew, her interest in the city waned. "Are we close yet?"

"You do not like being above the city?" Takoda's voice held a heavy dose of surprise.

"She's not used to it." Awan patted her hands where they dug into his biceps. She really should loosen her grip, but her fingers refused to listen.

"Of course." Takoda pointed again. "There is our residence."

She moved her gaze to the area, about to ask which house, when she noticed one had a hole taking up half of its backyard. As they descended, the size and depth of it became clearer. It was almost as big as an Olympic swimming pool, though no water filled the disturbed ground. As they came closer, the scent of rich dirt filled her nostrils. Oddly, it made her feel at home. It wasn't exactly earth per se, but it reminded her of it.

As soon as her feet touched the ground, she breathed deeply and let go of Awan. The sight of her suitcase and the sack of food coming to rest on the ground as well struck her as funny, and she held in a chuckle. It was as if she were Mary Poppins only without the umbrella. Now where had that childhood reference come from?

"Welcome to our home." Awan opened his arm toward the house, but she was far more interested in the giant hole.

She walked toward the edge, taking it all in, even the shovel like tool leaning against the far wall of the hole before she looked at Awan over her shoulder. "You did this?"

Clearly uncomfortable, he nodded. "I can fill it in again, so our courtyard can be more functionable."

Takoda came to stand next to her. "He did all of this in the short time I was visiting you." His mouth twitched upward, his enjoyment of Awan's need to let off steam that of two friends who tease each other often.

She was astounded Awan had done so much is such a short time. No wonder he hadn't complained about her grip on his arm. That he remained behind them proved his embarrassment over what she assumed he viewed as a lack of control. Her heart went out to him. "I wouldn't fill this in."

"You wouldn't?" Takoda eyes widened. "You'd leave it like this?"

She wasn't looking at him, but she could almost feel Awan's intense stare. "No, I'd adjust the shape a bit and create an oasis."

Awan footsteps behind her grew closer until he stood on the other side of her. "What do you mean by an oasis?"

She pointed toward the narrow spot at one end. "This could be a lovely pool. Over there could be a rock feature with water running over it and into the pool. And I'd give it a bit curvier shape like a meandering river." She waved her hand in a snake like fashion. "Then at that end, maybe a shallower area with steps leading up to a lounging area." As she pictured it in her mind, her excitement grew. "Or it could be really fancy and have a beach like entrance."

Her imagination was combining a couple of pools she'd been to while on vacations in the Caribbean. "You could even put in a slide and a bridge and a swim-up bar. With such a big area, the possibilities are endless." She gave Awan a huge smile.

"You'd like that?" His words came out hushed, catching her off guard. He gazed at her as if he'd give her both moons of Eden if she asked.

Uncomfortable with that thought, she turned back toward the gaping hole in the ground. "Who wouldn't? Don't you have pools in Tolba?"

Takoda nodded. "Yes. We have hot pools and cold ponds." We already have a hot pool."

That had to be a hot tub. "Outside or inside?"

He pointed to the far end of the giant hole. "On the other side of that mound of dirt."

This she had to see. Stepping behind him, she strode down the length of the hole and past the very large pile of dirt then halted. It *was* a hot tub! Quickly, she moved up to it and dropped her hand in the water. Ah, she'd really missed her hot tub on her patio at home. She'd emptied it on her first visit back to Earth since she wouldn't be using it for months.

Sensing Takoda was close, she turned to face him, her hand still in the warm water. "How do you keep it warm? There's no lid."

"It's the eyllen. We determined the appropriate size and number of eyllen pieces and they were inserted around the pool with the ground pressing them against the sides."

She examined the sides. It appeared to be poured concrete, but she knew better. Tolbans had created their own stone mixture to create their homes, something called toleric, and this was obviously the same material. "It's the perfect temperature." She pulled her hand out and shook the water off before wiping it with the bottom of her tunic. The working hot tub gave her the silver lining she needed to handle her new living situation.

That she was stalling to go inside to see exactly what her new living situation would be was obvious, at least to her. "If you like the idea for an oasis, I'd be happy to sketch out some ideas. You could even have the cold pond next to this hot pool so that stepping or jumping from one to the other could happen."

"You paint?" Awan's brows lowered in concern.

Why would painting be a problem? "No, I don't. I'm not an artist at all. But I renovated my home in Boston and can draw spaces well enough to get my ideas across."

His brows rose. "Then I think we should do this."

Takoda slapped him on the back. "Of course you want to. It will be a lot easier explaining it to our friends."

Awan grinned. "Exactly."

As Takoda chuckled, she understood better why the two very different men had formed a filoz. Somehow it worked. One's weakness was the other's strength. That was supposed to benefit the beloved since the filoz's primary goal was to make its beloved happy.

It all sounded perfect when she'd first learned about Dickinson Law, but now that she was about to enter the home of two men she barely knew as their beloved, she balked. Scanning the backyard, she tried to find something else to discuss to delay the inevitable.

"Now that we know what to do with my hole, I'll let you two move forward with it." Awan cringed. "I think I've contributed more than enough as is."

Takoda nodded. "We can do that." He gazed at her with confidence.

She wished she felt the same way.

"Now, would you like to go inside?" Awan held his arm out, inviting her to precede him.

She swallowed. It was time. For some reason, she sensed that stepping into their home would change her life forever, which was silly because if they had bonded, that particular event had already happened. "Of course." Her voice came out barely above a whisper. She cleared her throat and forced some enthusiasm into her words. "I'm very curious."

Takoda lifted her suitcase by the handle, grabbed the sack of food and led the way. They stepped into the shade of a large patrio before walking through the arched doorway into the home. She stopped just a few steps inside.

"Wow." It was so much brighter and far more colorful than

the Pleasure Dome, but the main living area was only two stories. The white walls reflected the light from windows placed at varying heights and colorful paintings were tastefully added to the walls. Actually, they appeared to be painted right on the walls.

The whole area would have been called open concept on Earth, with absolutely no walls or half walls dividing the space, not even a bookcase or art feature. The entire room was open. There was a kitchen toward the front of the house, with an island in it, a separate area for dining, another area for relaxing in what would be considered a living room and in the fourth area was an easel, a table, and cabinets. She'd call it an artist's corner if it actually had corners.

As she took it all in, her appreciation turned to apprehension. There were throws and pillows on the couches, an extravagant centerpiece on the dining table, numerous objects were on end tables and other pieces of furniture. Though everything was in its place, she couldn't help feeling like it was cluttered. No, not cluttered, lived-in, with memories and items that mean something.

"Do you like it?" Takoda's hopeful question brought her back to her hosts and their interest in her impression. That Takoda was concerned puzzled her.

If he didn't want her as his beloved, why would he care if she liked it? "It's beautiful." She took a couple more steps into the space between the dining and living areas. To her right, in the rounded wall that bordered the artist area and living room were three arched doors. She ignored them and moved toward the closest painting on the opposite side in the dining area.

Awan stepped next to her. "That's an interpretation of our Poetess saving us all from each other."

She'd heard the story of Emily Dickinson being brought to Eden. Supposedly, the poet had organized the women into a stronghold, and they didn't come out until the men agreed to stop fighting. The Edenists even had what was called Dickinson Law, which along with Crius Law, was obeyed by all Edenists no matter the city.

Though she'd found the story difficult to believe, in the painting it came to life. The colors were vibrant on the women's wraps and Dickinson stood out at the center of the large building in bright white. The nude men clamoring on the outside of what was a temple were in browns and tans, trying to get in or fighting with each other. She was no expert, but she'd visited many art museums and this could have hung in one of those. "It's very well done. This artist has talent."

When neither man responded, she turned toward Awan who gazed at the painting with sorrow in his eyes. Twisting around, she found Takoda looking at the ground, his shoulders slumped. She could almost feel the men's desolation. Beyond Takoda stood the artist area.

Well, hell. The artist must be Lyka, the third man in their filoz until a week ago. Great. Didn't she just rip open a new wound. *Nice start, Ro.* Obviously, studying the artwork would have to come later. Hastily, she moved away from the painting, refusing to look at the others filling the room, and instead made her way to the kitchen, or meal room as they called it.

"This meal room has everything." She forced herself to be upbeat, which was easy when it was such a fully equipped space. Opening what they called a cold box, she pretended to inspect the food. Recognizing the byunca juice that supposedly proved their bond, she quickly closed it.

"If there is anything you require, tell us." Awan stood at the kitchen island, obviously having recovered before Takoda.

"As long as you have kafez for the mornings, I'm happy with whatever you have." She cocked her head. "Is it true that women are not expected to cook?"

"Yes." He grinned. "Unless you wish to."

She waved her hand. "Oh no. Not my best skill. That's why I always order from meal domes."

"We can do that as well, but I do make an excellent namas bake, and Takoda's havling pig pie is a true delicacy."

Oh, that did sound good. Why did she have the feeling she would be gaining weight while they got to know each other? "Both of those sound delicious."

Takoda set the sack of food on the counter. "I'll put your box of belongings in Awan's room." With her suitcase in hand, he moved toward the arched door directly across from them and her mind rebelled.

"Wait. Why Awan's room? Why not my room?" Her voice was rising an octave again, and she swallowed hard. She didn't like feeling panicked. It rarely happened on Earth, but here on Eden the last few days, it had become more of a companion than she ever wanted.

He stilled. "Awan's room was designed for when we moved from simply being a filoz of men to a yenea, a filoz with a beloved. If we are bonded, that is where you will want your belongings."

There was that word "if" again. She wanted to kiss the man for using it. "I understand, but I thought I'd have my own sleeping room, at least for now."

Takoda's brow furrowed. "I don't understand."

Did he only do that with her or was it simply his go-to expression?

"Nor do I." Awan stepped from behind the island, his own confusion just as plain.

Crap, how was she supposed to explain? She walked around to the side of the island that had stools and sat. "I'm not sure what we talked about the night we met, but I'm pretty sure we didn't discuss this."

Takoda set her suitcase on the floor and moved closer. His interest would have been flattering if she didn't feel like a complete wimp.

"If it concerns you, we want to know." Awan leaned his butt against the back of the couch separating the artist area from the living room.

"Right. Well, this is a bit unusual. The fact is, I haven't really shared a living space since I was nine years old." There, she'd said it.

The two men still confused, looked at each other as if to see if the other understood. Were they really going to make her give details? Admit she was nervous about living with someone? Anyone?

"How can that be?" Awan's question was not what she expected and gave her a more comfortable side of the topic.

"My mother passed away from cancer when I was nine and my aunt took me in. She was a very successful woman, so she had a large home in Newton and an apartment in Boston. She settled me into her home, but had to work long hours, so she often stayed in the city. She was always home on the weekends and she had both a cook who made meals for me and a maid who came in twice a week to clean up after me."

She warmed to her topic. "It was a beautiful home, even

larger than this. I had my own 'office' as she called it where I could do my homework. Of course, when I left for college, I rented my own apartment and after achieving some success in my career, I bought a brownstone in the city." She smiled, very pleased with her accomplishments. Owning a brownstone in Boston was no small feat.

"Of course, I couldn't afford an updated one, so it took a few years to renovate, but now it's perfect. So you see, I've lived alone forever." She smiled reassuringly.

The two men stared at her in shock. She seriously didn't get it. "You have questions?"

Awan opened his mouth, but nothing came out.

"You lost your mother?" Takoda's sympathetic gaze was so unexpected, it jolted her back to her childhood.

Hell, she didn't want to think about how it *felt*. She'd compartmentalized that very well. "Yes, I did, but it's okay. I had my aunt, my mother's sister. I still had family."

"But you lived alone…as a child." Awan's voice was soft as if he still couldn't believe it.

And here she thought this was the easier side to explain. "I wasn't completely alone. Like I said, Aunt Georgi took care of me. Not only did she provide for my basic needs, but she also taught me how to think critically, be independent, and still be a lady." She shrugged. "I think I had the best childhood."

Awan finally spoke. "Of course you did. You are a beautiful and intelligent woman, so however you matured was exactly what you needed. It's just that the way we live while young is with our mother, who is most important, two or more fathers, and usually brothers. There is always family around us."

Takoda jumped in as Awan paused. "And in Tolba, we do not leave our family until we have found our filoz brothers. Then we make a home together so that we can invite a beloved to join us."

It was so opposite of her upbringing, she could understand why they were surprised by her explanation. Not only did they always live with others, but their main goal in life was to find a wife and procreate. In an odd way, it reminded her of her grandmother's era when women were raised to be housewives and mothers while the men worked. But here, the men not only worked but took on the role of housewives. It made sense that there were at least two to every woman in order to handle all of that.

She turned her palms upward and shrugged, smiling wryly. "Well, we *are* from different worlds."

Awan grinned and even Takoda's frown disappeared before he spoke again. "If you do not wish to stay with Awan, do you want to stay with me?" His voice raised at the end of his question as if he couldn't quite believe it, but was a bit flattered by the idea.

She scooted off the stool and walked past Awan to the door next to the one Takoda had headed for. "Is this your sleeping room?"

Takoda nodded.

As curious as she was to go inside and look, she would save that exploration for another time. Instead, she walked to the third door. "And was this Lyka's room."

Takoda didn't move, but Awan answered. "Yes. It was."

She opened the wooden door, half-expecting them to tell her to halt, but no sound came from behind her, so she stepped inside. What she found wasn't what she expected. All the rounded walls remained a pristine white, no paintings whatsoever. She would have expected an artist's room to be filled with color.

The bed was not overly large but appeared comfortable. There was a half-circle side table next to it and a small table next to the one window, which had a view of the courtyard and Awan's pool-to-be. The minimalist vibe in the room really appealed to her. She immediately felt comfortable.

With neither man coming in to tell her to leave, she moved to the open archway opposite the one she came in. It was a round bathroom with a sink large enough for two, two Tolban toilets and an open shower. At the other end from where she stood was another open archway. Obviously, Takoda and Lyka had shared this bathroom. If she were to stay in Lyka's room, that would be seriously awkward.

She turned around to look the bedroom over again and found both men standing in the arched doorway. "I like this room, but I know it would be hard for you if I stayed here, so I'll sleep on a longseat in the main room."

"No." Awan's quick reply startled Takoda as he snapped his head to look at Awan.

She opened her arms to indicate the room. "But this was Lyka's. Wouldn't it be hard for you if I slept here?"

Takoda grabbed his left biceps, his protective stance if she read him correctly.

Awan took a tentative step into the room. "Yes, it will be difficult." He glanced back at Takoda. "For both of us." He faced her again. "But Lyka is gone. He is never coming back. He is not dead though and we should not mourn him when he has found his yenea."

"Without us." The grumbled words by Takoda held anger, hurt, and resentment.

It made her wonder which was better, losing someone to death or losing someone to another and knowing there would never ever be contact again. Honestly, she wasn't sure. "I don't need to disturb anything if you want me to stay in here. I did not bring much besides my clothes."

Awan attempted a small smile. "It is yours until you feel comfortable with sharing my room."

Her heart melted at his willingness to put aside his heartache for her comfort. And what had she done for him? All she'd thought about was herself in this fiasco and yet she was the biggest culprit. She had the strangest inclination to hug him, but she kept control of herself. She wasn't a hugger. Everyone knew that.

Takoda dropped his arms and spun on his heel to stride across the living area. The sound of the front door closing punctuated the end to his footsteps in the house.

Awan sighed. "It is not you. He suffers in his heart with the loss of Lyka and Xavia."

That she understood. "What about you? Do you not?"

"I did. I do. But…" He looked past her before bringing his gaze back to her. "Now I have hope."

That she was his hope filled her with fear but also excitement. Would she ever stop having dual feelings when it came to this filoz, or would this push-pull feeling keep anything from ever happening? If she really wanted something to happen between them, then she needed to meet them halfway. She gave him a tentative smile. "I have hope too."

His own smile widened. "Then allow me to retrieve your belongings and while you settle in, I'll empty your sack and start our evening meal."

As he spun to follow through on his statements, she couldn't help but admire the movement of the muscles in his broad back or the roundness of his naked butt.

Would she be dessert? Not surprisingly, the thought excited her. Chastising herself, she refocused her attention on the room. If this had any hope of working out, she needed to get to know them first. It might seem backward, but she wasn't spending her life with two men simply for the sex. If she was willing to settle for that, she could have stayed on Earth.

She wanted what her mother never had, someone to share in her accomplishments, enjoy life together, and be an actual father to her children. Or rather fathers. The goal loomed large, overwhelming her.

Dropping onto the bed, she sighed. Maybe she was asking for too much.

Chapter Seven

Takoda sat on the high wall of Tolba, his legs dangling over the jungle side as he stared off into the dark greenery. The sky was just beginning to lighten, the jungle still dark and foreboding.

Somewhere out there were the brother of his heart and the woman he loved. As one of the few who could levitate, he could leave Tolba and search for them, bring them back, but to what end? They were happy with Davos.

He sneered, the betrayal still too hard to accept. Where had the dirgon taken them? How had he convinced them to bond? The shifting man had stolen his life.

Grabbing his left arm, he tried to ease the ache in his heart, but it didn't help. Why hadn't they fought for Lyka's release? He'd heard of two others who brought their family to bear on convincing the cheetans to allow them to stay. He never heard what the outcome was. Even if it wasn't good, he and Awan could have delayed the exile long enough to find a way to go with Lyka.

But they'd been too distracted by Xavia's disappearance. Neither he nor Awan could think clearly, desperately searching for her in Tolba, not knowing she'd gone with Lyka. Again, the searing pain of betrayal squeezed his heart, and he tightened his grip on his arm. When would the hurt stop? Would it ever stop?

They had had her in their residence, and she'd slipped through their fingers along with the brother of their heart. He couldn't help thinking his life would be different if they'd only bonded. Why hadn't they? What had he done wrong? It was easier to blame the dirgon than to face it might have been his fault.

Awan seemed to have forgiven them so easily. While Awan ached for what they'd lost, he didn't see the betrayal or the possibility that they had failed. Awan's faith in what was meant to be was unshakeable and one of the reasons Takoda had been drawn to his company while he went through his transition.

He'd never been as accepting as his schoolmates and once he started to come into his Kindred of Air ability, he'd become more rebellious. While others pushed him away, Awan let him in, accepting his ignorant statements and allowing him to work through his transition as he needed.

Just thinking about his own actions made him cringe. He admired Awan's acceptance while at the same time resenting it. Why couldn't he be like Awan, especially now when they had most likely bonded with Ro?

He should go home to her and Awan, but the motivation wasn't there. He'd only come up to the wall after two patrols had stopped him to make sure he wasn't Kindred of Eden. He was ready to lift them up and strand them on the top of the nearest residence. The only thing that stopped him was the concern that they would then restrict Kindred of Air based on his actions.

The predawn light began to penetrate the cleared area just outside the walls and the cleared area directly in front of him.

Movement out of the corner of his eye had him studying the jungle to the right of where he sat. Though he tried to peer into the dark foliage, he could see little, but there was something there. The leaves moved as it drew closer.

He remained completely still, a ridiculous hope filling his chest as he watched the progress. It was probably nothing more than a wild feroon or a pack of grendals, but still he watched. Leaves not far to the left moved as well and he looked out to see at least five trails. This was neither Lyka and Xavia come home nor animals. His muscles tensed and his protective instincts surged. All five disturbances were headed to a point directly beneath him.

Throwing his legs back over into Tolba, he levitated off the wall and floated to a spot far to the right. Keeping his body hidden behind the wall, he watched the convergence of movement.

At first, it stopped just inside the jungle. Then as if whoever was there scanned the area to be sure no one watched, men emerged and walked directly to the wall. There were five of them, no doubt all lawbreakers, but why would they come back to Tolba? They'd been exiled. Did they seek readmittance or something more sinister?

One man put his hand on the wall and pointed to the ground. Two shook their heads but another spoke. Then one of them appeared to laugh just as Helios broke over the horizon. In the next moment the laughing man appeared to turn into a spiral of wind and spun across the cleared area back into the jungle, cutting a swath as wide as a man's arms from fingertip to fingertip, but only as tall. It was if a tunnel had formed in the thick foliage.

The rest of the men gave chase, leaving Tolba's wall as it stood, but Takoda didn't like what he'd seen. This was serious enough to tell the cheetans. Yet even as that thought occurred, he found himself moving toward home, his instinct to protect those he cared about too strong to deny. Though he knew both Awan and Ro were safe…for now, he still needed to see them.

Not even questioning his instinct, he rushed over the two hatchocs to the rear courtyard of his home. As soon as his feet hit the ground, he ran for the door, threw it open, stepped inside, and halted. Why did he never remember how beautiful Ro was until he was in her presence? Her red hair was pulled up on top of her head, half falling out, and the short covering she wore revealed shapely bare legs.

"Takoda!"

Her voice had him rethinking his approach. He wanted to tell her they were all in danger, but that was not necessarily the case. Now the need to protect her from fearing anything surged forth. He forced himself to stroll forward toward the kitchen island where she sat. "It is me."

Her hand came over her heart. "You entered so fast, I thought someone was forcing you through the door and breaking in."

Breaking in? He didn't know that term but it fit what he'd just witnessed. Is that what the lawbreakers planned to do, break in? He paused at the edge of the meal area. "What is breaking in?"

She picked up a cup and held it with both hands. "It's when someone who has no right to be in your home, comes in and steals your belongings or causes you bodily harm. It can happen anywhere." She took a sip, watching him.

"It does not happen in Tolba." But could it? The question caused him worry. He would discuss it with Awan.

"I thought you were at work." She put the cup down. "Would

you like a cup of kafez? I'm only on my second cup, so there's plenty left."

He moved into the meal area, walking past the island to the counter where the kafez canister was located. Taking a cup from a shelf, he filled it halfway then moved to the cold box where he pulled out the anub milk and filled his cup to the top. After returning the milk to its proper place, he took a sip. The heat from the kafez made the milk foam and sweeten, a simple pleasure.

"Takoda, you didn't go to work, did you?"

He turned to face Ro. "I did not."

She studied her kafez. "I'm sorry I upset you." Her gaze rose to meet his. "I do not have to stay in Lyka's room."

That she would leave that space because of his feelings bothered him. "You do not have to. I…" The memory of the last time he tried to explain his feelings to her reminded him how he'd hurt her.

She stared him in the eye. "What? Talk to me. I'm sure we can talk without that blasted tequila."

He smirked. "I do not want to ever drink that again."

"You and me both. It was stupid of me to drink so much and to drag you down with me. I don't usually do things like that, but when I do, I really mess up." She gave him a self-deprecating smile.

He didn't like her thinking poorly of herself. "Awan and I didn't have to imbibe as much as we did either. Like you, it is rare that we have such drinks, but we were grieving."

"I know. I'm sorry you have lost those you love."

He nodded, not sure what to say without bringing up the pain again.

"Did you go to another Pleasure Dome last night?" Her question was asked with such a soft voice that he almost missed it.

"No!"

Her eyes widened in surprise.

He lowered his voice. "No. I would never go to a Pleasure Dome if bonded and since that may be the case, I have no plans to go." His shoulders slumped forward. "The night we met you was not planned either, but now nothing would induce me to visit one."

"Unless we discover we're not bonded after all. Then you could." She picked up her cup and had a sip.

Her quiet actions were the opposite of the tumult that whipped through him at the suggestion they weren't bonded. That made no sense. He himself intimated it but a moment ago. Why did he have no reaction to a lack of a bond when he thought it, but when she said it, he wanted to grab her to him and prove to her it was otherwise? He shook his head, completely baffled by his contradictory feelings.

Was this how Awan felt when he was "unbalanced?" If so, he found more empathy for his friend's feelings over the last few days. "Did you see Awan this morning?"

She grinned. "I did. He woke me up with a cup of kafez. It's as if he knew it was the perfect way to start my day." She grimaced. "I'm not fit for company until I have my first shot of caffeine, which I'm positive is what is in this delicious drink." She lifted her cup.

It was very much like Awan to think of others. "Have you tried it with anub milk?"

"I have. It's a bit too sweet for me in the morning. I like it black and strong to wake me up."

Her green eyes were definitely awake and bright as if she were about to set out on an adventure. He moved his gaze from her, finding it too transfixing and noticed the paper on the counter. His heart stopped for a moment as he recognized it as sheets from one of Lyka's artist pads.

Taking a deep breath, he forced the pain to the background, allowing him to focus on the marks across the paper. "What is this?"

She turned one sheet to face him. "I was thinking about Awan's hole." She gave a quiet chuckle but didn't look at him. "In this idea, I have the deeper end next to the hot pool and the shallow end with lounging area at the other, but I'm not convinced that makes sense."

"In this one," she moved another sheet toward him, "I flipped the idea. But I'm not sure about this either because it would make slipping from the hot pool into the cold pond impossible, especially because I gave it a beach entrance." She pointed to the area on her sketch.

"I can see your point." He examined the drawings side by side. He could easily see where it was in the courtyard and what everything was. As she said, she wasn't an artist, but the sketches were perfectly clear, except one area. He pointed to it on both drawings. "What is this?"

"That's a water feature. Do you think it's too much?" Her gaze fixed on him.

"Too much?" He shook his head. "I do not know what a water feature is. Do you mean a statue?"

"Oh, I hadn't thought of that, but I suppose it could be. I suppose a statue of a dolphin, I mean a layfeenya squirting water out of its mouth is an option, but I was thinking more along the lines of a waterfall."

She pulled one sketch closer. "Oh, actually, since there are some lovely trees on that side of the hole, we could make it a rock grotto with the water spilling over." Her voice rose in excitement as she looked at him once again. "You said you could levitate heavy things. Would you be able to levitate a rock about the size of, um, that table?" She pointed to where they ate their meals.

It was such a simple request to fulfill that he smiled. "I could."

She took the letti and applied it to the paper once again, drawing out the area closest to the courtyard walls. "We could even have the rocks set up like stairs so in addition to swimming through the waterfall and into the grotto, we can also jump off the top and into the cold pond." She finished adding lines then pointed. "What do you think?"

Her gaze was full of interest and he wanted to keep it that way. "I think we should make it be so."

She set down the letti and picked up her cup again. "See what kafez does for me. It gets my creative juices flowing."

Staring at her as she was, excited, her hair tousled and her smile wide, he felt drawn to her far more so than the night they met. Then she'd been sad, but now. It reminded him of feelings he had with…Xavia.

Turning away so she wouldn't see the pain he was sure would be in his eyes, he strolled to the windows at the back to view Awan's hole. His mind knew it wasn't fair to compare the two women, but his heart wouldn't stop interfering. He'd been truthful when he'd told Ro it wasn't her that kept him from wanting a bond.

Her bare feet as she padded across the hard floor warned him she approached. Part of him wanted to slip outside and avoid any contact, but he forced himself to remain where he was. It was the fact she could be his beloved whether he wanted it to be so or not that compelled him to do what he'd been taught. He must give her a chance, for all their sakes.

She stood next to him, studying the courtyard. Her fruity sweet scent wafted over and he breathed deeply.

"I was trying to incorporate the whole hole." She pointed to the table and chairs positioned not quite at the end of the courtyard. "But it could stop there. I really have no idea what it would take to do all this in Tolba. On Earth, it would take a small fortune, but since you don't use money here to make transactions, I may be reaching beyond what you and Awan would like."

"I believe that anything we can do to make the hole useful will be very appreciated by Awan. He has never lost his balance so far as to do this." He held his hand out toward the yard.

"Never?"

He glanced at her as she gazed out the window. "No, never." Not even when Xavia had disappeared. Though Awan had been out of balance and frantic that his scenarios wouldn't show him which was the correct one, he hadn't lost his sense of purpose like he had not knowing if they'd bonded with Ro. Did that mean something? Though Awan had seen the one scenario where Xavia had left with Lyka, they couldn't believe that to be the case and yet it was.

He didn't want to believe they were bonded. Was he simply blinding himself because he didn't want it to be true?

Ro's hand on his arm startled him and he flinched.

"I guess you were off in another world, so to speak." She smiled wryly. "I asked you if we could keep Awan in the loop, so he can feel better about the project."

He liked that idea. Making the brother of his heart feel better about what he thought of as a weakness was definitely good. He also liked that Ro wanted to do something for Awan.

Scrat. He needed to talk to Awan about what he'd seen at the wall. He'd been so distracted by Ro, he'd forgotten his purpose for returning home. "Yes, let us make it a gift to him, but now I must leave. I have to speak to Awan on another matter."

"Let me get dressed and I'll come with you." Ro turned and strode across the living area toward Lyka's room before Takoda could think.

"Wait."

She waved him off. "Don't worry, I'll only be a minute."

He couldn't take her with him. He didn't want her to know of the possible danger. It was their job to protect her, not scare her. He strode across the room and when he reached her door, he opened it only to halt.

She'd pulled on the leg coverings she always wore, but her torso was completely bare. A rush of desire spread through him so fast, the door handle in his grip bent.

"Takoda! A little privacy, please."

She wrapped her arms over her bountiful breasts, snapping him out of his stare.

He raised his gaze to hers. "Why do you cover such beauty?"

Her face flushed. "It is not our way on Earth to bare ourselves to everyone. You know that."

"I know, but I do not understand."

She sighed. "I get that. I'll try to explain it to you, but at the moment, I'd like to finish dressing."

"I will not stop you." At the thought that she might think he would force her to stay uncovered, his whole being rebelled. "You can do whatever makes you comfortable."

"I'm glad we are agreed. Now if you don't mind, can you close the door so I can finish dressing?"

He didn't understand what the door had to do with her covering her body, but he obediently stepped all the way into the room and closed the door.

"Takoda."

"Yes."

"I meant for you to close the door after you returned into the living area."

Again, he didn't understand the connection between the closed door and 'dressing,' but now didn't seem the time to ask. "As you wish."

Turning around, he let himself out and closed the door. He remained where he was, curious about the whole procedure. Within moments, the door opened and Ro walked through.

"I told you it wouldn't take long. I'm ready. I've been wanting to see the Discoverist Complex for months. I understand all progress in Tolba starts there. Will we be walking? I noticed it wasn't that far from here."

Still confused by her issue with the door, he nodded.

"Great. It's been a couple days since I've been out and about. Do you think we could stop at a shop on the way back? I'm running low on soap, I mean my lather-wash. I hope they have my scent in this hatchoc." As she spoke, she walked toward the door that opened upon the main pathway.

It appeared she would go with him. He didn't want her to,

but he couldn't deny her. He didn't remember things being so confusing with Xavia. Then again, Ro was not like Xavia.

As she opened the door, he darted across the room to be by her side. A woman alone in the busy streets of Tolba was not in danger, but she may be considered available. And she definitely wasn't available.

Standing just outside his home, he closed the door. "It is this way. Take my hand."

"I know the drill. My protector at the Pleasure Dome also insisted on taking my hand. It's a big thing here that a woman be holding someone's hand, but just so you know, I don't like the idea. It makes me feel like I'm being treated like a child." Despite her words of displeasure, her hand slipped into his.

He might have felt protective before, but with her hand in his, it was a far stronger emotion. She wasn't nearly as fragile as Xavia, but the idea of an unattached Edenist taking an interest in her, bothered him. With that thought in mind, he strode through the crowded stone street scowling at anyone who dared look their way.

"Hey, Takoda, are you in some kind of rush or something?"

At her words, he came to a stop and she walked headlong into him. As her body made contact with his, two feelings rushed through him at the same time, excitement and happiness. Stunned by the sensation, he wrapped his arms around her and held her close.

She looked up at him. "What are you doing?"

Staring into her eyes, he could lose his soul. Shaking his head to clear his odd reaction, he released her, but continued to hold fast to her hand. "I was keeping you from falling."

She studied him, clearly perplexed. So was he, but he wasn't about to reveal that.

"But why did you stop? One minute you're almost racing to get to our destination and the next you stop in your tracks. Is everything okay?"

Okay? Ah yes, she asked if all was well with him. The answer was a definite negative. "I merely wished to answer your question. I am in a bit of a rush. Am I walking too fast?"

"Yes."

Heat rushed to his face. "I apologize. I do not generally walk through the streets when they are so crowded."

"Because you levitate?"

He nodded. Then a memory flashed through his mind and he smirked. "One time when I was transitioning, I became so impatient that I started levitating people out of my way." He chuckled as he remembered the startled faces of the Edenists he'd moved. "After that, my fathers wouldn't let me leave without one of them or Awan accompanying me."

"I can just imagine how those people felt." She grinned. "But it must have made it a lot easier to get through the crowd."

He gave her a gentle pull as he started forward again at a slower pace. "It was, but it is not allowed. If every Edenist used their ability to move through the city, we'd have chaos. We have Kindred of Air who can push air and knock everyone down. We have Kindred of Mind who could make people move to the side. We have Kindred of Light who could reflect images back and make it appear as if it is twice as crowded and then stroll through the throng unimpeded." He shook his head. "I had a lot to learn."

"We all make mistakes growing up and even as adults." She squeezed his hand. "What's important is that we learn from them so they aren't a waste of time and we don't make them again."

Though her words made sense, he couldn't help wondering if she was thinking about the night of their possible bond. It bothered him that he still wasn't sure and didn't have a connection with her. Just a couple more days and if nothing happened, she could go back to the Pleasure Dome. Yet even at that thought, his whole body stiffened.

"Hey, not so tight. I'm no wilting flower, but you have a particularly strong grip."

He immediately relaxed his hand, embarrassed by his lack of control once again. Now he truly understood how Awan felt about his courtyard hole. He needed to focus on something else. "You said you've wanted to go to the Discoverist Complex. Why have you not?" He glanced at her to show he was truly interested.

She shrugged. "I was told that you have to be invited."

Invited? No one needed to be invited. The Discoverist Complex was open to all citizens of Tolba, even Kindred of Eden since many of that Kindred also labored there. He was about to ask her who had told her that when she tugged on his hand.

"Is that what I think it is?" She pointed at an open window of a meal dome.

He studied the man outside as he started to eat his nubbish. "I don't know. What are you referring to?"

She pulled him toward the shop. "Oh wow, I didn't know you had ice cream in Tolba. But you don't really have sugar, so how is it possible?"

The man with the nubbish moved away and they stepped up to the window. "Do you mean the nubbish?"

"If that is what you call that cold cream concoction, then yes."

Her innocence about Tolba melted his resistance. "Perhaps we can have this Edenist explain it to you."

Her eyes widened then she nodded. The Edenist at the window explained the combination of daemon bee honey and anub milk, answering every question she had. Her interest was strong and the more she learned, the more she wanted to know. He was completely entranced.

Finally, she turned to him. "Would it be possible to have some? I'm used to shopping with a protector. I'm not sure what we need to do."

At that moment, he would have levitated the entire building to grant her request. The Edenist behind the counter seemed to be flattered by her attention and no doubt was ready to spare some for her, but there was no way he'd allow that. Turning to the man at the window, he confidently explained his ability and offered his services.

It no time, Ro had a large cup of nubbish made with extra honey and he'd levitated eleven heavy barrels from the man's back courtyard storage into his cold box the size of a room. Not only was Ro pleased with her nubbish, she also appeared awed by his ability. When all was in place and she had finished her sweet, they resumed their walk.

She glanced at their pathway but focused on him. "I understand better now how your Air ability works. It's hard for me, and I'm sure other women from Earth, to truly understand what having an ability is like. We don't have these on Earth." Though she walked next to him, she paid little attention to the activity around them. "I know that Edenists gained their abilities after being brought to Eden by the Crius. Do you know how long it was before they gained these abilities? For example, is it possible for women to gain similar abilities?"

Her voice sounded so hopeful, he didn't want to answer truthfully, but that was the only answer he could give. "No, the Kindreds didn't appear for three generations."

"Oh well, it was worth asking."

He hated that she was disappointed. He searched for something that might make her happier and without thinking it through latched onto it. "But when women bond, they do connect with their men in ways that are only possible on Eden."

"You mean like how I always know when you are near?"

He barely heard her voice above the crowd, but he did, and he cringed inwardly. If she truly did know when he was near that meant they were bonded. "Is that something you never felt before? You said you thought it was intuition. Could that be it?"

She didn't respond, but she stopped looking at him.

Had he hurt her again with his question? "The bond does go both ways, though not necessarily in the same way or at the same time. I have yet to feel anything with you, so we may not be sure for another three days."

Despite his attempt to engage her, she continued in her silence, so he gave up and simply led the way. When they reached the complex, her spirits seemed to rise as she looked about her, bringing her back to how she was at the beginning of their journey.

He led her down four stone paths before she finally spoke. "This place is like a maze. How do people find their way around? I see no signs."

"It is no different than walking about Tolba. It's all about the bells when it comes to public places."

"The bells?" She came to a halt, so he stopped as well. "What do the bells have to do with anything? I mean, besides letting someone know you would like to come in?"

He pointed to the bells on the building closest to them. "Those bells are blue. That means we are in the section of the complex where discoverists work on water. If we continue this way, the bells will slowly change to violet where they experiment with air. If we walked farther, they would then turn to red where discoverists work on improving our health with food and plants and healing capabilities."

He pointed in the opposite direction. "These blue bells will change to green if we head that way. That's where they experiment with energy and so on." Now that she'd started showing an interest again, he wanted her to continue. He wanted her to like where Awan labored.

"So where does Awan work?"

He pointed directly ahead of them. "He is at the center of the complex, the Resource discoverists. It is arranged in a large circle and those who support all types of discoverists have their domes in here."

She let go of his hand and moved forward to look at the bells on the closest door. "These are white."

"Yes, as these discoverists do not actually discover new ways of doing things or how things work. They simply help all the others. Awan's dome is there." He pointed to the second on his left.

She immediately started walking toward it. For some reason, it bothered him that she was so comfortable not holding his hand anymore, but there was no need inside the quiet complex.

"This one?"

He strode toward her. "Yes."

Her hands found her hips. "So how do you know this is Awan's? This bell is exactly the same as all the rest."

He grinned. He couldn't help it. Her thought process was clear. She searched for a hole in the logic. He liked that. "Because the ringer on the bells has an A on it."

Her head snapped back toward the bells. "I totally missed that." Dropping her arms, she stepped to the bells and rang them.

In a few moments, Awan filled the doorway, his eyes wide with surprise as his smile grew. "Rowena, Takoda, please come in." He opened his arm to indicate they enter. "I'm very pleased that you came to visit."

At Awan's words, the reason for their visit loomed large in his mind and Takoda lost all enjoyment in his task.

Ro wandered across the room toward the open archway that led out into a shared courtyard. "This place is even larger than I expected." She turned around. "Maybe we could levitate when we leave so I can get an idea of exactly how it's laid out?"

That she was willing to be lifted again meant she trusted him more. He liked that. "I will be pleased to do that for you."

Awan moved toward the longseats in the center of the room. "Did you come to see the complex or me?"

Ro strolled to the longseat opposite of Awan and dropped onto it. "Oh, Takoda came to talk to you, but I came because I was nosey."

"Nosey?" Awan's confusion mirrored his own.

She pulled her leg up, so her foot rested on the cushion of the longseat. "Yes. It's an expression. I was curious about the Discoverist Complex and couldn't resist tagging along. I mean coming along with Takoda."

Awan looked at him over Ro's head and he signaled that it was not for her to hear. With the slightest of nods, Awan returned his gaze to Ro. "Then I will confer with Takoda outside and as soon as we're done, I'll be happy to satisfy your curiosity."

"That will work for me. I've been waiting a long time for a chance to see this part of Tolba."

Awan's eyebrows rose in question, but Takoda shrugged. Anyone on Tolba could visit the complex. The only stipulation was that someone familiar with it accompanied them so they didn't get lost.

"Shall we?" Awan motioned to the double glass doors that led out to the courtyard.

At the reminder of why he had come, Takoda strode across the room and out into the warm day. He waited until Awan had closed the doors before beginning. "I was on the walls this morning."

Awan's brows knit. "And all night?"

He flushed as he remembered his angry exit from their residence. "At least I didn't dig a hole the size of the Telemen Sea."

The brother of his heart chuckled. "True. I guess we each need to come to terms with our situation in our own way." He glanced toward the glass doors, the dark interior of his office making it difficult to see Ro. "I'm assuming you didn't explain your whereabouts to Rowena."

He shook his head. "I did not, but when she asked if I'd gone to another Pleasure Dome, I assured her I did not." It still bothered him that she would think that of him.

Awan's eyes widened before he seemed to understand the statement. "Though she has lived here for six Eden months, she has been sheltered from our society in many ways. It makes me wonder how she came to be in Tolba."

His mind skidded to a halt. He hadn't even thought about that. Had she been a chosen one of another filoz but never bonded with them? Is that why she was so hesitant about committing to the idea? Part of him was pleased that she fought the idea as much as he, but his gut twisted at the thought that she didn't want to be their beloved, which was as illogical as all the other feelings he had around her.

"You said you were on the walls. What happened?"

Awan's question brought him back to his concerns. "Yes, I sat upon the part of the wall that overlooks where the exiled are left." He didn't elaborate on what he'd been thinking while there. "As Helios began to shed his light over Eden, I saw a disturbance in the jungle. It was five lawbreakers all converging to one point at the edge of the jungle as if it had been preplanned."

"That may not be unusual. If I had been exiled, I'd probably journey back to the spot where I last saw my home."

"If that were the whole of it, I would not even be telling you about it, but there is more. Once together, they traversed the clearing together and stopped at the wall. They were talking about it, I'm sure. One had his hands on it and there was much gesturing."

Awan's whole body revealed his tension. "What happened?"

That was the question he'd been mulling over. "I'm not sure." He strode to the yahaw tree at the center of the yard before turning back. Finally, he shrugged. "I could not hear them, but after talking, one of them appeared to laugh then whipped himself into what I would describe as a landspout and plowed his way back into the jungle."

"A landspout?" Awan's eyes widened. "You mean like the waterspouts talked about in the ancient's stories only on land?"

He nodded. "I pondered the odd behavior all the way home. It is not like any ability I have known in Tolba, but I do not know them all. My thought was he might be Kindred of Air."

"That would make the most sense. But why did he go into the jungle? Could it have been emotional anguish?"

Takoda thought about the laughing man. "I don't think so. He seemed to enjoy himself and he left an open tunnel through the trees. My thought is that he was asked to do so in order for more lawbreakers to make their way to that one spot."

Awan glanced at the double glass doors. "I see why you are concerned. And you did not speak of this with Rowena?"

He shook his head. "I wanted to hear your thoughts before proceeding. Are you in agreement that the cheetans need to be alerted?"

"Yes. But you need to tell me every detail so we can decide who to discuss this with."

He strode back to where Awan stood next to two seats and sat. "I agree."

Chapter Eight

Rowena waited until the men were busy talking then began to explore. The office was relatively bare, especially compared to the hominess of their house. There was a desk with nothing on it and the two couches and coffee table. Against one wall was a small kitchenette with emphasis on small. The whole room was only a single-story dome.

Too tempted to go through the drawers, which would be exceptionally rude, she forced herself to look at the two paintings on the curved wall. They were obviously done by Lyka. One was a family portrait with Awan as the grown son. His mother appeared Eastern European and his two fathers were very tall. No wonder he towered at what she estimated as six-foot-seven inches tall. The other painting was somewhat abstract, but if she were to interpret it, it reflected balance and peace.

Turning around, there was nothing else to view. She leaned against the wall studying the two Edenists that might be her future. She had to admit she had good taste while drunk. Awan and Takoda were built like Greek statues with tans. Takoda reminded her of the statue of David, but with a much larger package. His hair even curled a bit like that. But Awan made her think of an Eastern

European boxer, silent but deadly, which didn't fit his personality at all.

What did fit was why she'd had such a terrible night's sleep. She kept seeing visions of her and Awan having sex. It revved her up with him pinning her against the wall and pumping into her. She kept waking up just before her climax. She'd actually left her room and walked to his, but at the last moment turned away. She forced herself to return to bed.

Unfortunately, the visions continued, and she'd finally had to pleasure herself to take the edge off enough to fall asleep. She'd dreamed of having sex with men before, but nothing so vivid that she'd been desperate enough to seek them out. It could be the bond. But if it was, she wouldn't have been able to resist, would she?

As Takoda took a seat, she groaned. This was the making of a long conversation. She never was good at doing nothing, and she'd waited so long to come to the Discoverist Complex. Micco had told her she could visit one day, but that hadn't happened. The hell with waiting. She could explore on her own. She grinned. It would be fun, now that she knew the colors of the bells were directional signs.

Pushing off the wall, she moved toward the exit. She glanced at the men in time to see Awan cross his legs, getting more comfortable. Really? Opening the door, she slipped outside onto the covered patrio. Taking careful note of the bell color, she strode out into the sun onto one of the cobblestone pathways and headed toward the blue bell section.

Micco had told her that visitors had to be invited and shown around, but since she was already in the complex, she saw no reason not to explore. Turning to her right, she strolled along the path until wonderous scents had her quickening her steps. The bells had turned blue and Takoda said the violet was next and then the red was where they experimented with food.

She followed her nose as the pathway split, looking for an open door. Micco had been very specific about how discoverists didn't like anyone to know what they were working on until they'd had success. It was one reason why he'd refrained from sharing his work with her though he and Sist had shared everything else. He'd said he would tell her when he achieved the outcome he was hoping for.

Her steps slowed as her mood fell. Takoda and Awan obviously didn't want her to know what they were talking about. Had she blown her chance, with Micco and Sist, at having everything like her mom wanted her to? Was there hope for her new yenea?

She stopped. How would she know? Maybe if the bond was confirmed? So, in a couple more days? And if it was true? Awan had already started to creep into her heart. The large man was so sweet with a calmness she gravitated to. His strength was that of body builder or Olympic athlete which she loved because it made her feel so feminine. Was their bond, as Awan firmly believed, meant to be? If that was true, why did she keep fighting it? Because Takoda was?

Maybe she needed to be brutally honest with herself. Why was she fighting the possible bond? First, she didn't know Takoda or Awan. That was legitimate. It was like having an arranged marriage back in historical times. It was no wonder she wasn't comfortable with that. She or her mother or even her grandmother had never been one to blindly accept society's expectations of her as a woman. In other words, she wasn't being selfish, just being herself. She could accept that.

Second, the reason that bothered her the most was her relationship with Micco and Sist. They'd been seeing each other every week for four months. Yes, it was true that a filoz often took at least a couple years before deciding to ask a woman to be their beloved, but that was because they watched their potential mate through the Crius portals. Only after all the men agreed did they make contact. But for Micco and Sist, they'd been in contact in what felt like forever.

She shook her head and started forward again. Maybe they weren't sure. She had thought she was until the morning of her anniversary on Eden. Suddenly, she'd developed cold feet. Was that because she was meant for Awan and Takoda? She still couldn't wrap her head around that fatalistic concept. To their credit, they had seen her at her worst, as in once in three to four years worst, and had stayed with her that night. Could mutual sorrow make a strong foundation for a relationship?

Her pace picked up as she took a right at yet another pathway split. It wasn't exactly a great first impression, though what she remembered from having sex with them, they were completely compatible in that area. Actually, they were the best she'd had, though that may have been because she'd had both of them together.

Even at the thought, she flushed. She wouldn't lie to herself. She was very attracted to them and experiencing what it was like to be the center of their attention in the bedroom broke down even her feminist walls. Maybe what they all needed to do was—

She stopped as a figure came into view across another courtyard. It was an Edenist striding along a parallel pathway a number of buildings away. She stared hard. It looked like Micco. Glancing at the bells, she noted they were purple changing to red.

That would be where Micco would work. Without a thought, she waved her arms. "Micco!"

The man continued walking, so she stepped off the path and ran across the dirt courtyard and between two buildings, just as he walked out of sight. Bursting out onto another pathway, she caught sight of him. She raced to catch up. "Micco! Hey, Micco."

The man stopped and glanced over his shoulder.

Not over there, over here. She continued to run toward him. "It's me, Rowena."

His eyes widened as he spotted her before he scanned the area, as if taking note of anyone nearby. Was he embarrassed to be seen with her? That thought had her slowing. But then he strode toward her with a welcoming smile on his face.

She walked forward, questioning her read of him. Maybe he simply had wondered where her escort was. He *did* say visitors were supposed to have a guide.

"Ro, what are you doing here?"

Though the question was said with a smile, it did sound a bit accusatory. Maybe she was breaking some serious rule. Just like a foreign country, it behooved her to understand Eden's rules. "I'm sorry I surprised you. I'm here with…." What should she call Awan and Takoda? "I'm here with some friends."

Micco took her hand. "I did not expect you. If I'd known you were coming, I could have made arrangements for you to see some of the successful projects in my area." With his head, he motioned behind him. "This isn't my dome. Mine is in the back." Again, he scanned the area. "Where is your protector?"

Crap, this was about to get uncomfortable, but she had to be honest with him. "I'm here with a filoz."

His eyebrows lowered. "A filoz?"

She'd have to be blind to not see the hurt in his eyes. "It's a trial."

He dropped her hand as if it burned him. "I did not know you had another filoz who wanted you."

She forced a chuckle. "Neither did I." She should tell him it was a one-night stand, but she just couldn't bring herself to admit that, especially since she didn't want him to think poorly of her. "When you and Sist came to see me last, I had thought, well…."

"Ah, you thought we might ask you to be our beloved."

She nodded, curious as to what he'd say to that.

"I admit, we have been discussing it." He didn't look away, but his gaze went glassy as if he was seeing something other than her. "The time is not right. Something else requires our complete focus now."

Her relief that she hadn't read his signals wrong quickly changed to hurt. "Something or someone?" She tried very hard to keep the sarcasm out of her voice, but from his returned focus on her, she hadn't been completely successful.

"It is larger than myself and not something I can discuss. We have refrained from asking you out of concern for your safety. That is all I can tell you." Though he appeared sorry, he was also completely confident he was doing the right thing.

But she wasn't stupid. Obviously, she didn't rate very high on the importance scale if she came in second to someone or something and didn't even rank high enough to be told what it was all about.

Once again, she felt the sting of rejection and she didn't like it. "I see. So, you were fine enjoying my company and my bed until when? Until next week? Next month? After I returned to Earth? If I'd known how low of a priority I was with you and Sist, I would have made an effort to meet more filoz."

His eyes widened. "No, do not think like that. You are very important to us." The fierceness of his words was reflected in his tone. "You are everything we want in a beloved."

Now she was just confused. "But?"

Micco rubbed the back of his neck, something she'd never seen him do. "We have to think beyond ourselves right now."

That admission had her hurt subsiding a bit. "What you're saying is whatever you're working on in there," she pointed to the building behind him, "takes precedence over your own needs and wants?"

His relieved smile confirmed her suspicion. "Yes, like that. Very much so."

Okay, *that* she could understand because she'd made her own profession a priority over finding someone to share her life with until now. "I get it." So where did that leave—

Takoda.

The feeling that he was near swept over her so suddenly, it derailed her train of thought. Searching the area, she turned around only to find it empty.

"Ro, what is it?"

She turned back to Micco. His look and stance had turned almost predatory. What the hell was going on? She couldn't explain that she sensed Takoda was near when he obviously wasn't. Just like back at the Pleasure Dome when—hell. Looking up, she found what she searched for. Above her and descending rapidly was Takoda and Awan. From the look on their faces, they were pissed.

Great. Now what was wrong?

She lowered her gaze toward Micco, but he was rising. Instead of being scared as she was when Takoda had first levitated her, Micco simply crossed his arms over his chest and stared at Takoda as they passed in midair.

She stepped back and faced Takoda as he came down hard on the ground.

"What are you doing?" He took three steps toward her and grasped both her arms. "Who is he? What was he doing to you?"

She tried to pull her arms from his grasp, but that wasn't happening. "Let go of me. We were just talking."

He let go but didn't move away.

"Thank you. Believe it or not, I had a life before the night we met and Micco was part of it. He's a friend."

Awan put his hand on Takoda's shoulder as he stood next to him but appeared just as angry. "Did Micco's filoz ask you to be their beloved?"

She glanced up. Micco simply watched them, too high to hear what they were saying. "Not yet, but it probably would have happened eventually." Unless, of course, she went back to Earth before they were ready.

Takoda turned toward Awan, dislodging his hand. "Take her back. I will speak to this Micco."

At Takoda's tone, an alarm as loud as a fire truck racing down Storrow Drive went off in her head. She pointed to Micco. "You bring him down now and you do it gently. Understand?"

Takoda's scowl grew deeper, but she refused to back down, locking her gaze with his blue one. Finally, he gave her a short nod.

"Good, and don't hurt him either."

Though his hands curled into fists, he nodded once again.

"Come." Awan's voice had grown deep, and a thrill of excitement buzzed through her.

The last thing she should be thinking about now was how sexy he sounded saying that particular word in that particular way. She glanced back up at Micco who had uncrossed his arms, but otherwise appeared unconcerned by Takoda's murderous mood. Knowing how much Edenists like to please their women, she had faith Takoda would behave within the parameters she'd set, but she had no doubt he'd make some kind of threat.

Finally, she turned to walk with Awan, not surprised when his large hand grasped her own. It was a bit tighter than when she and Takoda had strolled earlier. As they strode toward his office, he didn't say anything. He didn't walk too fast or have jerky movements, but she could tell he was angry. She just wasn't sure why. "How did you find me?"

His hand squeezed hers just a little tighter as if by reflex, but he didn't look at her. "I ran the scenarios. Nine showed me you were still in the complex." His voice lowered. "Two did not."

Guilt gave her a twinge. The last two had made him worry. She hadn't even thought about what they would think if they finished talking and she wasn't there. "I'm sorry. I'm not used to having to let others know where I'm going. To be honest, I didn't expect to run into Micco though I knew he was a discoverist."

Awan stopped suddenly, causing her to whip around since their hands were joined. "What is it?"

His gaze was intense. "How close were you to becoming part of this filoz?"

She suddenly could picture him digging the giant hole in

the back of his home. He always seemed so calm, but this was a different side of him, a dangerous side of him. The thrill that knowledge sent through her made no sense. "We were getting to know each other. Like you and I are."

"You are ours."

At his words, an image of Awan pinning her to a wall flashed through her mind. Her body responded immediately, suddenly wanting him in exactly that way. *Son of a bitch.*

Without another word, he started forward again, still keeping their pace measured.

She should argue that she wasn't theirs, but her heart wasn't in it. Was there really a bond? An image of Awan's mouth on her right breast filled her head and her nipples hardened. What was with all the erotic images? Her body was taking over, feeding off some sort of sexual energy Awan was exuding. Maybe it was the pheromones. Did he feel it too or was it just her?

Glancing at the color of the bells, she found herself picking up the pace. Had she really wandered that far away? Awan matched her stride even as another vision took hold. This time she was against a wall and he had two fingers deep inside her. Her breath caught and her sheath moistened even as she recognized the building with his office. She wanted out of her clothes and onto Awan more than air. What the hell was wrong with her?

She had no time to answer that question, nor did she want to. They'd reached his office, and he opened the door for her, but he didn't let go of her hand. In fact, once the door had closed, he pulled her to him and pressed her against the wall.

Relief and excitement flooded her just before Awan's mouth came down on hers. It was no exploratory kiss. His tongue took command of her mouth, seeking her total compliance. She grabbed the back of his neck, holding him to her until she couldn't breathe.

As if he sensed her need for air, he ripped his mouth away and caught her face between his two large hands as he leaned his forehead against hers. "I need to make you mine."

Her heart jumped as if it was all she ever wanted to hear. "Only if I can make you mine."

His nostrils flared and he lifted his head to stare into her eyes. "Yes."

An image of the erect cock that pressed against her stomach plunging deep inside her had her sheath tightening. "Too many clothes." She complained, her words coming out on a breath. Now she understood the Edenists' reason for walking about naked.

Awan didn't answer. He simply moved her away from the wall far enough to pull her tunic over her head before placing his hands on her ribs and pushing her back against it. Before she knew what he was about, he ripped her bra in half with his bare hands and his mouth latched onto her right breast.

Thrill after thrill raced through her as he sucked and nipped, her nipple growing so hard it bordered on pain. Just when she didn't think she could take anymore, he moved to her other breast. His teeth gently took her nipple and rolled it before pulling it toward him.

She arched in pleasure, her sheath so wet she was sure she had soaked through her leggings.

He let her nipple go with a pop. Then he spread his wide hands across her abdomen and pushed her leggings and panties to the floor. She'd barely got one foot out before his entire muscled body had pressed against hers, his cock pushing on her abdomen, making it clear how hard he was for her.

He didn't move as if he was trying to control his own need.

She didn't want control. She wanted him inside her. Now. Moving her hands from his back to his rock-hard butt, she squeezed.

"Rowena." His voice was a warning whisper in her ear.

She opened her mouth and licked at the chest muscle before her.

A guttural groan came from deep inside him just before he pulled his hips back and his fingers found her wet flesh. With an expertise of a man who knew his way around a woman, he gently eased two fingers inside her.

The invasion was both satisfying and titillating, but when he didn't move, the throbbing need in her core became unbearable. She tilted her head up. "Take me."

Within seconds, his fingers had pulled out. He bent his legs and the tip of his cock entered.

Yes! Her sheath widened to accommodate him as he slowly pushed inside, stretching her, filling her. Then when she thought she had all of him, he grasped her thighs, lifting her up, and wrapped her legs around him. Pressing her against the wall, he finished his entrance into her body.

Every nerve ending tingled at the complete possession. Her nipples crushed against his hard pectorals pulsed with heat. Locking her ankles around him, she lifted her face to look at him.

He gazed at her with a hunger she'd never seen before but felt clear to her core. No one had looked at her with such need. Even as she gazed into his amber eyes, a vision of him orgasming inside her flashed before her. Her sheath squeezed in reflex just as he lowered his head to take her mouth once again.

She closed her eyes, wanting only to feel.

He kept her pressed to the wall as he pulled out to his tip and held himself there at the same time his tongue retreated.

She plunged her own into his mouth, wanting him back.

He understood the message and thrust his cock into her in one quick, smooth glide.

Pleasure struck like a lightning bolt. She turned her head to gasp for air as he rocked into her again. The sensations racing through her body hit with an intensity that had her unable to think. He thrust harder and faster, spiraling her upward to her fast-approaching orgasm. The apex of feelings jumped with every thrust, her body not under her own control. And then it hit.

She broke apart from within. Crying out, she enjoyed every sharp pleasurable feeling that started in her core and blossomed outward.

Awan filled her, shouting out his own release.

Her orgasm intensified, taking all thought away beyond sheer satisfaction.

As the sensations dissipated, she opened her eyes to find him staring at her. It was an odd stare as if he couldn't quite figure her out.

She didn't stop playing with the short hairs at the base of his neck where her fingers rested. She tilted her head. "What?"

"You." He seemed unsure, as if what they experienced was unusual in some way. "You make me feel what I never have. I don't simply want you. I need you, crave you." His gaze intensified. "It's as if I haven't been a whole being before you."

His words filled her with joy while at the same time making her uncomfortable. "But why me?"

She expected to hear something about her looks or her personality or maybe even her body.

Awan remained bewildered for many seconds, and then, as if he'd had an epiphany, his face relaxed and a soft, loving smile appeared. "It is the bond."

Her breath caught at both his look and his words. Her heart recognized the look she'd always wanted to see, while her brain balked that there was a bond. "But—"

"Did you not feel my need for you even as we left Takoda?"

She frowned. They had simply walked away holding hands. Neither saying anything until…oh hell. She'd seen Awan making love to her, but that could have been her own imagination.

"Tell me, Rowena, did you not feel my need to press you to this wall, taste your breasts, and feel your wetness upon my fingers?"

Well, didn't that just answer that question. As much as she wanted to deny it, all that he said was true and her sheath moistened at his words. "I did." Her voice came out softly. She'd learned about the bond as every woman in the Pleasure Dome did, but to be bonded couldn't prepare one for the reality. They had stressed that each bond was unique.

He leaned in and kissed her lips gently before speaking. "It is an awe-inspiring change of life. If you are a little afraid, it is understandable."

She couldn't help challenging him, the thought that he'd bonded with another before made her unreasonably pissed off. "And you know this how? Did you bond with the woman who left you?"

Awan shook his head. "An Edenist can only bond once. The bond is for life. Xavia had not made the decision yet to bond with us."

For no reason at all, she hated Xavia and was angry with her for rejecting him, yet she felt a huge relief…until his words sunk in. "For life? As in, if I decided this didn't work for me, none of us could ever find someone else?" She had no prospects in mind at all, but the finality of it scared her.

He simply nodded.

The thought of leaving him and Takoda and forcing them to a lifetime without a mate was too cruel to think about. But before she could firmly grasp that, the sensation that Takoda was near forced her to ask. "Can this bond only work between part of a filoz?"

"No." He grinned. "Whatever Takoda chooses to believe is irrelevant. We are all bonded. This is why we had such a reaction to you being alone with another Edenist." Even as he said it, his hold on her tightened. In such an intimate position, it was easy to feel *everything*.

"So, you're saying you were jealous?"

"That word is inadequate to express how we feel. Takoda will be in need of—"

The door beside her opened. Instinctually, she pressed herself close to Awan to hide her body from the newcomer even though she knew it was Takoda.

His wild look caught her off guard. He immediately turned toward them and pinned her with his gaze. "You." He lifted his hand as his gaze moved to Awan. A silent communication passed between them and Awan removed her arms from his neck. At first, she was stunned that she remained against him until he unlocked her ankles and stepped from her embrace, leaving her hanging there, wanting more.

Only then did she understand that Takoda was levitating her.

He looked as if he wouldn't be able to draw another breath without being in her arms. She remained aloft, naked and vulnerable. But she didn't feel vulnerable as a vision of Takoda plunging deep inside her burst upon her.

She had a split second to glance at Awan's happy face before Takoda took his place in front of her. He opened his mouth to speak, but before he could get out a word, she said what they both needed to hear. "Yes."

His hands came up to her face even as she felt the tip of his cock push against her folds. His mouth came down on hers, his tongue thrusting inside at the same time his cock drove deep into her, knocking her breath from her lungs with the pleasure.

She moaned deep in her throat, the feel of him causing her to tighten her sheath.

Takoda didn't move, keeping her pinned to the wall, but his kiss was ravenous, even more desperate than Awan's. The feelings his need aroused inside her were hard to define. It was as if both these men counted on her to breathe.

She met Takoda's need with her own, her tongue dueling with his. He pressed into her as if he couldn't get close enough. She locked her ankles around him, wanting him to know she needed him just as much and tilted her pelvis.

He groaned before ripping his mouth away. "I cannot wait." The admission seemed to come from deep inside him as if it was the worst thing he could ever admit.

Her chest hurt for him. Anxious to put them both out of their misery, she gave him what they both needed. "Please don't. I want you now."

His body against her tensed for a split second as if in shock, before he pulled his hips back and plunged inside her again. His thrust sent off sparks throughout her, ready to light the tinder of her pleasure. But she had little time to enjoy those tiny shards of excitement before he thrust again.

Fires lit in every erogenous place as he withdrew then drove back in hard, again and again, until a conflagration of pleasure filled her, sweeping her up into his heat. She didn't know where he ended and she began as they went up in flames together.

Her orgasm hit hard, forcing her cry to be loud as she exploded from within seconds before Takoda groaned her name and plunged one last time, his pelvis pressing hers as he filled her with his release.

She held onto him, her body thrumming with the reverberations of her orgasm as he held her pinned between him and the wall, their breathing rapid and uneven. She opened her eyes to see Awan's heated gaze.

Son of a bitch. She'd forgotten she was with two men. And he'd watched everything. She dropped her gaze to see his cock hard and ready again. A thrill shot through her, causing her sheath to tighten, eliciting a groan from Takoda.

"Don't. I need a few minutes." His voice came out gravelly.

Before she could explain her reaction, Awan moved closer. "I don't." His eyes almost glowed with anticipation.

Could she? She never had before unless she had the night they'd all been drunk.

Takoda lifted his head from her shoulder and turned her face to meet his gaze. "Be with Awan while I recover."

The insinuation, that once Awan was done he'd return, had crazy sparks of excitement going off inside her. "I don't know if

I have the strength." As titillating as the idea was, she felt like an over-cooked noodle.

Takoda grinned. "You don't need strength." Slowly, he pulled out of her, stepping from her arms while she hung there, levitating. "Awan, give her what she craves."

As if he'd said the magic words, Awan's cock jumped, and her own body reacted, her nipples already hardening at the thought of being taken again and then again. She didn't know if there was a limit to how many orgasms a woman could have in a row, but if Takoda wanted to keep her floating, she was happy to find out.

Awan ran his hands over her thighs then moved them between her legs and spread her farther apart. His gaze remained fixated on her entrance as if he wanted to memorize every fold.

It was a heady sensation to be stared at with such focus.

But staring wasn't enough for him. His hands, still on her knees, moved toward her opening until his fingers spread her labia and revealed her very core.

Her heartbeat pounded so hard, she had to be vibrating with it.

Awan's thumb moved upward and stroked her clit, sending a jolt of excitement ricocheting through her.

She gasped at the intensity of the feeling. How could it be so strong when she'd just orgasmed?

This time, he didn't press her hard against the curved wall, but instead, he slowly entered her while watching his own cock disappear inside her.

The eroticism of that purposefulness was not lost on her. It made her want to give in to whatever he wished. She'd never felt so sexy and feminine.

Once inside her, he let go of her folds and braced his hands against the wall on either side of her head, keeping his torso away from her. "I promise not to go so fast this time."

She swallowed at what that might mean. If he expected an answer, he'd be disappointed because at that moment, he slowly pulled his hips away, sliding out of her to his tip then sliding back in. She grasped his arms, holding on as he moved out once again.

Despite how replete she'd been, her body buzzed like a vibrator on a slow speed, prolonging every pleasurable spike. The climb was slow but constant as he moved with practiced deliberateness, his cock pushing to its hilt then moving out to its tip completely each time.

She let her head fall back against the wall and closed her eyes, her total focus now on the building sensations between her legs.

Suddenly, a hand cupped her left breast, and she opened her eyes to find Takoda giving it the same intense perusal Awan had given her opening. His thumb moved up to her nipple and he stroked it back and forth in time to Awan's rhythm. The dual sensations in such slow progress added another level of orgasmic preparation.

Takoda's thumb left her breast as his hand moved down to where she and Awan joined. As Awan continued his slow and steady strokes, Takoda's finger found her clit.

Her breath hitched and her sheath tightened as the sharp excitement seemed to travel through her core, intensifying Awan's entrance into her body. When his rhythm picked up the pace, she knew he felt it too.

Takoda didn't touch her clit for four more strokes, making her crave the feeling even more. Then he did, and this time he didn't stop. His finger circled her clit, rubbing gently at first, even as Awan's thrusts increased.

Her entire body pulsed with heat, moving toward the precipice that would bring her the ultimate satisfaction. Her muscles tightened of their own accord as the feelings intensified. Just as she thought it couldn't get better, Takoda's finger pressed her clit hard just before Awan slammed into her.

The combination sent her flying over the edge in pure ecstasy. She gasped for air as her body trembled, the shocks of sensual bliss rocking her hard. Awan continued his hard and fast thrusts before coming to his own orgasm, filling her once again with satisfaction.

Eventually, she opened her eyes to find her head back against the wall in complete surrender. She had to force herself to move it to look at Awan, whose eyes were still closed. A small smile played about his mouth.

It took her a moment before she felt Takoda's stare. Turning her head, she looked into eyes so blue, she swore she could drown in them. She wanted to give him a grateful smile, but she didn't seem to have the energy.

"I want you again." Takoda's voice came out deep. This time it wasn't desperate so much as commanding and despite her weariness, her nipples hardened in reaction.

Awan's hand against her cheek brought her attention back to him. "You do not have to, but I know it will please us immensely."

Us? She tried to wrap her mind around the fact that having sex with one was like having sex with both, but she was still in feeling mode and her brain was preoccupied with the cock inside her and the promise of yet another opportunity to orgasm.

Then Awan pulled back completely, leaving her body. She had to bite her tongue to keep from telling him not to. How greedy could she get? Still, she floated in midair, a feeling she was quickly becoming comfortable with.

"It is up to you." Awan gave her a soft smile.

Was he teasing her? He had to know what it was like to have him leave when she wasn't ready for him to leave.

She switched her gaze to Takoda, whose face was not quite a scowl and more like a man who planned to get what he wanted, though he didn't say a word. It was that look that had her body responding. She'd never been a tiny woman to feel helpless around men, but right now, she felt as if she were a sex kitten and they were her cat nip. She didn't want any limitations on how much she could have. She needed to explore this new identity of hers.

Tilting her head, she let her eyelids half close and looked up at him beneath her lashes. "As you wish."

Takoda's nostrils flared and her body went on alert in a good way. He stepped before her, between her spread legs.

She expected him to enter her once again, but instead, she found herself floating higher until her breasts were even with his head.

Takoda didn't say a word. Instead, he stepped closer and swiped his tongue over a hard nipple.

A zing of pleasure swept straight down to her sheath. "Yes." Her word came out in a hiss.

As if her recognition of his ability was what he'd waited for, he latched onto her nipple with his mouth and sucked hard.

She grasped his shoulders and arched at the sensations, vaguely wondering how she could be revved up again so quickly.

He let out what sounded like a growl against her breast before moving to her other one to suck that one into his strong mouth.

Her pelvis tilted upward of its own accord, seeking what he would give her, but he ignored her silent plea to be taken and instead, stepped back, breaking her legs' hold on him.

Reaching out, he took each nipple between his fingers and pinched them lightly. The pleasure hit again and she wanted more. As if reading her need or maybe her pheromones, which had to be off the charts right now, he pinched them a little harder.

She hissed with carnal indulgence. It was all the encouragement he needed. He squeezed them even harder, and she moaned again unable to keep from moving her pelvis toward him again.

As if satisfied with her reactions, he stepped closer, lowering her until they were face to face. His blue eyes appeared almost black, they had darkened so much. His gaze was intense as he stared into her eyes.

He didn't touch her, just stared at her. A memory flitted through her mind of someone saying that the sexiest part of the human body was the brain. She was positive that Takoda had a very sexy brain.

Her lips twitched at the thought just before two fingers slipped into her sheath. She caught her breath at the unexpected intrusion. Excitement flowed throughout her body. How did he do that? There had been no indication in his eyes that he would touch her. She would watch him closer.

Then his thumb brushed against her clit. She couldn't help it. She pushed against the fingers inside her, wanting more. And he gave her more. Though he didn't move his fingers, his thumb circled her clit, playing her like a well-honed instrument. Just as she thought she'd reach her orgasm, he stopped and her body relaxed. Then he started playing her again.

It was exciting, frustrating, erotic, and completely new, the helpless feeling she had, knowing she would only reach her fourth orgasm when he wanted her to. After the third time, she lifted her hand to touch his nipple to entice him to finish it, but he caught it, linking their fingers together as he held her hand against the wall.

Not to be dissuaded, she lifted her other hand, only to be surprised when Awan linked his hand with hers and held it against the wall. She'd forgotten he was there, watching. Suddenly, she wanted them both to take her, something she never thought she'd want.

But the thought quickly flew out the window as Takoda's expert thumb fiddled against her clit, sending thrills through her body, her sheath tightening, even as she was helpless to participate in any way besides pushing harder against his fingers.

Again, he brought her to the brink. She didn't want to go there only to be let down again, but her body did as it pleased and the beginnings of her orgasm crept through her core, teasing her with its closeness.

Takoda withdrew his fingers altogether and in one swift movement, pulled her down hard onto his cock.

Her explosion was coupled with his own and they hit new heights together. She gasped as her body rocked against his, no longer in control.

His hands now held her butt to him as he filled her once again.

She let herself float on a cloud of satisfaction as her heartbeat slowed and she was finally able to pull in deeper breaths. Too weak to lift her head from his shoulder, she slowly opened her eyes to find Awan grinning at her, her hands now limp at her sides.

Unable to resist, she smiled tiredly at him.

He opened his mouth to speak when the bells outside his door rang. His eyes widened before he seemed to remember he was at work. "Takoda, take Rowena home."

Crap, she had to dress! "Wait, my clothes." Though she was freaked at the thought of some strange Edenist seeing her naked and still connected to Takoda, the thought of actually pulling on her leggings had her groaning.

Awan scooped up her clothes as Takoda slowly pulled out. Her feet touched the floor for the first time since Awan had lifted her around him and her knees buckled.

Takoda didn't let her fall as he floated them out the glass door Awan had opened before he strode back in to see who needed him.

Takoda was kind enough to float them above the small dome where he silently helped her dress, though he did most the work. She couldn't remember feeling this tired even after pulling two all-nighters in a row at work.

Once she had all her clothes on except her shoes which must still be in Awan's office, Takoda lifted her in his arms and they floated higher, past the Discoverist complex.

Takoda still didn't say anything and for that she was glad. So much had happened in so short a time and she needed to process it all. That her life was changed significantly now was a given, but how she felt about it and her own actions required serious thought. Something she couldn't manage at the moment.

Instead, she tried to focus on Tolba spread out beneath her, but even that couldn't hold her interest when her body was so tired. She closed her eyes, having complete faith that Takoda would get them home safely.

CHAPTER NINE

TAKODA SENSED THE INSTANT Ro fell asleep in his arms, her body completely relaxed, unlike when they'd joined. Even when she was physically tired, she'd still held herself as if unwilling to completely let go…except the last time. His need to have her accept him as he wanted her to had been as forceful as it had been unexpected. For some reason, he had to know that she was not only his but dependent upon him. He'd never had such a compulsion before, not even with Xavia.

Xavia was bonded to others and now he and Awan were bonded to Ro. He hadn't recognized the rage he felt upon seeing her speaking to the man called Micco. It wasn't until he'd stormed into Awan's place of labor and saw them entwined that it became clear.

His mind had only one thought at the time and that was to make her his. He couldn't remember if he said anything before he sunk into her ready body. Even if they hadn't been bonded before, they all were now. There was no possibility it wouldn't take after what they'd just done with Ro.

Carefully, he touched down in the rear courtyard close to the covered patrio. Keeping her suspended, he opened the door with one hand and floated them inside. He stopped, not sure where she would want to rest, her room or *their* room.

He looked down upon her face, resting against his chest. She was beautiful in her own unique way and more than a match for them physically. The urge to brush her cheek with his finger was strong, but he refrained. In the short time he'd known Ro, he'd recognized someone who thought much like him. Someone who questioned instead of accepted on faith. It had been a long time since he'd had a friend who thought as he did.

His heart warmed at the realization. He might never be able to love again but having her friendship would fill an empty place in his soul. He glanced at the three doors again and quickly moved to Lyka's old room, the twinge in his heart less painful this time. Gently, he laid her on the bed. If only she hadn't insisted on donning her clothes again, she'd sleep better now, but such was her wishes and he'd abide by them.

Brushing strands of dark red hair away from her face, he couldn't help holding onto them a little longer. They appeared as if they would burn him, but they were cool and silky in his fingers. Finally, he let them drop and moved toward the door. Without looking back, he closed it quietly and strode to Awan's room to use the rainbox to wash without waking Ro.

One he'd dried off, he headed for the meal area. He would make them all a filling meal of feroon steaks, ondile, and pegwa squash. He came to the preparation counter and pulled one of Ro's drawings closer. Then they could go out into the courtyard with her papers and understand better what her vision was for the cold pond. As she'd explained it, it was nothing like he'd seen in Tolba so far, and he'd seen more than many.

Pulling the steaks from the cold box, he added his favorite two plant leaves and set them back inside to take in the flavors. His mind wandered to Awan. He would undoubtedly say the ringing of his bells was meant to be, and maybe it was. Ro had been exhausted. Awan sometimes met with no one or could be busy all day with discoverists anxious for insight into which direction to move forward.

That Micco had never sought out Awan before had been obvious. They'd found him in the animal and food section. Surely Awan could help the man with the right direction to go. So why would Micco not use Awan's ability to help him succeed in his discoveries?

Chopping the pegwa squash, Takoda's gut tensed. The man had been far too calm when levitated and completely unphased as he brought him to the ground, careful to lower him slowly as Ro requested. Is that why Micco was so calm? He knew Ro would be sure no harm came to him? At that thought, his anger returned. Was this how it was for all bonded mates? He'd been educated in the bonding, but no one had mentioned the unreasonable rage that had taken over.

He may have been in the grip of mate protection, but he still sensed something wasn't right with Micco. The man hid something, most likely his research. What had Ro said? *I was told that you have to be invited.* Anyone could visit the Discoverist Complex. Did she hear that from Micco? If she had, that definitely meant he didn't want her in the complex without him. What did he hide from her?

He stopped chopping, his gut telling him he was close to the truth. What if his need to protect and claim Ro was not from the bond, but from an ancient instinct that sensed danger? At that, he shook his head. Even Awan would think that was too far afield. It could simply be that after seeing the lawbreakers planning something against Tolba, his own reactions were extra sensitive.

Throwing the ondile and pegwa squash onto a tray, he covered them in daemon bee honey and put them in the hot box. The lawbreakers' movements bothered him. He'd sat upon the outside walls of Tolba many times and had been witness to a few single men trying to find a way back inside. As far as he knew, the only one who had ever breached the walls of Tolba was Davos, the dirgon.

Even as he thought of the man-beast, his anger returned. He blamed him for taking away the family he was supposed to have. Now, without Xavia and Lyka, he had a broken heart.

And had bonded with Awan and Ro. The reality calmed him. He was truly bonded whether he wanted to be or not. When would he discover his connection to Ro? Or was he so broken, it couldn't happen? That gave him pause.

The door to the main throughfare opened and Awan stepped in. Takoda glanced at the level of Helios in the high western window of their home. It was still early. "I did not expect you back so soon."

Awan glanced at him before heading to his room. Just when Takoda thought he would ignore him, Awan stopped and spoke over his shoulder. "We have much to discuss."

While he agreed, Awan's face was tense which meant the topic of discussion was something he was very concerned about.

Turning down the heat in the hot box, he poured two glasses of ambrosia and brought them outside. As the door closed behind him, he reconsidered. If Awan wasn't happy, seeing the hole he dug while unbalanced, wouldn't help.

Returning inside, he set the glasses on the preparation counter as it was the farthest spot from Ro's sleeping room. Not only did he not wish to wake her, but he wasn't sure if the coming discussion was for her knowledge as well.

Awan strode through his open doorway and joined him. He sat on a stool, his hair still wet from the rainbox.

Takoda pushed the glass of ambrosia forward and Awan picked it up. After taking a couple sips with closed eyes, he set it down. "My visitor when you and Rowena left was a cheetan."

He stopped his own glass from reaching his lips. "What?"

Awan shook his head. "I was as stunned as you. Cheetans never come to the Discoverist Complex. They always send for us, but..."

He waited impatiently, knowing well that Awan chose his words carefully.

"The best way to describe the encounter was that it was not an official visit and more of a personal one."

"That doesn't make it less unusual." He finally took a sip of his drink.

Awan stroked his chin. "No, it does not. Moorg's questions concerned me. He hinted that he would be interested in scenarios on how well Tolba could survive if there were no Kindred of Eden at all."

Takoda's gut tensed. "What is he thinking? If all Kindred of Eden were gone, we wouldn't be able to survive. I don't need scenarios to understand that. Our ability to survive is based upon balance. With as many Kindred of Eden that have been exiled, I'd think he'd know that. Already there are problems with food supplies."

"This I know." Awan lifted his glass to his lips and took a long sip.

"Did you run the scenarios for him? What did they say?"

"I did not. He did not directly ask, and I did not volunteer. His visit and demeanor worried me. I do not know for certain, but I don't think Moorg wanted anyone to know he visited me."

He valued Awan's insight over all others. "Why did you think so?" If anything, that made the visit even more suspicious.

"He told me he would appreciate it if our conversation was kept between us."

Takoda set his drink down, the sudden stress in his body too hard to ignore. "This is not how the cheetans rule. Something is wrong."

Awan nodded. "I agree. But what do we do? Do we go before the cheetans and explain what happened? Would they believe me?"

Dread crept up his back. Tolba relied on the cheetans to govern the city fairly. That was why only the oldest and wisest became cheetans. If even one of them had other motives, it could destroy the fabric of their society. It was as if a lawbreaker had somehow become a cheetan, but that could never be. "Did you mention the lawbreakers I saw at the wall?"

Awan shook his head. "I should have, but I refrained. That is important information, and I didn't trust that it would be relayed with the urgency it needed."

"I believe you made the right decision. Now that this has occurred, I must go to the cheetans about the lawbreakers alone."

"Why?" Awan's brows lowered in his confusion.

"Because if you go before them, this cheetan will become nervous that you might say something about his visit."

"You are right." Awan took another sip. He didn't say anything else, but it was clear by his furrowed brow that his balance was affected.

Takoda put his hand on Awan's shoulder. "What is it?"

"I do not know. I'm conflicted. Moorg has always been a dependable cheetan. Yet he appears to want Kindred of Eden gone. When I figure it out, I will let you know."

"I will wait for when you are ready." He trusted Awan with his very life.

Awan took another sip of ambrosia before looking over his shoulder toward the only closed door in the residence. "Is Rowena well?"

He grinned. "She is. But she fell asleep before we made it back."

"I hope we did not overly tire her. Seeing her with this Micco was…unsettling."

"I do not think so." Takoda smiled at the memory of her cries of ecstasy. "I believe it was simply so much enjoyment. I am making feroon steaks for our evening meal to replenish her strength."

"And what about you? You must know we are bonded. Can you accept that?" Awan looked him in the eye.

"I know." He paused, trying to find the words to explain how he felt. Finally, he gave up. Instead, he pulled the sheets of paper over from the edge of the prep counter. "You haven't seen these. Ro did some preliminary drawings of what our cold pond could look like."

Awan's amber gaze remained on him a few moments longer before he accepted the change in topic and focused on the papers. He separated the drawings, studying them each separately. "This is extraordinary."

Once again, he found himself smiling, feeling a sense of pride for no logical reason. "I agree. I thought I would start on it tomorrow after I finish at the new hatchoc. I think the sooner it looks like we planned to do this all along, the sooner you will cease being embarrassed by your days of imbalance."

Awan flushed then grinned. "This will make it look like it was meant to be."

He rolled his eyes. Only Awan would—

The closed door to Ro's room opened. Her brilliant red hair was pulled back from her face and she blinked a couple times as if still waking. She scanned the open area until she saw them. "Wow, I never sleep in the middle of the day. I apologize."

Awan rose and strode toward her. "No need to apologize. You can do whatever you want. This is your home."

Takoda grimaced as Ro's eyes widened in what could only be considered panic. Definitely the wrong choice of words. Knowing how hard this bonding was to accept, he quickly interjected. "We're having feroon steaks. Do you prefer yours well-cooked or pink inside?"

Ro stepped past Awan. "I like a little pink. Is this one of your specialties?"

He nodded. "It is."

Awan followed her. "What foods do you enjoy?"

Ro hopped up on a stool. "I like most everything, though I have to say that the nubbish this afternoon was excellent."

Awan's brows rose.

Ro grinned. "You should have seen the owner of that establishment." She moved her gaze to him. "He was so happy when Takoda moved all his barrels in a matter of minutes."

The pride in her gaze caught Takoda off guard. "I'm glad that I can so easily provide you with your nubbish."

She focused on Awan who had moved to stand next to her. "Having Takoda around to lift heavy objects with his levitation ability is a real asset. Do you often get tapped for your ability to run scenarios?"

As Awan explained how often his services were requested, Takoda moved to the cold box to retrieve ambrosia for Ro. There was a comfortableness in their joint conversation yet a newness as well. It was the discovery phase of learning about one's beloved, but it usually happened before the bonding.

Retrieving a glass, he poured the ambrosia. Could Awan be right and Ro was meant to be their beloved all along? If so, why had he fallen in love with Xavia? Pushing the heavy thought away, he rejoined the conversation, offering Ro the drink, which she took readily.

After taking what could only be considered a gulp, she put it down and grinned sheepishly. "I didn't realize how thirsty I was. Thank you."

Awan caught his eye and they silently agreed that her thirst was caused by their afternoon lovemaking.

"What?" She waved her finger between them. "What is that thing you two do that I've seen other filoz do as well?"

"What do you mean?" Awan was first to answer her.

"You look at each other as if you know exactly what the other is thinking. How do you do that?"

Awan shrugged. "It is just natural."

She cocked her head, clearly skeptical, but before she could ask further questions, Awan picked up one of the drawings she'd done.

"Come, show me outside what your plans are for my hole."

She chuckled. "I wouldn't be embarrassed by it. It's going to become an amazing place to relax. Takoda, will you come too?"

He shook his head. "You two go while I prepare our meal. If you like, we can eat outside in the courtyard."

"I would like that." The smile she gave him filled him with warmth before she jumped off the stool and gathered up the other drawings. "Come Awan. Let me show you what this hole could be. On Earth we call it making lemonade out of lemons."

As the two closed the door, Takoda stared after them. Was that what they were doing by bonding with Ro? Were they trying to make something from what wasn't meant to be?

Conflicted by his runaway thoughts, he returned to making the evening meal. Feroon steaks he knew well. He much preferred staying with what he knew. The unknown, their future, the lawbreakers, the cheetans, even Micco, were the unknown and he very much wished he could unknow it all.

He looked through the far windows at Ro pointing to a spot on the far side of the courtyard. Maybe not all. He definitely enjoyed learning about Ro. Shaking his head, he moved to the cold box and pulled out the steaks. Food first. Everything else could wait.

Ro stared at the ceiling of her room, waiting for it to get light enough to read the poem painted there. Though she'd thought the room free of all paintings, she's seen the writing up there when she woke from her nap the day before.

She must have been incredibly tired her first night not to have noticed it and yesterday she was so embarrassed at having fallen asleep in the middle of the day that she'd rushed out of bed to apologize. Though to be honest, she'd had more of a workout with her filoz than any personal trainer could put her through.

Even as she thought of the tag-team sex Awan and Takoda had with her, her body tingled. It had been amazing and new in so many ways. Rarely had she let a man, never mind men, take over her pleasure so completely. She wasn't the submissive type, but something about their need for her had flipped her psyche upside down.

She'd been a bit nervous that they would expect her to bend at their will when not having sex as well, but last evening had been spent in comfortable companionship among equals.

Actually, they treated her as almost above them. It was a heady feeling yet an awkward one. She didn't want them to sacrifice their wishes for hers all the time, just as she didn't expect to sacrifice her own wants all the time for theirs. She wanted them to all be happy.

So why did you insist on sleeping in a separate room last night? And wasn't that the big question? One she'd have a difficult time answering if Awan and Takoda asked instead of bending to her preference. Despite an amazing day and an enjoyable evening, when they'd invited her to Awan's room, she couldn't do it. She'd needed time alone, away from them, or rather away from anyone. They had to be confused.

Their deep voices now were barely discernable through the toleric walls letting her know they had yet to leave for work. She could join them, say good morning and wish them a good day. Instead, she lay here waiting for the room to lighten so she could read the words on the ceiling when she could very well come back in later and do so.

There must be something wrong with her. Even though she imagined the welcoming smiles of the two handsome, well-built men as she walked into the main room, she couldn't seem to find it within herself to move. Could this be why she'd never found someone to share her life with? Was she so conditioned to living alone that the thought of sharing her space with them had her sabotaging her relationships?

Now that was something to ponder. Not that it mattered. It was too late. She was bonded…for life. A chill raced up her spine at the thought. She had everything she wanted, two good men who put her on a pedestal, even if deeper feelings weren't present yet, and she didn't have a clue how to be comfortable living with them. Just great.

The room had lightened considerably, so she read the beginning of what was clearly a three-stanza poem.

He touched me, so I live to know

That such a day, permitted so,

I groped upon his breast.

It was a boundless place to me,

And silenced, as the awful sea

Puts minor streams to rest.

The meaning of the first stanza struck far too close to home. Just yesterday she'd been swept up by the two men, thrilled yet completely lost in the pleasure she'd experienced as she became something she'd never been before. It definitely felt "boundless," which was rather ironic considering they were bound to each other.

Based on the little knowledge she had from one of her electives in college, the stanza pattern was typical of Emily Dickinson. That made sense since the nineteenth century American poet was credited with saving Eden back in the day. Was this Lyka's favorite poem? Did he feel this way toward the woman called Xavia?

A sudden need to know the import of the poem had her scrambling from bed. Though she wore no more than her oversized t-shirt, she threw open the door to her room, anxious now to talk to Awan, Takoda or both. She let her gaze sweep the large open living space.

No one.

She listened for the men's voices, maybe in the courtyard, but even as she turned her head toward the backyard windows, she sensed they were gone. Still hopeful, she strode to the back door, opened it and scanned the yard. Disappointment and a bit of frustration filled her. What was the sense of living together if they couldn't talk to each other? *You're the one who laid in bed so long.*

"Hell." That her disappointment was largely her fault didn't make it easier to accept. In fact, it made it worse and now she just wanted to redo the whole morning. Deflated, she shuffled to the kitchen area and poured a cup of kafez the men had made and left for her. Moving to the refrigerator, which Edenists called a cold box, she opened the door to find a note on a plate of baka buns.

She unfolded it.

For you and Cali when she arrives.

Now she felt completely selfish. She'd been so in her head about living with her filoz, not only had she forgotten Cali would visit, but she'd blamed the very men she didn't want to see for not being there. She needed to have her head examined. Meanwhile, they remembered and had been so thoughtful as to leave her a snack to have with her friend.

She headed back to her room, cup in hand. She'd never been one to shy away from learning new things, whether it was statistics in school or how to take out a wall during renovations. She'd always done it. Yes, she made mistakes along the way, but she'd finally figured it out. That's exactly how she would approach living with Awan and Takoda while on Eden. Their home was more open than hers, so it would be good practice before they all returned to Earth in order for her to resume her career.

Taking a few sips of the hot kafez, she quickly stripped and stepped into the shower, or rainbox as they called it. They never did stop and get her soap yesterday. She and Cali could do that. There had to be a place nearby. Maybe she could pick up something for the men to show them that she really did appreciate them and how understanding they were while she tried to adjust. The problem was what would she get? She still didn't know them very well. Too bad there were no greeting card shops in Tolba.

After drying off, she pulled on a pair of gray leggings and a royal blue tunic. Then arranging her hair into a messy bun, she picked up her cup and strode out into the main room. Purposefully, she passed by the open door to Takoda's room and stopped in front of Awan's.

This was where her "married" life was supposed to take place. Better to know what she was walking into then going in blind, even if it was just the space. Taking another swallow of her drink, she walked under the archway and into the large domed room.

Her first impression was colorful. Lyka had obviously had free reign in this room. Abstract paintings filled the curved walls with pinks, oranges, blues, greens, yellows and purples. She moved to the closest one and studied it. While it was abstract, there was a definite vibe to it. She took a couple steps back. "Oh."

From farther away the "vibe" was quite clear. It depicted three figures entwined together, the forms almost melding into one. Though there was no sexual detail, Lyka had captured the ultimate pleasure of a woman being taken by two men at the same time. Flushing with a sudden interest in what that might feel like, she stepped back, bumping into the bed.

Turning around she stared. It took up half the room easily. That made sense since it had been meant for four people. That it would only hold three, when she was ready to do the yenea thing, meant there would be plenty of room. Setting her cup on a small table against the wall, she sat on the bed.

It wouldn't be as scary if she were familiar with everything, so she lifted her feet up and lay back. It was even more comfortable than the one she'd slept in. She stared at the blank ceiling, a little surprised that Lyka had left that space empty between the many windows. Listening to be sure no one came home unexpectedly, she rolled over into the center of the bed.

Despite, or maybe because, of the paintings surrounding the room, there was a sense of symmetry. What was on the right was on the left, be it color scheme, window, or furniture. Even opposite the door to the room was an open archway that clearly revealed the bathroom. It wasn't lost on her that from the bed, the shower was not only visible, but there were no glass sides around it like the one she shared with Takoda.

Curious, she rose to investigate. No sooner had she taken a step in that direction then the crystals outside the front door rang. Grabbing up her cup of kafez, she hurried out of the room.

CHAPTER TEN

Ro moved to a front window out of habit. In Boston, she always checked before opening the door, but on Eden it was an unnecessary precaution.

Chiding herself, she quickly strode to the door and opened it. "Cali."

"Ro!" Her friend threw herself at her, making her stumble back.

"Hey, what's all the exuberance for. I've only been gone one full day."

Cali let go and stepped back, right into Kuruk, her protector. He grasped her shoulders.

"Oh, sorry." She stepped away again.

The man nodded and let go as if the occurrence happened quite often. Poor Kuruk. Cali was always moving and fidgeting. No doubt he had bruises from her.

"Wow, look at this place."

As Cali walked by her, she motioned for Kuruk to come inside. After he closed the door behind him, she turned to find Cali examining one of Lyka's paintings. She quickly walked to where she stood. "That's a depiction of the birth of the universe according to the Tolbans."

Cali's eyes widened. "It looks like a turtle."

Ro chuckled. "That's exactly what it is. You do remember that the turtle or tolba is an important symbol for this city, right?"

"Yes, but I didn't realize they thought the universe was born from a turtle and her eggs were planets." Cali's rolled her eyes.

"And they probably think our story of the Garden of Eden is quite odd as well." But if that were the case, was it coincidence that the planet was called Eden or had it been the original Eden? Was that why they didn't wear clothing? Such a weighty thought would require far more time and research to develop.

Instead, she hooked her arm in Cali's and brought her to the kitchen. "Come on, my filoz got us baka buns. I'll pour us some ambrosia and we can go out back and chat."

Cali hopped up on a stool. "Sounds good to me. You'll never believe what happened yesterday."

Ro took out the baka buns and ambrosia. Putting the buns in the inducer, which worked a lot like a microwave only it was powered by eyllen, she searched for a tray. "I'm gone for one day and something exciting happened at the Pleasure Dome?"

"Oh, not at the Pleasure Dome. It's the same old, same old there. No, Kenjada came by to tell me they have brought their woman to Tolba!"

The last was said with such excitement that Ro turned, giving up on her mission to find a tray. "They found a woman who wants all five of them?" After yesterday, just the thought of having five men in bed had her suddenly feeling tired. But along with that was relief. She been hiding from Cali her fear that Kenjada's filoz would want Cali. Cali might have the energy, but she was so small and after what she'd gone through, she deserved two men who doted on her, and only two.

Cali nodded her head. "Yup. Can you believe that? That's a lot more libido than I have." She winked. "But just imagine Christmas time. "Her friend's eye sparkled with excitement as if she anticipated a big Christmas celebration.

"You do know they don't have Christmas in Tolba, right?"

Cali waved her hand. "Oh, I know. They have that other holiday, but I'm sure as an Earth woman, if she wanted to celebrate it, they would."

She had a point there. Edenists would do anything for their beloved.

"Kenjada said he wants me to meet her. He said I'm their little sister and part of their family. Isn't that sweet?"

"Very." She resumed getting their food ready, pouring the drinks and taking the warm baka buns out. "I think that filoz is the only one in the history of Tolba to have a 'little sister.'"

"No, there have been a few others, but I'm definitely unique."

That was an understatement but in a very good way. Cali wouldn't even be alive today if Kenjada's filoz hadn't been in the right place at the right time to save her from her emotionally abusive and controlling boyfriend.

Ro set the three plates and glasses on the island counter. "We'll each have to carry our own. I can't find a tray."

"I may be small, but I think I can handle that." Though Cali jumped off the stool to pick up her glass and plate, Kuruk beat her to it, carrying it for her.

Cali shrugged.

"Wait until you see what we're doing out here." Ro led the way to the back and opened the door. She would have liked to have shown Cali her drawings, but she had no idea what Takoda had done with them after they all talked about them.

"Oh, gosh. That's a seriously big hole." Cali walked directly to the edge of the pool hole while Ro and Kuruk put the food down on the table.

She joined Cali. "It's going to be an oasis pool complete with beach entrance down there, a grotto waterfall over there, and bridge there."

"Wow, you've been busy for only one day. How did you get this hole so quickly?"

Preferring not to reveal Awan's actions since he seemed so sensitive about it, she shrugged. "Awan and Takoda want me to be happy."

This time Cali hooked her arm and pulled her to the table. "You have to tell me everything. Have you been able to figure out if you are really bonded? Did you all sleep in the same bed? Do they really cook for you?"

She took a big bite of baka bun to stall for time. At least Cali had given her a few questions instead of just one, which meant she could choose what to answer. "I can tell you with confidence that we are definitely bonded. With Awan, whatever he's craving I crave. With Takoda, I can sense when he's nearby which is very handy because he can levitate and is often hovering above where I wouldn't notice him."

Cali looked up as if expecting Takoda to be there.

"He's also a great cook. He made us a wonderful dinner last night. I'm going to have to start working out to avoid putting on pounds."

Cali sighed. "Wow, a man who will cook for you."

Though her friend missed it, she caught Kuruk's look of disbelief. He rarely ever spoke as protectors were meant to be seen and not heard for the most part, doing their job by their mere presence. Most were very careful not to interfere and keep a distance, but with Cali that was impossible.

"Awan cooks too. Last night he promised me namas. That's a shellfish that looks like a cross between a lobster and an octopus. Takoda swears it has a sweet white meat. I think anything with the slightest bit of sweetness is adored here."

Cali chewed on a bite of her snack as she nodded. When she finished, she leaned in. "Are you happy?"

Now that was a heavy question. "From what I know about them so far, yes. They are good men, even if I hadn't planned on bonding with them. But now that I have, I want it to work. Bonding is for life."

"For life?" Cali glanced at Kuruk for confirmation. He silently nodded.

"Yes. I want to make this work. This is my only chance to have what my mom had wished for herself and for me."

"Or maybe double what she wished." Cali winked.

Ro grinned. "True. I only have a couple weeks left before I have to go back to work. I want to learn all I can about Awan and Takoda and then show them all about my life on Earth. My home is a bit smaller than this, but I'm sure we can make it work."

Kuruk grunted and they both stared at him. He simply stared back.

Obviously, the man had an opinion, but was far too well-trained to voice it.

Cali turned to her. "How is it living with them? You said you've never lived with anyone before."

She finished chewing the bite she'd taken. "I don't really know yet. The house is a bit…" She wasn't sure how to word it politely.

"Cluttered?" Cali offered.

"Not really. Just lived-in and full." Yes, full said it perfectly. "Dinner yesterday was the first time all three of us spent any time together in it."

Cali nodded. "That makes sense. They both work, which is why I imagine they aren't here. I bet you'll have plenty of alone time. And then when you go back to work, the shoe will be on the other foot."

Again, Kuruk grunted.

This time Cali waved off Kuruk's vocalization. "Don't mind him. He's always doing that."

Ro glanced at Kuruk to see his lips twitching. Far from being insulted, he seemed to find Cali's remark humorous. No doubt, Cali talked to him all the time because that was what she was very good at.

"Sist came by this morning looking for you."

At the change in topic, Ro brought her attention back to her friend. "Sist?" Why would he visit Cali?

"Yes, he asked me if you were returning soon."

"That's odd. I ran into Micco at the Discoverist Complex yesterday, and he knows I'm with Awan and Takoda."

Cali contemplated that. "Now that you mention it, Sist did seem to be acting a bit off."

"How do you mean?"

"He kept looking around like he was afraid someone would

see him coming to visit you. Do you think Micco didn't tell him and he came to check on you?"

Ro caught Kuruk shaking his head. She agreed. Brothers of the heart did not keep things from each other. "Micco acted the same way when I ran into him. I thought it might be because I had no escort and he hadn't invited me."

Cali frowned. "I think it's silly that you have to be invited to the Discoverist Complex. That should be open to everyone. What they discover there affects the whole community."

At her obvious agitation, Kuruk laid his hand on her arm. "You do not have to be invited. You are free to visit anytime. Just tell me when you want to go."

Conflicting emotions raced through Ro. First, surprise that Kuruk had spoken that many words in a row while in Cali's presence and second that Micco had lied to her. "Are you sure?"

He nodded.

Cali didn't let it rest. "Are you saying that anyone, even women, can go to the Discoverist Complex any day or time they wish?"

Kuruk nodded again.

That didn't make sense. "Then why would Micco tell me I had to be invited?"

"He lied to you." Cali's words came out in a whisper.

She was as shocked as her friend. For all intents and purposes, Micco was out of her life, but the way he acted yesterday, combined with his furtive actions and now lying, didn't sit well with her.

"Obviously, he never meant to be your filoz." Cali's face went from stern to sunny in a split second. "I think you bringing Awan and Takoda to your dome was the best thing you've done since you arrived." She opened her arms wide. "Look at all you have now."

Ro glanced behind her at the huge hole and couldn't help chuckling. "You mean my mounds of dirt?"

Cali laughed. "But of course."

It felt good to joke and relax. After another hour of talking about everything from Edenist ways to the statue Cali had seen on her way to visit, they finally headed back inside.

Cali placed her plate in the sink. "Please thank your beloveds for providing the baka buns for us. I just love those. That was very thoughtful."

That reminded her. "I want to do something thoughtful for them, too. Any ideas? I've never lived with another man, never mind two men. What do you think I should do?"

"My jerk never appreciated anything I did, so I'm not sure. I guess you could cook them dinner." Cali grimaced.

Ro laughed. "Very funny. I want to be thoughtful, not kill them with my non-existent cooking skills."

Her friend leaned on the island. "I'm stumped." Cali looked over the counter to where Kuruk was, arms folded as he stood sentinel. "What would you want a woman to do for you?"

He didn't even blink as if he was used to odd questions coming from Cali. "I would like very much if she showed an interest in whatever it was that I enjoyed doing."

"Oh, good idea." Cali grinned. "So, in your case it would be your music?"

He nodded.

Cali turned back to her. "There you go. What are they most interested in?" She winked. "Besides you, I mean."

Well, hell. She had no idea. She didn't know her own husbands as well as Cali knew her protector. That was just sad. She leaned back against the counter. "I have no clue. I really suck at this."

"Hey, you do not. You haven't even known them a week yet, right? How much do they know about you? You're on even ground here. Just ask them."

"True. I could but is seems like the 'thoughtful' part of the gesture goes right out the window if I do that."

Cali nodded. "There is that."

With Cali's agreement, defeat filled her. How the hell was she going to make this work?

"You can ask one about the other." Kuruk's advice was a surprise not only because it made sense, but because he offered it without being asked. Maybe he was getting more comfortable around them.

Since he'd joined the conversation, she addressed her questions to him. "Would they know the answer? And more importantly, would they answer or simply tell me to ask the other myself?"

His lip quirked up. "Brothers of the heart know everything about each other and are willing to share. The only time we withhold information is when we are sure that our friend would prefer to be the one to explain."

There was personal experience behind that answer, but she doubted he'd explain further. "Then that's what I'll do. I'll ask Awan what Takoda's favorite thing to do is and Takoda what Awan's favorite thing is." She grimaced. "I just hope Awan isn't into meditation. I'm hopeless when it comes to turning my mind off."

Cali laughed. "I haven't even tried that. It would be a total waste of time."

She silently agreed, but didn't want to hurt her friend, so she simply smiled. "You made it a whole day without me. Think you can do so again tomorrow?"

"I'm not that pathetic. Knowing where you live makes me feel a little better. Though I think Kuruk may be a little overwhelmed with how much I'm talking to him."

The man in question shook his head. He was incredibly patient with Cali and Ro appreciated him for that. "You know, there are other women in the Pleasure Dome compound."

Cali shrugged. "I know." A sparkle came into her eyes. "But I'm not that desperate yet." She laughed loudly.

Ro smiled. "Now that I think of it. If I was able to put up with you coming over every day and talking to me non-stop, two Edenists should be a breeze to live with."

"Oh, I love you too, Ro."

She laughed with Cali, even noticing Kuruk's lip twitching. This was exactly what she needed, to just chill and relax about her situation. "I appreciate you coming today. I needed this."

"I was happy to." She paused, giving a quick look to Kuruk "But I won't be able to come the day after next. I got this guy to agree to escort me to the Dickinson Complex. I've never been there, and they are having what could only be called a movie showing."

"A movie? How?" Edenists had some advanced technology from the Crius, the alien race that had picked them up from Earth and dropped them off on Eden, but their own technological advances were far and few between because they simply used their abilities to create what they needed.

Cali's eyes lit with excitement. "There's a Kindred of Light Edenist at the complex who can project images on a wall. He's teamed up with a Kindred of Mind to create what they are calling a Moving Story, right?" Cali looked to Kuruk for confirmation.

He nodded.

"It sounds fascinating, so I want to see it."

It did. Ro had always thought of the Dickinson Complex as the artists' residence, which it was. She just hadn't realized how broadly that term was used. But she should have. She might have to check it out herself with her two men. "I think you should. Enjoy. I'll be busy finding out more about Awan and Takoda anyway."

"You mean your beloved?" Cali smiled slyly.

She couldn't quite think of them like that yet. Hopefully, someday though. "I mean Awan and Takoda."

Cali shook her head as she stepped back from the island counter. "The more you say it, the more real it will be."

"No, the more real it becomes, the more I'll say it."

Her friend sighed. "You have it all now, Ro. Honestly, I'm a little jealous." Her shoulders slumped as she turned to Kuruk. "I'm ready to go back now."

He immediately stepped aside to allow her to walk past him.

Rowena strode by him as well to catch Cali's arm. "Hey, are you saying you're ready to try a relationship?"

"No. Not yet. I'm just jealous because I don't feel I can yet."

She hugged Cali. "Maybe not yet, but you will because you won't let that bastard ruin your entire life. He's already taken too much of your time." She made eye contact with Kuruk who scowled as he nodded. Stepping back, she held Cali's hands. "You have come so far. I'll bet you'll be ready sooner than you think."

Cali's hesitant smile pulled on her heart.

"Trust me. You will. How can you not with all these amazing

men ready to do all you wish?" She held her arm out toward Kuruk. "Even Kuruk willingly listens to all you have to say. So you know there are men here for you."

Cali brightened at that. "You're right. I'll keep an open mind and heart if you will. Deal?"

She grinned. "Deal."

Kuruk opened the door and Cali started through but turned just as he stepped to it. Quickly, he stepped back, catching her shoulders to keep her from running into him.

"Oops, sorry." She leaned her head around the big man. "I'll be back in a few days. Have fun." She winked then strode back out the door, Kuruk following close behind.

Ro closed the door. The silence in the home was comforting. Now to continue her exploration of her home away from home. The more she could learn about the two men in her life, the better prepared she would be for their future interactions. Being prepared always helped mitigate the risks, and when it came to her heart, she wanted all risks eliminated.

Of course, that was why she'd stayed on Eden. How could she have her heart broken on a planet with men who practically worshipped their women?

〜◉〜

Awan finished putting away the clean utensils and hung the small towel on the drying rack. Leaning back against the counter, he stared at the closed door to Rowena's room, willing it to open.

Though they had spent five nights together in their residence, she managed to slip away into her room before he and Takoda headed for sleep. And every morning, she did not rise until after they both went about their labors. Takoda was far less patient than he was, but even he was growing concerned at the constant separation.

He tried to imagine what it would be like living one's entire life alone, but he failed miserably. It was too foreign to him. They wanted her to enjoy living with them and left her alone so she could wake alone, but the nights were difficult. To be bonded to Rowena and not have her in their bed felt as if they weren't whole. Being bonded meant being one. He'd already experienced twinges of imbalance from the situation.

Today, he had Muskwa training, which meant he had time to spend with his beloved and he wasn't leaving until he did. Crossing his arms, he determined to stay right where he was until she appeared.

The sound of water running made him grin. She *was* awake. Reassured she simply washed herself in the rainbox before emerging, he heated more kafez. It would be ready when she appeared.

It was a longer wait than he expected, but eventually her door opened.

She stepped out in a short top that revealed her ribs and a pair of what she called jean shorts with her hair pulled back neatly, clearly expecting the residence to be empty. "Oh, I didn't realize you were still home." She smiled uncertainly as she approached.

"I am." Turning, he poured her a cup of kafez and set it on the counter in front of her as she sat. "I wished to start my day with you."

"Me?" She lifted the cup to her lips and took a small sip. Her eyes closed for a moment before she opened them again and set the cup down. "Thank you. That first sip of caffeine is like heaven. It's what I need to face the day."

"Face the day? Do you mean sometimes you don't wish to? Is that why you sleep so long?"

She grimaced. "No, no. It's a bit of an expression to complain about getting up and going to work, but I actually love my job. I miss it." She shrugged. "But I'll be back before I know it and will wish I was here."

His heart froze, stealing his breath. "What do you mean go back?"

As if she hadn't just thrown him completely out of balance, she took another sip of kafez before answering. "I only have about two more weeks of my sabbatical and then if I want to keep my job, I have to return to Earth."

Is that why she kept herself distant from them? Because she planned to leave them and break the bond? He couldn't believe she could be so callous, but his tongue refused to ask the question he must.

She must have realized his quandary. "You're probably wondering how we will all fit in my brownstone. I do agree it is a little smaller than this palatial home, but I'll be working Monday through Friday, except when I have to fly to a location, so most of the time it will just be you and Takoda. If you really feel uncomfortable, I can look into finding a larger home, but in the city that's expensive. If you brought some of the savinstone with you, then we'd be fine. Gold prices are up right now."

It was as if she were speaking a foreign language. He struggled to comprehend. "You want us to come to Earth with you?"

She gave him a hesitant smile. "I was hoping you would. I mean, we're bonded. I didn't want to only visit here on the weekends. Aren't we supposed to live together?"

Relief flooded him. She did want them, she just had unrealistic expectations about how they would live. He could address that much easier than if she'd planned to break the bond. "Yes, we do need to live together."

She nodded. "That's what I thought. It's like marriage on Earth, though a bit different with all these special laws. I've heard of Crius Laws and Dickinson Laws, and—oh, that reminds me, I had a question about the poem painted on the ceiling in Lyka's room. That is if you don't mind talking about it."

He tried to remember which poem had been left up there. "I might need to read it to discuss it."

She waved her hand. "No, I think I can figure out what it's getting at. I was just wondering if it means a lot to you and Takoda. But I'm thinking maybe it meant something to Lyka?"

Her voice had softened as if she was afraid to hurt him. He never wanted her to hesitate to talk to him about anything. "No, it didn't. Every Bendis moon he painted a new poem from one of our Poetess' many. I think he was going in the order of the ancient text we have at the Dickinson Complex. He thought it important to keep her words of wisdom in plain sight."

"So there's no special meaning to it for you?"

"No. Does it mean something to you? If it does, we can have it painted on my sleeping room ceiling."

"No, not at all. I haven't even read the whole poem. I was just curious if it would give me insight into my new yenea."

Since the poem wasn't important, then he needed to find out what was so she could sleep with them. "The poem won't but sleeping with us will."

Immediately, she buried her nose in her cup.

Ah, so she was very aware of what she had been doing. "I know that you are used to living alone, something neither Takoda nor I can fathom. We do understand this arrangement is difficult for you and you are adjusting."

She finally looked at him in relief. "I'm so glad you understand. It's not you and Takoda at all."

Having her confirm what he had guessed at was reassuring, but it also brought questions to mind. "You said that you were on Eden because you hoped to bond." He pushed away a dark thought about Micco, convinced that would not have been a good match for her.

"I did, but that was only after I came here."

He tried to remember if she'd told them how she came to be on the planet the night they met, but nothing came to him. He had to ask. "How did you come to be on Eden?"

She chuckled. "It's a bit of a sad story, I'm afraid. I think I may need some breakfast first."

How could he have been so thoughtless? "Of course. I have henny eggs, havling pig, and pecone rolls. Is that acceptable?"

Her eyes widened and her smile grew. "I love all of that but I can't eat it all. Let's skip the pecone rolls."

Without another word, he set about making her food.

"I met Wym and Condor at a sci-fi themed party one night." She laughed. "Everyone was dressed in some kind of alien costume except them."

He kept his movements quiet so as to hear every word.

"They were actually dressed like Native Americans and were very convincing. You do know that Tolbans tend toward a slightly darker skin than mine, right?"

He grinned, but didn't turn around as he broke the henny eggs into the pan. "Yes, we are aware."

"They had a crowd of women around them when I arrived. I was dressed as a Betazoid from Star Trek, which means I didn't look all that different. No blue make-up, or wig, or even tail."

She chuckled again, obviously enjoying her story. "I noticed them right away, but with so many women around them, I just moved toward the bar to get a drink. Next thing I know they are flanking me and paying for my drink. To be honest, I was flattered."

He gripped the pan hard at the thought of his beloved with two other Edenists, but he managed to get the food onto a plate and set it before her.

"Oh, this smells delicious." She immediately picked up her fork and took a bite. Her eyes closed again. "Hmmm." After chewing she opened her eyes and swallowed. "This is amazing. You use some different seasoning than I've ever tasted."

His balance returned at her focus on him. "I do."

She waved her hand. "I've never tasted it before. Is this native to Tolba or is it imported from another city."

This time he grinned. "It is charwa. We grow it in Tolba."

"It adds a slightly smoky flavor that is excellent on these havling pig strips." She took another bite, totally enjoying her simple meal.

Pleasing her was easy. Just another example of why they were meant to be.

After a few more bites, she continued her story. "Wym and Condor remained by my side all night. It was as if they had been waiting to meet me and they refused to allow anyone else to take my attention away from them."

Wym and Condor. Those names sounded familiar for some reason, but he couldn't remember why.

"Anyway, at the end of the night, they asked if I'd like to see Eden." She shook her head. "I admit I had a few too many drinks, but I wasn't drunk by any means."

He couldn't help but think of the teekeela they'd drank together.

"I know what you're thinking, but no. I didn't have a drop of tequila. I just had more drinks than my usual conservative amount."

He smirked at how attuned she was to him already. "I believe you."

"Thank you." She took the last couple bites of her morning meal and pushed the plate away. "That was too good. I could eat that every day."

He opened his mouth to let her know he'd be happy to make it for her, but she held up her hand and shook her head. "Oh no. I don't need all those calories. Once a week at the most." She cocked her head. "Or maybe twice a week, but no more than that."

"I will be happy to make those arrangements." He grinned as he took the empty plate and began to wash it. "Please, continue."

"Sure. So, they invited me to Eden. Honestly, I never thought they meant another planet. I thought they were either inviting me to have sex or to a new nightclub I didn't know about. Boston has some great party places. Either way, I was intrigued, so I said yes. The next thing I know there is this invisible door between them and I'm seeing another building on the other side."

Rowena slid off her stool and stood. She held her arms out

the width of a portal. "You know how you Edenists stand just so far apart, so that was all I could see. I have to tell you, I sobered up pretty quick, but I was also excited. I've always believed there was alien life somewhere. How could there not be? But I never expected to meet any aliens myself. Never even thought about it."

He lowered his brow. "Did they not tell you about Eden before bringing you here?"

She shook her head. "No, but I didn't exactly ask either. Like I said, I made assumptions that were completely wrong."

It was obvious to him that Wym and Condor had watched Rowena for a number of years and decided to meet her. But unlike himself, Lyka, and Takoda with Xavia, they did not visit her often and explain Eden to her before bringing her to their planet. That was not the usual way to introduce a beloved to Eden. There was no steadfast procedure, but over the years, there were some practices that had been proven more effective than others.

"I stepped through the portal, very excited about what I would find." She turned away then and meandered toward Lyka's artist corner and the window that had a view of the dirt pathway in front.

Maybe it was time to change Lyka's space. Maybe they could make it something for Rowena.

"I spent the night on Eden without knowing much more than that it was another planet and that the law was every woman must have at least two men. The next morning, I woke up and Wym and Condor were gone."

"Gone? You mean to their labors, without telling you anything?" His protective instincts were rising at the thought of how confused she must have been.

Rowena turned away from the window. "No, they were gone. The home was not open like this." She swept her hand out to indicate their space. "It was divided into four large spaces. I woke alone and walked into the kitchen to see if they were in there, but they weren't. However, a strange man was helping himself to ambrosia from their refrigerator. I mean cold box."

He could feel his muscles tensing at the thought of Rowena alone with a strange Edenist.

"I asked him what he thought he was doing and told him Wym and Condor would not appreciate him helping himself." She scooched up her nose. "He said his name was Voren or Voram or something like that. He wanted to know my name. I wouldn't tell him. I just kept asking about Wym and Condor. Finally, he told me that he was there on behalf of the cheetans and that Wym and Condor were lawbreakers and being exiled."

A cold ball formed in his gut. "Were they both Kindred of Eden? Did they have the birthmark of two parallel lines with a curved line above and below?"

She nodded. "They did. I tried to argue with this Vor guy that they didn't do anything wrong, but he said they had, and he needed to know if I was bonded to them. I had no idea what bonding was and told him no. The next thing I know, I was escorted to the Pleasure Dome compound."

Awan forced himself to take a deep breath and let some of the anger go. He didn't want to scare her. "Did they give you a choice to stay then?"

Her face finally brightened. "Not at first. They had a woman come in and explain the basics of the planet. I was fascinated and kept asking questions. She did say I could return to Earth and they would have a Kindred of Mind erase my memories of Tolba. There was no way I wanted that. From what I'd seen, this place was intriguing and had so much potential for me."

She walked toward him, stopping right before him. "I still think it does. Of course, I had no idea what Kindreds were, but it didn't take me long to reason that on Eden I had a better chance of finding a man, or rather men, to share my life with than I did on Earth, so I elected to stay. Two protectors used their Crius chips to bring me back to Earth where I arranged for a six-month sabbatical from my job then I returned here."

Now he understood why she wanted them all to live on Earth. But that wouldn't be possible. "I'm glad you did."

She put her hand on his chest. "Me too."

Covering her hand with his, he couldn't stop himself from asking. "Then why do you not sleep with us at night?"

"To be honest, I'm afraid."

He raised his brows in surprise at her admission. "Afraid? What are you afraid of?"

"That's the thing, it's hard to explain." She gazed into his eyes. "I want to, but what if I do something that hurts your feelings, like get up in the middle of the night and return to my room?"

He smiled, shaking his head. "That would not hurt our feelings. We know you like to be alone a lot. Yes, we would prefer to wake up next to you in the morning and possibly enjoy you as a wonderful start to our day, but these are unusual circumstances and we all need to make allowances for each other."

She focused on their hands on his chest. "I would like to try, but I may get cold feet again."

He tilted her chin up with his other hand. "I will help you."

"I would appreciate that."

He gazed into the green depth of her eyes and felt strong stirrings in his own heart. Rowena had so many facets to her. He wanted to explore every one of them.

She stepped back, pulling her hand from his chest. "Shouldn't you be going to work now?"

He grinned, something he did a lot on Muskwa training days. "No, I do not need to labor today. Today I play."

She looked at him askance. "You mean it's your day off or do you play a game?"

He chuckled. "I train to compete. I am a Muskwa competitor. The Muskwa competition is only once a year, but we train weekly." He couldn't help standing straighter with his pronouncement. While any Edenist could play Muskwa with other Edenists, only those who were the best were allowed to compete before all of Tolba and he was in that elite group. He'd even been gaining on the current leader.

"You must tell me what Muskwa is. I've never heard of it." Rowena's eyes lit with excitement. "What kind of training do you do? Is it strength training or endurance training? How often do you play? Is anyone allowed to play? Can women play?"

He held up his hands and laughed, too pleased with her interest not to. "One question at a time."

Her gaze turned shrewd as she paused to think. "Would you let me come with you today so I can learn all about it?"

His chest filled with joy and he couldn't help himself. He pulled her to him and kissed her. When he broke away, her gaze lacked focus, increasing his happiness.

"Is that a yes?"

He laughed. "Yes. I would like very much if you would accompany me today. I will tell you everything about Muskwa."

"Excellent. Do I need to change?"

Confused, he shook his head. "I like you the way you are."

She shook her head. "I'm sorry. I meant should I change my clothes. like my shorts. Do I need to wear something different?"

His good humor returned. "If you like, you can leave your clothes here, but if you wish to wear clothes, it will not matter."

She stared wide-eyed. Finally, she responded. "Then I'll go like this." She gave him a sly smile. "I wouldn't want to be a distraction."

At her words, his mind filled with a vision of her enjoying her ecstasy and he caught his breath. "That is good reason. I just need to pack up food and drink and we can leave."

"Can I help with that? I'm not much of a cook, but I can pack with the best of them."

He shook his head. "I require a lot of sustenance during training. It's best I gather all the food."

"Okay, then I guess I'll go put on my sneakers. I'll be ready in a few." With that she walked back into her room.

He strode into the meal room and began emptying the cold box. He couldn't wait to show her Muskwa.

CHAPTER ELEVEN

RO LEANED AGAINST THE CLOSED door of her room, her heart beating so fast her blood was rushing faster than the T's red line at rush hour. She'd felt Awan's sudden passion for her like a wave crashing over her at the beach. It took her breath away. This bonding was more intense than she expected. Either that or it was specific to her and Awan's connection.

Her heart started to slow as her mind switched focus to Takoda. It bothered her that she had bonded to him, but he hadn't to her yet. Would it ever happen?

She pushed away from the door. She'd only known the men a week and spending more time with Takoda alone was on her to-do list. Quickly, she used the bathroom and put on a pair of sneakers. Walking on the packed dirt streets of Tolba was a lot rougher than wandering around the house bare foot or in a pair of flip flops.

Muskwa. It was an odd sounding competition. It made her think of mud wrestling for some reason. For all she knew it was much like table tennis or golf. She liked watching both because neither had many accidents. It was that risk manager inside her that she just couldn't seem to turn off. Sometimes it got in the way of her enjoyment, especially when viewing others.

"Are you ready?" Awan stood at the door as she entered the living area. That he was excited was obvious.

She quickened her step. "What's in that big bag besides food?"

"It is just food and drinks. I packed a separate bag for you, too."

"For me?" She walked through the front door, which he held open for her.

"Yes." He took her hand in his large one. "My training lasts half a day and I do not want you to grow hungry."

His thoughtfulness once again struck her. She'd dated a guy on Earth who ran in the Patriot's Day marathon. He'd asked her to come cheer him on, but never told her where would be the best place to stand or park or even where to meet him afterward.

Though Takoda definitely had the easiest way to go about the city, Awan's large physique made her own path rather easy as she followed behind him. The streets were seriously crowded in this hatchoc. It didn't ease up until they started to ascend a small gradual incline.

He stepped to the side to allow her to walk beside him. "This path will have less men."

She glanced behind them to double-check her observation they were ascending. "Are we going to one of the three hatchocs at the center of Tolba?"

"Yes. My training is in the Dickinson Complex, but my competitions are in the Cheetans' Complex."

Now that was interesting. "I thought the Dickinson Complex was for artistic endeavors and the Cheetans' was only for important governing matters."

Awan smiled and his posture straightened a bit more. "That is true. The Muskwa has been a tradition of our people since we were first brought to Eden. It was originally designed to determine the best warriors to lead the citizens in war. After the Fullamush, when it was decided to no longer wage war, the Muskwa evolved into a competition and also entertainment."

She tried to imagine baseball as an antique ritual but failed. "But you said the competition, which I would see as the entertainment, would be viewed in the Cheetans Complex."

He stopped and faced her. "I know on Earth you have competitions between different cities and countries and people go to watch and enjoy. It's different here. The training is the entertainment because it is considered both an artform and the creation of an artform."

She frowned, thoroughly confused.

Awan looked away for a moment then back at her. "The training is like the creation of a statue when you can watch it coming to life even if the artist makes mistakes and must patch them before finding perfection. The Muskwa competition itself is akin to a ritual, like your celebration at the end of your schooling."

"You mean graduation?" She'd been pretty excited when she'd graduated from grad school, but it had been a long, boring affair before that degree was in her hand. If that's what he meant, she could understand why it would be held in the Cheetans' Complex. "I think I get it."

He smiled. "Then let us continue."

Though the incline was gradual, it was higher than she realized when they had floated over the area the other day. Her step slowed. She was seriously out of shape. If she was staying longer on Eden, she would need to find a workout room or whatever they had in Tolba.

Awan, ever vigilant, noticed her pace and adjusted his own. Finally, they came to the top and walked beneath the archway proclaiming it the Dickinson Complex.

All mediums of art were displayed everywhere, on outside walls, the walking paths, and even in the artistically designed plants. Music came from one dome, while the scent of perfumes came from another. Most all the domes had openings as wide as an airplane hangar but arched, of course. Most likely they had a Kindred of Air Edenist come by at night and create an impenetrable wall of hard air like a window to protect the work inside from the elements.

After walking between two rows of large domes, they came to an open oval that was designed like a park with seating areas, plants, water features, and of course, artwork. "This is beautiful." She was surprised she got the words out because it literally took her breath away, causing her to stop.

"It is." Awan squeezed her hand. "If you wish, we can come back another day, but I do need to start my training so we can be back for the evening meal."

"Of course." She allowed him to lead her away, but she couldn't help thinking that Earth had a lot to learn from Tolba. While it was rudimentary in some ways, it was far advanced in others. She understood the strict rules keeping Eden from Earth, but it was a shame. She and her men would need to come up with a plan to keep their home world a secret when they all went to live on Earth.

Awan led her to a very large dome, which like the others had a wide opening. They stepped into the shade of the building and he turned to the right where there were stairs that led to an observation balcony that went all along the dome's curved structure at what would have been the third story. It was quite wide, allowing people to walk along and lean their arms on the chest-high half-wall that kept them safe. There were tables and stools with backs set by the balcony half-wall with more stools against the building's structure.

Awan had let go of her hand on the stairs and now it rested on the small of her back as they walked a few yards along the balcony. "You can choose wherever you'd like to stay."

Knowing he was anxious to get started training, she moved toward the first empty spot and looked over. Her breath caught. Below, as well as high up, close to where she stood, naked Edenists worked out on a variety of apparatus made to look like part of a forest, but it was clearly meant to test their strength and balance.

"If this is where you'd like to stay, I will bring over a seat for you."

She simply nodded in response to his question. It was like an Olympic training room on steroids, but with an outdoor appearance. If she didn't know better, she'd think she was halfway through a hike in the White Mountains of New Hampshire.

"Rowena, is something wrong?"

At the worry in Awan's voice, she tore her gaze from the spectacle below. "I'm fine. I have just never seen anything like this."

The tension in his neck muscles eased. "I will come back when I rest. Here." He hung a bag on the back of the stool he'd moved over. "If you need more to eat or drink, let me know when I come back."

Knowing how well he cared for her, she doubted she'd need

anything, except maybe a cold shower and that he couldn't give her...here. "I'm good. Go. I'm looking forward to watching you."

Again, he seemed to stand a bit straighter. "This is only a training, but I hope you enjoy it." With that, he kissed her briefly then turned and strode back to the stairs.

She stared unashamedly at his taut butt. Seriously. How did she get so lucky as to have two hunks? The answer was below. Living on Eden practically guaranteed that. Maybe there was something to Awan's belief that they were meant to be.

With that comforting thought in her head, she climbed up on the tall stool and took in the view of the training area. She didn't know what to focus on first. It was like going to a gymnastic meet with all the events happening at once, only in this case, not only were all the activities far more strenuous than that event, but the whole arena could have been something Disney would build for its Pocahontas experience, if it had one.

There was a conveyor belt that rose almost three stories up a mini mountain to a platform. It was at a forty-five-degree incline, the belt rolling from the top to the bottom. An Edenist had just reached the halfway mark as indicated on a tree when the belt and mountain moved and grew steeper. She swore she could see the man's quadriceps clearly outlined beneath his skin as he continued to move higher, despite the belt trying to move him down. As the belt changed position again, she could see him struggling and quickly focused on another spot, her risk alarms going off.

The spot her gaze landed on was a river running from one end of the dome to the other, right under the walls. The current was strong as an Edenist swam against it, his goal obviously the other end where boulders formed a convenient stair for exiting.

A shadow across the light coming in from one of the large windows in the ceiling had her looking up. She swallowed hard at the sight of a man on three parallel vines. He'd lost his footing and the vines swung with his shift in weight. Even as she watched, he regrouped and continued toward the high dome pinnacle where a platform hung suspended from the ceiling. Her instinct was to inspect the supports, but she couldn't see any.

The whole arena was like a themed amusement park, a jungle experience with a Native American vibe, but instead of rides it was filled with warrior Olympic events for superheroes. She gripped the wall as she caught sight of Awan approaching the man standing at the bottom of the mountain. Suddenly, the whole scene was far less fascinating and much more concerning. She scanned the entire floor of the building but didn't see a single safety net or any emergency equipment anywhere.

When she finished her inspection, she wanted to shut the whole operation down. Awan looked up at her at that moment and grinned. She forced herself to wave, glad he couldn't read her thoughts with his Kindred of Mind abilities like some of them could. This was her worst nightmare.

She had to remember he loved this. He knew what he was doing. She had to trust him. Not an easy task considering how few people she'd had to trust in her life. Luckily, they had all been worthy of her trust. She would bet Awan would be too, but as he approached the massive conveyor belt that rolled toward him, she tensed.

Suddenly, the belt changed. Rocks popped up sporadically along it like a rock-climbing wall. That mitigated her unease until water started to run from the top, all the way down the moving monstrosity. It was a damn waterfall!

Awan studied the torrent rolling toward him, the flow dropping into a split in the floor she hadn't noticed before. He walked toward it then jumped across the opening and ran up the first few yards as if he did it in his sleep. Unable to tear her gaze away from his graceful movements as he climbed the cascading waterfall without once using his hands, she stared in awe.

At the halfway mark, it moved creating not only a steeper incline but faster running water determined to knock her man off. He didn't miss a beat. He continued up the steeper slope at the same pace until the waterfall moved again. The sound of the rushing water could clearly be heard over any of the other events. Or maybe it was just her imagination.

Awan continued upward though at a slightly slower pace, getting closer and closer to the platform. When he was within three yards of the top, his foot missed a rock and his balance waivered as he quickly adjusted his weight and found purchase on another, but he had drifted another five yards downstream, so to speak.

She couldn't let go of the wall as she gripped it tightly, never letting her gaze drift away from him as he regained his ground. His thighs tensed with every step into the rushing water of the slope. Finally, he reached the top and jumped onto the platform. Then he faced her and smiled.

She could barely get air into her lungs, but she forced one hand to let go of the wall and wave. This was his favorite pastime?

Awan waved back before grabbing a rope hanging next to the platform and swinging across to the wall of the balcony she sat on. Jumping from the ledge, he sent the rope back the way he'd come.

She stared at him, his muscles pumped after his exertions,

water glistening on his skin, and a whole other feeling permeated her body.

"Did you like the waterfall climb?" Awan took the two steps to reach her.

She pulled air into her lungs, but her words came out as a whisper. "What if you'd fallen?"

His smile disappeared. "You were worried?"

She nodded. Hell yeah, she was worried! "Of course! There are no safety nets or fall cushions and you could have broken your neck." Her voice was bordering on hysteria. Part of her knew he wanted praise, but her heart raced with fear for him.

His wet, cool hands came down on her shoulders. "You must care for me then?"

"Of course I do. You're my beloved."

One hand left her shoulder to stroke her cheek.

She wasn't in the mood and pulled her head away from his touch. "You scared me."

He dropped his hands. "I am sorry. I did not think, did not know you cared for me. If I had known, I would have explained."

She put her hands on her hips. "Now you know. So explain." She had no idea where her unreasonable anger was coming from, but she couldn't stop it any more than she could stop her racing heart.

"Come, look." He moved to the balcony wall.

Reluctantly, she joined him.

"See that man next to the water-run? The one with the green armband?"

She examined the area. "I see three men with those armbands. Which one do you mean?"

"They are all life-protectors. Each one has a Kindred ability that will save a trainee should he fail at any specific challenge."

She scanned the men on the floor. There had to be at least five life-protectors for every individual person training. Her muscles relaxed. Turning, she looked at him. "That makes me feel a lot better. Thank you." She gave him a wide smile. "You did really well. I'm guessing there are different levels?"

He nodded, though he didn't smile back. "Yes. There are three with every challenge. All are to prepare us for whatever the course will be when we compete."

"You mean these are not the actual events?"

He shook his head. "Only those who create the competition know what they will be. They also design the training room."

It bothered her that he did not seem as excited as before. She really had started to care for him. "It's beautiful. I can see why it is in the Dickinson Complex now. I'm glad that you're safe. That means I can enjoy your prowess on the floor instead of worrying myself sick."

His facial expression didn't change, so she laid her hand on his wet chest. "Still, be careful."

His hand came over hers for a moment, grasping it, then he backed away. "I must go now."

"Do well."

He didn't answer. Instead, he turned and trotted down the stairs and out of sight.

Did she just screw things up because of her stupid training? The thought that her job could be an obstacle to her happiness bothered her. She should be able to have both. That's what men had. *On Earth.*

Ignoring her conscience, she settled back onto her stool. She didn't have long to wait before Awan approached the river. Again, he glanced up at her and she waved. *Come on, Awan. Snap out of whatever funk I put you in.*

He nodded in acknowledgement then moved to a bridge that spanned the river. It had no railings, which had her instincts jumping up and down, but she squashed them. "He's safe. Just enjoy his work."

Awan didn't jump in, which warned her he was waiting for something. A few minutes went by and the river changed. Not only did it speed up, but logs sporadically appeared to be swept downstream.

He wouldn't.

He did.

Awan dove into the river, coming up a few yards upstream before taking long measured strokes. As he met the first log, which was about as long as half the width of the man-made river, he batted it aside with one hand and continued his stroke. She found herself mesmerized by the smoothness by which he navigated the river and its dangers.

A weird sense of pride in him bubbled up inside her. It made no sense. It wasn't as if she had anything to do with his abilities, yet she couldn't wait to see Cali and tell her about this.

Was this pride part of the bond or something more? The men she'd dated on Earth hadn't sparked such a feeling in her. Then again, the men on Earth couldn't possibly do what Awan was doing. He was halfway to the other end when movement at the end caught her attention. What the hell?

A log, the complete width of the river, barreled down toward

Awan. She gripped the wall again. Something must be wrong. Did he see it? When another log the same length appeared at the end, it clicked. He was past the halfway point, so of course they had to make it harder. Concerned, but with a new faith in her beloved, she forced herself to let go of the wall. She needed to be rooting for him, not worrying about him.

The full-length log drew closer as Awan pushed through the strong current. Just as the log was within arms-reach, he went under.

She leaned forward, forcing herself to breathe. *Come on. Where are you?* Scanning the men with green bands, she saw no movement. *Okay, this must be normal.*

It didn't feel normal.

She kept her gaze riveted to the surface of the water. Movement upstream caught the corner of her eye and she whipped her gaze past two full logs. There she found Awan just in time to see him take a stroke and dive back under as a large log approached. She sat back and took a few deep breaths. She understood his technique now. He was not only strong, but smart.

When he finally reached the boulders at the end, he climbed out just in time to avoid another log. She jumped off the stool. "Whoo-hoo!" She clapped her hands and looked around, surprised the whole balcony wasn't cheering.

A few indulgent smiles were thrown her way, but otherwise the people returned their attention to the super athletes below. That was the only phrase she could think of for what Awan did. She jumped back on the stool and leaned over just in time to catch Awan looking up.

She gave him the thumbs up. When he didn't wave or even

return her smile, she calmed down. Maybe she wasn't acting appropriately. No one else seemed to be as excited with the feats of the athletes they watched.

Awan conferred with another athlete then moved to another training area. This one required balance and he handled it with ease. This time when he looked up, she waved, and he nodded back. Maybe waving was a more acceptable response. She watched him tackle three more stations before he disappeared from view.

Hoping it was his break, she finally checked the bag he'd left with her. She grinned. Fresh bread and ambrosia in a canister lay on top of a variety of cheeses, or what Edenists called tyree. She spread out the feast on the table, glancing toward the stairs.

She hated guessing what was wrong. Communication was key to a good relationship, or so she'd been told, so they needed to be open and honest. They did come from two different worlds and there was a lot they didn't know about each other.

"Is it enough?"

Whipping her head up, she found him standing next to the table. How did such a big man move so quietly? Ignoring his question, she smiled. "You were amazing down there. I have so many questions for you."

"You do?" He grinned, and the knot she didn't know was sitting between her shoulder blades released.

"I do. Like how long have you been doing this? What's your favorite type of challenge? Do you do training before coming to training? Are you the best there is?"

He laughed. "You do have a lot of questions." He opened his bag and set out enough food for four people.

She didn't begrudge him the food. He obviously needed it

after the workout he had. "But my first question is were you upset with me for being worried?"

He paused in the middle of setting down his drink. "Upset? No, I was not. I was…confused. I understand that you did not know about the life-protectors, but you didn't think I could be successful?"

She shook her head vigorously. "Oh, no. That wasn't it at all, though I imagine that was how it appeared." She wasn't sure where to start to explain. "I think you need to know where I'm coming from to understand."

"Please explain." He took a bite of what looked like a whole cooked henny.

"Back on Earth, my job, or labor is to keep accidents from happening. I basically have to think about every possible way someone could get hurt, whether it is my fellow workers or the people we serve. I've been trained to imagine what could go wrong."

He took a sip of what was in his drink canister and swallowed. "You ran scenarios similar to mine?"

"Similar but different. I have no special ability, so I have to think, given all that I know, how someone could get hurt. Sometimes there are only three possible ways. Sometimes there are twenty."

"Twenty?" His eyebrows lifted before he took another bite of food.

"Yes. And when I think about what could happen, it is never what will go right, only what will go wrong."

He put down his food. "Your labor is sad. Does it help people?"

His statement was so simple yet it encompassed her job in a nutshell. She'd never thought about it, but he was right. Her job was not exactly uplifting. "I receive my satisfaction knowing I prevented injuries or even death."

He nodded and went back to eating.

"Because I have been trained to think this way, when I watched you climb that mountain with all those obstacles, I was afraid you would be hurt. You have to understand, no man on Earth could have done what you did."

"And you thought I would be harmed and that worried you?"

"Worried?" She opened her eyes wide. "I was downright scared." She slapped her hand down on the table.

His gaze softened. "You care a lot about me then."

She nodded. "I do. I don't know much about you, but what I do know, I really like."

His hand covered hers. "I feel the same toward you as well."

It wasn't like he'd just proclaimed his love for her, but between his look and his words, her heart did a little jump. It was silly, really, but there it was.

He removed his hand and went back to eating. She started her own meal as well. Now that she'd relaxed, she found she was hungry.

Awan ate one container of food after another. It reminded her of a powerlifter she once dated only he added all kinds of protein shakes and vitamins as part of his routine. He was always talking about calorie intake and other health information. In fact, he'd been obsessive about it. She'd soon realized he didn't actually have room in his life for her and she stopped seeing him.

It wasn't like that with Awan at all.

"Do you care for Takoda as well?"

The question, coming out of the blue as it did, caught her off guard. "I think so. We've been working together on your cold pond and I've learned a bit more about him. He just seems more closed than you."

"Yes." The word came out as if he was distracted by something, but he looked right at her.

When he didn't elaborate, she had to ask. "Has he always been this way?"

"If you like both of us, why will you not sleep with us at night?"

Whoa, busted and put on the spot. Of course, he'd said they'd noticed, but she hadn't expected to get called on the carpet and it got her back up. "Is it required?" Even as the words came out, she kicked herself mentally.

His brows lowered. "No. It is wanted by all when bonded. Do you want to?"

That was a good question. "I do and I don't."

"I don't understand."

"Honestly, I don't either. I do want to be with both of you as a yenea, but I'm nervous. It's not just sharing a living space but sharing a bed. I'm still getting used to living in the same home with both of you."

He stroked his chin as he thought.

She found the old-fashioned habit endearing. "I know it's confusing. I'm sure I just need a little time. This all happened very quickly. It's not like you introduced yourselves to me on Earth like Wym and Condor did. We met and we bonded, so we need to get to know each other more." Though she only had another week or so and she had to get back to work, and then she wouldn't have as much time.

Not excited by that prospect, she switched the topic. "Do you think that Wym and Condor were simply exiled because they were Kindred of Eden?" They'd seemed so nice. She had a hard time seeing them as lawbreakers.

Awan finished chewing, obviously thinking seriously about her question. "I'm not sure. Not all lawbreakers are Kindred of Eden."

"But of the ones you know who have been exiled, did they do something wrong?"

Awan frowned. "Not all lawbreakers are exiled because of their actions. Some are exiled because they could be a danger to Tolba."

Wait, they were exiled before they committed a crime? "That's crazy. How would anyone know what someone else might do?"

"The cheetans are wise." Awan sighed heavily.

Crap, she'd forgotten Lyka was Kindred of Eden. Suddenly, it made her angry on Awan's behalf. She scowled at him. "And what exactly were they afraid Lyka might do, or did he actually break the law."

"No!" The word came out loudly and Awan lowered his voice. "Lyka was not a lawbreaker. He was—he is, a good man with a kindness that is unsurpassed."

"Really? So, what were the cheetans afraid he would do?" Though angry, she wasn't oblivious to the sorrow filling Awan's amber eyes.

"He had the ability to blend with his surroundings, in essence to be unobservable to others. The cheetans thought this could lead to discord if he heard information that was not for him to know and then related it to others."

Alarm bells went off in her head. Why would cheetans be

afraid of information being spread when she'd been told they acted on behalf of the city to keep all safe? Something wasn't right about this reasoning. "Did you and Takoda argue on Lyka's behalf?"

This time, instead of answering, Awan started to put his empty containers into his bag, focusing on what he did instead of on her. "It is not for us to question the cheetans. They know what is best."

Another wave of frustrated anger washed over her and she opened her mouth to argue, but just then Awan looked at her and his gaze left her with no voice.

"If Lyka remained, we would have never met you." Awan's large hand came up to cup her face. "You are why it was meant to be. I need you in my life. You are my nuttai."

All anger dissipated as warmth filled her heart, and she closed her open mouth.

"I must go and finish my training. I hope you will be pleased." He brushed her lips with the gentlest of kisses before turning away and striding for the stairs.

She watched him until she could no longer see him, her emotions a jumble. She didn't need to know what nuttai meant to know how he felt.

On one hand, she wanted to doubt that Awan could fall in love with her so quickly. On the other hand, he didn't have a deceitful bone in his body and if he said he needed her in his life, she believed him. It was a new feeling to be needed just because she was Rowena Lewis and not for her skills or what she could do for someone.

Putting away her own empty containers, she tried to understand how she felt. To have a man proclaim his love, though without the actual words, was humbling, frightening, and exciting.

That her one-night stand may have given her exactly what she'd wanted all along would be the ultimate irony.

But what a wonderful irony.

She turned toward the balcony wall once again, a feeling of anticipation building inside. She didn't just want to see what feat Awan would accomplish next out of curiosity. She wanted to witness *her* man's prowess on the training floor. It was as if she would share in his success.

For now, that was the only feeling she would allow. It was an exciting day on Eden and she would enjoy everything about it.

Awan entered the training area again and walked directly to the three vines that hung from the ceiling all the way to the floor where they were tethered. This particular challenge was not far from where she sat, so as he climbed to the top, he would see her.

Having seen him tackle six other challenges, she knew this one was far too easy for him. Anxiously, she waited to see what would happen to bring it up a level.

As Awan spoke to one of the life-protectors, another man untethered the three vines from the strong hooks in the floor. That would definitely make it more difficult.

Movement out of the corner of her eye had her glancing up. A clear slick liquid was flowing down the vines, coating them completely. *Talk about making things difficult!* Despite her growing confidence in Awan's prowess, she still made sure there were plenty of life-protectors below.

She'd seen one of them somehow provide an air cushion under one man's fall while another life-protector manipulated the river water when a man had been hit by a half log and sunk, only to be lifted out by the water and set back on the floor.

Assured there were enough life-protectors below Awan, she leaned on the wall to watch him start his oily climb. *You can do it. Come on, Awan. You're doing great!* Though she didn't vocalize her thoughts, she couldn't help cheering him on.

His movements and strength caused butterflies in her stomach. It was as if she were dating Superman. No, that would be more like Takoda with his levitation. Awan was more like a Thor with short hair.

Awan had just reached the halfway mark, and she tensed, knowing something else would come. Looking up, she checked to see if water would start pouring on him, but nothing happened. That's when she felt the heat. Whipping her gaze back to Awan, she stared at the flames creeping up the vines behind him. What the hell?! These men were crazy!

Awan didn't look down. He kept climbing upward, testing his grip with one hand before letting go with the other.

Once again, she found herself gripping the wall, her heart in her throat. From her vantage point, the flames seemed to be at his heels, the view was so distorted.

Still, he continued on at his pace, steadily grasping, ungrasping, and regrasping. He'd just tested one hand when his other slipped a foot, leaving him at a precarious angle and swinging by one arm, which the fire seemed to enjoy.

She wanted to close her eyes but refused. If Awan could keep his concentration to defeat this challenge, she sure as hell would watch every second.

Just as he drew level with the platform at the top, one vine disconnected from the ceiling. Awan quickly let go of it and with one arm swung himself up onto the top platform.

"Yes!" She jumped off her stool, unable to help herself. "You did it!"

He turned around at her shout and gave her a wide smile.

Her heart pounded and she threw him a kiss.

He grinned at her as the fire extinguished and what was left of the two remaining vines dropped to the ground.

Awan then grabbed a vine that attached to the platform and swung off, quickly lowering himself to the floor below.

She pressed her hand against her heart as if she could slow her heartbeat. That had been spectacular! She couldn't wait to tell Takoda when they returned home.

Below, Awan was moving off the floor, probably to get the slick oil off him and to prepare for the next challenge.

Thankful for the short reprieve, she climbed back on her stool and took a few gulps of ambrosia. She was worn out just from watching. Awan would probably sleep well tonight. After all that, he deserved to.

Maybe she should try sleeping with him and Takoda. Even if just for a little while. Just to get the feel of the whole thing.

"Ro?"

At the sound of that familiar voice, she turned around. "Micco? What are you doing here?"

He stepped up to her but didn't touch her. "Sist told me you had left your residence. When I saw you at the Discoverist Complex, I thought you were just starting an exploration with that filoz. But you have moved to their domicile?"

She couldn't ignore the hurt in his voice. Nor could she ignore that despite all she knew about him, despite how much she'd liked him, and despite their many nights together in bed, she felt nothing beyond friendship toward him. Friendship and guilt for hurting him, not that she'd meant to. She hopped off her stool and gave him her undivided attention. "I have. I have bonded with Awan and Takoda."

Micco's body jerked when she said the word bonded. "But how? When? I don't understand."

She turned away as guilt rifled through her, moving closer to the half-wall as she gathered her thoughts. There had to be something she could say that would help him.

He joined her there. "Ro? When did you meet them? I thought Sist and I were the only filoz in your life."

"I'm sorry. But I know that you have more important issues to tackle now. I don't want to be a distraction."

He shook his head. "When I saw you, what I said, it—" He stopped and stared at her. "I have to leave Tolba."

"What? Why?" Guilt flooded her. Did he feel so strongly that he couldn't live in the same city with her and her filoz?

He scanned the area, much like he had when they met at the Discoverist Complex. He took a step closer. "Please do not tell anyone as it must be kept secret. I can no longer live in a place where I am shunned."

Shunned? "Why do you think you're shunned? I promise you, I did not shun you."

He gave her a sad smile. "No, it is not you, Ro. It is the cheetans. Every day more and more Kindred of Eden are taken, named lawbreakers, and exiled. Though I speak against it, I have no true voice as I am Kindred of Eden. I can no longer live wondering daily if I will be taken away and never see Sist again. Or you." His dark eyes seemed to turn black as he gazed as her.

There was something too intense in those dark orbs that caused her to take a step back. She looked over her shoulder toward the open space, wishing Awan was with her.

"But you are bonded." The words came out as if Micco tried to convince himself of the truth.

She nodded. "I am." Her heart broke for him. She wanted to tell him he'd find someone better. She wanted to tell him—a vision of Awan throwing Micco over the balcony wall flashed across her mind, and she sucked in her breath. A craving to do it herself, which was impossible, started to grow. It scared the hell out of her. "You better go now."

"You are right. We lost you. It was my fault." Micco turned away, his shoulders slumped, his head lowered.

Crap, she felt like the worst person on Eden. Then she remembered what Awan had said about Lyka being exiled. "Micco."

He stopped but didn't turn around.

"Maybe it was meant to be."

He nodded then continued around the balcony.

She only half believed that, but she sincerely hoped since Micco grew up in Tolba, there would be some comfort in the idea.

Turning back to the open room, she found Awan watching Micco as he walked away. The craving to hurt Micco dissipated. She frowned at Awan. Could he have really wanted to kill Micco just for talking to her? If that were true, they had a lot to discuss. She wasn't impressed with overly jealous controlling men.

Awan finally stopped watching Micco and moved his attention to her. His lips split into a wide grin then he shrugged before moving to his next challenge.

What was that all about? Awan had to know she'd feel his

craving. Why would he find that humorous? Because there was no way she could follow through physically? Because, instead, she would get rid of Micco quickly?

Another Edenist attempting the vines in front of her suddenly slipped, falling toward the floor. She watched in horror until a bubble appeared around him and he floated safely to the staging area.

"Oh, you are too smart, Awan." She glared at him from where she stood, finally understanding why he was so proud of himself. He'd wanted to see Micco fall, knowing damn well one of the life-protectors would save him if he actually did, but it would still have scared him.

For a man who valued balance above all else, Awan had a mean streak. Either that or a very warped sense of humor.

Even as she contemplated that tidbit about him, he started his next challenge. She definitely needed to learn more about her filoz before bringing them back to Boston. The problem was, she was running out of time.

Chapter Twelve

Takoda rose above the Cheetan Complex, his hands fisting in frustration. His gut told him the lawbreakers he'd seen were different, but he had no way to prove it. The cheetans thought their walls were safe. Even when he'd pointed out the return of the dirgon, they still waved the threat away, saying they had their own abilities to counter any attack.

If he only had himself to worry about, he would be far less concerned, but now he had a beloved, and despite the fact that he couldn't love her, he would defend her with his life.

But it was even more than that. He feared for everyone in Tolba. Was it not better to be prepared and have nothing happen than to not be prepared and have disaster strike?

Even as he floated down to his rear courtyard, he made a decision. Ro needed to know as much as he and Awan. By not telling her, they were putting her at risk in the same way the cheetans were putting the citizens of Tolba at risk.

As he landed softly next to the cold pond, he grinned. He'd arranged to have a Kindred of Water come fill the finished pond on the morrow. Working on the design and implementation with Ro had opened his eyes to many aspects of her intellect and personality. All of which he enjoyed.

He walked toward the door. Now if he and Awan could just convince her to sleep with them, he would feel more comfortable with their future and bring her to meet his mother and fathers.

The door opened before he reached it.

"I knew you were near." Ro smiled at him then looked behind her before facing him again. "Awan and I were just about to get in the hot pool. I told him after his workout, his muscles deserved it."

Her words flew over him like a lintue bird, his mind too focused on her in two small scraps of cloth. Immediately, his body heated. How could such small coverings be more enticing than her naked body?

"Why don't you join us?"

He snapped his gaze to meet hers. "I will."

Ro sauntered over to the hot pool and climbed in, her rounded ass making him want to grasp it.

Bounding over and kicking off his translucent footwear, he quickly stepped into the hot water.

She was already sitting down, the water lifting her breasts to float just beneath the surface.

"Ah, you have returned." Awan set a pitcher down on the table beneath the patrio. "I'll bring another glass." He immediately strode back inside.

"Have you ever seen Awan train for the Muskwa?" Ro's voice had him swiveling his head back to focus on her.

He lowered himself into the water and sat next to her, wishing the round pool was slightly smaller. He laid his hand on her thigh. "I have. He is one of the best."

She gave him a wide smile. "I believe that. Is there something like that you love to do?"

Her question surprised him. There was his labor, but that was something everyone did for the good of the community. He enjoyed helping people like the nubbish seller, but that was simply using his ability to barter for a product. Finally, he shrugged. "Nothing like that."

"There isn't anything that brings you joy over everything else?" Her gaze was intense like she wanted him to have something.

He grinned. "There is that one thing all Edenists find the most joy in, making love to their beloved."

Ro's mouth opened slightly as if his words had stirred her. If that was so, he was pleased, and he gave her thigh a slight squeeze.

"She's looking for something particular to you." Awan approached the pool, three glasses of ambrosia in his hands. "Of course, we all enjoy our women, but she wants to know what makes *you* happy."

As Awan set the glasses on the new shelf surrounding the hot pool, Takoda tried to think of something he did that made him happy. It seemed like forever since he'd thought about happiness.

"What about your jungle-watching?" Awan settled in next to Ro on her other side.

She raised her brow, clearly curious. "Jungle-watching?"

"It is nothing." Why would Awan bring that up?

She placed her hand on his beneath the water. "If it makes you happy then it's something. Tell me."

Her focus was too enticing to ignore. "I like to sit atop the walls of Tolba and watch Helios spread out his last rays over Eden. Sometimes I will get up early and go there to see Helios rise, also. There is a wild beauty to the jungle that can be awe-inspiring."

"That sounds gorgeous." She spoke to both of them. "Even

when I'm in the city back home, I often will take a weekend to head up north to enjoy the beauty of the New Hampshire mountains. I can understand your joy in that." She let go of his hand and reached for the glass Awan handed her.

It occurred to him that she'd not been out of her hatchoc until she'd come to their residence. "Have you ever seen the jungle?"

She shook her head. "Only what I saw from the air the first time you brought me here, but I wasn't really paying attention. Levitating appears to take some getting used to." She crinkled her nose. "But I think I just need practice. Would you be willing to take me with you to see the sunset, or rather Helios sink below the horizon? Or do you prefer to be alone?" She scanned his face, obviously trying to read his thoughts on the matter.

Usually, Takoda preferred to be alone. He often gazed out and thought of Xavia and Lyka. But he wanted Ro to see the beauty and power of their surroundings. He wanted to share that with her. He could take her to another wall of Tolba that could be special to them. "I would very much like to show you the jungle."

She smiled almost in relief. "I can't wait to see it."

Had she been afraid he would deny her? A tinge of guilt crept into his conscience. He hadn't given her much encouragement except through their physical connection. It wasn't her fault that he loved another.

"But not tonight." Awan lifted his glass. "Tonight, Rowena has agreed to share our bed."

A rush of excitement ran through him. Part was due to the idea of having her beside him, but part was the fact that they would sleep as a yenea. A filoz with a beloved who were bonded shared a bed every night. It wasn't just tradition, it was a need generated by the bond, and he'd felt that missing piece since she'd come home with them. "I look forward to this."

Ro's gaze left his to focus on her drink as if it was something she'd never seen before.

Takoda wasn't sure if her action was due to embarrassment or nervousness, but he recognized her reticence and it dampened his anticipation. He looked over her head at Awan, who nodded. He'd either noticed her reaction or was aware of the problem. Takoda pointed to himself. Was he what made her uncertain?

Awan shook his head, which relieved him more than he expected. Awan would tell him at the appropriate time. In the meantime, he needed to let them both know what had happened with the cheetans.

He raised his glass. "This was an excellent idea. It's exactly what I needed after my meeting with the cheetans."

Awan's brow lowered, obviously not happy about his choice of subject.

"I think it important that we are all aware of what happened there."

Ro's green gaze returned to him. "Why did you meet with the cheetans? It must have been important."

That she understood so much about their culture already made it easier to relate to her. Easier than when Xavia first came. He shook himself at that thought and continued. "I met with them because earlier this week when I sat upon the wall, I witnessed lawbreakers congregating just outside of Tolba."

"Is that so unusual?" Her anger came out in her tone. "I'm sure many of them would prefer to be back inside, especially those who had yet to break the law in the first place."

On this, they agreed. "It is common for me to see a lone lawbreaker or even two come back to Tolba and contemplate breeching the walls, but it is wishful thinking. They are too tall and solid, and without portal chips, it is impossible."

"Except for the dirgon." Awan's unexpected addition to the conversation was said in an arctic cold voice.

Takoda wasn't surprised. They might view themselves as to blame for not fighting harder to stop the breaking apart of their filoz, but it was the dirgon who made that separation permanent.

Ro set her glass on the shelf behind her. "What exactly is this dirgon I've heard about?"

Fearing what Awan might say, Takoda answered quickly. "A dirgon is said to be an ancient animal that lived on Eden thousands of years ago. It was the result of a mating between a dire wolf and a dragon. It had never been proven it existed, but one of our past discoverists recreated that beast in his son. The man, Davos, changes into a dirgon at will."

Her eyes were wide, but when he mentioned the changing, she cocked her head. "That's a lot like our mythical werewolf. Only in that case, he can't help his change which occurs with a full moon."

Awan shook his head. "Selene and Bendis have nothing to do with it."

"Wait." Ro looked at Awan and back to him. "It was this Davos who bonded with Lyka and Xavia, right?"

Takoda nodded, not trusting himself to speak as the old anger surfaced again.

"Do you think he will help these lawbreakers get back into Tolba?" Her furrowed brow made her fear clear.

Takoda blinked. It hadn't occurred to him that Davos might

want to help lawbreakers. "He definitely could. He has the ability to fly over the walls even without portal chips."

"I don't think he would." Awan sounded confident.

Ro snapped her gaze back to Awan. "Why not? He sounds pretty scary to me. Half giant wolf and half dragon?"

Awan nodded. "He is a scary site to behold, but it is the man that I speak of. If he is bonded with Lyka and Xavia, he cannot be someone who would support lawbreakers."

Takoda had to admit, Awan had a good point. "That is true, so we do not need to worry about the dirgon as far as lawbreakers breeching the walls, but this group I saw who approached the city is another matter. They came from a variety of directions and met at one spot at the edge of the jungle. They either had predetermined the day and time or they were somehow called together. I have never seen this before and I watch the jungle often."

Ro, who had turned toward him when he started to speak, squeezed his hand. "And you took this to the cheetans to make them aware, so they could protect the city?"

"I did." He sighed. "But they did not think the information I bestowed warranted any additional precautions, not even patrols."

Ro stiffened next to him. "How could they ignore you? Do they have others who regularly watch the jungle?"

Takoda shook his head.

"Then that's even more reason why they should listen to you. What is their problem?" Ro's hair on top of her head, bobbed with her movements.

At her defense of him, his heart warmed. "I'm afraid they are too complacent. I helped build the walls around the new hatchoc. They are strong, but they are not invincible."

She folded her arms beneath her breasts. "Maybe they consider a breeching simply what is meant to be." She snapped her head around to spear Awan with a cold look.

The man, to his credit, seemed uncomfortable. "Our cheetans would never accept a threat to the community as inevitable. That is why they still exile lawbreakers."

Ro lifted her hand from his thigh and waved it above the water. "And Kindred of Eden who may, perhaps, accidently, break the law one day." Her tone made it clear that she found the exile of that Kindred as odious as he did. However, she did not appear frightened.

Takoda hoped that was because she had faith in Awan's and his abilities to protect her. "I will make it part of my routine to watch the jungle, though I cannot be there every rise and set of Helios."

Ro stared at the water, obviously deep in thought, but about what, he had no idea. Suddenly, she stood. "I've got it."

The water lapped over the edge of the hot pool at her sudden movement. She turned to face them. "My job on Earth is risk management." She focused on him. "I already told Awan, but what that means is I'm always looking for ways to keep people safe. However, it sounds as if the cheetans are in no hurry to take any additional precautions, so you can do what we do on Earth when citizens want to protect their communities when their local police departments don't have the funding to do daily patrols. They create crime watches." Her green eyes sparkled with excitement.

She stood there, dripping wet, her nipples clearly outlined by the wet cloth covering them and all he wanted to do was be inside her. Forcing himself to stay on topic with what excited her, he moved his gaze back to her face. "How do we do that?"

"That depends." She paused as she thought. "If men are willing to use their portal chips, they can take turns patrolling the walls."

Awan grunted. "I don't think many will. It is frowned upon to use the chips within the walls, so that we can use them to come and go to Earth. The cheetans want the chips to last as long as possible."

She backed up and sat on the edge of the pool, crossing her legs. "Then we would need to get creative. There must be other ways to get to the top of the walls besides levitation."

Now this he knew. "There are. Many Kindred of Water, Air, and Eden can use their abilities to get to the top of the walls, but we would have to identify them and then convince them that there is a threat."

She uncrossed her legs and set both hands on her knees. "Then that's where you start. It's a lot more than what the cheetans are doing."

Takoda grinned. Her intelligence just added to her beauty, and he couldn't resist her for another moment. Drifting toward her, he placed his hands on her shins and pushed her legs apart to kneel on the top underwater step. "You are brilliant." Taking her face in his hands, he kissed her.

Her hands, which had drifted to his sides, now ran up his torso until they wrapped around his neck.

She smelled of sweetness and tasted of ambrosia, fueling his desire. Her tongue exploring his mouth, tasted him in return.

Without warning, she broke the kiss and smiled up at him. "Thank you. This just happens to be an area I know a lot about."

She leaned to the side to look behind him. "What do you think, Awan?"

Takoda moved aside as Awan floated to kneel next to him. "I agree with Takoda. You are just what Tolba needs." His voice lowered. "What we need."

Her eyes widened as if she just realized what they were thinking, or could it be that Awan's craving for her was transmitted to her? If so, the hot pool was about to get hotter.

Surprising them, she stood. "I think I need a cold shower and definitely some sustenance if you're thinking about what I'm thinking about."

She stood above them, her red hair almost on fire as Helios splashed the sky with his orange and red palette, signaling the end of the day. Then she laughed before turning and walking to the table to use her drying cloth.

Takoda started to rise, but Awan's hand on his arm, stopped him. He looked at the brother of his heart, raising his eyebrows in question.

"Let her go." The words were soft as if Awan didn't want Ro to hear them.

He remained where he was but watched their beloved until she disappeared inside. Then he turned to Awan. "Why?"

"She is trying very hard to please us. If we enjoy her now, she may slip away to her own bed again tonight. She has said she will try sleeping with us. We need to let her get ready as she wishes. In the night, we can distract her with pleasure in my room to make it easier on her."

Takoda drifted back and picked up his glass, pondering what Awan said. He kept forgetting that living with others was new to her. The last few nights, he'd found himself resenting her distance, which didn't actually make sense since he didn't expect to truly love her. He'd been taught to put his woman first and yet that was not what he'd done.

Had the damage done to his heart affected his mind as well?

Ro adjusted the neckline of her large t-shirt for the fifth time before finally leaving the bathroom, her bare feet not making a sound on the stone floor. Stopping in her bedroom, she scanned the room. It wasn't really her room. She only used it until she could get used to sleeping with not one but two men. And tonight, she'd promised to try.

She looked up as if she could gain the courage she needed from some celestial force and noticed the poem on the ceiling again. The second stanza was exactly how she felt now.

And now, I'm different from before,
As if I breathed superior air,
Or brushed a royal gown;
My feet, too, that had wandered so,
My gypsy face transfigured now
To tenderer renown.

Eden was superior to Earth in so many ways, yet backwards as well. She had traveled, looking for a man to enhance her perfect life and instead found two that were far more than she'd expected. Was her search over? It could be. After all, the third time's a charm. She smiled at the old saying, hoping it was true.

The men's voices in the other room had her moving her gaze back to her closed door. She really had no choice. The bond she'd allowed to be created meant that Awan and Takoda had to be it for her, or they would forever live apart and alone.

As opposed to scaring her, that thought made her more determined than ever to make her relationship work, and that meant sleeping in their bed. It had been her determination that had made her successful in her career, so it could only help in this case.

Resolute, she opened her door and strode out.

Awan was in mid-sentence and stopped, his gaze flowing over her like the warm water in the shower.

Takoda turned. "Your hair. It reminds me of our first night." His blue eyes darkened.

A thrill ran through her. "That's because I only leave it loose at night. It gets in the way during the day."

"It is beautiful." Awan walked past Takoda and stood before her. Gently, he touched her hair as if she were as delicate as a dragonfly.

Now that was an odd thought since she more resembled a Japanese beetle. Then again, standing next to Awan, she always felt delicate. "Thank you."

Awan's large hand slid beneath her hair to her neck then moved up to cup the back of her head. His face lowered and his lips touched hers in a gentle kiss.

The phrase "gentle giant" came to mind before his tongue swept inside her mouth. She opened to him, even as he wrapped his other arm around her and pulled her closer. Little tingles started deep in her belly as they tasted each other fully.

"I remember." Takoda's whispered words floated by her ear as he stepped behind her. His lips found her neck and his hands held her hips.

Suddenly, the tingles in her belly sparked.

Awan lifted his head and gazed into her eyes. "We want to give you pleasure tonight."

Her breath caught for a moment. Two muscular, handsome, intelligent, caring men wanted to make love to her at the same time? She had to be dreaming. But she wasn't dreaming. She was simply on Eden. Here, this was normal, a situation sought after by every man born on the planet.

Takoda lifted his lips from the back of her neck. "Will you allow it?"

His breath passed by her ear, causing her to involuntarily lift her shoulder in response. She met Awan's gaze. "I would like that." Then she looked over her shoulder. "Very much."

Immediately, Awan stepped back as Takoda wrapped his arms around her and floated them into Awan's bedroom. No sooner had her feet touched the floor then Takoda's arms loosened. He took the bottom of her t-shirt and lifted it over her head.

She pulled Takoda's head down as soon as her hands were free. She stepped closer as her lips met his and her tongue swept inside. His citrusy scent filled her nostrils as his hands came to rest on her hips again.

Even as her toes curled at their shared kiss, the scent of ginger wafted in just before Awan's muscular body made contact with her back, his already hard cock pushing against her spine.

"We will make you ours together." Awan's voice had deepened and his implication of things to come caused her entire body to shiver.

It didn't go unnoticed because Takoda broke their kiss and grinned. "You want us both joined to you."

Heat filled her cheeks. She'd never admitted that to anyone. It was just a fantasy…until she'd landed on Eden.

A guttural sound came from deep within Awan's chest, causing her to look over her shoulder. His amber gaze promised carnal delights she'd not even imagined. "It is the most intimate of joinings."

She didn't have time to imagine what he meant before his mouth locked onto hers and his tongue took over. Next thing she knew, she'd been turned around and was back in his arms. He pulled her tight against him.

She wrapped her arms around his neck, loving the feel of her breasts pressed against his rock-hard chest. Pure desire coursed through her veins, making her feel a bit lightheaded.

Breaking the kiss to breathe deeper, she discovered she wasn't light-headed at all. Takoda had levitated them into a horizontal position. She turned her head to the side to find him motioning with his hand and she and Awan floated over to the middle of the bed.

Awan raised a brow. "Did I not tell you how beneficial it is to have a beloved who can levitate?"

She smiled. "No, you didn't. But I completely agree."

As they were lowered onto the mattress, her knees slipped to Awan's sides and she sat up on his upper thighs. The view was impressive. Even thinking about the feats he'd accomplished at the Muskwa training had her feminine genetics melting. So much for all her feminist independence. It must be because Awan was the first man to make her feel small. She seriously felt like a cavewoman claiming her mate. She couldn't refrain from touching the large hard cock in front of her, just waiting for her to place herself on it.

Awan moved his hands up to cup her breasts, effectively dislodging hers from his body. She would have complained, but as his thumbs rubbed across her nipples, the spikes of pleasure had her swallowing hard.

The bed dipped to her right, and she turned her head to find Takoda lowering his mouth to hers. She titled her head up, happy to kiss him. Just as his mouth took over hers, he grasped her hands in his and pulled them behind her.

She moaned as she gave herself over to him and Awan, who now had begun to roll her nipples between his fingers. She explored Takoda's mouth with her tongue as he adjusted his hold on her so he had both her hands in one of his.

Awan's hands shifted even as he spread his legs slightly, forcing her own apart more. She was about to break the kiss, when Takoda's free hand held her cheek and his kiss deepened.

Feeling cherished in a very sexual way, she complied with his wishes and he was soon nipping at her lips. She let her head tilt back as he released her cheek and continued his kisses along her neck.

Large fingers at her entrance told her Awan had left her breast for a reason. Her heart rate sped up as he found the moisture of her readiness and spread her labia.

Takoda's hand around hers tightened even as his kisses to her neck became harder. Part of her tried to remember why that might not be a good thing, but the feeling of being possessed by him was too strong.

Then Awan's two fingers moved to her clit, and she bucked. With both of them making love to her, every touch was a surprise, a very pleasant one.

Takoda moved his mouth to her ear. "Enjoy. Let yourself feel it all."

The words caused electricity to race up her spine. She was definitely feeling every nuance of both men. As Awan's fingers once again stroked upward to her clit, the excitement raced through her and seemed to be echoed in the tensing of his thighs beneath her butt.

Takoda's mouth captured hers once again, making love to her with his tongue at the same time his free hand found the crease of her butt cheeks and a finger moved between them to her anal star.

Her breath caught at the sensation of liquid over that sensitive spot, his slight pressure mirroring what Awan did to her clit. Her whole body was on fire. Pulling her head away from Takoda's kiss, she sucked in air. "If you keep this up, I'll come without you."

As if that was their very intention, both men moved their fingers away and then back to their favorite spots to tease her more. Takoda's finger pushed between her butt cheeks until it slipped inside.

A loud moan came from the back of her throat as the sensations his movement caused ripped through her already sensitized body. Then Awan rubbed her clit in determined rapidity, spiraling her excitement beyond the bounds of stability and her body exploded.

She yelled, unable to help it as the ultimate pleasure overtook her. She let herself ride the peak and grasp every erotic spike before letting her mind have control once again. She leaned forward, placing her hands on Awan's substantial chest as she took deeper breaths and her body calmed.

"Did you enjoy that?" Awan's quiet voice held amusement.

She looked him in the eye, a wise remark on the tip of her

tongue, but at the last minute she swallowed it. "I did. Very, very, much." She barely refrained from winking.

Awan's face tensed and his hard cock jerked, hitting her body.

That's when she realized Takoda was not touching her anymore. She felt his absence keenly. "Where's Takoda?" Sitting up, she turned her head to the left and right.

"I'm here." He spoke from above her, as usual, and slowly descended until he was standing over Awan's chest, his own hard cock the same level as her mouth.

She gave him a sly grin. "So I see." She had a cock in front of her legs and one in front of her face. She couldn't resist. Lifting herself above Awan's erection, she grasped Takoda's thighs and slowly lowered herself.

Awan's substantial cock spread her sheath and filled her to the very core as she came down to his pelvis. "Oh, yes." By the movement inside her, she could tell Awan thought so as well.

Maybe she was being greedy, but the new sensations flowing through her caused a need to have both men at once. Without questioning those feelings, she pulled Takoda's hips toward her and opened her mouth to taste his tip.

A feeling of rightness filled her as she pulled him into her mouth. Having them both inside her, was her giving to them instead of taking. She slid her mouth as far as she could then back again, sucking him along the way. The tenseness of the muscles beneath her hands told her he enjoyed it.

As she took him in her mouth again, she lifted up off of Awan and came slowly down as she pulled to the tip of Takoda again. Her own body reacted even as she focused on giving pleasure to them. On her fifth stroke down on Awan, he grabbed her hips and Takoda cupped her head.

Disappointed, she let Takoda go. "Is something wrong?"

He nodded then shook his head. Letting go of her, he levitated away. "Too close to my release."

Pleased, she refrained from smiling. "But you can find your release in me. I don't mind."

He slowly lowered himself to the floor. "I will." He moved to the table on the side of the room and opened a bottle.

She was about to ask what it was when Awan's hand cupped her breasts again. She whipped her head back to him.

His gaze was focused on her body. "Landisbaum, but you are beautiful."

She bit her cheek to keep from smiling at his swearing compliment. "And you are…" she searched for a word that was more specific than simply telling him he was handsome. "You are enticing."

His nostrils flared and his hands on her breasts squeezed slightly. Then he let go and pulled her down on his chest. "My nuttai, you fill my world."

Her heart responded. He was always hopeful and excited by what they could be, and right now, she completely agreed. Not sure how to respond, she lowered her lips to his and kissed him gently, wanting him to know that she was falling in love with him.

Awan's return kiss held so much promise, her heart filled with joy. She broke away smiling.

He gazed back at her, his own smile just as wide. Then without warning, he rolled them over.

She gave a short cry of surprise then laughed, everything

feeling so right. Again, she needed Takoda to be a part of it. "Takoda, now where did you go?"

"I'm right here." He laid on the bed next to them.

She reached her hand out to him and he grasped it. "Good. I need you both." Though she'd meant it in a general way, Takoda's gaze darkened, and her sheath tightened around Awan.

Takoda let go of her hand and stroked down her leg. "And you shall have us both."

Instinctively, she pressed her pelvis against Awan. "Yes." The word was but a breath, but he heard.

He raised his hips and slid inside her again.

She closed her eyes as she wrapped her arms around him and spread her legs wider to accommodate him. His penetration was deeper than when she was on top and as he pulled away again only to slide back in, she felt more than sexy. She felt loved.

He speared her again, his mouth coming down on hers to kiss her. It was both sensual and loving.

An image flashed through her mind of Awan inside her as he was and Takoda inside her as well from behind. The titillating image had her opening her eyes only to find she and Awan were no longer on the bed, yet he was still able to pull back.

But he didn't slide in again. Instead, he gazed into her eyes as if waiting for the scene he craved to come to be.

Takoda's finger, once again on her butt, had her widening her eyes. He spread a cool liquid lube down her crease and to her anal star once more.

Her breath caught as she understood Awan's craving and why they floated. Takoda would enter from beneath her.

She stared at Awan, his gaze so heated by what they were

about to do that she thought he would come right then. Instead, he slowly pushed back inside her.

Her breathing was rapid as she waited for what was to come. Finally, Takoda spread her butt cheeks. She held her breath, anticipation making her sheath weep. Awan's eyes promised her an ecstasy like no other.

Takoda's cock pressed against her anal hole and shocks of excitement went off in her core.

He whispered beneath her. "Feel it all. Do not fight it. Welcome the pleasure."

At his words, she relaxed into it, knowing he wouldn't let her down. And he didn't.

She welcomed him in and his cock slipped inside. She and Awan floated down until she could feel Takoda against her back and inside her. Her body, brain, and soul sighed in satisfaction.

Takoda's arms came around her and his hands grasped her breasts, even as Awan pulled his hips back.

Awan's entrance into her was slow and steady, causing lightning strikes as he pushed her sheath wide against the cock in her ass.

Takoda massaged her breasts, keeping her nipples in a hardened state that caused her sheath to tighten. Awan continued his strokes, increasing his rhythm just a little at a time, letting her feel it all over and over again.

She couldn't think. Her body's pleasure ricocheted everywhere.

Awan strokes grew more rapid and harder, his own breathing heavy as he built towards his climax.

She grasped his arms next to her as the feelings inside her cascaded on top of one another until her climax broke over her like a waterfall. Every nerve-ending lit up and she screamed.

But it didn't stop as first Takoda and then Awan filled her with their release. Each one set her own orgasm beginning again.

Instead of feeling wiped out by the triple orgasm, her body seemed to have wound up, and she opened her eyes as she breathed, not able to speak, but feeling so amazing she could do nothing but smile.

Awan finally opened his eyes, matching her smile with one of his own. Takoda's hands, resting on her breasts, gave her a slight squeeze and she laughed. Never had she felt so free, so sexy, so loved, and that all was right with the world. Whatever world that happened to be. She chuckled again at the thought.

Takoda spoke from beneath her. "You enjoy the Eden way then?"

The Eden way? "Yes, I do."

"Good." He sounded satisfied himself.

She didn't blame him.

Awan finally spoke as well. "Now you see yet another reason for why it is good to have a beloved who levitates."

She laughed again, feeling more carefree than she ever remembered, way before she'd been driven by achieving her life goals.

Within seconds, Takoda had turned them on their side and lowered them to the bed. All of them connected, a true yenea.

Takoda was first to disconnect from her. She felt his absence as if his physical withdrawal from her body also distanced him from her mentally. She hoped that wasn't true.

Awan withdrew next, but she didn't mind that as much as their connection was strong.

She had just sat up when she found herself in Awan's arms

again, only this time he carried her to the bathroom. Takoda turned on the rainbox and squirted soap into his hands, his grin mischievous. "Awan, I'll wash the front and you can wash the back."

"That is a plan I can follow." Awan set her down in the middle of the spray.

She put her hands on her hips and faced them both. "Don't I have a say in this?"

They looked at each other then looked at her. "No." The word was said in unison. And with that, Awan raised both her hands over her head and grasped them in one of his large ones.

Her whole body reenergized with excitement. Maybe sleeping with her men wouldn't be that hard to get used to after all.

Chapter Thirteen

AWAN WALKED BACK INTO HIS room, the hot kafez he'd made for Rowena sending its rich sent into his nostrils. Though he rarely drank it, she truly enjoyed it. Setting it down on the side table next to his bed, he stood for a moment, enjoying the perfect balance of his life.

They were now whole again. He did not think it possible after Lyka and Xavia were taken from them, but Rowena balanced him and Takoda in many ways. True, she was cautious about everything, but he was confident she would come to love them both. Already, she cared.

He studied her as she slept. Lying on her side, she had one leg thrown out across the bed while both hands were tucked underneath her head. Her sunset-red hair covered the pillow. He loved that she was not fragile, something he had always wished for in a beloved.

Takoda had wanted to wake her to enjoy her once again, but he'd been able to dissuade him. It was important that she feel she could *sleep* with them. If they'd woken her, she may have returned to her room.

He shook his head as he finally moved toward the rainbox.

"

Her odd childhood and her labor on Earth made her hesitant, but when she allowed herself to simply be, they all lived in perfect harmony.

Turning on the water, he adjusted the temperature with the lever. They would leave her to herself today, which should make her feel more comfortable. He planned to talk to his friend Kenjada to learn more about Wym and Condor, the two men she said brought her to Eden. If the day allowed, he'd also take a walk to the red section of the Discoverist Complex and look in on what Micco was working on. He agreed with Takoda, the man hid something.

He stepped beneath the large square where warm water fell like rain. Pushing the lever for his spice-scented lather-wash, he scooped it up and began to wash. He faced the sleeping room to see if his movements had woken Rowena, but she still lay as he'd left her. He grinned. After they'd washed her while making love to her, she'd finally become tired. Turning back, he gathered more soap and cleaned his face.

Seeing her reach her ecstasy so many times last night had made it difficult to fall asleep, especially as she pressed her ass against his cock. Even at the remembered feelings of her touching him had his cock growing hard now. Quickly, he washed it and continued with his ablutions.

There was only one obstacle that he could see to their continued happiness and that was her deadline to return to Earth. They needed to know more from her before they could suggest an alternative course of action. He didn't fully understand her need to return there, but he did recognize that it was very important to her, which meant it was important to all of them.

Deep in the recesses of his mind, he knew that something

about her return to Earth was what had caused her to invite them to her dome that night. She had been miserable, and they had yet to truly understand why. For the elevendieth time, he wished he could remember all—

Feminine hands touched his waist then wrapped around his abdomen, causing his muscles to tense. All thoughts of Earth scattered as Rowena pressed herself against his back.

"Hmm, now this was a great view to wake up to."

He took a deep breath as his cock stood out from his body. "Did you sleep well?"

"Uh-huh." She pressed a kiss to his back. "How could I not. You two wiped me out."

He tried to look over his shoulder at her. "We did not mean to tire you so much."

"Oh, it wasn't all your fault. I was obviously a willing participant." One of her hands lowered down his abdomen toward his erection. "It was rather rude of me not to offer you the same treatment I gave Takoda."

He swallowed hard as her hand wrapped around his cock and stroked it up to the tip. He should say something, but he didn't want to say the wrong thing and stop her movements.

She pulled her hand back up him. "Hmm, nice." Then she lowered it and cupped his sac.

His whole body tensed, the anticipation of her next touch keeping him immobile. Luckily, he didn't have to wait long.

She dropped her hand and moved to stand in front of him. Flicking her wet hair over her shoulder, she set her hands on his chest running them upward to his nipples where she rubbed her hands back and forth.

His balls tightened, but he remained completely still, or rather most of him.

Her hands roamed further upward, over his shoulders and down his arms to his hands. "I have to say, I was quite turned on watching you triumph in every single Muskwa challenge. I wanted to yell to everyone that you were part of my yenea."

His heart swelled at her words. "I am pleased I made you proud."

Her hands moved to his hips and then lower to cup his erection. "Proud, yes, but also it made me want to do this." She knelt before him and her lips surrounded the tip of his cock.

"Rowena."

She looked up at him and slowly took him deep into her mouth. Then she pulled back, her teeth lightly scraping him as she went.

He fisted his hands to keep himself still.

Her gaze left his as she sucked him back into her mouth, one hand wrapping tightly around his base while the other handled his balls.

He held himself back by will alone. If she wanted to play with him, he needed to let her.

Her mouth began to slide back and forth over him, her tongue flicking beneath the edge of his tip as she pulled back, sending shock waves up his ass. When she pulled him back in, she sucked hard then released and sucked again before scraping her teeth against him and flicking him once again.

He kept himself as still as a statue as long as he could, but his release was imminent. As she pulled back to his tip, he quickly pulled away. Without another thought, he scooped her up into his arms, her laughter fueling his desire.

Dropping her on the bed, he knelt between her legs. "I must."

She grinned. "You lasted longer than I thought."

At the glint in her eye, he understood. This is what she wanted. Relief, humor, and need swept through him as he leaned over her and pushed into her moist warm sheath. As he delved to the hilt, his whole world seemed to come together like the creation of Eden.

Rowena's legs wrapped around his waist and her arms grasped his neck. "Make love to me."

Landisbaum! She was all that he ever wanted. Unable to resist such perfection, he lowered his head and kissed her with everything he felt. Her mouth tasted of kafez and the unique flavor that was her. Her body molded to his as he pressed her into the softness of the bed, their wet bodies filling in each other's gaps.

Not releasing her mouth, he pulled his hips back and pushed back in, his body reveling in hers. Again, he pulled out and pushed in, her legs pulling him closer as if she couldn't get enough of him. He acquiesced to her need and pressed his pelvis hard against her.

"Oh, yes, Awan."

His name on her lips fueled his fire beyond control. Lifting his hips again, he plunged deep into his woman, his nuttai, his beloved.

Her breathing came out in gasps and her sheath tightened around him. Barely holding himself in check, he thrust again, breaking their kiss as his whole body released his happiness into hers.

Her scream of pleasure coincided with the tightening of her sheath and she spasmed around him, prolonging his release. It was as if all his strength had left him in that one pivotal moment and he quickly rolled them so he was on his side, not trusting himself to keep from collapsing on her.

Her face lay against his chest, her hair covering it, but her chest moved rapidly as she pulled air into her lungs. Eventually, her breathing slowed and she swiped her hair from her eyes to look up at him. "I can see there are advantages to sleeping together all night."

He grinned, pleased that her first night had been a pleasant one for her. First times always left a lasting impression. "Yes, there are."

"Last night you called me your nuttai. You've said that before. What does it mean?"

Placing his hand over hers on his chest, he smiled softly. "It is an endearment. It means my heart."

She pulled his head down and kissed him lazily. His heart opened at the sweetness of the gesture. When she was done, she lay back. "I'm so glad I don't have to go to work today. I wouldn't have the energy. I don't think I could call in sick for having too much sex."

He chuckled. "That is not unusual here."

She propped her head up on her hand. "Are you serious? Men don't go to their labors because they had too much sex the night before?"

"Or morning. Or they leave early to go home and pleasure their beloved."

She crinkled her nose at that. "That's the only flaw I see with this planet. The women are expected to stay home while the men labor all day. How boring."

The blanket of serenity that had enveloped him slid away.

He'd forgotten her expectation that they return to Earth with her. He could tell her labors were very important to her, but he didn't see how they could be applied on Eden. Everyone's abilities made dangerous situations rare.

She rolled completely out of his embrace and stood, bracing her hand on the wall next to the bed for support. "I didn't exactly shower in there." She motioned toward his rainbox with her head. "So I'll just go to my room and get cleaned up and dressed."

Her unconscious withdrawal had his euphoria completely dissipating. It didn't occur to her that she could use *their* rainbox.

She leaned over the bed. "Hey, everything okay? A moment ago, you were smiling. I hoped I had something to do with that, but now you've stopped."

He bolstered his spirits. He had to remember this was still new for her. Eventually, she would share everything with them, and they could change the use of Lyka's old room. "I just need a minute to recover."

She grinned crookedly then placed a quick kiss on his lips. "I totally understand." Straightening, she turned and sauntered out of the bedroom.

At least she didn't look for her clothing from the evening before. That was a positive sign.

Stretching, he listened for her movements in the other room, but with Takoda's room between them, he didn't hear anything. Reluctantly, he rose and washed again. He had labors to accomplish today and Rowena being alone would make her more comfortable.

Striding into the meal area, he set out a plate of tyree and havling pig on a toasted bun for her. He stood still, watching her door, willing it to open, but it remained closed. Sighing, he finally forced himself to leave his residence and maneuver through the crowded pathways of Tolba toward the Discoverist Complex.

Before he headed up the hill, he turned right onto a less crowded path, his pace quickening. He was anxious to talk to Kenjada, not only to discover what happened to Wym and Condor, but also to meet his new chosen one. Had she become their beloved yet? Maybe his friend could give him some advice on his own relationship and the odd situation he found himself in now.

Ro paced the length of Awan and Takoda's home. For three days now, she'd been left alone and at first the new filled pool had been like being on vacation on some Caribbean Island. The alone time had been wonderful, but today she missed her men. It irritated her that she wanted them to come home early, just so she could talk to them. This wasn't her. She *liked* being alone.

But it had been almost six months now since she'd last worked and her mind was probably mush. Cali had only stopped by briefly the day before on her way to see how the new hatchoc was coming along.

She was happy that Cali was less dependent on her company since she'd be returning to Earth next week. Of course, they could all return to Eden for vacations or even weekends. It wasn't as if it took any time to portal between the two planets. She liked the idea of spending weekends on Eden.

Though it would be fun to meet up with Cali, it seemed like Kuruk had taken her place. Though he didn't say much, he definitely gave Cali the attention she needed and more importantly the support. It worked since Cali was curious and interested in having a filoz of her own but wasn't ready yet.

Kind of like herself. After her first night sleeping with Awan and Takoda, she hadn't made it another full night in their bed. It made her nervous that she couldn't seem to stay with them all night unless she was exhausted from having sex. Both nights she'd woken and felt stifled, so she'd slipped out and went to bed in Lyka's room.

It was obvious they were disappointed. Takoda asked her outright what was wrong, but Awan's patient understanding had her wishing she could be different. What if there was something genetically wrong with her? All the women in her family, and that's all there were, women, had never had husbands for very long, if at all. It didn't mean the bond couldn't work, but they might all have to adjust their expectations.

She paused in her pacing and looked up at the windows high in the domed walls. It was barely after noon. She had at least four hours before Awan or Takoda came home and she was bored. Flopping down on the couch, she sighed. Hopefully, the rain would hold off tonight so she could finally go with Takoda and watch the sunset from the walls of Tolba. That was something she'd been looking forward to.

Maybe she should go to her Pleasure Dome house and figure out what needed to be brought over. Not that the men would approve of her walking all the way over there without at least one of them. She rested her head back on the couch, her bun acting like a pillow, and closed her eyes. It was amazing how much her life had changed in the last couple of weeks.

Lifting her head, she opened her eyes and her gaze fell upon the book about the animals of Eden. She'd brought it out two days ago meaning to look up the dirgon and got sidetracked. She really needed to return it to the Knowledge Dome soon. She'd had it forever.

She leaned forward and picked it up off the coffee table. Crossing her bare legs beneath her, since she wore her short jean shorts, she made herself comfortable. She'd read halfway through it and didn't remember the dirgon, but then again, she'd been more interested in the zander, so she hadn't been paying close attention.

Opening it up to the beginning, she perused the pictures and explanations about a myriad of animals that would be equal to prehistoric times on Earth. The dire wolf was one of the first animals in the book along with a waloma which looked like a giant stinging insect. She shivered, happy they were extinct. Then there was the zander, which was the size and shape of a pterodactyl, but it had brown feathers with gold tips all over it and its head was all gold feathering.

There was also an awasaw which was about twice the size of a grizzly bear, shaped a lot like that creature, but had light tan stripes breaking up its dark brown coat. She flipped the page to find a bezor, skog, and a zeban, which the book said had the dexterity with its hands to match that of Edenists. How they could know that was beyond her.

On the next page she found the dragon. It wasn't like the mythical dragon of Earth. It seemed more like a brontosaurus with giant leathery wings. The write up didn't mention anything about breathing fire, but it did mention the destruction it could cause with its wings or tail.

Determined to learn more, she continued through a number

of pages describing other types of animals before she finally reached the dirgon. It was an odd creature with the front half looking like a wolf and the back half like the prehistoric dragon creature. According to the text, it was the mixing of those two animals in order to keep them from going extinct.

It didn't say anything about Edenists being able to shift into one, but obviously they did since a dirgon completely wrecked—

She looked up. Takoda was near. Dropping the book on the couch, she jumped up and strode toward the back door. She reached out to open it and halted. What the hell?

Turning away, she forced herself to return to the couch. Since when did she get excited to have a man show up? The men she dated on Earth hadn't made her drop what she was doing when they arrived. In fact, if they came over unannounced, it usually irritated her.

Maybe that meant that what she felt for Takoda and Awan was real. Or maybe she was just bored. Unable to decide if she should go to the door or sit back down, she was caught standing in front of the couch when the door opened.

"Ro." Takoda smiled, perfectly comfortable showing her he was happy to see her.

She really needed to get out of her own head. "Hi, you're home early."

He strode over to her and took her in his arms, the scent of citrus enveloping her. "Yes, I am. I visited Awan to ask about his next Muskwa competition and he told me you craved our company, but he is required at his labors right now."

Awan knew she craved their company? "How could Awan know I missed you?" She wasn't really craving it. Was she?

His smile quirked up on one side. "It's the bond."

"I thought the bond was Awan feeling balanced with me."

He chuckled. "No, I believe that is simply Awan. Now, he can feel your cravings as you feel his."

That was interesting. "So do you know when I'm near?" Mentally she crossed her fingers it was so.

He took a deep breath and tightened his hold. "Not like how you can tell I'm near, but I definitely can smell you. It makes me want to take you."

Tingles spread out across her whole body, quickly overpowering her disappointment. "And is that what you came home for?"

Surprisingly, he shook his head. "No. I saw the sky is clear of rain clouds and I couldn't wait to have you join me on the wall for the Helios' descent."

Her heart started a little happy dance in her chest. "I've been looking forward to this for days."

His deep blue eyes lit with appreciation before he lowered his mouth and gave her a sensuous kiss. His tongue played with hers as he leisurely enjoyed her. The taste of Tolban ale filled her with anticipation.

He broke the kiss. "First, we will need to pack our evening meal." Letting her go, he strode into the kitchen and quickly pulled items from the cold box. She strolled over to watch him as he made warm sandwich pockets and filled containers with Tolban ale.

There was something so sexy about a naked man preparing a meal. In her dreams, she'd never imagined this could be her life.

When he was finished, he packed it into a bag, much like Awan had done. "Shall we?"

She gave him a warm smile. "Absolutely."

He led her to the back door and as soon as they were outside, he took her hand, leading her past the patrio. "Are you ready to ascend?"

She grasped his arm with her other hand. "Yes, I'm ready."

Slowly, they rose above the yard, their new pool looking even more like a small beach from above.

"Your design is very pleasing."

At his words, her cheeks heated. "It wasn't that original. I just took a couple ideas I'd seen used before and put them together."

"That does not lessen your design. Why do you not accept that it is well done?"

She continued to look down at their creation, biting her next words about it how it wasn't just her. Why couldn't she simply accept the compliment? The pool was well-designed, even if it wasn't her specialty. "You're right. It came out even better than I expected. Even Awan enjoys it." She finally looked at him.

He smirked. "I'm glad we were able to make use of his giant hole."

"Me too. He's so happy about it, he said he had invited a friend of his to come over to see it."

Takoda started floating them over the domed houses of the hatchocs. "I have a feeling you may be asked to design another one."

The thought of designing another had her excited. It spoke to her creative side, like when she'd made the design for the renovation of her brownstone. "Speaking of designing, would it be possible to see the new hatchoc you've been working on before we settle in for the sunset?"

Their forward motion paused. She glanced at him to see if her request was a problem. He was gazing at her, his expression almost soft. "You want to see where I labor?"

She nodded, her voice suddenly refusing to come out.

"I would be honored to show you."

But they didn't move. They simply hung there in midair as the people of Tolba went on with their lives, oblivious to the connection forming above them. She was positive that was the strange feeling in her chest. It had to be a connection with the man who didn't think he could form one ever again.

Finally, he seemed to recall himself and his lips quirked up. "It's back this way. The head of the turtle faces east toward the new day."

"That makes sense." Not really, but she was still trying to get her brain to function.

They floated toward the other end of Tolba, directly over the three primary complexes on their hill to the opening in the old wall, which appeared almost eleven feet thick. That had to have been a chore to take down.

"It is still in the very beginning stages." Takoda pointed as he spoke. "There will only be five curved pathways with residences and a common space for all to share in the center here."

"You mean like a cold pool and play areas for kids? Or do you mean like a park with trees and greenspace?" As the idea formed, she described it. "I can see a cold pool over here with a few salis bushes along the edge and then a covered patrio to allow families to relax out of the sun. There could be more dense trees over there with a play area for children. I think it could be very inviting and make for a great community vibe."

He floated in front of her. "I see what you envision. I do not think anything that beautiful has been planned. I am going to share your ideas with the master planner."

She shrugged. "It's not that unique, on Earth—"

Takoda kissed her, catching her off guard and she immediately melted. He filled her senses.

When he stopped, his brows lowered. "No more. I do not want to hear any more why your ideas are not good. They are very creative."

Crap, she hadn't realized she did that. "Understood. I will try to stop."

"Good." Takoda turned back toward the hatchoc and floated them over to various places, explaining what part he played in the construction. He said it matter-of-factly, not like he was bragging, but she was still very impressed.

"They are lucky to have you and your ability, otherwise this would take a lot longer."

"True. I am happy to do my part to help the city. With this new hatchoc, there will be less crowding on the main pathways and another area to visit."

The Edenists' interest in the community as a whole had fascinated her since she'd started living in Tolba. It all seemed to blend well with their barter system and productivity. They all offered their talents and abilities to make living for all a comfort and pleasure. So different from Earth. At least, most of it.

He turned them around, back the way they'd come. "I will show you where future hatchocs will be located as we move toward the end of day."

"I'd like that."

As they floated over the city, he pointed out where the four "feet" of Tolba would eventually be added.

She was about to ask what would happen once all those expansions had been filled, when another Edenist floated toward them.

The man smiled at her then nodded in deference to Takoda.

He nodded back, but his hand held hers just a bit tighter. She had to admit, she liked how he and Awan protected her. "That's the first man I've seen levitating like you. That ability must be very prized."

His hand relaxed a bit and he definitely stood straighter. "It is. There are only a few of us. It is such a helpful ability that trading for items like nubbish or anything else you wish is very easy. However, it is a significant responsibility as many need our help."

"Do you know all the others who can levitate?"

He slowed their forward progression as they approached the far wall. "I do. We are fortunate that there are others with different abilities that can accomplish similar tasks. For example, some Kindred of Eden can use living plants to lift heavy objects and a few Kindred of Mind can do the same with their minds."

Now that he pointed that out, she could see why technology had not caught on. There was no need for it with so many men with various natural abilities.

Takoda gently brought them down onto the wide wall. "Helios is already touching Eden to say good night."

He was right. Their sun had just begun to dip below the planet shimmering on what appeared to be water. "Is that an ocean?"

"It is the Telemen Sea, the largest body of water on Eden. It will reflect the colors Helios decides to gift us with. It is never the same."

She was glad she wasn't afraid of heights. Though the wall was eleven-feet wide and he had set them down in the middle, there were no railings, and it had to be at least eleven stories high. Before her was a completely barren area for at least two hundred yards. Except for the typical tan dirt also found inside Tolba, there was nothing.

Then, as if someone had drawn a line in the dirt, thick jungle crowded right up to it. It couldn't be anything natural. No doubt some Edenist ability kept the jungle at bay. But the jungle stretched out before them for what could be twenty miles. It was impossible to tell. It was everywhere, a dark green living thing that seemed a bit ominous in the fading light.

A movement in that darkness to her left caught her attention. "What's that?" She pointed to the spot near the edge of the jungle that met the packed dirt. A single salis bush moved but no other leaves did. "Is it an animal?"

"It may be." His voice was barely a whisper as they stood there watching the spot.

Just as the shadows covered part of the empty ground, a man stepped out. He scanned the area around him, including behind him before approaching the wall. He looked up at it as if gauging what he could do. Then he laid his palm on the cyndistone and lowered his head. After a few minutes, he pressed the same palm to his chest.

The actions squeezed her heart. Was he one of the Kindred of Eden who didn't deserve to be exiled?

As if the man understood there was no way into the city, he turned away and strode back into the jungle. Something about his walk seemed familiar. It was probably from living in Tolba so long.

She turned to Takoda. "Do you think he was a lawbreaker?"

He didn't answer at first, he just moved his gaze from the jungle to the horizon. "No, I don't."

As if he didn't wish to talk about it, which she could understand, he pointed. "Look. The day is ending."

She turned her head to study the sliver of water where it touched the horizon. Clouds she hadn't noticed, hovered over the sea, reflecting a pale yellow and orange light back toward the setting sun and lighting up the water. "It's beautiful."

When he didn't respond, she glanced up at him as he stood beside her, his face in profile watching the dance of color in the sky. There was something almost reverent in the way he stared at nature's beauty, and another piece of who he was clicked into place for her.

She returned her gaze to the horizon to find the colors had spread and changed, brighter oranges and streaks of red joining the sky's canvas below the clouds. The sun, or Helios, as the Tolbans called it, was quickly sinking, only a third of it still visible.

Takoda squeezed her hand. "Watch the final rays sink below the water. A bright blue flash will occur, signaling the start of night, and all the colors will begin to glow."

Having turned her head when he spoke, she quickly returned her gaze to watch the spectacle. It was only a matter of minutes, the sun seeming to sink faster as it got closer to disappearing. Then, as Takoda foretold, a bright aqua-blue wave of light flashed over the sea and jungle. If she had blinked, she would have missed it.

As he predicted, the colors began to change. This was no Earth sunset. The deep oranges and red that had been closer to the horizon morphed into a sizzling fire, spreading like a fan from the ocean into the sky. The tips of the flames turned such a deep red hue, they began to look purple. The clouds, instead of hiding the colors, reflected them like glitter.

Enthralled, she couldn't take her eyes off the horizon as the changing colors seemed to play with each other, swirling then separating then blending until the lighter colors sank beyond the sea. The higher tips joined together to create a deep purple, like the color of wine grapes, and they grew darker until it all merged with the night sky.

She had no idea how long they stood there, an hour? What she did know is she'd never seen such a spectacular display. "Have you ever brought anyone else up here?" She tensed at the thought that Xavia had shared this with him. She was an idiot for asking.

"Only my mother." Takoda's answer both relieved and surprised her.

He continued. "You two are the only ones who have asked to see the end of day with me." His voice had softened as if in wonder, and her heart jumped to attention.

She laid her hand on his hard chest. It was warm, and she could feel his heartbeat beneath her palm. "Thank you for sharing this with me. I can appreciate why you come here. To be alone with this beauty is both humbling and exciting."

Though there was little light, she could see his nostrils flare. "But I am not alone tonight."

She wasn't sure if it was his heartbeat or her own that picked up the pace, but she suddenly felt an emotional connection between them that enhanced the sexual excitement running through her body. "Takoda."

Chapter Fourteen

He clasped her hand on his chest as if it could explain the stirrings he felt in his heart. Sharing Helios' ritual with her had made the experience take on a whole new meaning. It was both a reflection of her and a reflection of Eden to have the two together.

Pulling her hand to his neck, he grasped her to him. As he lowered his head, she opened her lips, her other hand wrapping around his neck as well, welcoming him into her heart and body. The awe that filled him rivaled that of the jungle around him.

He needed her like he needed air, food, and water. He needed her to live. The realization was too much to have alone. He broke their kiss. "I can't imagine my life without you in it."

Her eyes widened at first, then her gaze grew intense. "I can't imagine mine without you."

He lowered his lips to hers once again, this time taking all she offered as he let his feelings for her loose.

Her mouth wasn't enough. Leaving her intoxicating taste, he trailed kisses along her jawline, her neck, and her collarbone. Reaching down, he pulled her top cloth up and lifted it over her head only to throw it down on the wall. Without hesitation, he continued his taste of her body, breathing in her sweet scent.

"Beautiful." The word came out of its own accord and he lifted her arm to kiss her biceps, the inside of her elbow, her palm. Grasping her about the waist, he levitated them both to a horizontal position so his mouth could capture her breast, his tongue exploring its unique texture.

Ro's hands rifled through his hair, letting him know she was pleased with his ministrations.

There was so much about pleasing her that he wanted to learn. His heart recognized an ancient need and he was powerless to ignore it. He moved his mouth to her other breast, her hands now on his shoulder gripping hard so he sucked her harder, wanting all of her.

In stark contrast, he released her and pressed light kisses beneath her breasts and along her rib cage. Her womanly shape was outlined in the flare of her hips. He kissed that flare before moving to her belly where he couldn't resist licking at her navel. A soft moan from her filled his senses and he tucked that small pleasure away in his memory to use another time.

Her leg wrappings were a barrier to his journey. Gently, he pulled them down her long legs, the scent of her readiness calling to him. As he made his way along her thigh, she spread her legs in invitation, one he was sure to accept eventually. But first he wanted to taste all of her.

He kissed her knee, her shin, her ankle, even her foot, before traveling back up her other leg. In the recesses of his mind was the need to touch all of her. As he returned to the juncture of her thighs, she bent her knees, allowing him open access to the core of her femininity.

It was an invitation he wouldn't resist. Pushing his shoulders between her legs, he used his finger to spread her labia, kissed her clit and her opening before pushing his tongue into her.

"Yesss." Her hiss pleased him, and his cock grew stone hard.

Pleasing her became paramount as he licked at her, savoring her wetness and her sex. Licking around her clit caused her hips to rise and her hands in his hair to grip him to her.

His need rose, revealing itself. He needed her to want him. Determination swept through him as he slipped two fingers inside her and laved at her clit. When he added light nips, her body shuddered.

He lifted his head. "Release for me, Ro. I want to taste your ecstasy."

A moan was her only answer.

He went back to her, licking and nipping as small noises came from the back of her throat. Feeling her near the edge as her sheath tightened around his fingers, he took her clit between his lips and sucked.

"Oh. Oh. Ohhhh." Her yell was swallowed by the jungle as she released around his fingers. Her body arched in her ecstasy. When her spasms slowed, he pulled his fingers out and licked them.

Not waiting for her breath to even out, he positioned himself over her, his cock at her entrance, but he did not push in. He kept himself over her, leveraged on his elbows, waiting.

She opened her eyes and looked at him. "Now. I want you inside me now."

It was all he'd waited for. It satisfied his need. Slowly, he slid inside her moist sheath, his psyche at peace.

Ro wrapped her legs around him, pressing him deeper.

His heart swelled. Dropping his head, he kissed her lips

gently, nipping at them before dropping kisses along her jaw and earlobe. "Forever."

Her sheath contracted around him. "Come with me, Takoda."

He couldn't hold back any longer, his balls tight, his body ready. Pulling out, he thrust back in. Her sheath held him, resisting his slide out, only to welcome him again. He watched her face, her eyes closed, her lips parted, as her body built with him.

He held back with sheer willpower alone as each thrust threatened to send him into oblivion. As she tightened around him, he let his release mingle with hers, losing himself inside her.

"Takoda?" Her voice was soft and a little scratchy as she brought him out of his euphoria.

"Yes."

Her hand rifled through his hair. "You are wonderful."

She didn't understand that he needed no words. She'd given him all he needed already. She'd given herself to him. He smirked. "What I am, is hungry. Would you like to eat?"

Her quiet laughter filled his soul. "Yes, I would."

He wrapped his arms around her then and held her for just a moment. He didn't know why. Then, reluctantly, he leveraged himself and pulled out of her warmth, his body well-sated.

Sitting up, he pulled her up and set them on the hard wall.

"Wow, I didn't realize how comfortable your levitation can be." She lifted her ass off the wall.

He handed her the covering she used for her torso. "You can sit on this."

She shook her head. "I'm not sitting here naked while we eat just so my butt will be comfortable on my tunic, thank you."

He lowered his brows. "Why not?"

"Why not? Because…because…" She looked around. "I'm not sure why."

He laughed at that, the joy of her realization worth sharing.

Though she still donned what she called a tunic and her leg wrappings, progress was occurring. Before long, he could see her living in their home naked, even if she covered up when around others.

He levitated the sack of food over to them and began distributing it.

"What is that?" Ro pointed to the pastry filled with henny, vegetables, and spices.

He grinned. "It's a rhoade. Here." He held out the still warm pocket of bread filled to the brim.

She took a bite. "Hmmm, I'm tasting henny with something like chickpea, a mild curry, mild garlic, coriander, a strong flavored potato and a tinge of hotness, maybe a tiny amount of red pepper, or whatever you use here."

"I believe you've described it correctly, though two of the items you mentioned I do not know." He held out the pocket and she took another bite.

"I definitely like this." She held out the container of Tolban ale he brought. "Want some?"

He nodded, taking a drink before biting into the rhoade. He handed back the container and watched as she drank from it as well.

Though he hadn't meant to, he shared their entire meal, each taking a bite from the same food. It felt right.

THE INTIMACY OF THEIR DINNER was not lost on her. It was the perfect finale to an amazing evening. "Does Helios provide such beautiful entertainment every night?" Though she spoke to Takoda, she stared at the sky, noticing the stars for the first time as if someone turned them on one by one.

He squeezed her hand. "Only when it doesn't rain. When the clouds cover the sky while Helios retires, the sky rebels with multiple shades of gray and the night never truly turns black." He turned her toward him. "Then the lights of Tolba reflect against the clouds and keep the city partially lit.

"I noticed that the last few nights when we were in the hot pool. It was like twilight."

"Even when you left our bed?"

Though his words were spoken with no accusation, she still felt a sting as he broke the spell. "I know it's hard for you to understand. I just feel…" she tried to find a word that would best describe it. "Smothered."

She sensed more than saw him stiffen as there was little light on top of the wall. "It's not you. I'm just used to sleeping alone. I need to adjust to it, just like you do when you enter the cold pond."

"I do not understand."

She smirked. "You go into the cold pond slowly, letting your body acclimate to the temperature, especially when it hits a particular spot."

He remained quiet for moment, obviously thinking about what she said. "I think I understand. Awan and I are the cold water."

Actually, they were seriously hot, but for this analogy, it was best she keep it simple. "Yes. My mind is like your body getting used to the cold water, only in my case, I'm getting used to sharing a bed."

"I hope it does not take you long. We like having you in our bed. It feels right when you are there."

This time her belly did a somersault. Her hopes for her dreams skyrocketed. There was a very good chance she could have what her mother had always wished, a successful career and a man to enjoy life with, only in her case it was two men and an amazing planet.

She leaned forward and kissed him, sharing her happiness with one of the men who would always be there for her and she for him. Finally, she broke it off. "Of course, once we get back to Earth, I'll have to have a custom bed made. My king size bed will be a little small for the three of us."

He sat back. "Back to Earth? Why would we sleep on Earth?"

She took his hand, wanting to reassure him that her feelings wouldn't change once they were on her planet. "So I can go to work. I only have five days left before I have to report back. I thought we could leave in a couple days, so I can get things ready."

He pulled his hands from hers. "You want to leave us?"

She shook her head, though she wasn't sure he could see it. Selene was just a sliver in the night sky and the ambient light from Tolba didn't reach very high. "No, of course not! I want you and Awan to come to Earth to live with me. Didn't he tell you?"

Takoda rose. "We cannot live on Earth."

A shiver of dread shot up her spine and she stood as well. "Of course, you can. My home is not as large as yours, but we can come to Eden on the weekends. There are many humans who have a weekend home, though to be fair, it is usually just outside the city, not off the planet." She attempted a smile to lighten the mood, but she wasn't sure she succeeded.

"You do not understand. It is Crius Law. It is to keep our planet from being known. More importantly, it is to keep us safe. We cannot live on Earth. The metals of Earth are deadly for us."

What? How did she not know this? "But you visit Earth to find your beloved. I know from Cali that the filoz who found her stayed on Earth a week to get to know their soon-to-be beloved. How can you do that if Earth is toxic to you?"

"We are very careful about where we go and we don't stay long to minimize the exposure."

Her entire happy homelife as she dreamed it disappeared like a magician's act. She definitely felt as if someone had played a trick on her. "You're telling me there is no way you can live on Earth?"

"No."

The word was said with such finality that she wanted to cry. *Get a hold of yourself Ro. You're a smart woman. How else did you end up with a great career and two great men?* There had to be a way around this dilemma. "Okay, so we can work around this. I can go to work during the day, just like you and Awan go to your labors and then you two can just portal me back here when I'm done."

Even as she said the words, a hundred issues with her idea rose to block her. What about when she needed to work late? Or what if she had to travel? Would she keep her brownstone? The thought of giving it up after all the work she'd put into renovating it had her stomach somersaulting.

A fear she'd never had before suddenly loomed large. For the first time, she was afraid of dying alone like her mother and grandmother before her. Not to mention the aunts and cousins, all female, who completed their life that way. That was long after decades of old age in retirement, filling their days with tasks instead of meaning.

It took her a few minutes to realize that Takoda remained silent and stood five feet away. When had he stepped back? His withdrawal bothered her. "Thank you for telling me. I must have missed that in my orientation to Eden. Either that or they may not have said anything." Come to think of it, Micco and Sist never said anything either, and they definitely knew that she'd planned to live on Earth.

Irritation rifled through her. If she ran into them again, she'd be giving them a piece of her mind. Pushing away thoughts of her past relationship, she focused on Takoda because his silence made it clear he was dwelling on it. Probably still thinking she was going to leave them. "This is obviously going to take some thought. Maybe Awan will have some ideas as well."

When he still didn't respond, she changed the subject. Distraction may cause problems in the workplace, but in relationships, she'd found it to be an effective tool for uncomfortable situations. While this rated as far more than uncomfortable, it was worth a try. "When does the Bendis moon show itself again? I can see that Selene is almost through her cycle. Doesn't that mean the pink moon will be up again soon?"

He didn't answer for a long time, causing her tension to rise. Of the two men, she could see him brooding for days.

Finally, he spoke. "This month we will have one black night with neither moon, but then Bendis will fill the sky. The following night Selene will return."

"Why do you say this month? Is it different depending on the month?"

He squatted and gathered up the containers from their dinner and placed them in the bag. "Selene is dependable, but Bendis has his own schedule that has nothing to do with Selene."

No wonder she could never figure out when the pink moon would arrive. She loved going outside when the planet was covered in a pink glow. "The last time Bendis rose, I met you." Her voice softened of its own accord at the memory.

Takoda took her hand. "Yes. I believe that was the worst night of my life until we met you."

She wanted to ask if he was happier now and pleased that everything had happened the way it had, but she wasn't quite that brave. "I admit that I am happy I sought out your company that night. I must have been following my women's intuition to choose you and Awan of all the men milling about the Pleasure Dome."

They started to float upward as he took them off the wall and back over the city. "Why *did* you choose us?"

She thought back to that night, happy she could remember the beginning of it. "Well, you two were definitely the best looking of all the men there, at least to me. But to be honest, I was so depressed that I didn't want to smile and you two were the only ones in the whole dome without smiles. I wasn't used to seeing frowning men in the Pleasure Dome."

"We hadn't planned on staying, but—that is not normal."

Now she was confused. "What isn't normal?"

"That." He pointed with his other hand to a building on the hill that was obviously lit from within.

She tried to figure out where it was exactly. "Is that the Discoverist Complex?"

"Yes. That building is in the red bells section."

That was where Micco worked. "Is it unusual for people to work late?"

"It is. Labor should be limited so as not to interfere with the joy of living." He said it almost by rote as if he'd been taught that value from a very young age.

They drifted toward the brightly lit building. Like many of the domes, this building had windows high in its walls. In fact, this one had a large round window at the very apex of the dome. That might be for high noon sunlight if they were growing plants.

Excited to see what was inside, she kept her gaze on the giant window as they floated closer, Takoda was obviously also curious.

At first all she saw were the inside walls, but then a strange looking animal came into view. Before she could study it, the lights went out.

Takoda halted their forward progression. "They know we are here and do not want us to know what work is being done." His voice made it clear he was not happy with this development.

"I thought many of the discoverists keep their projects a secret until they have some success and can share it with others."

Takoda stiffened, his hand clenching hers tighter. "Who told you that?"

Crap, now what? "Micco."

"Scrat."

When Takoda didn't elaborate and started them toward home again, she balked, tugging on his hand. "Wait a minute. What does that mean?"

He shook his head. "It is an expression we use when we wish things were different. I think you call it a swear."

She waved her free hand. "I know what scrat means. I meant why did you say it?"

They floated down to the backyard. "I will explain, but we need to include Awan as well."

As soon as their feet touched the ground, he let go of her hand and started for the house.

She was right behind him. If it was serious enough that he wanted them all to discuss it, she didn't want to miss a moment. Stepping through the door, she almost collided with Takoda, grabbing his arm to keep her balance as she moved around him. Once she did, she halted as well. "Awan?"

Awan sat on the couch. In his hand was a small green bag that he pressed against the back of his head.

She ran over and sat next to him. "What happened? Are you okay?" Of all the people she thought might get injured, Awan was the last.

He started to nod then winced. "I will be fine." He grimaced. "Just gave my opinion where it wasn't wanted."

Takoda came forward and sat on the chair adjacent to them. "What do you mean?"

"I mean I met Kenjada and his filoz at the Latzeran meal establishment and I asked him about Wym and Condor, the men who provided Rowena with her crossover to Eden. I knew I'd heard their names before."

She cocked her head. "Why would you ask about them?"

He gave her a self-depreciating smirk. "I needed to know who introduced you to our planet. Kenjada remembered them and explained what had happened. Their exile was postponed for five months."

"What to do you mean, their case? Do mean they were still in Tolba all that time?" Now she felt like a jerk for not trying to find out where they were and visiting them. "Do you mean I could have helped them stay in Tolba?"

Awan's gaze moved to Takoda then back to her. "No, you couldn't have helped unless you were bonded."

"Obviously, that wasn't the case, but it could have been if I'd known."

Awan's face fell. "Do you wish it were so?"

She thought back to her relationship with Wym and Condor. They were fun, but she barely knew them at the time. They'd only had one night together. "No, I am happy with my filoz now." She smiled, hoping she reassured them. "I'd only met them that night. Back then I knew nothing about Eden or bonding. I'm glad that I have lived here long enough to appreciate this life and the bond."

Awan smiled, but Takoda remained deep in thought.

She pointed to Awan's head. "So far, nothing you said explains that."

"True." He readjusted the bag.

From the condensation on it, she had no doubt he'd filled it with ice.

"Kenjada told me how Wym and Condor had claimed to have a chosen one and that they needed to stay. Their families also got involved, one of which is a cheetan. But in the end, since there had been no bonding, the cheetans decided to stand by their decision to exile them."

Again, she couldn't help wondering if she'd at least been there to argue that things might have turned out differently. But she couldn't imagine being with anyone other than the two men with her now. "And that caused a fight to break out between you and Kenjada?"

"That will never happen." Takoda's comment had her raising an eyebrow at him. He got the hint and explained. "Kenjada and Awan grew up together."

Awan smirked. "Yes, we are like brothers, but not brothers of the heart." He turned back to her. "What started the argument was I told Kenjada that it was meant to be so you could be our beloved, but a Kindred of Eden overheard and took offense to my comment."

She would have taken offense as well, but she wouldn't have hit him, even if she didn't know him. "I can understand that. So you argued?"

"I did, but he and his filoz were having none of it."

Filoz? "So Kenjada's filoz and you fought this other filoz?"

He looked away. "No, Kenjada has a Kindred of Eden in his filoz. I fought the other filoz myself, but only after they attacked."

She widened her eyes. "And how many in that filoz?"

"Four."

Takoda laughed. "You are slipping, Awan. Only four and you have a bump on the head?"

Awan scowled at him. "One of them was Kindred of Mind and smashed a table on my head from behind."

Her gut started to tense. "This sounds like an unfair all-out brawl."

"Just a short one." Awan looked to Takoda

"What he means is, everyone quickly dispersed because if a Kindred of Eden is found fighting with another Edenist, he is automatically exiled. Fighting is not acceptable in Tolba for any reason. It is a very rare occurrence since the Fullamush."

She placed her hand on Awan's thigh, truly concerned, but part of her was angry for the Kindred of Eden. "And what if *you'd* been caught, Awan?"

He glanced at Takoda again. "I would have been given additional labors at a cheetan's request."

She pulled her hand back. "But the Kindred of Eden men would have been exiled? That's wrong on so many levels."

"You are not happy I am here instead of at the cheetans?"

Awan appeared so hurt, her chest tightened. "No, of course not. I'm very happy that you're here and no one is the wiser." She cupped his cheek to add to her reassurance.

His shoulders relaxed, but she could tell, he wasn't completely convinced. When had that happened that she could read him so well?

"We have more troubles with the Kindred of Eden." At Takoda's pronouncement, she tensed. His tone made it sound like they were the enemy.

She no longer had feelings for Micco, but she still considered him a friend and she couldn't stand someone being found guilty without evidence. "We don't know that. Just because they were working late doesn't make them public enemy number one."

Awan's hand covered hers as if he wanted her to relax, but that wasn't happening.

The big man shook his head at Takoda. "What is Rowena referring to?"

"They were at the Discoverist Complex. As we returned here, I noticed light shining from a dome in the red bells section. Ro believes they were simply laboring late, but I don't."

"Why?" Awan kept his focus on Takoda though his hand held hers.

Takoda glanced at her before speaking. "As we came close enough to see inside the open roof, the lights went out."

She couldn't resist adding her two cents. "That could simply have been a coincidence. How would they know we were about to get close enough to see what was going on inside?"

Takoda stood as if by literally talking down to them, he would be right. "A Kindred of Mind or Kindred of Heart could easily sense us approaching even if they didn't know we were above. Even a Kindred of Air could sense our movement or a Kindred of Eden with a keen sense of smell like a grendal might have smelled your sweet scent."

Crap, she forgot about all the special abilities Edenists had. It did appear that they had shut the light out just as she'd seen that odd animal. Could it be a new breed for food?

Awan looked at her. "If they darkened the dome that means they hide something. There is no reason to hide anything in Tolba. We are one community working for the good of all."

She didn't like where this was headed. "But if it was a Kindred of Mind, Heart, or Air who sensed us, that means that they are with the Kindred of Eden, so how bad can it be? It's not like the Kindred of Eden are plotting to take over Tolba. In fact, from what I've seen, it's the other way around." She pulled her hand from Awan, too agitated to touch at the moment.

Takoda, who had paced a few steps away turned back. "What do you mean 'the other way around?'"

She rolled her eyes. "Maybe it's because I'm an outsider or because I come from Earth, but it's pretty apparent that there has been a growing wave of prejudice against Kindred of Eden."

She stood as well as her mind went down the path of possible outcomes. "There are three ways this could end. The first, which is highly unlikely, is that Tolbans wake up and realize that all Kindred are needed in order for this society to move forward. They will suddenly stop exiling Kindred of Eden unless they actually break the law."

Getting into her argument, she walked over to where Takoda stood and faced him. "The second is that the Kindred of Eden decide they've had enough and start fighting back."

Takoda nodded, which made her blood boil. "Yes, what you say could happen. They could take over Tolba, except you're forgetting one thing. They are far outnumbered since so many have been exiled over the years."

Awan rose now as well. "This is true. There are far less Kindred of Eden than their used to be."

"Exactly." His confirmation made her feel supported. "And what will they do when new Kindred of Eden are born? Will parents try to hide their children's birthmarks by burning them? I bet even now parents worry when their baby is born if he'll have the Eden birthmark. And if he does, they groan, wondering what will happen to their son. Or maybe eventually the cheetans will have the hatchoc patrols take the children away at birth to be exiled."

Takoda scowled. "That would never happen."

Could her men be truly that naïve? "You'd be amazed at what fear and hate can do. It's happened in Earth's history." She could feel her anger escalating and took a deep breath to garner some kind of control. Awan and Takoda were not the enemy. They were simply ignorant. "The third option is the Kindred of Eden take over a hatchoc and keep everyone else out so they can live in peace. My guess is this would be exactly what they would prefer."

Both men stared at her incredulously.

"What?" She held her palms out facing up. "It happened on Earth to our Native Americans, and only halted after someone with brains realized it was wrong to commit genocide."

Takoda's eyes widened. "Your bells."

Her bells? "What are you talking about?"

He moved to one of the paintings on the wall in Lyka's artist corner and pointed.

Despite her anger, she followed to get a closer look. When she first viewed the painting, she assumed it was another part of Tolban history, but now as she studied it, it was clear this scene went back to when the Crius took the Tolbans from North America.

Takoda's finger lay just beneath a symbol on a tree trunk. "This is the same design as the bells on your door at the Pleasure Dome compound."

He was right. It was the same exact design. Next to the trunk was a stand with a prone Native American beneath which was a white patch. Could it be snow. Was the symbol important to the dead? "That must mean that the Crius actually saved your people because almost all of them were wiped out on Earth."

She viewed the painting in a new context. Now the men lurking in the bottom corner made sense. She moved to get a closer look. She'd assumed they were more Native Americans, but now that she realized the import of the scene, she clearly made out their European dress and if she wasn't mistaken, it wasn't a weird tree next to them but a musket.

She turned to face the men. "There are no Crius here to save your people this time. First, it's Kindred of Eden. Next it might be Kindred of Air. Who knows where it will end, but I can guarantee you this, it won't end well."

Takoda's blue gaze and lowered brow proved he was beginning to see what she was trying to say.

Awan rubbed his chin. "But we are not humans. We are Edenists. We have evolved."

For some reason, his answer irritated her. "Obviously, you haven't evolved that much."

Takoda came to stand next to her. "I think what Ro is trying to say is that we need to reserve our judgment right now. I think we should gather more information."

That was part of it. Maybe she was jumping to conclusions. "Yes, you definitely need more information, like who was this cheetan that came to see you, Awan, and does he have a problem with Kindred of Eden for some reason?"

He shook his head. "I do not believe that Moorg has had any negative interactions with Kindred of Eden."

She scowled at him. "But do you know that for a fact? "

"It's probably best that I see what I can discover on that." Takoda grimaced and glanced at Awan. "Moorg is already aware that you know what he's thinking."

Awan nodded. "True. I could instead simply visit the dome you spoke of and see what discoveries they are working on."

Feeling somewhat vindicated, her energy left. "I'll let you two continue this conversation without me. I'm going to bed." She headed for Lyka's room.

"Rowena."

She turned to see what Awan wanted.

"Are you not going to sleep in our bed?"

Wow, she'd completely forgotten. What did that say about how well she was adjusting? Of course, that was when she'd thought she'd be adjusting on Earth. "I need some time alone."

Despite the hurt look in his amber gaze, her gut was telling her being with them was not the right thing for any of them right now. "Good night." She looked at Takoda. "I'll see you tomorrow."

Turning back toward Lyka's room, she strode inside, turned on the eyllen lamp and shut the door. Her heart ached at how much she cared for them, but her brain wouldn't stop spinning. Quickly, she washed up in the bathroom she shared with Takoda and closed the curtain she'd erected over the door.

Relationships were no easier on Eden than they were on Earth. In fact, with two men, it made it doubly complicated, and with the bond, it made it permanent. She changed into a big t-shirt and climbed into bed.

Was it her? Was it only because she carried the baggage of Earth's history that she jumped to foregone conclusions? She had to be open to the possibility that she was way off. Edenists *were* far more civilized than humans even if they had hardly any technology. Tolba was the perfect example of how they all worked for the common good. So where did that leave the individual?

Obviously, for individuals like herself, who had successful careers and a life on Earth, they were left with only two choices, stay with her men on Eden or leave them and enjoy her career.

She rolled over onto her back. She couldn't accept either of those choices. There had to be some kind of compromise. At first, making this work had been about not relegating Awan and Takoda to a life of unhappiness. But now...now her heart was involved far more than she'd realized. They each spoke to a part of who she was and with them she felt complete, cared for, possibly even loved. Everything her mother had hoped for her.

But her mother had also expected her to enjoy her own career. That had been her plan. Succeed in the career and then find a man to enjoy life with. If she stayed on Eden, she'd have to give up a ten-year career that she'd worked hard for. What would she do in Tolba, sit by the pool and drink ambrosia all day? Then enjoy a dinner prepared for her and two men making love to her?

There were women who'd kill to have that kind of life. What the hell was wrong with her? Maybe she was genetically predisposed to work. No, not to work, to succeed in life. It was the challenge and the success of overcoming it that fulfilled her. Why couldn't she have both?

She needed to think of this crossroads as another challenge to be overcome and conquer it like Awan met his Muskwa challenges. Staring at the ceiling, she let her mind wander to the final stanza in the poem Lyka had painted. So far it had spoken to her experience. Maybe there was wisdom to be found in Dickinson's words:

Into this Port, if I might come,
Rebecca, to Jerusalem,
 Would not so ravished turn—
Nor Persian, baffled at her shrine
    Lift such a Crucifixial sign
To her imperial Sun.

Now she was stumped. Was Tolba her port and did it mean she shouldn't turn back to Earth or because she had been thoroughly ravished more than once, she should return to Earth? She wasn't Persian, more Welsh, but she was definitely baffled. What sign was she lifting and who was her sun? Helios? Her mother?

And why was she trying to find an answer in a poem written over a hundred years ago? This was stupid.

Rolling onto her side, she turned off the eyllen light and closed her eyes. Better to get a good night's rest. She'd talk it over with Cali tomorrow. At least her friend knew where she was coming from.

Chapter Fifteen

Awan closed the door as the young discoverist left his office, an excited jaunt in his step. If only he could feel the same way.

Moving to the table, he picked up the empty glass and brought it into the meal area to wash it. It bothered him that Rowena didn't come out of her room before he'd left. He'd waited for her as long as he could.

Takoda told him what she'd said about laboring on Earth and coming home afterward. He didn't like the idea at all. They'd discussed finding Rowena labor in Tolba, but that would be difficult.

Since his particular Kindred of Mind ability was so helpful to the Discoverist Complex, he'd met this morning with the Kindred of Heart that oversaw all the needs for the discoverists, but that meeting had ended in disappointment. The man's arguments against having Rowena become a resource had been valid, though he'd found ways around them, even offering to share his space with her, but to no avail.

In just the past few days, he'd felt two cravings from Rowena about her labors on Earth. Her labor was as important to her as his and Takoda's was to them. But women in Tolba didn't labor.

They were to be treasured, protected, and pleased. What pleased Rowena was to labor. It was just another reason why he loved her.

He stilled, the half dry glass in his hand.

He loved Rowena. His chest warmed with peace at the thought. Yes, he loved her. He wasn't surprised. It was another element of proof that they were meant to be. Finishing the glass, he put it away.

If his love was to be reciprocated, he had to accomplish two things. He had to find Rowena labor that would make her happy and discover if anything untoward was happening in the red bell section of the complex.

With confidence in his purpose, he strode from his office and down the complex until he reached the place where they had first encountered Micco. There were five large domes and a number of smaller ones. Takoda had said the late-night light had come from a larger one, so he entered the first one he came to.

Inside were a variety of plant boxes on different sized platforms hanging on the sides of the dome, each one the length and width of the average man. The colors growing from them ranged from white to deep purple with everything in between. Some of the plants he recognized, but others he'd never seen before. Looking up, he found the entire peak of the dome was open to the sky, or it could be a window. It was hard to tell from where he stood.

He walked to the closest box, where a Kindred of Eden pinched off an orange leaf and bit it before running his tongue along his teeth.

"I've never seen that before."

The Edenist grinned. "This is a jotte. One of the cheetans

brought it back from Alantice for us. We are trying to determine if we can grow it here."

"Is it a food?" The plant itself was a big round ball with the orange leaves layered on top of each other.

The Edenist shook his head. "Not exactly. It is flavoring for food. It makes your mouth feel hot inside."

He wasn't sure he would be having much of that if they did figure out how to grow it. "It looks like you are having some success with it."

The Edenist nodded. "We are. Not all plants from the other cities do well. It depends a lot on the conditions." He pointed. "There we have plants from Naralina that are doing very well. We did have a couple specimens from Kif, but that was years ago. Unfortunately, none of them lasted."

"I imagine that can be disappointing."

After the Edenist went on to explain more specifics, Awan finally got to his purpose. "Can you tell me if Micco labors in here?"

The man shook his head. "No. He's working with animals. That's the dome behind this one."

Awan thanked him and left, pleased with what he'd learned. Since most of the discoverists came to him for scenarios, he didn't visit many of the domes. He'd have to rectify that. He had a feeling Rowena would enjoy hearing about them or even visiting with him.

Finding the building where Micco was supposed to be, he entered. It was set up much like the one he'd just left, with various landing levels, but he didn't see any animals, and there was a distinct difference between this dome and the last. The moment he walked in, every Edenist turned to look at him, and there were no smiles of welcome to be seen.

His instincts told him to tread carefully here, and the back of his head started to pound where he'd been hit the night before.

A Kindred of Eden started to approach but was pulled back by Micco. The man walked with authority, obviously overseeing the labors here. "You are one of Ro's yenea."

Not exactly a welcome, but not confrontational either. He tried to keep his mind open as Rowena wished. "Yes, I am Awan. You are Micco."

The man nodded. "Did Moorg send you?"

Instantly, two pieces of information clicked into place. Moorg had asked him if Tolba could function without Kindred of Eden and here was Micco, very defensively, thinking that same cheetan had sent him. That told Awan there was at least one cheetan who must want this Kindred gone. "Moorg? Why would he send me here?"

Micco waved his question away. "No matter. What is it you wish to know?"

Many questions came to mind. What were they doing working late at night? Where were the animals they were supposedly researching? What exactly were they trying to discover? But that's not what came out. "Why did you not bond with Rowena?"

Two emotions crossed Micco's face so quickly, Awan would have missed them if he had blinked. The first was deep regret. The second was relief. Was Micco relieved the question wasn't about his work?

"Sist and I were not ready yet. We knew she planned to leave soon. We were discussing it when you made our decision irrelevant." The final word came out with a clear accusation.

It was considered the ultimate insult to take another's chosen one. Had he and Takoda done to Micco and Sist what Davos had done to them? It did not sit well with him. "You had made her your chosen one then?" She hadn't said anything…as far as he could remember.

Micco stared at him a moment before finally speaking. "No. We did not." The defeat in the man's countenance made his regret clear.

This time it was Awan who was relieved. "We would not have intentionally taken another's chosen one."

Micco shrugged. "I guess it was meant to be." There was anger in his voice.

He hoped Micco would see the truth in the words despite his inclination to fight against it. "I have faith in that."

Laughter was the last response he expected, but that was what he received.

"Did you hear that?" Micco turned and addressed the others still watching them. "He has faith it was meant to be."

A low murmur echoed throughout the dome and even what sounded very close to a groan. Awan's protective instincts rose. Just like with Moorg, something wasn't right. It had to be the discoveries they were focused on. "Are your labors here not to move Tolba forward?"

Micco turned back to him, immediately alert. "Of course. Our work with animal genes will definitely move Tolba." His smirk didn't make sense. "If you wish, I can have one of our discoverists go into specific detail for you." He jerked his head to the side. "But I don't think that's really why you came."

How much did the man know? Did he know that Takoda saw them working into the night or was he guessing? "You are correct.

Since I rarely come to see what is happening in the complex because people usually come to me, I thought I'd start visiting each dome, maybe even bring Rowena with me. Why is it that you have never come to use my abilities? Every other discoverist dome has sent someone to me at least once?"

"I didn't need your ability." He lifted his arm to encompass all the men in the dome. "We are confident in our path."

He scanned the levels and saw most men nodding. "I see." He returned his gaze back to Micco. "I hope your confidence brings your labors here to fruition."

Micco grinned. "Oh, it will. That I can promise."

More perplexed than when he came, he determined there was nothing else he could learn. "Then I will leave you to your labor. I look forward to hearing about your outcomes."

"It will be very soon." Micco's smile remained in place, but there was more meaning to his words.

Not able to figure out what he was missing, Awan simply nodded, then strode back to the door. He'd just opened it, when Micco spoke.

"Awan. Please tell Rowena I am sorry."

He glanced over his shoulder and nodded, the regret on Micco's face one of the few easy to read emotions he'd witnessed during their entire conversation. Closing the door behind him, he strode back toward his office.

There was far more going on in Micco's discoverist dome than simply discovery, but what it was remained a mystery. What was clear to him was that they didn't want anyone to know and that in itself portended ill. But was it toward Tolbans in general or his own yenea in particular? Either way, he felt his balance tilting and there was only one person who could bring him back to his equilibrium.

Without another thought, he passed by his office and strode toward the exit. He informed the Edenist stationed there that he would be gone for the rest of the day. Once in the main pathway, he moved quickly through the throng, only one thought in his mind.

Rowena.

Rowena studied the picture in the book called *Animals of Eden*. It reminded her a little of the creature she'd seen last night as Takoda and she drifted closer to the Discoverist dome. It was close, but not exact. Of course, she only had the split-second sighting of it. The one she saw appeared to be a pretty orange. It appeared to be a monkey with wings.

A monkey with wings? Maybe she was channeling her last viewing of the *Wizard of Oz*. Monkeys didn't have wings. Even the picture she studied looked more like a lion with wings, closer to the mythical griffin on Earth.

Taking another sip of her kafez, she gazed out the back windows at the beach pool she'd designed. It had to be her best design yet. Then again, she'd had a lot to work with, just like her home in Boston.

She missed her work. Lying around relaxing all day wasn't her thing. She had to convince Awan and Takoda to simply portal her into work and portal her out. Any special arrangements with travel would have to be accommodated. It was that simple.

Only it wasn't because they were sure to balk. On one hand, she was confident of their feelings for her now, especially after the other night on the wall with Takoda. He'd been the one she was least sure of.

Yes, she was still adjusting to living with them, but she had to admit that coming home to them every night held a lot of appeal. And if they wanted this to work, they had to bend. She definitely had.

Then what would she do with her beautiful home? She could rent it out or sell it, but that seemed so final. Something was still holding her back from making the total commitment. If she could put her finger on it, she might be able to figure it all out before she went back to work.

Taking another sip of her kafez, she set the cup on the coffee table and crossed her legs up under her. Her purple leggings clashed with her red tunic, but she didn't care. She was comfortable. She turned the page and perused the drawings of animals. Nothing matched what she'd seen. Maybe she needed to go back to the first half of the book, on the prehistoric animals.

She'd just flipped to the beginning of the book when the crystals outside the front door chimed. Setting the book down, she rose. It couldn't be Cali because she wasn't coming until tomorrow.

Moving to a front window, she checked to see who it was. "Sist?" Quickly, she walked to the door an opened it. "Sist, what are you doing here?"

"I need to talk to you." His usually smiling face was serious and he glanced behind him as if to make sure no one noticed him. It was so much like what Micco had done at the Discoverist Complex. She opened the door wide. "Of course. Come in."

He glanced behind him one more time then stepped inside and closed the door.

His behavior caused her stomach to tense. This was no social call. She backed up to allow him to come further inside, but he stayed directly behind the sturdy wooden door. "Sist, what is it? Is someone after you?"

"No, not me. I came because of Micco."

The memory of how Micco looked the last time she saw him caused her heart to start beating rapidly. "What about Micco?"

He reached for her hands like he used to, but quickly pulled them back. "He won't forgive himself for failing to make you our beloved. He's being irrational. He's not seeing things as he needs to."

She wouldn't have believed Sist if she hadn't seen the look on Micco's face when he visited her the day she went to Awan's Muskwa training. "What can I do to help? I may be bonded, but you two are still my friends."

Some of the tension left Sist's face. "I too wish events had occurred differently, but I am grateful for your friendship."

By the way he said it, she felt as if she was the only friend they had. "You can count on me. What can I do?"

"Can you tell him that you are happy in your new yenea? Make him understand that what you have now fulfills you. I think if he understood that you have what you always wanted, he will be able to see more clearly."

Even as he said the words, she recognized them as the truth. She *was* happy and she *did* have all she'd ever wanted. "Of course, I can. When should I go see him?"

"Today. It has to be today. At his dome in the Discoverist Complex."

At his anxious tone, she took a step back. "Why today?"

He lowered his voice. "Micco is on the list to be exiled tonight."

"What?" Her moral compass rebelled at the thought. "Why? What did he do?"

For the first time since she'd met him, Sist sneered. "What did he do? He was born Kindred of Eden. That is his crime."

She felt as if someone had punched her in the stomach. Nausea threatened, but she took a deep breath. "But he's a discoverist. They're supposed to be revered."

He sighed. "That may have protected him, but since we lost you, he feels he has nothing left to lose. He's been very vocal in his opposition to Kindred of Eden being exiled."

Guilt crept into her conscience. "Is there any way to stop it?"

"No." Sist shook his head. "But before he is exiled, he needs to know you are happy or I'm afraid he won't survive beyond these walls." He waved his hand up high.

Holy crap! Micco out in that dark jungle for no reason whatsoever. It wasn't right. Tears stung her eyes. "Of course, I'll come. I can come right now."

"No." He glanced toward the front windows. "It's best you not be seen with me by either the patrols or your beloved."

She understood. This had to be killing him. Sist was Kindred of Heart and his heart had to be breaking right now. "I promise. I will go see Micco before Helios sets."

"Thank you." He started to smile then grabbed her arm. "You can't tell anyone that we know Micco is being exiled. It could endanger the Edenist who informed us of this."

"Not even my beloved?" She didn't like the idea of lying to them.

"Especially not them." His worry was etched into his furrowed brow.

She didn't like it, but she understood. She could simply leave in another hour after Sist left and before either Awan or Takoda came home. "You have my word. I will leave shortly."

He let go of her arm. "Thank you. Remember, you must come before night as that is when they plan to take him away."

She nodded, her throat suddenly unwilling to open to allow words to come out.

He gave her a sorrowful smile. "You are a very special woman, Rowena Lewis."

She blinked as tears filled her eyes. By the time she could see clearly again, Sist had slipped out the door.

Wiping her eyes with the back of her hand, she strode into her bedroom. She'd need shoes and a different top. No need to draw attention to herself. Grabbing a deep purple tunic that matched her leggings, she changed. She took down her bun and pulled her hair back in a simple ponytail. Then she walked into the bathroom to wash her face. No need to look like she'd been crying when she arrived there.

She'd just finished her ablutions when the sound of the front door opening caught her attention. Her first instinct was it was an intruder, so she quietly moved toward her open doorway.

"Rowena. Rowena where are you?"

At the sound of Awan's voice, which seemed a little panicked itself, she stepped out into the main room. "I'm right here. What's wrong?"

Awan stood in the middle of the room, his eyes wide, until he saw her. Immediately his neck muscles relaxed and he smiled warmly. "Nothing is wrong. I just needed to see you to regain my balance."

She sauntered toward him and smirked. "What, you don't want to dig another hole?"

He laughed as he put his arms around her. "I don't think there's room in our back courtyard for another hole."

She winked. "You could always dig a hole beneath our home and then we could have a basement."

His brow furrowed. "I am not familiar with a basement."

She patted his cheek. "It's not important. What is important is why you felt so off balance that you came home in the middle of the day to see me. That's not like you."

His arms released from around her as he moved toward the kitchen. "It is because I believe something is happening that is not good for Tolba, but I'm not sure what."

She crossed her arms over her chest. "That doesn't seem like enough to throw you off balance."

He looked up from pulling a container out of the refrigerator. "It is what most plays with my balance — not knowing."

She walked over and pulled out a stool to sit at the island. "Did you run the scenarios?"

He handed her a cup of ambrosia. "No. I didn't. I was so unsettled that I came home as fast as I could to see you."

Seriously, how did she get so lucky? "And do you feel better now."

He nodded before taking a couple gulps from his own cup. "I do."

"Good. Then you can run the scenarios. What was it that bothered you?"

He returned the container to the fridge. "I went to two of the discoverist domes led by Kindred of Eden." He quirked his mouth up on one side. "The discoverists usually come see me, so I have yet to see their discovery projects in person. I was thinking you would like to come with me to see what is new."

Though she was thrilled that he wanted her to tag along, suspicion filled her. "Why did you go to the Kindred of Eden ones? No wait, I know. You wanted to figure out what was going on last night in the dome with the lights on late."

Awan nodded. "Yes, that is correct. It is a very unusual occurrence. I decided to start there."

Her whole body tensed. "And what did you find there?"

"My first stop was a dome filled with a variety of plants. One of the men came to me and explained what they were doing. He seemed pleased I had shown an interest. They have plants from other Eden cities and are attempting to grow them here for additional food sources."

She forced herself to take another sip of her drink despite her stress level intensifying. "Why do I think there is a 'but' coming?"

"Because you are an intelligent woman." He paused as if looking for the right words. "But when I walked into Micco's dome, it was completely different. Everyone immediately stopped working to stare at me, and they weren't wearing smiles of welcome. Then Micco came forward and asked if Moorg had sent me."

"Did he?" She couldn't keep the accusatory tone from her voice.

"No. I have not seen him since he came to see me." Awan rubbed his chin. "But it was an odd question."

She couldn't wait for him to continue. "So did you ask him if he'd been working late last night?"

"No." He looked down at his cup. "I wanted to know if he had made you his chosen one."

In an instant, her guilt disappeared. If Micco and Sist had made her their chosen one, basically their fiancé, then she would never have slept with Awan and Takoda. But they hadn't even done that. She'd forgotten about that step in the process on Eden, probably because she missed it completely with her current yenea.

In Eden, the men made their woman a *chosen one* whether she agreed or not. Then they wooed her and asked her to become their beloved. Micco and Sist and done neither. "No, they didn't."

His gaze came up to meet hers. "That is what he said."

There was relief in his eyes, proving that he too had worried about how they'd come together. She needed to be sure Takoda suffered from no such guilt as well. "So in other words, you didn't find anything wrong."

"No, but there is something wrong there. I felt it here." Awan put his hand on his well-defined abdominals.

"And that's what threw you off balance? You didn't see or hear anything wrong, but your gut told you there was?" She could understand that.

Awan nodded.

"Then run the scenarios for the Kindred of Eden working in Micco's discoverist dome." She smiled at him.

"I will." He was looking at her when he said it, but then his eyes went yellow and she cringed at the sight. It was very weird.

Finally, his eyes returned to their amber color, but he didn't smile or even nod.

"What did you find?"

"I found…" his voice trailed off as he focused on the back windows.

"Awan?" Obviously from his faraway look, it wasn't joyous news. Knowing that Micco was being exiled didn't help her slowly churning stomach.

He finally faced her again. "Of eleven scenarios, there are eleven completely different possibilities. That is rare. Of all the possibilities, not one is good for Tolba."

Well, hell, now she was anxious to see Micco. Maybe he would tell her what was up. "You can share those with me, right?"

"Why? You are safe. Takoda is safe. You have no need to worry."

He had to be kidding. "Wait a minute. Just because you two aren't Kindred of Eden, doesn't mean I turn a blind eye to their plight or to my friends."

Awan's brow furrowed. "I understand how you feel. When Lyka was taken away to be exiled, I wanted to do something to stop it, but it was meant to be. Now, his life is filled with love. So too are we meant to be."

He couldn't be that steeped in such a fatalistic belief. He couldn't. She hopped off the stool and walked around the island to take both of his large hands in her. "Awan, I understand how much you believe this, but what is happening is wrong. It is *not* meant to be. I told you last night what some of the outcomes could be. None of them were good for those people. Can't you see that?"

"You are wrong." He shook his head and spoke with absolute certainty. "There is a plan that we cannot see yet. The Kindred of Eden and Tolba will be where they are meant to be."

She dropped his hands. "Those who refuse to learn from history are bound to repeat it. That is a saying on Earth."

He lifted his head a notch, a stubborn pose if she'd ever seen one. "We are of Eden and are more evolved. We are not meant to travel down the same path your species did. That is why we are here."

Irritation morphed into anger. "You're here because the Crius saved your people from extinction. You have a responsibility to live up to their faith in your worthiness."

"Me?" He was truly perplexed.

"Yes, you. You and all the people of Tolba."

He shook his head. "You misinterpret our history. We are here because we thrived here and we will continue to. You must have faith that all will be as it should."

She threw up her hands. "Well, I don't have that faith. I come from a people who make their own decisions, and when faced with adversity, we don't lie down and let it come, but stand up and fight it, conquer it, to make their world a better place. You can do this here."

Awan sighed as if trying to argue with a child. "It is not our way."

She barely kept herself from growling. "So you want me to give up a career I love, that I worked my whole life to attain, to live here with you in a city where the people won't stand up to injustice?"

His neck stiffened at that. "You are our beloved. You belong with us, no matter what happens in our city."

Oh, hell, no. "Are you saying you refuse to do anything to help the Kindred of Eden?"

"I will not."

She stormed away but spun back when she got halfway across the room. "And you expect me to accept that about you and live here happily?" Her voice rose a full octave at the end of her statement, her disbelief so complete.

He held out one hand, palm up. "It is who I am. At least I love you."

At least he what? A feeling of warmth started to melt her heart when her brain took over. "What do you mean at least *you* love me?"

Awan's gaze wouldn't meet hers. "Is my love not enough?"

Realization dawned. "You're saying Takoda doesn't love me. Am I right? Is that what you're saying?" She couldn't keep the squeak from her voice. How could Awan know?

"I can only speak for myself."

"Oh no. No, you don't. You just spoke for Takoda."

He shook his head. "Only Takoda can speak for Takoda."

She fisted her hands, beyond frustrated, angry, and hurting. "Then take me to see him right now. We need to have this settled before I decide if I'm returning to Earth in a few days."

Awan strode toward her but she put up her hands. "Don't."

"But you can't return to Earth. You are our beloved."

The hurt in his eyes almost undermined her anger, but she held onto it. This was too important. "Take me to Takoda. Now."

He stared at her as if expecting her to back down, but she wasn't backing down. Finally, he nodded and opened his arm toward the door.

She strode past him, swallowing the bile in her throat as her stomach churned upon itself. It wasn't just her anger causing her upset.

The pain of learning Takoda still didn't love her after all they'd shared had her almost sick. And that the man behind her, who loved her so thoroughly, refused to stand up for what was right made her question how she could love him so much.

Awan took her hand and they headed out the door. She almost told him to stop, not wanting to know the truth, but she clamped her teeth together. She refused to end up like Cali had, living in her own world of make believe until it was too late.

She was a Lewis. All the women in her family for generations had faced discrimination and prejudice to fight for what they wanted. If she aspired to having all that they had plus men who loved her, she had to do this.

She had to find out now.

Chapter Sixteen

Takoda lowered the toleric blocks next to where the men were building the bottom level of a residence. Looking down the row of partially completed buildings, he couldn't help but think about what Ro had said. Was sectioning off a hatchoc just for Kindred of Eden really where they were headed? It was so foreign to their community that it was almost impossible to imagine. Every baby boy born could have any of the Kindred birth marks. Would the cheetans take babies from their mothers? He shook his head. They'd never do that to a woman.

Yet as he stared at the row of soon-to-be residences, he couldn't help imaging this hatchoc being sealed off from the rest of Tolba. The vision reminded him of a story he'd once heard as a child of the end of a humanoid race. It had just been a story, but he hadn't been able to sleep that night.

"Takoda."

At the sound of Awan's voice, he spun around. The brother of his heart stood there looking hopeless and next to him was Ro. Something was wrong. "Awan, Ro. What is it?"

"I asked Awan to bring me here to talk to you." She looked

around to see many people watching them. "Is there somewhere we can talk?"

"Yes. I can bring us all to the top of the wall."

"No."

At Awan's refusal, he raised his brow. "No?"

"This is between you and Rowena. I will return home and await you both there." His gazed moved to Ro and remained on her.

What had happened? "Very well. Come." He took Ro's hand, but it felt cold even though it was warm and Helios hadn't set yet. As he floated them up to the top of the wall, Awan turned to walk back home, his shoulders slumped.

Finding a spot in the middle, he lowered them gently and turned to her. "What is it? What happened between you?"

She let go of his hand and took a few steps back, her gaze everywhere but on him.

His whole body went on alert, but he didn't speak.

Finally, she met his eyes, her green gaze so intense, he had to force himself not to look away. "Awan says you don't love me."

His breath left his lungs and refused to return.

"Is this true?"

He forced himself to breathe in so he could answer her. "I care for you very much."

She didn't look away. "But you don't love me."

"I told you. I cannot love you or anyone else."

Her head titled. "Because you still love Xavia?"

He couldn't seem to get himself to answer.

"How long were you all together? Longer than us?" She pointed to her chest.

"No. Xavia was with us for two days before Lyka was exiled. Why? Does it matter?"

"Two days?" Her incredulity was obvious. "Only two days. And in that time, you can…care for her more than all the time we've had together?"

Why did her question cause him guilt? He loved Xavia with his entire being. "You need to understand, we watched her through the portal for three years. We knew everything about her. Then we visited her many times on Earth before we explained where we were from and invited her to Eden. That is how a chosen one is chosen."

"I see." Tears welled in her eyes.

He moved forward to comfort her, but she stepped back. "Ro, I was honest with you after our first night."

"And were you honest with me the other night on the wall when you told me how you couldn't imagine your life without me? Or was that just pillow talk?"

Her anger was tangible as was her hurt, and he wanted more than anything to hold her. "I don't know pillow talk. I only know that you make our lives complete in a way I never expected."

Her hands fisted at her sides. "Really? That's a great way to encourage me to stay here and give up all I worked for on Earth. Why should I give that up for a man who doesn't love me and one who thinks injustice is meant to be? Not exactly a winning combination to trump a rewarding career on a planet where my efforts are valued."

He was confused. "You *are* valued. What are you talking about? Do you mean what's happening with the Kindred of Eden? I agree with you. We need to do something about it. I promise, I will. I don't want Tolba to be a repeat of Earth."

Her shoulders dropped as if what he'd said was disappointing. Again, he moved toward her to take her in his arms, but she stepped back again.

"Don't. I don't want your comfort. I've lived alone my whole life. I've made important decisions with none but my own counsel. I need to make this one alone too."

He dropped his arms as a chill raced up his back. "What decision?"

She straightened her shoulders and glared at him. "I have a job, labors that fulfill me waiting for me back on Earth. But neither of you seem to be open to the idea of me continuing that while being a part of this yenea. That means I now have to make a choice. Go back to Earth, to a position I love where I feel like a productive member of society and live in a home I designed to enjoy forever. Or stay here with a fatalistic man who loves me and one who shares my views but can't."

His entire body suddenly felt like he stood at the pole of the planet. He struggled to keep breathing, his heart racing and his breath shallow. The view of her life as she envisioned it became suddenly as clear as solidified air and his part of it was not enticing.

She didn't look at him as if she was already back on Earth, weighing her options to herself. "Some women would say I'm asking for too much. Maybe I am, but it's what I deserve. I gave up a lot to spend an entire three Earth months to find the men meant to be with me. My first pair disappeared before I woke up. The second pair never made me their chosen one, even though I was open to it. And now the third pair can't get on the same page for me."

She chuckled a bit hysterically. "You know what they say, three strikes and you're out."

Panic started to fill him. "But we are bonded. That is unbreakable."

For the first time since he brought her on the wall, she softened. "I know. I hate that if I return to Earth, none of us will ever have another love. Though you never wanted one anyway. But I never meant for that to happen." She held her arms out wide. "I never meant for any of this to happen." Her shoulders sagged in defeat. "Maybe what I wanted wasn't meant to be."

Now his panic intensified with hurt. She would reject them. Not only would it bring him pain but Awan would be heartbroken once again. There would never be love in their lives.

He grabbed onto his left shoulder. Why couldn't he love her like she wished? What was wrong with him?

"Please take me back to the Pleasure Dome."

His entire body rebelled at the thought. "But you belong with us."

"I'm not sure of that anymore."

His heart pounded at her words. She had been sure at some point and they had destroyed it. No cheetans were to blame this time. "Let us—"

"No. I need to think. I have to be alone, truly alone." She gave him an intense stare. "Will you take me there?"

There was more to her words than simply a question. She was asking him to respect her. If only he could explain how much he did respect her. But she didn't want words from him unless they were the ones he couldn't say truthfully. Instead, he nodded.

Letting go of his shoulder, he held out his hand.

She walked forward and took it.

Without another word, he floated them off the wall and

beyond the new hatchoc. As they passed their home, his chest hurt. He silently waited for her to change her mind, but she didn't say a word. She didn't even squeeze his hand as they floated by.

They should be returning to Awan, not over the hill to another hatchoc. Yet he did as she wished. He had no choice.

He slowly descended into the courtyard before her door.

As soon as her feet touched the ground, she let go. "I will let you know my decision. I only have a few days before I must return to my labors if that is my decision."

He didn't want to leave her. Reaching for anything to say, he grasped his first thought. "Awan will want to talk to you."

"No. I've realized something very important. You and he must remain true to who you are. I cannot make Awan care about those being exiled any more than I can make you love me. What I must decide now is if who you are is who I want to share my life with."

She laid her hand on his arm. "And you should decide between you if I'm really the one you want to share your life with. I know I am no prize in the relationship category, but this is who I am." She dropped her hand. "Go. Tell Awan what I said. I promise, if I go back to Earth, I will ask you and Awan to open the portal and no others."

If. She said *if*. That tiny spark of hope is what he would cling to. What he would beg Bendis for tonight and Helios for in the morning – for his beloved to stay. He nodded once. "I will tell Awan."

"Thank you." She turned away from him and walked into her residence.

He watched as the door closed, no last look from her beautiful green eyes.

By the Crius, what was wrong with him! Furious, he levitated quickly into the sky and back the way he'd come. He would do what she suggested. He would talk to Awan and they *would* find some way to convince her to stay.

She'd become very important to them, to him. He was truthful when he told her he couldn't see his life without her. If only he's met her first.

Awan would know what to do for them. He could run the scenarios. The portal between them all wasn't closed yet.

He descended quickly, landing with a thud on the hard packed dirt in the back courtyard.

He stared in shock, his heart thudding like it would leave his chest. "Scrat, Awan! What are you doing?"

Awan looked up from the hole beneath their residence, his eyes wild. "She wants a basement."

∼◦Q◦∼

Ro opened her eyes. She must have fallen asleep after giving in to her tears. It certainly hadn't helped. Now she just felt tired and her eyes gritty. Getting up from her couch, she walked into her bathroom and washed her face.

Washing her face three times in one day had to be a record. She froze and moved the cloth away.

Son of a bitch! There was barely any light coming in the window. Micco!

Frantic now, she dropped the cloth and ran out of her home. Entering the Pleasure Dome, she found a few men had already wandered in. Ignoring them, she strode up to the Lead Protector and requested an escort.

Though he didn't say anything, she could tell he was surprised to see her. Right now, she didn't care. She needed to see Micco.

And what? Tell him that you're happy? Well, hell. She'd never been good at lying, but this could mean the difference between life and death for him. She'd just have to suck it up.

In no time, a Protector came and they headed out. She recognized the glow in the sky now that she'd seen the full beauty of an Eden sunset. Her heart squeezed at the memory, but she pushed it away. One problem at a time.

Next would be the dark purple which would turn to black. She hoped the hatchoc patrol would be late. She needed time to convince Micco she was happily bonded.

As they strode up the hill, she forced herself to think of all the great qualities Awan and Takoda possessed. Awan's thoughtfulness, strength, love, and Takoda's support, sensitivity, and interest in her ideas did make her life happy. She would focus on all that when she talked to Micco.

Once in the Discoverist Complex, she led the way. At Awan's door she stopped. "This is where my beloved works. He can take me home." She opened the door and stepped into the empty office.

After waiting thirty seconds, she cracked the door open. The protector was gone. Without a second thought, she strode toward the red bell section, anxious now that the reds in the sky had given way to purple.

Finally, she made it to the place where she'd met Micco on her first visit. He'd said he worked in the dome behind the one in front of her. There were no lights on in this one. Was she too late?

Running around the large building, she slowed to a fast walk as light streamed from the windows of the next dome. Hopefully

Micco was still there. Opening the door, she stepped inside and stopped.

What the hell? It was as if the book she'd been reading on the animals of Eden had come to life. Or at least the first half of the book. On every hanging platform inside the dome was a prehistoric animal.

When the large dragon across from her on the ground level caught sight of her, her throat closed. She reached behind her for the door, but a paw clamped down on her hand.

She looked up into the black eyes of an awasaw. She found her voice then and screamed. The furry striped grizzly changed before her eyes, losing its fur and morphing into an Edenist with grey eyes and a serious scowl.

He turned his face upward. "Micco. We have a problem."

She followed the man's gaze toward the ceiling in time to see a giant bird take off from the top platform. As it navigated its way down between the other animals, she recognized it as a zander. Even as the bird began to morph, her brain put the puzzle pieces together. "Micco," she breathed, stunned.

He strode forward. "Ro, what are you doing here?"

His worried expression confused her. "I came to see you. Sist told me you were blaming yourself for not making me your chosen one. I wanted you to know that it's okay. I'm very happy with my yenea."

"Yes, at the Dickinson Complex you said it was meant to be."

She did say that, didn't she? "I know, but you looked so dejected. I wanted to come and tell you that I'm very happy with Awan and Takoda." Her words rang true in her heart. The question was, could she remain happy with them?

Micco nodded to the Edenist who was an awasaw and the man stepped away. "Thank you for telling me this. Sist told you I am on the list for exile, didn't he?"

She nodded. "He did. You are lucky to have him."

"Yes, he is." At the sound of Sist's voice, she spun around.

"Sist. Sorry, I didn't see you. I was a bit preoccupied with all these fascinating animals." She turned back to Micco. "This has been your work. Edenists who can shift into prehistoric animals. Why did you hide it from me? I think it's wonderful." She glanced at the dragon. "As long as they don't eat anyone." She smiled tentatively.

Micco's brows drew together. "I didn't want you to know because it is not safe to know. We are hunted like the very animals we are."

"Hunted?" Did Tolba have some dark hidden sport she didn't know about?

Sist stepped up beside Micco. "What he means is that Kindred of Eden are being tagged for exile, but the reason they are being exiled goes back to another shifter, the first shifter."

Holy crap. "You mean Davos, the dirgon."

"Yes." Micco nodded. "Davos didn't do anything wrong, but his ability and size caused fear in others. That's when they started exiling us for no reason."

She glanced behind him again. Some of the Edenists had shifted into men again, but others remained in animal form. They were very unique, but yes, scary looking animals. "Are you saying if the cheetans knew there were so many of you, they would exile everyone?"

"Yes." Micco gave her a sad smile. "I always knew you were intelligent."

If he knew she was intelligent, why didn't he tell her about his shifting Kindred? "How long are you going to hide everyone? Eventually, someone will figure it out."

Micco looked at Sist. Again, there was that silent communication between them. Finally, Sist responded. "Just until tonight."

She cocked her head. "Why tonight?"

"Because tonight neither Bendis nor Selene will light the sky." Sist smiled. "The dirgon can come in the night and lead us all to our new residence. A place where Kindred of Eden are welcome."

Now she understood. "You are going to another city. That makes sense."

Micco shook his head. "No. We cannot risk other Kindred being afraid of our ability. We go with the dirgon to the sanctuary he built for all of us."

"Then I'm happy you will have a safe place to live."

"It will be more than a safe place." The awasaw joined the conversation. "We will still have our Crius chips so we can bring our chosen ones to Eden." He opened his arm to the dome as if to encompass all the men there. "We will finally be able to live free as we were meant to be."

Meant to be. She kept hearing that Tolban phrase. It was almost like brainwashing. Would Awan agree that all these Kindred of Eden were meant to leave Tolba? "Is this all of you then? Will you all be free tonight?"

Micco's brows lowered. "Not all. There are more, but they still have faith that the cheetans can be swayed to live side by side with them." He frowned. "I do not."

She could see his dejection, but also anger. She understood. "I can—"

"Micco, they come!"

She looked up at a man standing on the top platform Micco had vacated. The darkness in the window above him told the real tale. The hatchoc patrol was right on time.

"We must leave. Now." Sist motioned to the room.

Filoz of two, three, four, and even five, started to open their portals. Set by set stepped through and disappeared.

There were still four more including Sist and Micco when the door behind her opened and three men strode in.

Micco grabbed her arm and pulled her back with him.

"We are here for Micco." The lead Edenist pointed at Micco. Another one with the Kindred of Mind birthmark started to raise his hand only to stop as his mouth dropped open.

She started to turn when large claws wrapped around her and she found herself flying upward. She grabbed hold of the massive bird's leg as her stomach somersaulted with the speed she was lifted. She tried to keep from throwing up as the zander flew through the now open roof. The last thing she saw below was the shifters disappearing through their portals with Sist.

The wind against her face was strong as the bird flapped its giant wings, taking her far higher than Takoda ever did. She much preferred levitating to this. As Micco flew past the Tolban walls, her heart revolted. She couldn't be in the jungle. She needed to go back.

In no time, they were descending again, on the wrong side of the wall from Awan and Takoda. Panic and fear set in with the realization that her men were nowhere near and had no idea where she was.

Surprisingly, Micco gently set her down before landing nearby.

She bent over and promptly vomited, her stomach having had all the upheaval it could handle for one day.

Micco set his hand on her back and she stepped away, wiping her mouth with the edge of her tunic, all that she had, happy at least her hair was tied away from her face. "You need to open a portal so I can go back to my beloveds." She scanned the dark jungle, remembering the single lawbreaker she'd seen while with Takoda. She shivered. "Now."

It was a very dark night. It made it difficult to see his face, but his voice was adamant. "We cannot."

She froze, unable to think for a minute. "You cannot? What do you mean you cannot?" Her voice was rising as fear edged in. "Of course you can. Just stand next to Sist and open a portal to my home and I'll walk through it. Done deal."

He stepped closer and the regret on his face became clear. "Why did you come tonight of all nights?"

"Why?" She scanned the men gathered there, most having shifted back into their bestial form, probably for protection. "Because Sist asked me to."

Even in the dark she could see his eyes widen. "Sist?" He turned toward the men. "Sist!" The word was loud and came out like a hiss.

Footsteps approached and Sist joined them. "Yes?"

"Why did you ask Ro to come to our dome tonight?"

The man shook his head. "I did not ask her to come tonight. I asked her to come during the day."

"Ro, is this true?"

What the hell was going on here? "Yes, but I was delayed. I knew it was getting dark, but I didn't want you to beat yourself up over losing me when you were being exiled."

"Beat myself up?"

That did sound strange when she thought about it. "It means that you wouldn't forgive yourself and mope around, I mean be sorrowful for a very long time which might affect your ability to survive out here. I wanted you to know that it was okay because I was happy with my yenea."

Micco turned toward Sist. "Why didn't you tell me?"

"You had too many to worry about."

Feeling completely confused and not a little nervous, she stepped closer. "What's going on here?"

Micco returned his attention to her and sighed. "It was Sist who needed to know if you were happy, not me."

She looked at Sist. "Then why didn't you ask me at my residence? I would have told you I was happy."

"Because I didn't want you to know how much it hurt me that you didn't wait for us to choose you."

She should have known Sist would be more affected by what happened. He was Kindred of Heart after all. One of the Kindreds she'd thought she wanted. "I'm sorry. I didn't know you felt so much for me. I was planning to leave and I knew you both were aware of that, yet you didn't make me your chosen one."

"I know." Sist's shoulders fell.

She resisted the urge to give him a hug. He was still much bigger than she was and it wouldn't be right since she was married on this planet.

Micco laid a hand on Sist' shoulder, but spoke to her. "That was my decision. I wasn't sure you'd be willing to live outside the Tolban walls with us."

That he'd been planning this for so long and hadn't even

hinted at it to her further solidified her impression that bonding with him and Sist would not have been good for her. She needed men who kept her in the loop and were truthful, like Awan and Takoda.

"You were right. I would not have wanted to live out here." She gestured to the pitch-black wall at the end of the clearing. "Though I am happy that you will have a safe place to live out here, I wish to go back to my home in Tolba now."

Micco shook his head. "We cannot allow you to return. You have seen what we are. You know there are others like us. We cannot allow that information to reach the cheetans' ears and put the rest of our Kindred in danger. It would even effect those who cannot shift."

True panic climbed into her heart. "But I'm bonded. You can't take me away from my beloveds."

"I'm sorry." Micco turned away and strode to the men waiting for his next commands.

She looked to Sist, who avoided eye contact and followed the brother of his heart.

Standing there, her gaze flitted to the darkness of the jungle before she quickly turned away and gauged the wall towering far above her. Beyond it, the stars glittered against the night, mocking her with their bright happiness.

She just wanted to be back in Awan and Takoda's home. She didn't even want to go back to Earth any more. With her back literally against a wall, her heart far outweighed her mind. What she needed were Awan and Takoda, not her career. Is this what her mom had felt before she'd passed?

Tears trickled down her cheeks. She wiped them away as she

looked up at the stars. *Awan. Takoda. I really, really need you right now.*

Suddenly, a large black mass moved overhead, blocking out the starlight.

Chapter Seventeen

Awan jerked to a halt, his feet finding the bottom of the cold pool. "Rowena."

"She's not here." Takoda took another gulp of Tolban ale and set the empty glass on the table.

Taking the two steps to the side, Awan pulled himself out. "I know. But she's craving us."

"What?" Takoda's head snapped around. "What do you mean?"

He grabbed the cloth he'd set on the chair, hope filling his chest. "It's the bond."

Takoda rose unsteadily. "Are you sure? She was very specific in her instructions to us."

"I am. We need to go to her right now." He started past Takoda when his arm was grabbed.

"Wait. You have to be sure. When I left her at the Pleasure Dome, she made it clear that *she* would contact us."

He shook off Takoda. "She just did. I know what I felt. It was a strong craving." He reflected on the sensation, a vision of the stars filling his head and a need so deep it was…desperate. "She needs us. We go now."

His own anxiety must have broken through Takoda's stupor because immediately they floated into the sky and were heading across the city. The craving had not been a pleasurable feeling like the rest they'd shared. This one scared him.

Landing a little hard on the ground before Rowena's dome, Awan didn't hesitate. He strode forward and without ringing the bells and opened the door. "Rowena, we are here."

Silence greeted them. Unwilling to accept the obvious, he strode into the sleeping room and washing room, but there was no one. He came back out and pinned Takoda with his gaze. "Where is she?"

Takoda's brow furrowed. "I left her here. She is supposed to be here."

"Cali." Without another word, Awan left the dome and headed for the Lead Protector to find out where Cali's dome was.

They entered the Pleasure Dome and wound their way through the throng of men and women there.

"Awan! Takoda!"

He turned his head to find Cali standing on a longseat waving. Immediately, he changed direction.

"Hey, what are you doing here." Cali tried to look behind them. "Where's Ro?"

His heart sank at the question.

Takoda stepped around him. "That's what we wanted to ask you. Have you seen her today?"

Cali frowned. "No. I was planning to see her tomorrow." Her face changed and she lowered her eyebrows. "Did you lose her?"

The accusation in her voice mirrored the own in his heart. "Takoda brought her to her dome here earlier today, but she is not there now."

"That's not like Ro. She doesn't generally go out at night. At least she's smart enough to take a protector. Let's ask."

As much as Awan wanted to push everyone aside to get to the dais at the end of the room, he made his way through the throng carefully. Cali followed with Takoda behind her. By time he made it there, he had no patience left. "Did Rowena leave with a protector today?"

The man scowled at him and opened his mouth but shut it as Cali stepped up. "Please, we can't find her. Do you know where she went?"

The man's face softened. "Yes. She took a protector to the Discoverist Complex, but she didn't return with him. She said she'd leave with her beloved who labors there."

Awan's heart filled with dread. Why would Rowena lie?

"She went to see Micco." Takoda's words squeezed his chest.

"Why?" The word came out on a breath.

"That's what we're going to find out." Takoda stalked toward the exit.

"Hey, what about me?" Cali tugged on his arm.

"When we find her, we'll bring her back to our residence. You can wait for us there."

"Right. Got it." She turned back into the crowd, obviously looking for someone.

He quickly headed for the exit, anxious to confront Micco again. Emerging onto the empty pathway, he found Takoda had disappeared. Then he started to rise and he looked up. Though few were out, levitating would definitely be the fastest way to get there.

Once he was as high as the brother of his heart, they sailed over to the center hill and the Discoverist Complex. Takoda floated them directly to Micco's dome which remained lit. Without stopping, he lowered them through the wide opening at the top.

As they descended, they inspected every platform. By time they landed on the ground, it was clear the dome had been abandoned.

Awan didn't like it. "They left quickly."

"Yes, but where is Ro?" Takoda started to pace, his agitation making his movements jerky. "I cannot lose another woman I love. We have to find her."

Awan stared at the brother of his heart. "You love Rowena?"

Takoda stopped pacing and for a brief moment, his face relaxed before panic filled his eyes. "I do." His eyes filled with unshed tears. "I did not understand my feelings for her until just now when faced with the prospect of having lost her."

His own heart filled with rightness. "What about Xavia?"

Takoda scowled. "I was wrong. Quickly. Run the scenarios."

Awan focused inward on Rowena and where she might be. As the scenes played out in his mind, he froze with dread.

Takoda's voice came through. "What is it? What did you see?"

He let his eyes adjust. "Every scenario is completely different, but there are three that have her in danger."

"Where?" Takoda's eyes narrowed. "We must go to her, now."

The fear in Takoda's voice mirrored his own. "The Cheetans Complex, the new hatchoc, or beyond the walls of Tolba."

Takoda's head jerked. "She's outside Tolba!"

His heart started to pound. "Landisbaum, how do you know?"

"I know, here." Takoda put his hand over his chest. "It is the bond."

Even as they began to float upward again, Awan couldn't

accept that their beloved was beyond the safety of Tolba. "You said you felt no bond with her."

Takoda faced him. "I didn't until now."

"But why now?" He didn't want it to be true that their beloved was in the jungle without them.

"I think it is because I finally admitted I love her. I didn't think I could, but I was wrong. That I might never see her again has forced me to acknowledge the truth. I love Ro with everything I am."

A strange peace settled over him as if he was back in balance because all was as it should be, but it wasn't. Still, his fear for Rowena abated. "And so as she knows when you are near, you know where she is?"

"I do. She's just outside the walls on the western side."

Takoda started to move them in that direction. "Tell, me Awan." Takoda's voice was soft. "Is this meant to be? Should we leave Ro where she is so as not to disrupt some larger plan?"

Pain sliced through his chest at the question. There was no doubt in his mind even as his long-held belief cracked and crumbled. "No. We find our beloved and bring her home. We are bound by Eden. She is *meant* to be with us."

"I agree." Takoda clapped him on the back and sped them toward the west wall.

Awan reached for the balance he knew Rowena would bring, so he could think clearly. "If you set us on the wall, we can portal there."

"No. I want Ro to know I am near and all will be well."

At Takoda's words, the feeling behind Rowena's craving for him and Takoda resurfaced. "Yes. I believe she is scared. She is calling for us."

No sooner were the words out than Takoda moved them

quickly over the edge of Tolba and beyond, but he stopped at the sight below them. Rowena stood against the wall, a great black beast facing her.

At that moment she looked up and Awan felt her craving again. "She needs us. Put us down between her and—"

His air left his body as he was grabbed up in massive claws.

"Awan!"

Takoda's shout jerked him into action. He started to peel the giant claws away from his body. The loud screech above him didn't deter him. As the giant bird flew close to the jungle canopy, it let him go.

With no light to guide him, he grabbed for anything to stop his fall. His hand grasped a tree branch and his momentum spun him around it. He let go and grabbed again, his hand closing around a vine. This time he held on as it swung him around and into another branch.

For a moment the air was knocked from him once again, but he held on, grasping the vine with both hands and sliding lower. This time when he swung back, he didn't hit anything. As soon as the vine slowed a bit more, he lowered himself to the ground.

Looking through the dense foliage, he turned, not sure of where he was. Then light appeared and penetrated the jungle. Quietly, he crept forward.

"Micco!" Ro screamed as the zander lifted Awan high into the air. She had no idea how he and Takoda knew she was there, but her relief at sensing Takoda turned to anger in an instant at Micco. If he hurt one hair on Awan's head, she would make him regret it, zander or not.

As Takoda came closer, men around the dirgon shifted. Holy crap. But just as fear edged its way back, the beasts were lifted and thrown on top of one another.

Yes! Score one for Takoda. She reached her arm up and pointed, hoping he'd simply levitate her, but he was preoccupied by a wall of water headed for him. Where had that come from? She scanned the men nearby. One of the other men of the shifter's filoz was holding his hand up. She was about to run for him when one of the beasts, the flying monkey, took flight. "Takoda!"

He glanced down, forgetting about the water and got soaked as he descended quickly to the ground behind her.

"Stop!"

At the loud voice coming from the dirgon, she whipped her gaze around to face the giant wolf. Though she'd seen him land and thought he was about to eat her, she'd stood her ground, refusing to believe an Edenist would harm a woman, dirgon or not.

"Everyone return to your natural form."

She studied the dirgon. His mouth didn't even move. Suddenly, on top of his head, a man appeared who wasn't there a moment ago. Whoever he was, all the shifters listened, except the dirgon.

Just as she started to relax, a growl came from the beast. "Who is the woman?" The very deep voice reverberated through them all. Now *that* was the dirgon speaking.

Takoda wrapped his arm around her waist. "This is Ro, our beloved."

"Takoda?" The man on the beast stared. "Give me some light."

Out of nowhere, a light appeared above them like a tiny star.

She scanned the men standing around and saw a man lowering his hand.

Takoda whispered in her ear as he pointed to the man on top of the beast. "That's Lyka."

Her heart skipped. She rested her hand on his about her waist. "Are you okay?"

He didn't have a chance to answer because a woman appeared next to Lyka.

Ro's heart sunk. It had to be Xavia and she was stunning. Long dark hair framed her face, eyes tilted up at the corners giving her an exotic look, and her body was perfect. No wonder Takoda could never get over her.

She felt like an ugly Amazon next to a woman who could have been a top model in New York. Hell, in Milan or wherever the top models lived.

"Takoda, it is you?" Xavia started to move forward as if she would come down and greet him, but Lyka grabbed her arm. "Where is Awan?"

Takoda pointed at Micco, who now stood next to the dirgon. "Wherever he dropped him." The accusatory tone was clear to everyone.

She gasped, the thought of Awan lying broken on the ground somewhere caused her panic to rise again. They *had* to find hm.

"I didn't drop him." Micco looked directly at her. "I couldn't hold him. He wiggled his way out of my grasp. I made it to the jungle before he slipped out."

"Enough." The single word came from the beast.

Enough? She couldn't let that pass. "No, it isn't enough. Awan is in the dark jungle, probably injured or worse. He has to be found."

Takoda gave her a squeeze. "We will find him. He is alive or I would know it."

His words were so confident, she was able to swallow her panic, but she still couldn't help imagining Awan gravely hurt.

Lyka moved back to the neck of the beast and taking Xavia on his back, climbed down a rope that hung there, probably for that very reason. As soon as he touched the ground, the dirgon began to shift.

She wasn't the only one to watch in wonder. It was even more remarkable than when the awasaw shifted because the dirgon was bigger and more interesting. The wide leathery wings folded in first and then the long dinosaur like tail shortened before the head and body reconfigured into a man with long black hair and ice-cold blue eyes.

A very large and unhappy man by the scowl on his face.

He strode forward until he was directly in front of them. "You are not a lawbreaker and not a Kindred of Eden or part of the filoz here. Why are you here?"

Xavia joined him. "This is Takoda, from Lyka's old filoz. Takoda, this is Davos."

Despite feeling like the ugly duckling, Ro did notice that Xavia did not claim Takoda. Not that it mattered since the woman already had his heart.

Takoda's body filled with tension next to her. "I came for my beloved."

Something in the way Davos' eyes narrowed pissed her off. It was as if he didn't believe Takoda. She pointed at Micco, still angry at him for repaying her kindness with a kidnapping. "That's right. Because that man abducted me."

Davos turned his angry gaze on Micco. "Is this true?"

Micco strode toward them. "I had no choice. She now knows about our shifters. If anyone discovers this truth, those still in Tolba will be hunted down and exiled, just like you."

From the bristling of Davos, Micco had gone too far.

Davos' voice lowered to a deeper octave, proving he was pissed. "I will not take anyone with us who does not wish to go."

She thought for sure that Micco would back down.

Instead, he stepped up to Davos as if he could stare the taller man down. "I cannot endanger the shifters still within the walls."

A strange rumbling sound came from Davos.

"Excuse me." Xavia pushed her way between the two men and faced Micco. "Why not simply ask her not to tell anyone?" Xavia looked at Takoda. "And why not ask Takoda and Awan not to tell anyone?" She returned her gaze to Micco. "Do you think my former filoz untrustworthy?"

Oh, the woman had guts. As much as Ro didn't want to like Xavia, she was impressed.

"I do not know your former filoz." Micco remained stubborn.

Getting frustrated with him, Ro couldn't keep silent any longer. "Micco, don't be an ass." She stepped away from Takoda, but he captured her hand. "I'm happy to keep your secret and I'm sure Takoda and Awan will too, just as soon as we find out where you dropped him." She scowled at him. "He could be bleeding to death right now and all you care about are your own Kindred. How do you expect others to care about yours when you don't care about others?"

"I—"

Warming to her subject, she interrupted. "As it turns out, you aren't the only one who cares about your Kindred. My yenea lost Lyka here and were so distraught they drank so much they couldn't remember what they'd done. Takoda and I have been discussing what we can do to stop this ridiculous exiling that is not only hurting Kindred of Eden but their filoz and Tolba as a whole."

Micco held his hands out. "I didn't know."

"You also probably don't know that Moorg has been asking about what would happen to Tolba if there were no Kindred of Eden at all. He's obviously hoping that Tolba could do fine without any of you there." She hooked her thumb over her shoulder toward the looming wall.

At her pronouncement, Davos stepped forward. "What is this?"

Takoda spun her around behind him so fast, she felt dizzy, but he kept his feet planted. "It is true. The brother of my heart had a visit from Moorg personally, but Awan didn't volunteer to run the scenarios."

Davos' brow wrinkled in confusion. "Scenarios?"

"Yes." At the sound of Awan's voice, Ro stepped beside Takoda to find Awan.

He walked out of the darkness and into the circle of light. His abdominals were scratched and bleeding and a long gash swiped diagonally across them.

"Awan!" She started to run toward him, but Takoda didn't let go of her hand. She scowled at him. He only shook his head, so she faced forward again.

Awan strode toward them, weaving between the Kindred of Eden men and their filoz. He had no limp and despite his bloody torso, he appeared as strong and intimidating as he always did.

When he finally stopped next to Davos, it was obvious he was about an inch taller than the man. For some reason, she was proud of him for that, probably due to some prehistoric gene passed down to her from a cavewoman ancestor.

He stared Davos in the eye. "I am Kindred of Mind and my ability allows me to see eleven possible futures according to Eden. I did not run the scenarios for Moorg, but I just ran them for us." He looked at her. "You were right."

Her heart thudded in her chest as he turned his head back to face Davos. "All scenarios except one have all Kindred of Eden being exiled. My ability allows me to share what I have seen. Do you wish to see?"

For the first time since she'd seen the dirgon hovering in the sky above her, she sensed a shift in him. She couldn't put her finger on it, but she'd swear he was unsure.

Xavia stepped next to him and held onto his arm. "We need to know."

Davos studied Awan as if not sure he could trust him then gave the smallest of nods.

She had no doubt that Awan's eyes changed to the eerie yellow when he laid his hand on Davos' arm. When Davos' eyes widened it was clear he'd been given the same knowledge Awan had.

Without another word, Awan turned his back on Davos and strode directly to her and opened his arms. She welcomed his embrace, gently holding him, her relief that he wasn't on death's door causing her eyes to fill with tears.

He lifted her chin from his chest. "You were right. This is *not* meant to be."

His admission made her cry even harder. She knew how much

it took for him to give up on his belief, but he had…and he'd done it for her. He lowered his head and kissed her, his love and faith in her filling her up until she thought she'd burst with happiness.

His lips left hers just as Takoda walked by them.

Awan let go of her, but kept one arm around her as he turned them to face the now pensive Davos.

"We can help." Takoda spoke to Davos though he glanced at Micco. "For those facing exile, we can give them safe haven."

Micco raised his brow in interest.

Davos shook his head. "I already do that."

Lyka joined the conversation as he strode to join his yenea. "Yes, but only after the Crius chips have been removed. What if, like with these men, we were able to help others leave who wished to do so before that occurs?"

She suddenly realized how lucky Davos was that Xavia had left Tolba with Lyka. If she hadn't, they wouldn't be mated. Neither Davos or Lyka had Crius chips to portal to Earth to find a woman. She was beginning to see how critical the situation was for the whole Kindred now. "You would have to know who was slated for exile." She faced Micco. "Like you did. How did you know?"

He moved his gaze from her to Davos, who once again gave that short nod. Micco addressed her. "There is a man laboring with the cheetans who communicates with us."

Awan walked forward with her and they were soon discussing the logistics of keeping people safe until Davos returned. It was agreed that her yenea would hide those who were due to be exiled. After Awan ran the scenarios on whether they would be discovered at their residence and determined they wouldn't, she had to interrupt.

"But what if there are this many who need to be hidden until the next dark night?" She opened her arm to indicate the two dozen men standing with them.

Takoda, for the first time that night, smiled. "Oh, we will have plenty of room. Only Kindred of Eden need to be hidden. The rest of the filoz can wait for the appointed night."

He was being rather optimistic. "Yes, but we only have two extra rooms. What if there are six who need sanctuary?"

Takoda actually chuckled. "That will not be a problem. Ask Awan."

She looked up at him to find, even in the limited light, a blush making its way across his face. "Awan?"

He shrugged, clearly uncomfortable. "I dug you a basement."

A basement? When the memory surfaced of her explaining where he could dig if he became out of balance again, she grinned and put her hand over his heart. "Thank you for that."

The conversation continued until a plan was set and all that was left was to implement it.

Davos signaled for the light to be extinguished, and they were all left in the dark. It took a moment for her eyes to adjust, but she didn't mind as Awan's arm was still wrapped about her and Takoda held her hand.

When she was able to see, Lyka was standing in front of them. "I am happy for you." His words were clearly intended for his former filoz, but she felt included as well.

Takoda reached out his arm. "We are happy for you as well."

Lyka grasped arms with him then turned away to follow Davos, who waited to lead them all to his settlement he called Una.

Xavia said something to Davos then left him to approach

them. "Ro, I'm so pleased that you found these two. I can see you fill their hearts with joy. Know that I will always be grateful to you for that."

Not a little shocked, she didn't know what to say.

Takoda answered instead. "Be happy as well Xavia. Our love for Ro and hers for us is all we need."

Xavia smiled and with a friendly nod, turned to join her yenea.

Takoda tugged on her hand. "Come love. It is time to return."

Ro stared at him. "You said *our love* for me. I thought you said you couldn't love me."

He lowered his head, not meeting her gaze. "I was wrong." His head came up and he stared into her eyes. "I love you."

Thankful Awan's arm was around her to keep her knees from giving out, she pulled his head down and kissed him with all the love she felt. When she let go, she tightened her grip on both of them, so thankful she hadn't lost them. "Let's go home."

Takoda raised them off the ground and floated them up to the top of the wall of Tolba where he set them down. They all studied the dark jungle, looking for those forced to flee the city.

In her heart, she knew they felt the sadness too. "Awan, you said there was only one scenario where the Kindred of Eden wouldn't all be exiled. What was that?"

He shook his head. "It was very complicated, but know that the plans we made tonight are the first step in not only saving the Kindred of Eden, but the city of Tolba itself."

She smiled slyly. "And will you share all the steps with us?"

"Of course. I will also share with you how much I crave you being beneath me while Takoda is below you."

A vision of being sandwiched between the two men with both of them buried deep in her body flashed through her mind, igniting every sexual nerve ending at once. "I wholeheartedly agree with satisfying that craving."

Before she knew what they intended, she found herself levitating above the wall. She laughed. "I didn't mean immediately, but what the hell?" Throwing her arms wide, she welcomed the men of her heart and the start to a whole new life.

EPILOGUE

TAKODA WISHED TO HAVE THE last people leave, but those gathered in their rear courtyard made Ro happy. He'd had at least three of their visitors request her services. That, coupled with what his planner had requested would hopefully fill the missing piece in her life.

Though she tried to hide it, both he and Awan were aware she missed her labor. Awan had had three cravings from her in the last week even as she planned Cali's birth celebration.

Ro sauntered over to him in what she called a bathing suit. Though she went nude in their hot pool and cold pond when they were alone, she made it clear that when others were present, she would cover herself.

She laid her towel over the chair at the table where he stood. "Don't worry. Kenjada and Cali will be leaving soon."

He took her hand and pulled her to him. "Now how did you know that was what I was thinking?"

She chuckled. "Your feelings are written all over your face."

He touched his face but didn't feel anything on it.

She laughed. "It's an expression. I mean I could tell what you were thinking by your facial expression."

She had come to know him in many ways. He changed his expression as he thought of taking her on the table right there to see if she really could read his face.

"Takoda, stop that. We may not have the craving connection, but I can still tell what you're thinking and that will just have to wait until our last guests leave."

He grinned, very pleased with her answer. "I will hold you to that."

She pulled out of his embrace to watch the last people still in the cold pond.

Cali took that moment to jump from the top of the rock grotto, causing her protector, who stood under a tree, to tense. She came up laughing and swam to the side. Though she was obviously talking to Kuruk, Takoda couldn't hear her words over the splashes and conversations of the others. For that, he was grateful. The woman talked a lot.

"I just had an exciting conversation with Kenjada."

Ro's tone of voice made it clear to him that though she spoke casually, she was about to talk about something important. Another trait he'd come to understand. He took her hand to let her know she could tell him anything. "What did you discuss?"

"First, you'll be happy to know that two of the men in his filoz are willing to take turns patrolling the walls. I think we have the start of our Lawbreaker Watch."

Her thoughtfulness at supporting his concerns, filled his heart. "This is excellent. I trust Kenjada and his filoz."

She nodded. "I figured you would. I know we need to be very selective."

Her understanding of the situation was definitely a benefit

to them. "And what else did you find exciting in your talk with Kenjada?"

She turned back to face the cold pond. The man they spoke of ran and jumped into the deepest part of the pond, sending a wave of water over everyone. The laughter was loud, but Takoda stayed focused on Ro.

He squeezed her hand to let her know he still listened.

Finally, she faced him. "Kenjada would like me to design a very large cold pond for his yenea. There are six of them, so it would be a big project. I told him I'd be happy to. I've been feeling a bit lost and…"

He relaxed. "I know. Is this something you want to do? It is not exactly what your labors were on Earth."

Her green eyes sparkled with excitement, reminding him of yesterday afternoon as the three of them made love on the patrio. "I would love designing another outdoor area. It's a bit like starting over in a whole new career. It's a challenge, and I can learn so much. I'd like to redesign some space in the house so I can have an office. Do you think I should use Lyka's old room or yours? Of course, I'd leave the bed there in case we have guests." In other words, in case a Kindred of Eden needed sanctuary.

There was another place that might work better. "Instead, what if you used Lyka's artist corner. He always said it had the best light. Would that be enough space?"

Her eyes widened. "Are you sure you wouldn't mind?"

"No. It's time to change that area of the house." It was past time actually. Lyka was gone, but he was happy just as they were.

"Then I'd love to. Since we are bringing my small dresser from my brownstone, we can also bring my worktable from my home office. My aunt won't need it once she moves in. She's just happy to have a free place in town."

"We can transport whatever you need. You may want to make a list of items because three other guests have asked for your talent as well."

"Really?" She sounded breathless.

The anticipation of her reaction to the news he had made him smile. "Yes. I was going to wait to tell you after everyone left, but I talked to my planner. He was so impressed with your design for the common space of the new hatchoc, he has requested your labors in the design of the next four."

"Oh wow. I'd love to do that! I'd have to study up on common spaces a bit more." Her gaze drifted as she planned. "Maybe a quick trip to Earth to buy a few more books."

He chuckled. "You better obtain more than a few. My planner wants you to design the whole hatchoc."

Her mouth opened, but nothing came out as she stared at him.

He didn't want her to feel she had to do it. No woman *had* to labor in Tolba. "You don't have to, if you don't care to. You do what you want."

"Yes!" Her shout ended on a laugh as she hugged him hard then gave him a kiss that had his body taking notice. When she broke away, her eyes were shining with unshed tears. "I would love to." She cupped his neck. "Thank you." Her words were soft before she kissed him again, a tender, I-love-you type kiss.

By the Crius he was thankful she'd come into their lives! Not only did he have a new beloved but a friend growing as close to him as Awan.

"Hey you two, get a room." Cali's voice had them breaking a part as she strode toward them, still drying herself with her cloth.

Ro turned, but kept one arm around him. "Hey, if you want this, you'll have to find your own."

"Yeah, I know. I know." Cali waved off the comment before covering her whole head and drying her hair.

Kuruk, who had followed her, stopped to stand behind an empty chair not far away as he watched her.

"Are you thinking what I'm thinking?" Ro's whisper in his ear made it hard to focus on her words.

He glanced at her and her head jerked in Kuruk's direction. "I think there's feelings there."

As he confirmed what she noticed, his mood fell. It was acceptable for a protector to choose a meekwee for his own filoz as long as it was not the one he protected. If what Ro said was true, Kuruk could be looking at a cheetan punishment.

"I don't think she has a clue though." Ro said the words before smiling at Cali who threw back the towel and smiled back.

Her friend practically skipped toward them. "That is an awesome pool. When I find my filoz, I'm going to insist that they have you design one for us." The woman poured herself a cup of the ambrosia sitting on the table.

Though Ro laughed, Takoda could see Kuruk thinking. Would there be more need for his beloved's talent? At that thought, he squeezed her against him to get her attention. "Remember, here on Eden our labors stop when Helios goes to sleep." His tone may have come out a bit stern by the surprised look on her face.

She scowled, but then her face softened. "You're right. I will remember that. And of course, I will always be available for an afternoon delight like we had yesterday." She wiggled her brows.

Her words relieved him. "Good, because we plan on having those."

She gave him a sly grin. "Speaking of a three-way delight, where is Awan?"

Cali spurted out the ambrosia she'd just gulped. "Three-way? Who said we were talking about that? Watch your language among those of us with only one-ways." She winked at her joke.

Ro's petite friend did have an interesting way with words. "Awan went to the front. Our crystals rang."

Though Ro didn't lose her smile, he felt the tension through her hand. They had finished the 'basement' well before the celebration, but it wasn't ready for Kindred of Eden yet. If anyone had come for sanctuary today, they would be put in Lyka's room.

Cali turned to Kuruk. "Do you have crystals or bells on your door?"

As the man explained the difference, Awan walked out the backdoor and stopped at the edge of the patrio. He scanned the guests and when he found Kuruk near them, he strode straight to him. The two men spoke in low tones that none of them could hear.

Cali stepped closer to Ro. "What do you think that's all about?"

Ro shrugged. "I'm sure if you ask him, he'll tell you."

Cali looked uncertain. "Only if it's something about the city. He clams right up when I ask him about anything personal." She pouted. "All I know is he has a brother of his heart and lives in the same hatchoc as the Pleasure Dome complex."

"I know you know more than that." Ro tilted her head. "Like his favorite thing to do is his music, right?"

Cali brightened immediately. "True. Now that I think of it, there are a few things I know about him." She rolled her eyes. "The trick is not to ask him straight out. I have to get him talking about something else related."

Ro lifted her hand, palm upward. "There you go. You already have him figured out."

"Hardly." Cali opened her mouth to continue, but Awan and Kuruk approached.

From the look on Kuruk's face, Takoda knew something was wrong.

The man walked up to Cali. "I must leave now. Would you like to return to the Pleasure Dome complex with me, or would you prefer to stay? Awan has offered to escort you if you wish to stay."

Cali didn't hesitate for an instant. "I'll go back with you."

If he hadn't been watching, Takoda was sure he'd have missed the fleeting grateful look that Kuruk gave her. Now he understood what Ro meant about having one's thoughts written on their face.

"I'll walk you out." Ro hooked her arm with Cali and the three started for the door.

Awan stepped close and as soon as the door closed, he spoke. "It is not good."

Takoda waited, knowing Awan would tell him all.

"The man at our door was a healer. He'd just come from tending the brother of Kuruk's heart."

Takoda sympathized with the man. "What is wrong with him?"

"I do not know the specifics." Awan shook his head. "But the reason for his pain comes from being a Kindred of Eden."

Immediately, Takoda glanced toward the newly planted yeehaw tree and salis bushes that covered the week-old disturbance in the ground caused by the building of their basement.

Awan simply nodded at him. "We are putting Ro at risk."

Taking action was still new for the brother of his heart, so Takoda tamped down the disappointment Awan's comment provoked. "True, but it is better for us to be in danger together than to lose her."

"Your reasoning is sound."

"And don't forget that if—" he stopped as Kenjada approached, the rest of his filoz drying off by the cold pond. Takoda addressed Kenjada. "I understand you have requested a design done by our agapayto." He used the more formal word to be clear how important Ro and her time was to them.

The man grinned. "I have. We have not had so much enjoyment since we first became a filoz, and to have our beloved and little sister with us has made this a special day."

Awan clapped his friend on the shoulder. "I'm glad you have had a pleasant time. You and your filoz and Cali are always welcome at our home."

"And you all to ours as well." Kenjada looked over his shoulder where the rest of his yenea moved toward him. He turned back to them. "Is Cali feeling well? She left without letting us know."

Takoda barely kept himself from glancing at Awan. "Yes, she is fine. I believe it was Kuruk whose filoz requested his presence."

Kenjada's concern evaporated. "That is good to hear. We will leave you now as Helios is soon to make ready for bed. Thank you for making Cali's birth day special for her."

The backdoor closing caught their attention as Ro sauntered down the steps. She held out her hands. "Kenjada, thank you for coming."

The man took her hands and nodded. "You are a good friend to our Cali."

She smiled at all who now stood with him, including the woman who was their beloved. "And you are all a wonderful family to her."

As they finished their goodbyes, Ro led them into the residence.

Takoda's itch returned, but it was no longer because he wished to tell his beloved about her labor opportunities. This itch was to fulfill his promise to Ro. He pulled out the two chairs still left at the table and moved the empty pitcher.

"What are you doing?" Awan waved toward the chairs he'd just moved.

"I promised Ro that as soon as the last guest left, we would take her on this table."

Awan sucked in a breath and grinned.

Within moments Ro came running out the door. "Awan! I felt that."

Takoda laughed. That Awan could practically call their beloved to them with a simple craving reassured him that Ro laboring longer than she should would never happen.

He met Awan's smiling gaze and as one they walked forward and took her hands. When they all reached the table, Awan untied the ties at her hips while he untied the back of her top, lifting it over her head.

They dropped the strips of cloth on a chair and turned as one to enjoy the view of their beloved, their agapayto, their reason for breathing.

Awan leaned in. "She has made us whole."

Takoda responded. "She has made us love again."

Ro hopped up on the table, setting her pretty ass on it. "You know, I can hear you, right?"

Takoda nodded. "We know."

He and Awan stepped forward in unison. She cupped each of their cheeks. "Don't forget the most important part. We are bound, forever, as one."

The End

For updates, sneak peeks, and special prizes, sign up to receive the latest news from Lexi Post at
http://bit.ly/LexiUpdate

READ ON FOR A SNEAK peek of *Burning for Eden*...

BURNING FOR EDEN

Coming soon

Chapter One

RHYE, WHAT HAVE YOU DONE?

Kuruk's chest tightened with fear. He couldn't lose the brother of his heart as well. The entire right side of Rhye's body, including his face, was covered in jansen tree paste. The slight rise of his chest was the only indication he still lived.

Holding back the tears by willpower alone, Kuruk nodded to the healer who beckoned him from the archway. Reassuring himself that Rhye's breathing remained regular, he finally moved from the foot of the bed and left the sleeping room.

As soon as he was out of the room and in the living area, he rounded on the healer. "What the wabanak happened?" He kept his voice low but didn't hold back his anger.

The healer's gaze was sympathetic. "He's been burned on almost half his body. Most is superficial, but there are a few places that concern me." The man's brow furrowed. "I will know better how he will fair in a couple of days."

"A couple days?" Kuruk lowered his voice again, struggling to tamp down the anger and fear. Fear was his enemy. He'd learned that while still a boy. He needed to focus on the anger. He pointed to Rhye's sleeping room. "How did this happen?"

The healer shrugged his shoulders. "I do not know. There was an accident. I was called to the site and immediately had him brought through a portal to here. There were too many others about, and other healers tended those less injured." The man frowned again. "They were very loud in their pain, but your filoz member in there didn't utter a word, and he was by far the most harmed."

Rhye? Not utter a sound? That wasn't like him. Kuruk's gut tightened, making him feel ill. He crossed his arms over his chest to hide his own weakness. "If Rhye didn't say anything, that means he lost consciousness."

"No, he was awake, but he was focused on the others who were hurt. I have given him biwil for the pain and kerasi juice to help him sleep. He needs sleep so his body can heal. That is vitally important right now." The healer set a paper on the table next to the longseat and started for the door.

Panic swept over Kuruk. He strode after the man sweat coating his face. "Wait, where are you going?"

The man's brows rose. "I am going to my residence. I have not eaten yet and it is dark."

Eaten? Just the thought of food had bile rising in Kuruk's throat. "But what about Rhye? You have to stay here and care for him."

The healer gave him a sad smile. "There is nothing more I can do now until we see how much he will heal." The man paused and looked away, the unspoken words obvious. *If Rhye healed.* Finally, the healer continued, pointing to the living area. "I have left instructions for you. Keep him hydrated and continue the biwil and kerasi juice. For food, if he's hungry, though I doubt that will be the case, only give him liquids."

Instructions? Liquids? He tried to get his mind to focus past the knowledge that the healer was leaving.

"I will be back in two days. At that point, I should be able to address what are the most important needs." The healer glanced at Rhye's sleeping room, then as if accepting he'd done all he could, he opened the door.

"Wait." Kuruk stepped up, barely refraining from pulling the door from the man's hand. "What if he gets worse? Or if I have questions?"

The healer held up his forearm where the swirl of the Kindred of Mind birthmark was evident. "Just call me. Use these words: Healer Ebel, you are needed. And I will come. I left that on the instructions too."

"Healer Ebel, you are needed. Very well." That did give him some reassurance.

The healer laid his hand on Kuruk's shoulder. "There is no one better to care for the brother of your heart than you right now. Have faith."

He nodded, unable to say anything past the tightening of his throat. Rhye was all he had left.

The click of the door closing snapped him from his painful thoughts. Quiet filled their small residence. He made his way back to Rhye's sleeping room to check on him.

Nothing had changed. Rhye lay as he had been, his chest rising and falling in steady rhythm.

Returning to the living area, Kuruk looked around. Spotting

the paper the healer left, he sat on the longseat and picked it up, but he couldn't read it, the water in his eyes blurring out the words. Dropping it back on the table, he leaned back and stared at the domed ceiling.

The bustle of daily life continued just outside the thoroughfare door of their home, but all those sounds were muffled, and silence permeated every rounded corner of the residence. His own heartbeat reverberated through him, solidifying the fact that he was alone in this.

Rhye had been with him since he was old enough to remember. Through every good and bad event, they'd always upheld one another. They bolstered each other, drank together, talked and argued or sat silently supporting each other. But this silence wasn't support. This silence was stifling, reminding him that he had no one. No one to help him save Rhye.

Or was there? Did he dare?

Read on for a chapter of Beast of Eden.

Beast of Eden

Chapter One

What the hell had she done?

Xavia Jones glanced over her shoulder as the portal closed and revealed the vast, dense jungle outside the impenetrable walls of Tolba. The jungle didn't bother her, animals were her thing, but the large shadow that moved over them all did.

Looking up, she shaded her eyes, trying to see what it was.

What it was, was huge! It blocked the sun, making it impossible to distinguish its features. She was a hundred percent sure they didn't have anything like it on Earth. It looked like a flying brontosaurus, but with a wing span wider than a commercial airplane's and with a furry head the size of a tyrannosaurus rex skull.

While the scientist in her found it fascinating, the woman in her was more than a little afraid, and she crossed her arms over her stomach, wiping her sweaty palms on her shirt.

As the animal flew away, she faced forward. Unfortunately, she couldn't see anything but Lyka's broad back and the naked backs of more than a dozen other Edenists who had just been exiled from the walled-city. And now thanks to her impetuous nature when it came to prejudice, she found herself outside the safety of those walls, too. Not a good place to be after arriving just two days earlier on a new planet filled with naked hunks who held women in the highest esteem…in the city.

The men watched the beast and didn't see her, since even at five-feet ten-inches, she was far shorter and smaller than any Edenist. Quietly, she crouched, finding a view between the men where she could see the sky in front of them.

And then she wished she hadn't.

She stayed low as the giant flying animal circled one more time before finally landing fifty yards away in the dense jungle. The ground shook, and she lost her balance, falling on her jean-covered butt. "Ouch." She clapped a hand over her mouth, but she was too late. The feet in front of her turned.

"Xavia?" Lyka's surprise wasn't unexpected.

He turned forward, scanning the men in front of him before he crouched beside her and whispered. "What are you doing here? You shouldn't be out here. It is dangerous. You were supposed to stay with my filoz."

At the mention of their supposed filoz, her anger burned anew. She scowled. "Some filoz. If that's how they prove their loyalty, I'd rather be here with you."

Lyka's golden eyes softened before he frowned. "It is not safe."

That was an understatement. And if she hadn't let her anger get the better of her over the injustice of Lyka being exiled, she'd probably still be safely inside Tolba. But once again, she just couldn't stay quiet. On Earth, she'd lost more than one job over her inability to keep silent when prejudice reared its ugly head. She'd have thought she'd learned her lesson by now to at least bite her tongue.

Movement between the men's legs caught her attention. "I think we have company." She kept her voice low, not wanting the others to know she was there.

Lyka quickly blocked her view and rose, pulling her up behind him. He settled her hands on his waist as he used his chameleon ability to make her blend in with him. The first time he'd done that in Costa Rica when she was studying a particularly skittish rodent, she'd been afraid, but as she experienced the benefits of his unique talent, she'd appreciated it more and more.

Right now, she was more than a *little* grateful, despite how hard it was to ignore his sandalwood scent and his sinful nakedness. As a scientist from Earth, the closest thing to a "discoverist" on Eden, she found the rest of the naked Edenists in Tolba merely curious animals, but Lyka and his filoz were a different story altogether. They caused her the typical butterflies-in-the-belly reaction. Maybe, because as they'd said, she was their *chosen one*.

The sound of heavy footsteps had her peeking around Lyka's broad back. Damn!

Two Edenists approached the group, as naked as the rest, but the one striding purposefully toward them was stunning. He had straight black hair that disappeared behind his shoulders though the sides of his head were shaved. A significant growth of black stubble traveled from his sideburns down along his chin and over his top lip. His eyes seemed to shoot silver daggers, but it had to be the reflection of the sun. She could only assume the two must have ridden the huge monstrosity that had flown overhead.

As the Edenist approached, his stride didn't slow and the Tolba exiles parted until he halted before Lyka. She immediately pressed herself against Lyka's back, her fear far outweighing any desire she might feel at having Lyka's butt against her stomach.

"Where is she?" The very deep voice sent an unexpected shiver through her.

Lyka's body tensed. "Where is—Davos?"

The new Edenist didn't say anything for a long moment. "Lyka? I should have known that even a cheetan's son would be shown no mercy."

"I thought you were dead. We all did."

"I'm sure many wish I was." Again, there was silence.

Now that it was clear the two men knew each other, she relaxed a little, but still didn't dare take a look at Davos up close. She wasn't exactly known for her bravery and though Lyka could extend his camouflage onto another's skin, it didn't affect eyes.

Davos kept his voice low. "I must ask you again. Where is she? I hope she is behind you because if you sent her into the jungle, she won't make it past sunset."

"Why do you think there is a she?"

That was a very good question. She waited to hear the answer, but none came. Instead, after a few more seconds, a hand clamped down on her arm and pulled her forward.

Before she could even squeak, Lyka had grabbed her around the waist and held her against his chest, breaking Davos' grip.

She looked up into the coldest ice blue eyes she'd ever seen. Though she was still camouflaged, her eyes gave her away. Davos scowled, making him look even more ferocious. He must be one of the criminals of Tolba. Another shiver raced up her spine.

"She can't be here." The words were a low whisper.

Lyka spoke from behind her. "I know that, but she is."

That didn't help. Davos' jaw moved back and forth as if he were grinding his teeth to keep from yelling out his anger. A few tense seconds later he moved his gaze to Lyka. "Keep her hidden. And for Bendis sake, block her pheromones."

His last word came out in a hiss. Then as if he expected to be obeyed without question, he turned around and pushed seven men away from the group. The others watched him, but she didn't dare speak for fear they'd notice her. She looked up at Lyka over her shoulder in silent question, but he shook his head. Either he had no idea what was happening, or he did and didn't want to discuss it at the moment.

The other Edenist who had come with Davos, a man with short brown hair and a beard, inspected the seven men. She could see two were Kindred of Eden, but the others weren't. She assumed that those really *were* criminals.

The Edenists' punishment of exiling those who broke the law held merit, or she'd thought so until they decided Lyka was a lawbreaker, as they called them. Lyka wouldn't hurt a flea. Did they have fleas on Eden?

"Who are you? The welcoming committee?" One criminal laughed. "Any chance you have sweets and a Pleasure Dome nearby?"

"Janek, take them." Davos' command was sharp.

"Wait, what about them?" One of the seven separated Edenists, who was Kindred of Eden, pointed toward the group she was in. He was obviously concerned that he was being separated. She didn't blame him.

Davos strode up to the man, staring him down. "I will take care of them."

There wasn't another word as Janek led the seven men off into the jungle behind her.

Confused, she looked at Lyka again, but he was frowning. He probably didn't know what was going on either.

"Come. We have a long way to go before Selene rises." Then with a wave of his hand, Davos turned away and headed in the opposite direction of Janek, obviously anxious to travel before the white moon lit the jungle.

The Edenists looked at each other briefly then followed.

Lyka took her hand, keeping her concealed with his ability as he leaned in to whisper. "I must block your pheromones so the others do not realize you are here. When you grow tired, let me know and I'll carry you."

She swallowed hard. Lyka had told her about the Edenist ability to block women's pheromones back when she needed to get close to the African spiny mice. She was fine with that. It was what was unfolding that made her nervous. "Where are we going? Is it safe?"

He looked at the unscalable and door-less walls of Tolba before he scanned the surrounding open area. He brought his gaze back to her. "I don't know. But I do know that anything is better than staying here waiting for a wild animal or lawbreaker to attack. Or worse, starving to death."

She nodded, her throat too tight to speak.

He gave her half of his beautiful smile then he disappeared into the scenery, her only connection their clasped hands. As he started forward, she hurried along.

Maybe agreeing to come to Eden had been the wrong choice.

A woman? Holy Bendis! Had Lyka been touched by the pink moon? The jungle was no place for an Earth woman! He had his hands full with the ever-growing population in Una. Janek had made some modifications, but finding another place to live had become urgent.

Six more Kindred of Eden would fill them to capacity and that didn't take into account the woman. The urge to take to the skies made his hands twitch. It was the only place he could find peace, but it would have to wait.

He shook his head as his pace increased. A woman would cause chaos among the exiles. Even if she was a chosen one, she couldn't stay, but he couldn't leave her in the jungle. Why in Selene's name had Lyka brought her?

At the rate Tolba was exiling Eden Kindred, there couldn't be many left. He'd thought those in a filoz who had an Earth woman were safe. Obviously, the cheetans of Tolba had reached new heights of paranoia. Leaders should rule with their minds, not their fears.

"Where'd you go?" A male voice sounded from far behind him.

Davos spun around. Ithio! Yelling would get them killed. Without responding, he ran back through the bush. He found the group just as the Edenist was opening his mouth to yell again.

He clamped his hand over the man's mouth and hissed while dragging his thumb across his own chest. "Silence."

The man's startled eyes grew wide before his brows lowered and he pulled away. Obviously about to argue, he was suddenly pushed aside by what appeared to be nothing.

Lyka appeared, his chameleon ability fading as he faced the man. He spoke in a very low voice. "I suggest we follow Davos' directions until we are safe, unless one of you knows the jungle better than an exile of elevendy years."

"How do you know you can trust him?" The man who had yelled looked furtively at him before returning his attention to Lyka.

"Because he didn't kill us the moment he found us."

Davos scanned the men, who were clearly uneasy after that pronouncement. He didn't have time for this. "You have two choices. Either come with me or stay here."

He started to turn when he noticed Lyka looking down. Though the man was completely impossible to see while camouflaged, the woman's brown eyes were easy to find. The fear in them angered him further. He addressed Lyka. "*You* have no choice."

Lyka nodded, taking some of the irritation away, but not enough.

Davos started for Una again. He didn't care if they followed or not. They were just more responsibility added to what he already had. When would Tolba stop throwing out their Eden Kindred? Was there no one left in the city who spoke reason?

He trudged through the jungle, anxious to be home and let Kellic take over. Kellic was happy, welcoming, and sympathetic. All things he wasn't. Had he ever been?

Lyka took the opportunity of letting the other men pass him to help Xavia onto his back.

"Are you sure I'm not too heavy?" Her question, whispered in his ear, sent a shiver of desire racing to his groin, but he ignored it, her safety far more important.

He let his chameleon take over as he answered. "No. You are no heavier than a head puff."

"And I'm Albert Einstein."

He searched his memory for the name, but he hadn't been very attentive in school. However, it didn't take schooling to know she doubted his answer. Instead of responding and risking more conversation, he simply started after the others.

She wasn't heavy. What she was, was distracting. Her long black hair brushed his shoulder and arm. Her soft, lithe body, even clothed brought to mind her delicate face, which was what had caught his attention years ago when he first spotted her through the portal. She had slightly slanted, crystalline bronze eyes that reflected her intelligence, a slender nose and full lips that she rolled in when thinking or nervous. She brought out his protectiveness and a kindness he hadn't known he possessed.

But right now, it was his protective instincts that he needed to focus on and ignore the feel of her on his back. Determined to keep her safe, he caught up with the men ahead, quickly walking by them until he was directly behind Davos.

He had no idea what life had been like for his former childhood friend and neighbor, but obviously he'd survived. That alone told him that Davos was his and Xavia's best chance of staying safe. If she needed to be protected, there was no one better to do it than Davos. The fact that the man was angry that he had to protect her, hopefully meant he still believed in and maybe followed Dickinson Law.

Lyka hadn't seen his neighbor since he was exiled just before his fourteenth year. He'd liked Davos. They'd been in school together and had planned to go to the Pleasure Domes when they were old enough. He'd actually thought they might form a filoz.

Then Davos started going through his transition and Lyka barely saw him. The few times he had, the boy he'd known had changed.

Lyka had been irritated at first, and a slightly hurt, until his own transition started. Some men had it easy, but for him, where a physical change occurred, it was harder to master control. He could only imagine what Davos had gone through. And then suddenly his friend was gone, exiled.

His parents just said that Davos had broken the law and was a danger to those in Tolba. Then he was welcomed by Awan and Takoda, his filoz, and he'd let his hurt go, or so he thought. He hadn't realized he still was bothered by being dismissed until he saw Davos walking toward him.

The man in question started to slow. He glanced back, not seeing Lyka, but his gaze caught Xavia's before he stopped.

Lyka moved to the side, well aware that the men behind him couldn't see him or his chosen one and might walk into them. They gathered in front of Davos. They'd been walking for at least fourteen hours and they were clearly ready to rest. Many of them had abilities that could have aided their travels, but they had obviously thought better of using them until they knew where they were going.

He allowed himself to resume his natural appearance, keeping Xavia hidden, and waited for Davos.

"Why did we stop? Are we spending the night here?" An Edenist, who Lyka recognized from his own hatchoc in Tolba, spoke quietly.

Davos looked each of them in the eye before he spoke. "I am about to offer you a place you may call home as long as you want.

We call it Una. It is filled with others like us, banished from Tolba simply because we are Eden Kindred. This is a safe place. However, we have two rules that must be followed without question."

Davos waited, but no one spoke. He gave a short nod at their patience. "If you are ever away from Una and a lawbreaker finds you, you must never lead him back here."

The men looked at each other, digesting that information.

"The second rule is if you feel it is impossible to live in Una without fighting another Edenist, then you agree to leave."

The rules seemed made to keep everyone safe.

"What if we don't agree or don't follow the rules?"

Lyka tensed. Though it was a legitimate question, it wasn't really the best time to ask. Xavia's arms tightened around him, her understanding of the situation clear in that brief action.

Davos, surprisingly didn't single the man out. Instead, he looked at every one of them before answering. "If you do not agree, you may leave now."

All the men shook their heads.

"If you live in Una and do not follow the rules, you will be killed."

More than one man drew in his breath in an audible gasp. Death at the hands of another was abhorred in Tolba, considered the ultimate hubris to put one's self on a level with Mother Eden.

The reaction of others was mixed. Some were as surprised as he, but others looked doubtful and a couple seemed to take it as a challenge. Those last obviously knew nothing about Davos.

"Before we continue, I will ask each of you if you agree."

Lyka waited as each man swore he would abide by the rules. Davos finally came to him. "Do you swear upon Helios, Selene, Bendis and Mother Eden that you will obey the rules of Una?"

"I do."

Davos glanced over Lyka's shoulder, frowning once again at Xavia before resuming his place at the lead.

Xavia squeezed him around his neck, making it clear she needed to speak. He blended into the scenery and let everyone pass but didn't let them get too far ahead. If she needed reassurance after Davos' parting look, he could wait a moment and comfort her. "What is it?"

"What happened to that giant flying animal? I would think we all could have flown on its back instead of trudging through the jungle. Did Davos leave it behind? Did it fly home? Does he have control of it? What do you call it?"

Her words sent her breath past his ear, reminding him of how soft and delicate she was, and how her questions could anger the very man that promised them safety. "Tolbans call it the Beast. Now no more questions. I know you are curious, but we don't want our words to alert an animal of our presence. We are vulnerable right now."

"Sorry. I'll be quiet."

He didn't want her to feel she was wrong, but his primary task at the moment was keeping her safe. *If* safety could be assured in the jungle. He could address her feelings once that was assured. He moved faster to catch up with the group.

Davos continued on for another hour before the white light of Selene started to filter through the jungle vegetation. Finally, he slowed again, but he didn't stop. He simply walked out of the thick jungle into a clearing almost half the size of Tolba.

"Wow." Xavia's whispered wonderment matched Lyka's own.

Before them was a large dome as high as any Tolban wall, but it was entirely made of living trees, vines, and plants. There didn't appear to be any way to enter it.

"It looks like a wigwam of nuclear proportions." She kept her voice low so only he could hear.

So far, none of the men he traveled with yet realized she was with them. If any of them had been Kindred of Mind or Kindred of Heart, that wouldn't have been the case. Many in those kindred could read minds or feel emotions. As far as he was aware, since he had masked her pheromones, no Kindred of Eden should be able to sense Xavia without seeing or hearing her.

Since he was unfamiliar with the term wigwam, he simply squeezed her leg. To him it looked like a mountain of plants in the middle of an open field. They had small structures, about his height, inside Tolba, but they were for waste that would be used in the gardens. They even had stone Pleasure Domes, but nothing like this.

He appreciated the intelligence and Kindred ability it took to create a living dome for multiple men. He assumed by now that Davos did not survive by himself, which meant others resided inside.

"Do not stand in the open." Davos, who had continued to walk slowly toward the plant house, turned to see if they followed, but every one of them still stared in awe. "Rutting feroon and grendals are about, and we've encountered a boarox, so it is not safe to remain out here." He turned back around and continued toward his home.

A boarox? Boarox were animals of the colder climes, if he remembered his lessons correctly. They also ate anything that breathed, including Edenists. He was too stunned by that pronouncement to move, but the rest of his party quickly surged ahead.

"Lyka?" Xavia's whispered question jerked him into motion.

He had no doubt she'd want to know about every animal Davos mentioned. As a discoverist, her studies on Earth were focused on animals and their abilities to adapt over hundreds of years. She called it evolution. Her intense focus on her planet's nature was part of what had drawn him to her.

But right now, he just wanted to keep her alive. He scanned the jungle line surrounding the open area for danger. Inside the walls of Tolba, there was no reason to fear attack. It was a city of harmony,. All had their place in the prosperity of each other.

The only ones who left the city were some of the cheetans, and they used portals to travel to other cities. None of those who were exiled with him had ever experienced the jungle. What they knew of it was what they'd learned in school. Unfortunately, he hadn't retained much of that. Now they would have to adapt…like Xavia's animals.

The thought would have been humorous if the circumstances weren't so deadly. Xavia's arms tightening around his neck alerted him to the movement at the front of the plant house. Tree branches separated and vines pulled aside to form an arched opening, revealing a large dimly lit expanse inside. The awed silence of them all was noticeable against the sound of a nearby idonee, the night bird making its plaintive call from behind them.

Davos never slowed. He walked through the sudden opening and disappeared from sight.

Before any of them thought to follow, the entrance was filled with another Edenist as he strode out toward them. "Welcome to Una." He appeared a bit older than Davos and much more welcoming. He had brown hair and green eyes which creased in the corners as he smiled. "I'm Kellic, another like you, exiled for being Kindred of Eden. Welcome to your new home. I promise it is safe and comfortable. We've been expecting you."

The men looked at each other. Finally, one in front asked the obvious question. "How did you know we would be arriving?"

Kellic raised one eyebrow. "We are not so ignorant out here as the Tolba cheetans might expect. Come, you will learn all, but first you need shelter and sleep. This way." His last words were said with more force but still with a warm smile.

Lyka let the others precede him as he whispered toward Xavia. "Close your eyes until I say otherwise or Kellic will see you." No doubt she was as curious as he to see inside the marvel that was Una, but his camouflage abilities did not include the eyes of others. Only his eyes changed when he wanted to hide himself.

As the last one to pass Kellic, Lyka nodded his thanks and stepped through the opening.

Kellic immediately followed, brushing past him to stand at the front of the newcomers. He kept his voice low. "We have accommodations for all of you." Two other men came to stand next to him. "This is Nudak and Zael." Kellic pointed to the two men in the front of their group. Then he pointed to two of the newcomers. "You and you follow them. They will bring you to your sleeping space. I'll take—"

"Zael?" A man from the back walked forward.

Zael looked at the man who approached. "Ogin? I did not expect to see you." The two men hugged briefly.

Kellic grinned. "Zael, go ahead and show your friend his space. I'll take this man. The rest of you wait here."

As soon as the men had left, Lyka backed closer to the entrance, which had completely disappeared. He whispered over his shoulder. "You can look now. It is like nothing I've ever seen."

Also by Lexi Post

Sci-fi Romance

Cruise into Eden
(The Eden Series: Book 1)
Unexpected Eden
(The Eden Series: Book 2)
Eden Discovered
(The Eden Series: Book 3)
Eden Revealed
(The Eden Series: Book 4)
Avenging Eden
(The Eden Series: Book 5)

Beast of Eden
(Eden Series Tolba: Book 1)
Bound by Eden
(Eden Series Tolba: Book 2)
Burning for Eden
(Eden Series Tolba: Book 3)

Paranormal Romance

Masque
Passion's Poison
Passion of Sleepy Hollow
Heart of Frankenstein

Pleasures of Christmas Past
(A Christmas Carol Series: Book 1)
Desires of Christmas Present
(A Christmas Carol Series: Book 2)
Temptations of Christmas Future
(A Christmas Carol Series: Book 3)
One of A Kind Christmas
(A Christmas Carol Series: Book 4)

On Highland Time
(Time Weavers, Inc. Book 1)
A Pocket in Time
(Time Weavers, Inc. Book 2)

Contemporary Cowboy Romance

Cowboys Never Fold
(Poker Flat Series: Book 1)
Cowboy's Match
(Poker Flat Series: Book 2)
Cowboy's Best Shot
(Poker Flat Series: Book 3)

Cowboy's Break
(Poker Flat Series: Book 4)
Wedding at Poker Flat
(Poker Flat Series: Book 5)

Christmas with Angel
(Poker Flat Series Book 2.5, Last Chance Series: Book 1)
Trace's Trouble
(Last Chance Series: Book 2)
Fletcher's Flame
(Last Chance Series: Book 3)
Logan's Luck
(Last Chance Series: Book 4)
Dillon's Dare
(Last Chance Series: Book 5)
Riley's Rescue
(Last Chance Series: Book 6)

Aloha Cowboy
(Island Cowboy Series: Book 1)

Military Romance

When Love Chimes
(Broken Valor Series: Book 1)
Poisoned Honor
(Broken Valor Series: Book 2)

EDEN – ENGLISH DICTIONARY

agapayto – A wife, but more. A woman who has a connection with every man in the filoz. More formal name for beloved.

amobe – An invisible to the eye, flat blob like creature that cleans places by eating dirt, including skin, hair, fur and dried stains.

ambrosia – The drink of Eden. It has a mango coconut flavor with a trace of spice in the aftertaste.

animmit – Tiny insects that devour animal and Edenist waste.

anub – A small white animal whose milk is very sweet and foams when interacting with heat.

awasaw – A prehistoric Grizzly bear but larger and with tan stripes.

baka bun – Similar to a jelly donut only filled with citrusy fruit jams like lemon and orange that energize.

Bedia – An endearment meaning "beloved."

beloved – A less formal name for agapayto (wife). A woman can refuse to be a beloved.

Bendis - The large moon with pink light often called the second moon.

biwil – A strong herb that takes away pain.

blood sign - marking of lawbreaker band - a circle of blood with an x over it.

boabi – Furry animal that looks like a koala bear with ears as long as a Basset hound and black eyes. It curls into a large round ball when frightened. Tigrans like to play with it, but direlots will eat it.

boarox – An animal as big as a bison with no hair and black splotches on its legs It has a large droopy upper lip that covers a mouthful of white shark teeth.

bonabus vine – A leafy vine with small flowers like bluebells that give off a calming scent.

bonding – The sexual act that connects a beloved with her filoz if she is on Eden. This is a biological connection that can never be broken.

breast binding – bra

brother of his heart - best friend who he will share a beloved with

burning ceremony – celebration of an Edenist's life with everything the deceased liked from food to songs to favorite free time activities. Then the dead is placed on a pyre and burned. People take turns watching the fire so the man is never alone as his spirit rejoins Eden.

By the Crius - expression of surprise, frustration, anger, etc.

byunca – tart fruit like a cross between a lemon and a cranberry caball - A large blue bird with long tail feathers, bright yellow eyes with red irises and black pupils.

charwa – a seasoning with a smoky flavor from the charwa plant found in many of the cities.

cheetan – a Edenist leader in Tolba

chictaw – a small yellow songbird with a black beak and white breast that could fit in the palm of one's hand

chosen one – A woman who is like fiancée, but the Edenists choose with no agreement from the woman.

cold box – refrigerator

connar boulder – The hardest rock known to Eden.

Criuson Law - The law set up by the original settlers of Eden.

Crius – The aliens who took people from Earth during the ancient times dropped them off on Eden

crossover - The first time the chosen one goes through the portal to Eden.

cyndistone – A teal, granite-like stone.

Cythera or Cys for short - Women of the Pleasure Temples.

daemond - honey bee

dally greens – A vegetable similar to Brussel sprouts but with an overtone of onion.

decods - like leagues (3 miles are a decod.)

Depoteese - Director

Dickinson Law – Laws instituted after the Fullamush when the men fought over women.

dirgon – Half dire wolf and half dragon

direlot – A ferocious and cunning animal that most closely resembles a wolf but has two heads and two tails.

Discoverists – Scientists but not only in the scientific field.

Eden day - 22 hours

elseire - Bird with purple wings when in flight but folded up looks green.

eyllen - energy rock source

feroon - A big beast with tusks, furry and as large as an elephant but no trunk, fairly docile.

filoz - group of men (2-5) who are close like a family

fithee – A long brown snake-like creature that burrows into mountainsides with both ends.

Fiya – Endearment closest to "sweetheart."

Fullamush - The great war that almost destroyed the planet but the women and Emily Dickinson brought peace (story in Unexpected Eden).

gokokhoko – A bird like an owl but larger with feathers in various shades of green.

grapet – A purple vegetable that havling pigs like (used as bait).

grendal – An animal like a wild boar but larger, has brown tusks and squeals, travels in herds.

hatchoc – A division of Tolba equal to a neighborhood.

Haven – A walled settlement founded by Nassic and Wareson who escaped Naralina and gathered other "lawbreakers" who were falsely accused to form a society.

havling pig – Smaller pig-like animal that wanders alone.

head puffs - pillows

heat top - stove

Helios - Sun

henny - chicken like bird

Hermday - Wednesday

hestas – Blankets made of see-hrough material that is very thin, but quite warm.

High Hall – Center (highest) building in the Ruling Circle complex of Naralina.

Holy Bendis - An expression of surprise, frustration, anger, etc.

idonee – nightingale

inducer - microwave

infragile vine – An unbreakable vine a day after it's cut from its live piece.

ithio - idiot

jansen tree – A short tree with straight branches that has leaves and roots that are good for tea and healing.

jotte – A spice grown in Alantice that makes food spicy hot.

jump-off ledge – In Loraleaf where men pick up the vines left on a hook to swing across or down.

kafez - coffee but stronger

keeoki – Endearment meaning "my love".

keepers - guards

kerasi – A mild sleep inducing fruit (cherry flavored) red.

khityki - kitten

Kif - Capital of Eden for 2 years until it switches to the next city

Kindred – a broad group that every Edenist is born into but doesn't know his specific abilities until his transition. A family will have multiple kindreds within it.

landisbaum – swear, usually used positively

landspout – Like a waterspout but on land - tornado

Latzeran Sea - large body of water known for its depth

lather-wash - soap

lawbreakers - what the Edenists call criminals – those exiled from cities

layfeenya - dolphin like creatures with much bigger tails

letti – A quill-like instrument that works similar to a pen as it is filled with ink and has a small ball inside that keeps the flow steady.

lindyshine – Small bright purple flowers that grow among moss and smell similar to lilac but more woodsy.

lintue – A small green bird that flits about the leaves of trees. They have soft chirps unless calling a warning.

liquidator - bartender

living area - living room

logar - horse with a horn

longseat - couch

Loraleaf – An older settlement in the trees founded by Jahl, Khaos and Sandale as an alternative to the city of Naralina which contains men who followed them from the city.

lumens – Insects that glow. The female glow golden from the start of sunset until dark. The males glow blue from darkness until dawn.

magee tree – A large tree that grows to over 100 feet high with a trunk over 20 feet in diameter and lives hundreds of years.

meal room - kitchen

meekwee – Tolban word for single women who live at the Pleasure Dome complex.

mimi – Feroon meat and spices cooked in a piece of material in boiling water.

Muskwa – A ritual competition of strength, balance, and cunning. Similar to a military bootcamp course, but with a greater variety of tests. Origins in the determination of who would be the best warriors.

namas - A shellfish that looks like a cross between a lobster and an octopus. It has a sweet white meat.

Naralina – The white and gold walled city that men of Haven and Loraleaf hail from.

naswa – A tiny vine with yellow leaves that causes the skin to itch if touched.

nubbish – A dessert like ice cream, but made with honey instead of sugar.

Nuttai – An endearment meaning my heart.

ondile – A vegetable like a carrot only they are white.

ozwa – A biscuit, but it has mashed byunca fruit inside, which are very tart.

pander bush – A bush with large dark green leaves.

patrio – A patio, sometimes covered, sometimes not.

pecone rolls – A cinnamon pastry with tiny nuts.

pegwa squash – like acorn squash only yellow inside

peeswa snake – A snake with saliva that stops bleeding.

pyomite – A purple translucent stone with lime green veins.

racide – A poisonous plant with large orange flowers.

rainbox – shower

rancels – The exchange token backed by each city's largest export. Most commonly used between cities (only used between individuals when bartering, giving, or owing won't work).

rhoade - A meal in a pocket made of chicken, chickpea, a mild curry, mild garlic, coriander, a strong flavored potato and a tinge of hotness like a tiny amount of red pepper if made on Earth.

rhybat – A small rodent with super large ears that is afraid of its own shadow.

Ruling Circle of Naralina – The oligarchy Council of 5 for the city of Naralina.

sable worm silk - thread

salis bush - Looks like a small weeping willow.

Samuvian desert – A large cactus filled desert.

savinstone - gold

Scrat – A swear, like "shit."

Selene - moon with silver light

sherry flower - Light pink flower with strong scent that grows on a thin stem (very fragile).

shevi – Lemony breakfast food with avocado tasting pieces inside a puff pastry.

shilla - lube

shiner – A lantern powered by eyllen.

sirie – A gold and orange butterfly, parent of the siris caterpillar.

siris webbing – A silky soft webbing made by large, amber-colored, furry caterpillari often used for head puffs (pillows).

sitki - barn

Stass! - whoa!

table cover - table cloth

Talia - Tigran Theron befriended while living in his cave.

Telemen Sea – Largest body of water on Eden and closest to Tolba. Where Alantice is situated.

tigran - Sabretooth sized cat with chameleon abilities that loves to be petted.

tigranweed – like catnip to tigrans

toleric – Mud and ground infragile vine blocks that are unbreakable.

tyling – Ham and cheese sandwich.

tyree – A dairy product like cheese with less salt and each type with a different spice.

Valex pit – A mythological pit for refuse, evil deeds, and ignorance

villain's mark – blood sign

waba – Small dome hut that holds compost.

wabanak – A swear like "shit." More common in Tolba.

waterhole - swimming pond or stream

walstone – White stone they built walls of Naralina with.

welchet – A small mammal that looks like a porcupine, but its quills are actually soft. It has two tusks that grow out from the bottom of its jaw for digging grubs, and it has six legs. It's very fast.

yahaw – A tall tree that has branches only at the top that spread out like a canopy. Great for shade.

yenea – A filoz with a beloved or agapayto.

About Lexi Post

Lexi Post is a New York Times and USA Today best-selling author of romance inspired by the classics. She spent years in higher education taking and teaching courses about the classical literature she loved. From Edgar Allan Poe's short story, *The Masque of the Red Death* to Leo Tolstoy's *War and Peace*, she's read, studied, and taught wonderful classics.

But Lexi's first love is romance novels. In an effort to marry her two first loves, she started writing romance inspired by the classics and found she loved it. From hot paranormals to sizzling cowboys to hunks from out of this world, Lexi provides a sensuous experience with a "whole lotta story."

Lexi is living her own happily ever after with her husband and her two cats in Florida. She makes her own ice cream every weekend, loves bright colors, and you will never see her without a hat.

www.lexipostbooks.com

www.ingramcontent.com/pod-product-compliance
Lightning Source LLC
Chambersburg PA
CBHW070736190726
48292CB00002B/293